THE DARCY BROTHERS

THE COMPLETE SERIES BOX SET

ALIX NICHOLS

FOREWORD

Thank you for picking up the complete **DARCY BROTHERS SERIES BOX SET!**

This box set includes four fun and sexy romantic comedies:

- Find You in Paris
- Raphael's Fling
- The Perfect Catch
- Clarissa and the Cowboy

Follow three French aristocrat brothers - stuck-up Sebastian, bad-boy Raphael and vengeful Noah - as each meets his match where he least expects to, and falls head over heels in love!

BOOK 1: FIND YOU IN PARIS

What does it take to fall in love with your enemy? a) His private jet. b) His six-pack abs. c) His unsuspected charm.

WARNING: Just like in *Pride and Prejudice* that inspired this book, expect to find one rich, brooding and handsome Mr. Darcy and one feisty small-town girl who can't stand him. Unlike *Pride and Prejudice*, this book also contains artful nude photos of said Mr. Darcy, a fake marriage and nights of wild passion in Paris.

BOOK 2: RAPHAEL'S FLING
One bookish assistant. One cocky CEO. One Christmas party that changes everything…

GUARANTEED: Belly laughs, hot love scenes and a happy ending for this lust-to-love romance full of humor and passion. "I stayed up way too late to finish this book!" — Amazon Reviewer

BOOK 3: THE PERFECT CATCH
When brooding goalie Noah meets perky realtor Sophie, sparks fly hot and fast…

"You will laugh and cry, and you won't be disappointed!" — Cutting Muse Blog

COMPANION NOVELLA: CLARISSA & THE COWBOY

The heat between archeologist Clarissa and hunky farmer Nathan is explosive. But the worlds they live in couldn't be further apart…

This story is a hot and hilarious opposites-attract romance in which Dr. Penelope "Clarissa" Muller from Book 1 takes center stage.

BOOKS BY ALIX NICHOLS

SCIENCE FICTION ROMANCES

Keepers of Xereill

The Traitor's Bride

The Commander's Captive

The Cyborg's Lady

CONTEMPORARY ROMANCES

The Darcy Brothers

Find You in Paris

Raphael's Fling

The Perfect Catch

Clarissa and the Cowboy

Playing to Win

Playing with Fire

Playing for Keeps

Playing Dirty

La Bohème

Winter's Gift

What If It's Love?

Falling for Emma

Under My Skin

Amanda's Guide to Love

COPYRIGHT

Editing provided by Write Divas

FIND YOU IN PARIS

THE DARCY BROTHERS BOOK 1

PART I
PROPOSITION

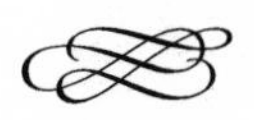

CHAPTER 1

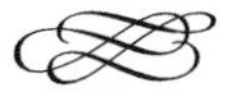

DIANE

It is a truth universally acknowledged that a young man in possession of a vast fortune must be an entitled SOB born into money. Either that or a rags-to-riches a-hole who bulldozed his way to said fortune, leaving maimed bodies in his wake.

The ferocious-looking PA returns to her desk. "Monsieur Darcy is still in a meeting."

"That's OK." I smile benignly. "I can wait."

I place my hands demurely on my knees and stare at the portrait adorning—or should I say disfiguring—the wall across the hallway from where I'm seated.

Pictured is Count Sebastian d'Arcy du Grand-Thouars de Saint-Maurice, the oldest son of the late Count Thibaud d'Arcy du Grand-Thouars de Saint-Maurice and the inheritor of an estate estimated at around one billion euros. Said estate isn't your run-of-the-mill stock holdings or start-up fortune. Oh no. It's made up of possessions that were handed down—uninterrupted and snowballing—all the way from the Middle Ages.

Even Robespierre and his fellow revolutionaries didn't get their greedy little hands on the d'Arcy fortune.

What are the odds?

Upon his father's premature demise ten years ago, young Sebastian moved back into the town house in the heart of Le Marais and took the reins of the family's main business. A twenty-three-year-old greenhorn at the time, you'd expect him to make tons of bad decisions and sink the company or, at least, diminish its value.

But no such luck.

Instead, Sebastian Darcy took Parfums d'Arcy from number three to the number one European flavor and fragrance producer—a feat that neither his illustrious grandfather nor his star-crossed father had managed to accomplish.

According to my research, also about ten years ago, the new count chose to go by "Darcy," abandoning the apostrophe and the rest of his status-laden name. I'm sure he only did it to fool those *beneath* him—which includes most everyone in a country that guillotined its royals—into believing that he sees himself as their equal.

The hell he does.

Sebastian Darcy is a stinking-rich aristocrat with instincts of an unscrupulous business shark. This means he qualifies in both the SOB and the a-hole categories.

No, scratch that. He *slays* both categories.

And I hate him more than words can say.

The straitlaced man on the wall seems to smirk. I shudder, my nerves taut to the point of snapping. Will they kick me out if I spit at the photo? Of course they will. I steal a glance at the PA stationed between me and Darcy's office. She looks like a cross between a human and a pit bull. I'm sure she'd love to stick something other than paper between the jaws of her sturdy hole punch.

My hand, for example.

But I didn't come here to fight with Darcy's PA. I'll keep my saliva in my mouth, my eyes cast down, my butt perched on the edge of the designer chair, and my knees drawn together and folded to the side.

Like the meek little mouse I'm trying to pass for.

After waiting three weeks, I'm careful not to arouse any suspicion in Pitbull's mind so she won't cancel my appointment with Darcy.

Eyes on the prize, Diane! Don't forget you're here to declare war by spitting in Count Sebastian Darcy's face, rather than at his photographic representation.

I look at the photo again, arranged in perfect symmetry between the portraits of his grandfather, Bernard, who founded the company, and his father, Thibaud, who almost put the lid on it. I know this because I've done my homework.

During my week-long research, I dug up every piece of information the Internet had to offer about Sebastian Darcy and his family. I was hoping to find dirt, and I did. The only problem was it was already out in the open—common knowledge, yesterday's news.

And completely useless as leverage.

Pitbull looks up from her smartphone. "Monsieur Darcy is delayed. Do you mind waiting a little longer?"

"No problem." I smile politely. "I'm free this afternoon."

She arches an eyebrow as if having a free afternoon is something reprehensible.

How I wish I could stick out my tongue! But instead I widen my already unnaturally wide smile.

She frowns, clearly not buying it.

I turn away and stare at Darcy's likeness again. In addition to the now-stale scandal, my research has revealed that Darcy is close to his middle brother, Raphael, and also to a longtime friend—Laurent something or other. Our vulture-man even managed to have a serious girlfriend for most of last year. A food-chain heiress, she looked smashing at the various soirées, galas, and fundraisers where she was photographed on his arm. Darcy was rumored to be so into his rich beauty he was about to propose. But then she suddenly dumped him about six months ago.

Clever girl.

He has no right to be happy when Dad's life is in shambles.

I won't stop until I crush him, even if it means I go to jail—or to hell—for using black-hat tactics. It's not as if they'd let me into heaven, anyway. I've already broken the arms and legs on Darcy's voodoo doll.

There's no turning back after you do that sort of thing.

The next step is to let the world know who he really is and hurt him in a variety of ways, big and small. And then, just before delivering the deathblow, let him know he's paying for his sins.

That's why my first move is to show him my face and make sure he remembers it and associates it with *unpleasantness*. That way, when the shit hits the fan, he'll know which creditor is collecting her debt.

Pitbull breaks me out of my dream world. "Monsieur Darcy's meeting is running late."

"That's OK, I can—"

"No," she cuts me off. "There's no point in waiting anymore. As soon as the meeting is over, he'll head to the 9th arrondissement, where he's expected at a private reception."

I stand up.

She glances at my bare ring finger. "Mademoiselle, I can reschedule you for Friday, December twelfth. It's two months away, but that's the only—"

"Thank you, but that won't be necessary," I say.

I know exactly which reception Sebastian Darcy is going to tonight.

CHAPTER 2

SEBASTIAN

THREE MONTHS LATER

"It might snow this afternoon." Octave holds my coat while I wrap a scarf around my neck. "Will monsieur be taking his supper at home?"

As always, I wince at "monsieur," but I do my best not to show it.

Grandpapa Bernard hired Octave before I was born. Roughly Papa's age and a bear of a man, Octave has worked for my family for thirty-odd years, rising from valet to *majordome*. He's seen Raphael, Noah, and me in all kinds of embarrassing situations young boys tend to get themselves into. I've asked him a thousand times to call me Sebastian.

All in vain.

Octave Rossi claims his respect for my *old* family name, my *noble* title, and my position in society is too strong for him to drop the "monsieur."

So be it.

"Yes," I say. "But I'll come home late, so please tell

Lynette to make something light. And don't stay up for me."

He nods. "*Oui*, monsieur."

Chances are he'll be up until I get home.

Since I moved back into the town house after Papa's passing, Octave has been helpful in a way no one, not even Maman—especially not Maman—has ever been. All the little things, from paying electricity bills and hiring help to undertaking necessary repairs and planning reception menus, are taken care of with remarkable efficiency.

When he offered to assist me with my correspondence, I insisted on doubling his salary. My argument was that he'd be saving me the expense of a second PA for private matters.

He caved in only after I threatened to move out and sell the house.

I trust him more than anyone.

"Hello, Sebastian! To the office?" my chauffeur, Greg, asks.

He, at least, doesn't have a problem calling me by my first name.

"We'll make a detour," I say as I climb into the Toyota Prius. "I need to see someone first."

I give him the address, and he drives me to the Franprix on rue de la Chapelle in the 18th arrondissement. Greg parks the car, and I march into the supermarket, scanning the cashiers' counters lined parallel to the shop windows.

There she is!

Diane Petit smiles at a customer as she hands her a bag of groceries. She'll be finishing her shift in about ten minutes, according to the private eye I hired to locate and tail her. I'll talk to her then.

Right now, I pretend to study the selection of batteries and gift cards on display not far from her desk. What I'm really doing is furtively surveying the firebrand who smashed a cream cake in my face in front of a few dozen people last October. At the time, the only thing I registered about her through my surprise and anger was *foxy*.

I've had ample opportunity to pour over her pretty face and eye-pleasing shape in the numerous close-ups the PI has supplied over the past few weeks. I've studied Diane in all kinds of situations and circumstances—at work with her customers, hanging out with her friends, and roaming the streets with her camera, immortalizing everyday scenes of Parisian life. She's hot, all right, but there's also something endearing about her, something unsophisticated and very un-Parisian.

In spite of her extravagant outburst at Jeanne's bash, Diane Petit seems to be an unpretentious small-town bumpkin through and through.

I've learned a good deal about her since that memorable evening. I know she works part time at this supermarket, lives in a high-rise in the 14th, and hangs out with her foster sister Chloe, a coworker named Elorie, and a waitress named Manon.

She enjoys photographing random things, going to the movies, eating chocolate, and drinking cappuccino.

More importantly, I know why Diane did what she did that night at *La Bohème*.

And I plan to use it to my advantage.

Someone gives me a sharp prod in the back.

"Why are you here?" Diane asks as I spin around.

"To give you a chance to apologize."

She smirks. "You're wasting your time."

"No apology, then?"

"You're here to let me know you're on to me, right?" She puffs out her chest. "Read my lips—I'm not afraid of you."

"That's not why I'm here."

"How did you find me, anyway?"

"I hired a professional who tracked you down within days."

She tilts her head to the side. "And you've waited three months before confronting me. Why?"

"I wanted to know what your deal was, so I gave my PI the time to compile a solid profile." I hesitate before adding, "Besides, your foster sister was shot, and you were busy looking after her. I wanted to wait until Chloe had fully recovered."

"You've met Chloe?" She sounds surprised.

"Of course." I shrug. "Jeanne introduced us."

She blows out her cheeks. "What do you want, Darcy?"

"Just to talk."

"About what?"

"I have a proposition that might interest you."

She looks me over. "Unless your proposition is to give me a magic wand that would turn you into a piglet, I'm not interested."

"I obviously can't do that, but what I can do is—"

"Hey, Elorie, are we still on?" Diane calls to a fellow cashier who passes by.

Elorie smiles. "Only if you and Manon let me choose the movie."

"Fine with me, but I can't vouch for Manon."

While Diane and Elorie discuss the time and place of their outing, I resolve to draw Diane somewhere else before making my offer. Preferably, somewhere that's on my turf rather than hers.

"Can we go someplace quieter?" I ask Diane after Elorie leaves.

She sighs. "OK, but don't take it as a good sign."

"Understood."

I do take it as a step in the right direction, though.

She follows me outside and into the car.

"To Le Big Ben, please," I say to Greg.

He nods, and thirty minutes later, Diane and I are seated in a private booth at my favorite Parisian gentlemen's club, which I also happen to co-own with Raphael as of three weeks ago. We've kept the old manager, who's doing an admirable job. I've continued coming here with Laurent or Raph, as a longtime patron who enjoys the subdued elegance of this place and its unparalleled selection of whiskeys. The staff may not even realize the club has changed hands. It's easier this way—and it removes the need for socializing with them.

"So," Diane says after the server brings my espresso and her cappuccino. "What's your proposition?"

"Marry me."

She blinks and bursts out laughing as if I just said something outrageous. Which I guess it was without prior explanation.

Maybe I should start over.

"Here's the deal," I say. "You and I will *date* through April." I make air quotes when I say "date."

She looks at me as if I've lost my mind.

"You'll *move in* with me in May," I continue. "About a month after that, we'll get *married*."

Diane makes a circular motion with her index at the side of her head and mouths, "Nutcase."

"A month into our marriage, I'll *cheat* on you," I

continue, undeterred, with a quote unquote on *cheat.* "And then you'll *leave* me."

She gives me a long stare. "Why?"

"It doesn't concern you. What you need to know is that I'm prepared to pay fifty thousand euros for a maximum of six months in a pretend relationship."

"Why?" she asks again.

"You don't need to know that."

"OK, let me ask you something I do need to know." She arches an eyebrow. "Why *me*?"

I shrug.

"If you continue ignoring my legitimate questions," she says, "I'm out of here before you finish your espresso."

"You're perfect for a plan I'd like to set in motion," I say. "And as an incentive for you to play your role the best you can, I'll quadruple your fee if my plan succeeds."

"How will I know if it succeeds if you won't even tell me what it is?"

"Trust me, you'll know." I smirk. "Everyone in my entourage will."

Diane leans back with her arms crossed over her chest. "Can't you find another candidate for your shady scheme? It couldn't have escaped your notice that I humiliated you in public."

"I assure you it didn't," I say. "But what's really important and valuable here is that it didn't escape other people's notice, either. A picture of my cream-cake-covered mug even ended up in a tabloid or two."

She gives me a smug smile.

"At the time, I told everyone I didn't know you, but I can easily change my tune and *confess* we'd been dating."

"This doesn't make any sense."

"Believe me, it does—a whole lot of sense—if you consider it in light of my scheme."

"Which I can't do," she cuts in, "because you won't tell me what your scheme is."

True. "Anyway, I'll tell everyone we've talked it over and made up."

She says nothing.

"Mademoiselle Petit… Diane." I lean in. "Your parents—and yourself—are *not* in the best financial shape right now. I'm offering an easy solution to your woes."

"Ha!" she interjects with an angry gleam in her almond-shaped eyes. "Says the person who caused our woes!"

She's right, of course, but not entirely. Before going in for the kill, I did offer to buy out her father's fragrance company. The offer wasn't generous by any measure, but it was reasonable given the circumstances. Charles Petit's artisanal workshop wasn't doing terribly well. In fact, it was of little interest to me, with the exception of the two or three of his signature fragrances that were worth the price I'd offered. Charles is a lousy businessman—but he's a true artist. He *created* the fragrances he sold, and he also created for others. I would've offered him a job in one of my labs had I not been one hundred percent sure he'd decline it.

As it happened, he also declined my fifty thousand, calling me a scumbag and a few other choice epithets I won't repeat in front of a lady. Fifty thousand euros isn't a fortune, but seeing as he stood no chance against me, he should've taken the money.

It was better than nothing.

But Charles Petit proved to be more emotional than rational about his business. And he ended up with nothing. Worse than nothing, actually. I heard he took to drinking, got kicked out by his wife, and had a heart attack. Or was it a stroke?

Anyway, my point is, at least some of those misfortunes could've been avoided had he sold his company to me.

I open my mouth to say this to Diane, but then it occurs to me she must already know about my offer. She probably also shares Monsieur Petit's opinion that it was indecently low.

"Can we skip the whole dating and marrying nonsense," Diane says, "and go straight to the part where you grovel at my dad's feet, thrust a check for two hundred thousand into his hand, and beg him to take it in the hopes he might forgive you one day?"

I sigh and shake my head.

She stands. "The answer is no."

"Why don't you think it over? I'll be in touch next week." I set a twenty on the table. "May I offer you a ride?"

"Thank you, Monsieur Darcy, you're very *kind*." She bares her teeth in a smile that doesn't even try to pass for a real one. "But I prefer the *métro*."

CHAPTER 3

DIANE

"Will you remind me again why we're on a *bus* just before the rush hour?" Elorie gives me a sour look, hugging her counterfeit Chanel bag to her chest.

I admit, it was a mistake. But I'm not admitting this out loud.

"It takes us straight to the bistro I've been telling you about," I say. "Like a taxi."

Elorie snorts. "Taxi, my foot! When I take a cab, I sprawl comfortably and give this baby"—she points at her bag—"its own seat. Whereas now—"

She jostles the woman on her left. "Madame, you're stepping on my foot!"

The woman apologizes and shifts a couple of inches, which is no mean feat, considering how packed the bus is.

Elorie turns back to me. "You said the bistro was in the 9th, yes?"

I nod.

"At this rate, it'll take us an hour to get there."

I'm about to suggest we get off and find the nearest *métro* station when two school kids jump out of their seats and make their way to the exit.

We take their seats immediately.

"Ah," Elorie says. "This is better. Not a taxi by a long shot, but still."

We're on this bus because I'm taking Elorie to celebrate at *La Bohème*, my favorite bistro in Paris. Perhaps even more than its amazing cappuccinos and out-of-this-world chocolate mousse, I love that bistro because it's home to two terrific chicks—Manon and Jeanne. Headwaiter Manon is my gym and movies companion, and she's the sweetest person I've ever met. Proprietor Jeanne's personality is so mood enhancing she should charge a supplement every time she tends the bar. Jeanne also happens to have a brother, Hugo, who happens to be my sister Chloe's fiancé. In other words, she's almost family.

How cool is that?

Regardless, I'd half expected her to declare me persona non grata for crashing her latest reception and assaulting one of her guests. The guest in question—Sebastian Darcy—is her husband's friend and political backer, which makes my smashing a cream cake in his face an even bigger affront. But Jeanne just laughed the incident off, saying the bash had been too stuffy and in serious need of an icebreaker.

Which I kindly provided.

The Manon-Jeanne combo makes me feel truly welcome at *La Bohème*. So much so that I forget I'm far away from home in a metropolis of eleven million people, suburbs included. The vast majority of them are crammed into tiny apartments and deeply convinced they're the most evolved representatives of the human race. Here in Paris, if you say *bonjour* to a stranger on the street, they think you're either a nutcase or a hooker.

"How's *the quest* coming along?" I ask Elorie.

The quest is shorthand for Elorie's newfound mission —locate an eligible billionaire and get him to marry her. Elorie defines "eligible" as currently available, reasonably young, and passably good-looking.

She launched the project three months ago on her twenty-sixth birthday, and she's been working hard on it ever since. Not very successfully, judging by the sound of it. But what's three months when looking for a soul mate who meets such high standards and such specific… specifications?

"I've made good progress," Elorie says.

I bug out my eyes. "I want a name!"

"Not so fast, *ma cocotte*. My progress is theoretical at this point."

"Oh."

"Don't you *oh* me." Elorie wags her index finger from side to side. "Would you launch a business without conducting a market study first?"

"I guess not." I narrow my eyes. "Do you approach all your dreams as a business?"

She shrugs. "Not all—only the ones worth pursuing. Anyway, as the saying goes, if you practice without theory, you shall fall into the ditch."

"There's no such saying."

"You sure?" She puts her chin up. "Well, there should be. Anyway, I stand on much firmer ground today than three months ago all because I've done enough research to write a thesis on the topic."

"Maybe you should write one," I mutter.

Elorie is the most entertaining person I've ever met and I love her, but her pragmatism does rattle me sometimes. Then again, I'm well aware I'm a country-fried prawn who still hasn't wrapped her head around big-city attitudes.

"Ha-ha, very funny!" Elorie pauses before adding, "Anyway, I've now read all the tutorials and how-to articles I could get my hands on, and I've analyzed several real-life case studies."

"I'm impressed."

"Me, too," she says with a wink. "I've never taken anything so seriously in my whole life."

"*Mesdames, messieurs,*" the bus driver says into the speaker. "This bus will not continue beyond Opéra. You can wait for the next one or take an alternate route."

People gripe and boo and begin to move toward the doors.

I spread my arms in apology.

Elorie rolls her eyes.

We get off and continue our journey using the most reliable means of transportation in Paris—our feet. The air is cold and humid, which is no surprise in February, but at least it isn't raining.

I look up at the leaden sky and tone down my gratitude—it isn't raining *yet.*

"Feel like sharing your theoretical findings?" I ask, tucking my scarf inside my coat in an attempt to shield myself from the cutting wind.

Elorie considers my request. "OK. But only because you're my friend and you always pay for the drinks."

"Aww." I place my hand on my heart. "You put 'friend' before 'drinks,' you wonderful person."

"Listen up—because I won't repeat this," Elorie says, choosing to ignore my irony. "The single most important action you can take is to hang out where billionaires do."

"In Swiss banks?"

"For example." She nods, unfazed. "Don't tell me you believe Kate would've snatched William if her clever mom hadn't sent her to the University of St Andrews, where the cream of British nobility goes?"

"I must confess I haven't given the matter much thought."

"Then thank me for opening your eyes."

"Thank you," I say dutifully. "But we have a problem—I'm too old for college, and it isn't my thing, anyway."

"That's OK," she says. "It was just an example."

"Phew." I'm doing my best to keep my expression earnest. "What a load off!"

She glances at me sideways and shakes her head. "What I'm telling you isn't funny, Diane. It's precious. I'd be taking notes if I were you."

"Sorry, sweetie. Go on."

"I'll give you a few pointers," she says. "Go horseback riding, join a golf club, or book yourself into a high-end ski resort. If you're targeting a specific man, go exactly where he goes."

"Some people would call it stalking."

"*I* call it lending fate a hand."

"OK," I say. "What about the rich perverts who frequent BDSM clubs? Should I get a membership for one? And what about the polygamists who make their wives wear burkas? Where do you draw the line?"

"Where he buys me Louboutin pumps, Prada sunglasses, and Chanel purses to wear with my burka." She arches an eyebrow. "If I can travel the world in his private jet and have my own wing in his palace plus three or four maids at my beck and call, then sure, why not. Bring on the burka."

I stop and put my hands on my hips.

Elorie stops, too.

"Aren't you a little too cavalier about this?" My voice betrays my feelings—equal parts incredulity and concern. "Let me be more specific. We're not talking a *burkini* here. We're talking the works with gloves and an eye grid. And *other* wives."

Elorie tilts her head to the side, thinking. "Ten maids, my own palace, and my own jet."

I'm too dumbfounded to speak.

"What?" she says. "Don't look at me like that. Everyone has a price, and so do you."

"I don't think so."

"Of course, you do. You're just too ashamed to admit it, which is kind of sad."

Does she really think that?

"Or maybe you're fooling yourself that your affections can't be bought," she says, her expression pensive. "Which is even sadder."

"Please, believe me when I say I don't care about money." I stare her in the eye. "I don't mind having some—just enough to get by—but I wouldn't make the slightest sacrifice just so I can marry a rich man."

Elorie rolls her eyes, clearly not buying it.

"If you want to know the truth," I say, "I find rich men repulsive. They're so full of themselves, so convinced of their superiority! They gross me out."

"What, all of them?" she asks, raising an eyebrow.

"Without exception. They mistake their dumb luck for divine providence and their lack of scruples for business acumen."

Elorie narrows her eyes. "It sounds like you're talking about one rich man in particular. And I think it's Sebastian Darcy."

The moment she mentions his name, I realize I've spent the past few weeks doing exactly what Elorie just advised me to do—researching a rich man. But there's a difference. I haven't been investigating him for a chance to marry him. I've been probing into his life in the hopes of finding a weapon to destroy him.

I didn't find any.

And then, three days ago, he showed up at my workplace and handed me one.

Sure, what he's offered is a stick rather than a hatchet. But it's up to me to take that stick and sharpen it into a spear. Our ancestors killed mammoths with spears—I should be able to skewer a man.

"He's superhot, by the way," Elorie says. "I'd marry him even if he was a mere millionaire."

"He's a jerk."

"Who isn't?"

I start walking again. "So you meet the billionaire of your dreams, then what?"

"Duh." She rolls her eyes. "Then I make him fall madly in love with me."

"Of course! How?"

"By being gorgeous, self-confident, and classy."

I clear my throat audibly.

"What was that supposed to mean?" she asks, turning to me.

"We're cashiers." I give her a hard stare. "We may be called *cute* but *gorgeous* and *classy are* beyond our reach."

I expect her to object that you can be classy on a budget, but instead she puts her arm around my shoulders and gives a gentle squeeze.

"Finally," she says with an approving smile. "Diane

Petit has demonstrated there's a realist hiding in there, underneath her *principles* and other bullshit."

Her words sting a little.

"My dear," Elorie says as we turn onto rue Cadet. "I'll reward your bout of honesty by giving you the single most precious piece of advice anyone has ever given you. Or ever will."

I halt again and fold my hands across my chest. "I'm all ears."

"I'm sharing this," Elorie says, "because we're besties and because I want you to owe me one."

I shake my head. "You can't link those two reasons with an *and*. They're mutually exclusive. It's either because we're besties *or* because you want me to owe you one."

She sucks on her teeth for a brief moment. "I want you to owe me one."

"OK, what's your precious advice?"

"It's a shortcut that very few women are aware of."

"Yeees?"

"You need to develop a real interest and a certain level of competence in what the billionaires you're targeting are passionate about."

I pull a face. "Things like football?"

"If that's what floats his boat."

"I see."

"It can be all sorts of things." Elorie begins to count on her fingers. "Sports cars. War movies. Guns. High tech gadgets. Video games."

"I think they're a waste of time," I say.

"It doesn't matter what you think. What matters is what you say." She moves on to her right hand. "Mixed martial arts. Wine. Politics. Porn. Art photography."

My eyebrows shoot up.

She giggles. "That last one was a mole to check if you were paying attention. Nobody—except you, that is—cares about art photography."

"I know men who do."

"Are they filthy rich?"

I shake my head.

"Ha! Thought so."

We reach *La Bohème*, and I stop in front of the entrance, pulling Elorie by her sleeve to stop her from walking on.

"OK," I say. "Let's finish this conversation before we go in. Let's say you've become a wine connoisseur or a sports car buff. How does that guarantee your billionaire will fall to your feet like an electrocuted wasp?"

"It's science, dum-dum." She cocks her head. "Say your man loves Star Wars and football. You give him a well-timed Yoda quote, and his mind goes, 'Ooh, she's special.' Then you give him an analysis of the latest Paris Saint-Germain victory, and his body releases even more happiness hormones. And before he knows it, his brain learns to associate that euphoric state with you. This leads him to conclude you're Mademoiselle Right, which, in turn, leads him to propose."

"Neat," I say.

And what about the billionaire who proposes not because he gives a shit if you're Mademoiselle Right or Mademoiselle One Night, but because he wants to use you in some shady scheme?

I push open the door to the bistro and decide to keep that last observation to myself.

CHAPTER 4

DIANE

"So what are we celebrating?" Elorie asks after we settle at the bar and Manon hands us two tall glasses of *vin chaud*.

The steaming mulled wine smells of cinnamon and orange. It makes my frozen insides relax with comfort and my brain thaw with a pleasant mist in a way that's satisfying beyond words.

Who needs orgasms when you can just take a walk out in the cold and drink this ambrosia?

I grab the spoon in my glass and pull out the half slice of orange begging to be eaten. "Have you heard of *Voilà Paris*?"

"The gossip magazine?"

"They call themselves a women's magazine, but yes, gossip is their main stock in trade." I bite into my orange slice. "They bought some of my pics last month, and now they're hiring me on as a freelance photojournalist."

Elorie frowns. "You're going to be a paparazzo."

I shake my head, unable to speak because of the wine in my mouth.

"They publish articles, too, not just celebrity gossip," Manon says.

I swallow the wine. "The deal is if I produce fun pictures with original captions, they'll let me put them together into a story."

"Congratulations, Diane!" Manon high-fives me and jogs away to take care of other customers.

"Yeah, congrats," Elorie says with a lot less enthusiasm. "Does this mean you'll resign from the supermarket?"

"I can't. Freelancing pays for movie tickets and drinks, but there's also the little matter of rent."

Elorie nods, perking up.

We hang out at *La Bohème* for another hour and then head home. Elorie catches an RER train to her parents' suburban cottage, and I take the *métro* to Chloe's apartment in the 14th. In fact, I should stop thinking of it as Chloe's. Now that she's moved in with Hugo and I've taken over the lease, the place is officially mine.

The next morning, I wake up with a headache that's too strong for the two glasses of mulled wine I had last night. Then I remember I hardly slept, weighing the pros and cons with regards to Darcy's offer just as I'd done the night before and the night before that.

I pop an aspirin and head to the shower.

Darcy's proposition has been on my mind nonstop for three days now. No matter how I turn it, taking him up on his offer is a no-brainer. Basically, there are only two ways this can go. Option A, I play his game and pocket the funds for Dad. Option B, I pretend to play his game, but in reality, I seize the opportunity to poke around his house and dig up some dirt on him. Once I have the info and the evidence, I'll get it published in *Voilà Paris* or leak it to a more serious periodical, depending on the nature of the scoop. This will, hopefully, do some serious damage to Darcy's finances or, at least, tarnish his reputation.

Maybe both. And thus avenge Dad.

My brain prefers Option A, while my gut craves Option B. But here's the best part—I win, no matter how the dice roll, and Dad gets either money or satisfaction. Or both, if I can find dirt and be patient enough to hold onto it until after I am paid. That would make me a villain, and a nasty piece of work, but who says being ruthless is men's prerogative?

Sebastian Darcy is a vulture. He deserves a taste of his own cruelty.

It's in that crucial instant, right after I've shampooed my hair and just before I rinse it, that I decide I'll marry him.

We meet in his office because Darcy's schedule for today has only one thirty-minute slot that could be freed.

"I'm glad you were able to see that my offer represents a unique opportunity for you and your family," he says, motioning me to the *informal* area of his ginormous office with comfy leather armchairs and a designer coffee table.

His arrogance is unbearable, but I hold my tongue. If I want my plan to succeed, I need him to trust me.

Pitbull enters with a tray loaded with drinks, pretty

little sandwiches, and mouthwatering pastries. She gives me a perplexed look, which tells me she remembers me from my cancelled appointment back in October and wonders if she's pegged me right.

"Could you maybe clue me in on the whys of your offer?" Rather than sitting down, I go to the floor-to-ceiling window and take in the breathtaking view. "It would help to know what I'm getting myself into."

"I explained last time," he says. "And I can assure you it's not illegal or dangerous."

I turn around and give him a stare. "You didn't explain anything. You just said 'I need you to be my pretend girlfriend for a couple of months and then my pretend wife for another month or so.' "

"And that's as much as you need to know," he says, his voice dry. "Take it or leave it."

Fine. Don't tell me. I'll find out on my own.

"Will you please sit down?" He points to the sofa. "I'd like you to look at the contract."

Ah, so there's a written contract. Well, what did I expect?

I amble over to one of the armchairs, plonk myself down, and pick up an éclair. "I'm not going to sign your contract right away."

"I don't expect you to." He sits down opposite me. "You can study it tonight and call me tomorrow morning, but you can't discuss it with anyone. That's why you'll need to sign *this* before you can see the contract."

He nudges a sheet of paper across the coffee table. The title at the top of the page says, "Nondisclosure Agreement."

How clever of him.

I read and sign the agreement while Darcy wolfs

down a few sandwiches, explaining he hasn't had time to eat yet.

Who knew billionaires were such busy people?

"We'll use your dramatic appearance at Jeanne and Mat's party to our best advantage," he says, wiping his fingers with a napkin.

"How?"

"I'll tell everyone we'd been seeing each other discreetly for a few months until you were led to believe I'd cheated on you. But now the misunderstanding is cleared up and we're back together, madly in love."

I narrow my eyes. "Why go out of your way to give a reason for what I did when you can just fall *madly in love* with a fresh face who won't require any explaining."

"Because what you did suggests you're the kind of woman who doesn't put up with cheating."

"And that's good becaaaause…?"

"I can't tell you, but trust me, it's good. In fact, it's perfect for my plan."

I sigh. "Whatever you say."

"Let's look at the contract now, shall we?" He glances at his watch. "My meeting starts in fifteen minutes."

I open the manila folder and stare at the document inside it.

"Most of it is legalese that we can go over next time once we agree on the terms," Darcy says.

I nod.

"You can go straight to this part." He turns several pages and points at a paragraph with bullet points. "Please read this and let me know if you have questions. Or, if you prefer, I can just walk you through it."

I scoff at him. "Coming from a family that's been

sending its children to private schools for generations, you may not be aware that France has had free universal education since the 1880s."

He blinks, clearly taken aback. "I'm sorry. I didn't mean to offend you."

"No, it's me who's sorry to shatter your aristocratic illusions," I say. "But cashiers can read."

"I was just trying to be helpful," he says.

I know he is. And it aggravates me. I'd be much more comfortable with him if he'd stop hiding his ugly face behind this mask of polite concern.

Darcy looks at his watch again and taps his index finger on the highlighted passage. "Read this at home, then reread it, and write down all your questions. I'll call you tomorrow night."

Aha, now he's showing his bossy side.

I'm so intimidated.

Not.

"*Oui*, monsieur." I bow my head with exaggerated obedience, noting in passing that Darcy has handsome hands—lean wrists, large palms, and long fingers.

At least the right one, which is currently pinning the contract to the table.

Let's hope his left hand is teeny-weeny. Or super fat. Or excessively hairy.

He doesn't deserve two handsome hands.

"The gist of this paragraph," Darcy says, "is that you recognize you're entering a financially compensated transaction with me, which is couched as a relationship, but is *not* a relationship, be it physical or emotional."

A relationship with an a-hole.

God forbid.

"Consider it recognized," I say.

"It also says here somewhere..." He slides his finger

along the lines and halts on one of the bullet points. "Here—it says you commit to moving in with me at about the two-month mark on our timeline."

"Do I have to?"

"This has to be credible for it to work." He makes a sweeping gesture with his other hand, which, unfortunately, is as nicely shaped as the first. "A month after that, I'll propose, and another month after that, we'll marry."

"It'll look rushed. Besides, how are you going to stage a town hall ceremony and—"

"I won't have to. We'll fly to the Bahamas for a week and get *married* there." He uses air quotes.

"Wow, you've thought this through."

"I have, indeed." He clears his throat. "As you can see, the bullet point just below states that sex is not a requirement but you *will* need to touch and kiss me in public."

"Good."

He raises his eyebrows in surprise.

Crap. That came out all wrong.

"What I meant was it's good that sex isn't required. It would've been a deal-breaker."

He nods. "That's what I thought."

"Do I *have* to kiss you?"

"Yes. It doesn't have to be torrid. But if we never kiss, our relationship won't look convincing."

"OK, if we must." I sigh. "So we date, move in together, and smooch on camera. Then what?"

"Then we wait for… a certain person to make his move."

"How very enigmatic." I roll my eyes. "You do realize I'm going to hate every moment of our time together, right?"

"You won't be the only one," he says. "In any event, if nothing happens within six months, we'll break up and I'll pay you for your time. But if my plan works, you'll walk away a rich woman."

Or if *my* plan works, you'll be left a ruined man.

PART II
ISLAND

CHAPTER 5

DIANE

"Did Belle Auxbois at least say she'd think about it?"

I turn to glance at Dad, who's slumped in the passenger seat, fuming. I take it the pop star made no such promise. It doesn't surprise me. The diva demonstrates typical rich-person behavior—exploit whomever you can, whenever you can, for as long as you can. Come to think of it, this credo must be the most important qualification for joining the Rich Club.

The only real difference between Belle Auxbois and Darcy is that her fake sweetness and angelic voice have misled millions of people into thinking she's a nice person.

Dad and I are in his car, and I'm driving him home from his physical therapy session. The poor man hates these sessions with all his heart. I don't blame him. His therapist is a hulk of a woman with sadistic propensities. She would've made a formidable Grand Inquisitor in another time and place, wringing confessions of witchcraft and heresy from innocent souls. But luckily for the medievals and unluckily for us, Troll Queen isn't an officer of the Inquisition. She's employed by a public hospital just outside of Marseille.

It took me six weekends with Dad and trips to the hospital's rehab center to figure out her deal. This meant hours of watching her walk and talk—in fact, "bark" would be a better word for her unique communication style—and listening to grown men and women begging for mercy behind her door.

Have you ever tried to read a book while your beloved daddy screams, "Please, I can't take it anymore!" next door?

I have.

And I didn't enjoy it.

Anyway, Mamma Grizzly is convinced that stroke rehab protocol has to be painful to be effective. And God forbid someone confuses what she does for a living with massage. Because, you see, madame isn't a masseuse. Hell, no. Her job is *not* to rub and knead people into comfort. Her job is to twist and contort patients into recovery.

To be fair, Dad *has* improved dramatically since the dominatrix first laid her hands on him. He can now move his fingers and speak more distinctively.

And that's the only reason I haven't sued her. Instead, I always make sure my smartphone is fully charged before we head to the hospital. When we get there, I stick my earplugs in my ears and let System of a Down outshout Dad.

"What exactly did Belle say when you called her?" I ask again.

He turns to me. "It's a no-go. She cited the contract."

That damn contract! Why hadn't he shown it to me

before signing?

"Did you try to appeal to her humanity? Explain how much it would mean to you in your current situation?"

"Yeah, I did." He sighs and turns away to stare at the road. "She said she was sorry, but she couldn't do it."

"Not even to admit you gave her a hand? Or that she consulted you?"

"You see,"—he lets out a bitter snort—"Madame Auxbois was featured on some morning show a couple of days ago, where she told the *whole country* she'd concocted the perfume in her kitchen. All by herself."

I blow my cheeks out. "That's ridiculous."

Stupid cow!

I glance at Dad's defeated face, and my heart aches with pity. If I want to help him—and God knows I do more than anything in the world—I must get better at channeling my anger into something constructive.

Count your blessings, Diane.

For one, Dad's arm is on the mend, and his speech has improved so much it's hard to imagine I had trouble understanding him a year ago. He's joined AA and hasn't had a drop of alcohol since his stroke.

And last but not least, I'm about to get an unhoped-for chance to hurt his archenemy—Sebastian Darcy.

We met briefly yesterday to sign the contract and iron out the details. I tried all the powers of persuasion I'm capable of to waive the requirement of living under his roof. But he was firm. He said his immediate circle had to believe we were consumed by mad passion. It was crucial to the success of his scheme. I'm deducing—clever me—that his scheme targets someone in his entourage.

I also tried to persuade him to let Chloe and Elorie in on our charade. Chloe is family and Elorie is my best friend in Paris. They know me well, especially Chloe. It would be hard to lie to them.

The answer was no way. The only person in the loop besides the two of us is his brother Raphael, but only because they hatched the plan together. Aside from that exception, no one else must know. Every additional person who has the info increases the risk of a leak and, consequently, the failure of his plan. With an icy gleam in his eyes, he reminded me I had committed to secrecy by signing the nondisclosure agreement and he had every intention of holding me to it.

You do that, genius.

Whoever drafted that agreement—I suspect it was Darcy and his bro all by themselves, seeing his obsession with confidentiality—left a loophole. The text focuses too much on the fake relationship and things around it. But there's nothing in it that says I must keep my lips sealed with regards to unrelated trivial secrets I might stumble upon, such as tax evasion or financial fraud.

Or less trivial ones, such as murder.

I almost drooled as I pictured myself finding proof that the senior Darcy's death wasn't accidental. Lo and behold, he was killed in cold blood by his oldest son, Sebastian. The golden boy will be investigated, found guilty, and sent to prison where he'll rot for rest of his days.

Wouldn't that be a hoot?

"Any other questions?" Darcy asked, breaking me out of my favorite fantasy.

I'd told him my biggest concern was how Dad would handle the news of our *association* once it reached his ears.

"He'll get over it," Darcy said, all dry pragmatism.

"He'll stop talking to me." I wrung my hands. "He'll think I'm a traitor."

"If it's any consolation, my mother thinks I'm a traitor."

Does she now? Is that why Marguerite d'Arcy has been holed up in Nepal doing charity work for over a decade? *Voilà Paris* called her "the French Mother Teresa" in the feature they ran about her a couple of years ago.

"Why would she think that?" I asked.

He sighed and waved my question off. "Long story."

I made a mental note to investigate.

Before we said good-bye, Darcy informed me that our first "post-reconcilliation" outing will be a "small, informal gathering" to celebrate his brother Raphael's twenty-ninth birthday. I pointed out I didn't know anyone in his circle. He said he'd invited Jeanne and Mat. Mat is an up-and-coming politician he believes in and backs. I'm friends with Jeanne. We can spend most of the weekend chatting with the couple. That way, neither of us will appear stiff to anyone watching.

I nodded, dropping my head so he wouldn't see me roll my eyes.

Because, honestly, who are you kidding, man?

You never smile. I've never seen you slump or stoop, be it in photos or in real life. Regardless of what you say or do, your body language, accent and manners scream, "Stuck-up aristocrat."

You don't just appear stiff—you're Count Stiff. No, you're King Stiff.

Brace yourself, your Majesty.

I'm here to depose you.

CHAPTER 6

DIANE

I sip my iced tea and stare out the bay window at the waters of the Mediterranean. I'm no longer in Dad's cheap divorcé pad deep inside the ugliest industrial suburb of Marseille. This place is lush and unspoiled by construction folly. In fact, the only construction here is an unobtrusive energy-efficient villa overlooking the beach.

The "small, informal gathering" Darcy had told me about turned out to be a weekend party for over fifty guests. Held on a Greek island.

A *private* Greek island.

The guests were flown to Crete this morning by *private* jet—of course—all white leather and overwhelming sleekness. While up in the air, I met Darcy's middle brother, Raphael—the CEO of a large audit firm—his best friend, Laurent, and a bunch of other people, all of whom eyed me with unrestrained curiosity.

After we landed, I was eager to see the sites, but it looked as if I was the only one who'd never been to

Crete before. Even Jeanne, the only other "normal" person in this jet set, had visited it when she backpacked around Europe at twenty.

"Another time," Darcy had said to me, all bossy and curt, before we were all ferried to Ninossos, farther south, on board a *private* mahogany-paneled yacht.

How else was a poor rich man to transport guests to his island?

"Papa loved this place," Darcy says, planting himself next to me. "The weather is mild here almost all year round."

I can definitely believe that, considering how sunny and warm it is right now in the middle of winter. The island is small and kept in its natural state, except for this villa. Perched on a hillside and separated from the sandy beach by terraced gardens, it offers a breathtaking view over the sea.

What's not to love?

"It's Raphael's now," Darcy says.

I give him a sidelong glance and turn away quickly, embarrassed by the effect his jeans and shirt are having on me. *Dammit!* When he wears one of his bespoke suits, I can tell myself it's not him, it's the cut. The second I catch myself eyeing his torso, I bring up the image of a Savile Row tailor wielding his magic scissors and turning amorphous men into hunks.

The problem is no sane person with functioning eyes would call the man standing next to me amorphous.

I force a sneer. "Is the boat his, too?"

He nods.

"And the jet?"

"We co-own it, the same as Le Big Ben."

"I hadn't pegged you as someone who's into *sharing*, even with family members."

"You're wrong—I do share, and not only with family. My other jet is used for corporate travel by all Parfums d'Arcy managers and sales reps."

I shake my head, tut-tutting. "How disappointing. Billionaires aren't what they used to be."

He says nothing.

I sneak a peek at him. Darcy's expression is as stony as ever. It's not as if I expected him to crack up or anything, but… I don't know… maybe smile a little?

Forget it.

Who cares what he thinks, anyway?

I point at the picture-perfect young people who sunbathe and entertain themselves in a variety of beachy ways a couple dozen meters from the villa. "I'll go find Jeanne."

"Of course," he says. "I'll go chat with the caterer and the local staff and make sure everything's ready for the party tonight."

I scrunch my eyebrows. "Shouldn't Raphael do that? It's *his* birthday."

"Raphael should relax and enjoy himself," Darcy says. "It's his *birthday*."

Righto.

With a canned smile, I hand him my empty glass and head outside.

The first thing that jumps out at me as the soles of my feet touch the sand is just *how much* Raphael is enjoying himself. Reclining on his back, the birthday boy is letting a topless Scarlett Johansson doppelgänger on his left smear sunscreen onto his tanned chest. While she's at it, a topless clone of Natalie Portman on his right giggles at something he said.

Seriously?

I look around. Am I the only one who finds this utterly ridiculous?

Oh, wait! Maybe the trio is reenacting *The Other Boleyn Girl.*

Yes, that must be it.

I avert my gaze, scanning the beach crowd for Jeanne.

Honestly, what did I expect? Rich men are all like that—spoiled and obnoxious. I'm sure Raphael's older brother engages in similar pursuits when he isn't in a fake relationship with a girl who shudders at the thought of kissing him. To say nothing of engaging in a threesome with him. My antipathy to Darcy aside, I'd have to be unconscious or dead to be involved in a threesome with anyone—even a man I lusted after.

If I ever met such a man.

"Hey, Diane!" Raphael waves enthusiastically while "Scarlett" and "Natalie" peer at me, giving off distinctly hostile vibes. "Over here!"

Er… *I don't think so*. "I'm looking for Jeanne."

"Mat's wife? I saw her inside." He stands up and saunters toward me in all his bare-chested glory.

I wonder if his brother's muscles are as well defined as his. Then I wonder why I'm wondering this.

"You should ask Seb to give you a tour of the island," he says, looking me over.

I give him a pointed *cut-the-crap* look.

He shrugs with a hint of defiance, as if to say, *I'm just playing my part and so should you*.

Oh, well, I guess I should. There are doppelgängers within earshot, after all. And, judging by how quiet they've suddenly grown, they're all ears.

"Great idea." I force a smile. "Do you come here often?"

"Whenever I can. This is my favorite place on Earth."

"What's the deal with the *third* Darcy brother?" I ask. "He wasn't on the plane, was he?"

Raphael shakes his head, his grin fading a little.

"I haven't had the pleasure of meeting him yet," I say.

It's clear he doesn't relish the turn our small talk is taking, but I can't help myself. "Will he be arriving later, on a *regular* flight with all those poor millionaires crammed in business class?"

"Noah isn't coming," Raphael says, his smile strained now. "He had some… important business to take care of."

Birthday boy takes a sudden interest in his feet, as if he just discovered he had toes. It doesn't look as if he'll say more on the subject.

Never mind. None of the Darcy secrets will resist Diane Petit's power of observation.

You just wait.

"Raphael, come back here," Scarlett Johansson calls out, pouting. "You promised to return the sunscreen favor."

Natalie Portman mirrors her pout. "And I'm still waiting for my foot massage."

Raphael looks at me, obviously relieved. "I'd love to chat more, but I have promises to keep."

"Off you go," I say.

Behind me, someone jogs toward us. Before I have time to turn around, that someone puts his arm around my shoulders.

"Let me show you around this rock." Darcy says, pressing a kiss to my forehead. "Come, *chérie*."

I knit my brows. "Didn't your governess teach you that sneaking up on people is bad manners, *chéri*?"

A smile crinkles Raphael's eyes as he turns toward Darcy. "Is everything under control? Food delivered and servers lined up?"

Darcy hesitates. "If you really want to know, there was a small issue with the swimming pool. The caretaker couldn't get the new heating system to start."

"It's no big deal," Raphael says.

"You invited people to a poolside party, didn't you?" Darcy's tone is so distinctly older brotherly it reminds me of Lionel. "You don't want to let them down."

"You're right," Raphael says before turning to me. "We should all thank whatever deity we believe in for people like Seb. They make the world a better place."

Yeah, sure.

"Speaking of a better place." Raphael wrinkles his nose at Darcy. "Did you actually manage to fix the pool heater?"

"I managed to find the user manual," Darcy says. "And Kostas fixed the heating system."

Raphael taps his brother's shoulder. "I'll leave you to your girlfriend."

"Come." Darcy pulls my hand. "I want you to meet Laurent and some other friends."

I give him a canned smile. "I can't wait!"

What I really can't wait for is to go back home and barf.

CHAPTER 7

DIANE

It's ten in the evening and the party is in full swing.

Darcy and I stand between two ancient olive trees, in a small circle of dressed people, most of whom are friends of Darcy's. The majority of his brother's crowd are in swimsuits and flock around the pool and the DJ, who's converted one of the decks into a dance floor.

I would've liked to plunge into the pool, too, and maybe dance a little. I'm closer both in age and attitude to the boisterous "Raphaelites" than the stuck-up "Sebastianers." But what I want to do is irrelevant. I'm here for work—not pleasure. That's what I tell myself every time Darcy wraps his arm around my shoulder or sets his hand on the small of my back to show his friends how much "in love" he is.

Does he think they're stupid?

I don't know about men, but I'm almost sure the women have us figured out by now. Our embraces are devoid of tenderness. The looks we exchange are cold, and the endearments we say to each other sound painfully fake.

But it's Darcy's problem, not mine. My contract says nothing about "good acting." As far as I'm concerned, all's well.

The DJ starts a new disk. It's by an unfamiliar artist, but one I'll certainly be looking up. The beat is so hard to resist that all of Raphael's standing and sitting friends begin to groove. One by one, the swimming ones come out of the pool, too, and join in the fun. The two Boleyn girls rock their nimble frames suggestively, no doubt to please their "king."

Where is the birthday boy, by the way?

I turn my head toward the barbecue grill. There he is, cooking batches of seafood, meat, and vegetables. Said batches—cleaned and skewered for him—are being ferried from the kitchen and, once off the grill, served by the catering staff.

I look away, trying not to sneer at this rich man's version of *hands-on* work.

A splash draws my attention to the pool where a vision in female form emerges. She makes me think of Botticelli's *Venus*. Minus the supersized shell. Plus a red bikini.

No part of her is beautiful, strictly speaking. But there's such confidence in her posture and in the way she surveys the crowd that you can't help wondering: *Am I missing something?* Could she be a royal princess from one of those napkin-sized countries around the Mediterranean? I try to run a facial recognition search in my mind, pulling up all the princesses I'd seen in gossip magazines when I'd done my "research."

No one matches Venus. Maybe she isn't royalty, after all, but simply the first woman I've met whose self-esteem feeds on something other than her looks. Could be money, wit, professional aptitude, unequalled skill or expertise in some area… Whatever it is, she has tons of it.

All around, heads turn and conversations falter.

Venus steps onto the deck and wrings her mane of silky hair, her gesture full of easy elegance.

Darcy follows my gaze. "Genevieve Lougnon, heiress to the Lougnon Champagne house. She's Raph's best friend since childhood."

Laurent gives me a wink. "My jaw dropped, too, when I saw Genevieve for the first time. But don't worry—you'll get used to her aplomb. Eventually."

Laurent is a surgeon and as middle-class as it gets in Darcy's inner circle.

Jeanne and Mat join our small group.

"You know," Mat says to Darcy. "I almost declined your invitation."

Darcy raises an eyebrow in surprise.

"It's one thing to have you back the Greens' European Parliament bid—for which I'm eternally grateful," Mat says. "But it's another to let you jet me to a poolside party on your private island."

"It's Raph's," Darcy says, ever the nitpicker. "I thought the Greens were outside the rich-poor divide."

"No political party really is, regardless of what they claim." Mat shrugs. "But it would, indeed, have been worse if I was a socialist."

"You think this could backfire?"

Mat gives him a wink. "If hard pressed, I'll say I only agreed to come here so I could study your top-notch low-energy house."

"You know what's funny?" Jeanne says to Darcy.

"Mat actually did spend three hours this afternoon crawling all over the house and taking notes."

"Unfortunately,"—Darcy smiles—"nobody will believe him."

It's the first time I've seen him smile. His face lights up and transforms in a most unexpected way. There's mirth in his eyes. His lips, usually pressed together in a hard line, part and show white teeth. His body relaxes, and the permanent stick up his posterior seems to dissolve as if by magic. He looks almost… charming.

"Unfair but true," Mat says.

Jeanne gives her husband an affectionate look—the kind neither Darcy nor I can ever produce for each other, even if our lives depended on it.

"Hey, hon." Jeanne turns to me. "I heard from Chloe about your dad's struggle to get credited for his new perfume. What a bummer."

I shrug. "Belle Auxbois said she'd sue him if she saw his name mentioned anywhere in relation to it."

"So it's in the contract?" Mat asks. "Wasn't he aware of her terms when he signed it?"

I sigh. "It's not that simple. The contract says she may 'wish to but doesn't have to' credit Dad. It's written in fine print, tucked away on one of the last pages. When he read it before signing, he saw what he wanted to see."

"Poor Charles." Jeanne gives my arm a squeeze. "He assumed she'd recognize his 'help' like the other celebs he's worked with in the past, right?"

I nod.

"The road to hell is paved with assumptions," Darcy says.

Neither his tone nor his expression betrays an ounce

of the sympathy that Jeanne and Mat's comments conveyed.

Self-righteous ass.

He does have a point, of course. I've lost count of how many times Mom and I have told Dad he needs to quit being such an idealist and learn to plan for contingencies. We've also begged him to expect his clients and business partners to try to screw him over.

Because most of them will, given the chance.

So, yeah, I do agree with the point he's making, but my agreement doesn't make his remark more palatable. I guess it's the way he delivered it—injecting it with such superiority—that turned my stomach.

He must think he's so much better than Dad! Than all of us lowborn provincials. Bile rises in my throat. I know I should let this slide, but the itch to bite back is stronger than me. Must have something to do with family honor, I suspect.

The Darcys versus the Petits.

I pick up a seafood platter and hold it up for my *boyfriend*. "Let he who is without assumption cast the first prawn at me."

He stares into my eyes, saying nothing.

I shrug and put the platter down. "I'm not feeling well. Must be the oysters or just a stomach bug."

"I can give you some of my SMECTA," Jeanne says quickly. "I never travel without it!"

"It's OK—I'll be fine tomorrow morning. What I need is sleep." I wave my hand. "Night-night, everyone."

The group wishes me a good night, and I withdraw into the house.

Did I mention I'm sharing a bedroom with Darcy?

Thankfully, it's huge and has a nice big couch in

addition to the king-size bed. Darcy kindly offered to sleep on the couch. I agreed immediately, not bothering with the *no, you take the bed* nonsense. His comfort is the least of my concerns.

But I don't go to the bedroom just yet.

Inspired by Mat, I engage in some "crawling and climbing" of my own, starting with the walkout basement and the kitchen. After that I move on to the living room on the ground floor and upstairs to the bedrooms. Knocking gently on one door after another and sneaking in when there's no reply, I cover each level as fast as I can. And as thoroughly as I can. Unlike Mat, my goal isn't to learn how this villa saves energy.

I'm looking for dirt.

Who knows, I may never return to this place, so tonight is my chance to find a room stocked with cocaine packets or a freezer filled with body parts, or at least a bundle of compromising letters.

When I step into a bedroom across the hallway from mine on the first floor, I hear familiar voices and freeze. They're coming from outside. The window is ajar, and the people talking underneath are none other than Darcy and Raphael.

I crouch under the window and listen.

"Your fake girlfriend—she's cute," Raphael says.

"Define cute." Darcy's voice sounds funny. I think he's a little drunk. "Do you mean *diverting* with her rustic southern accent?"

"No, I mean good-looking."

"Rrrreally?" Darcy slurs. He *is* drunk. "I wouldn't call her good-looking. Perky, yes. Fresh-faced, maybe. But certainly not good-looking."

"You serious?"

"A woman needs a good measure of *class* to be

considered good-looking." Darcy pauses before adding, "Diane Petit doesn't have a nanogram of it."

Ouch. That stings.

Raphael mutters something and then says louder, "So, under no circumstances would you date her for real?"

I find myself holding my breath.

Just my vanity, no doubt.

Darcy takes his time before answering. "I can imagine exactly *three* circumstances where I'd date her for real. First, I go crazy. Can happen to the best of us. Second, I'm coerced. And third, the survival of humanity depends on it."

Raphael chuckles. "Sounds as if you don't have much regard for your future wife."

"It's mutual between us," Darcy says.

It is, indeed.

CHAPTER 8

DIANE

Earlier today, I woke up to chirping birds and murmuring waves. Darcy was already out. Twenty minutes later, I joined the guests having a sumptuous breakfast on the patio. Their faces showed various degrees of hangover, ranging from Genevieve's zero to Raphael's one hundred with everyone else in between.

I greeted Darcy with the sweetest "good morning, *chéri*" I was capable of and sat down next to Jeanne as the chair next to him was already occupied by Laurent.

Three cheers for the man!

A couple of hours later, we arrived in Crete—no sightseeing this time either—and boarded the co-owned jet. At around five in the afternoon, Darcy's chauffeur dropped me off in front of my building, and I was finally home, frustrated and depressed after my luxury getaway.

I feel a lot better now, ensconced in a beauty salon with Elorie, both of us getting massages and manicures.

"So, what's the occasion?" she asks as a nice-smelling lady in a white tunic applies red nail polish to her pinky. "Must be something big."

I focus on my thumb, which is being painted blue. "Why do you say that?"

"You bought me a drink after you got a job offer from that online magazine. Now you're paying ten times more."

I smile and shake my head, still looking for the best way to deliver the bombshell. Elorie will find out about Darcy, anyway, either from a common acquaintance or a photo in a tabloid. It's crucial that I tell her first.

"Did you win the EuroMillions jackpot?" she asks. "That must be it. How much was it?"

I smile. "I won zilch, as usual. But I did sell a few photos through an online depository, and I finally got paid for the wedding I immortalized three weeks ago."

"All right, that explains the *how* of this." Elorie narrows her eyes. "But it doesn't explain the *why*."

OK, Diane—ready, set, roll.

"I've been hiding something important from you," I say. "And now I want to come clean and apologize."

"I knew it!" She let out a smug puff. "Spill the beans."

"I'm seeing someone. And it's getting sort of… serious."

Elorie's jaw slackens. "No way! Since when? Who is he?"

"His name is Sebastian," I say before adding under my breath, "Darcy."

She leans in, eyes wide in disbelief. "Come again—Sebastian who?"

"Darcy."

"Darcy as in d'Arcy du Grand-Thouars de Saint-

Maurice, the billionaire count at the helm of Parfums d'Arcy?"

I nod.

"The a-hole who ruined your father?"

"Yes," I mumble.

She turns away and keeps her gaze on her nails for a long moment.

I know what she's itching to say and I dread it.

"Hypocrite," she finally spits out without looking at me.

What can I say in my defense?

Nothing at all.

Elorie pulls a face and says in a squeaky nasal voice, "I'm Saint Diane. I disapprove of your materialistic dream, Elorie. I would never date a billionaire. Money means nothing to me."

Time for another lie. "It's not about his money—I fancy him."

"No kidding." She smirks. "Why would anyone fancy a tall, dark, and handsome billionaire? Who happens to be single. And young."

And a jerk.

But that's beside the point.

She purses her lips. "Where did you meet him?"

"He's a friend of Jeanne's husband, Mat."

Elorie blinks. "Jeanne from *La Bohème*?"

"The very same." I take a fortifying breath—here goes one more lie. "It started as casual sex a few weeks ago and grew into something bigger… really fast."

Elorie says nothing.

"Will you forgive me for keeping you in the dark?" I ask.

She keeps silent for a while and then smiles. "Still waters run deep, eh?"

I smile back.

"OK," she says. "I'll forgive you on one condition."

"Shoot."

"Introduce me into his circle."

I grin at Elorie's ever pragmatic attitude. "Consider it done."

"OK," she says. "You're forgiven."

I blow her a kiss.

"Let's rewind to where you said it was getting serious," she says. "What did you mean by that?"

That I'm marrying him in exactly two months.

"Just that we're not hiding anymore, which, by the way, will make it easy to bring you into the fold."

She nods, her eyes bright. I can almost see smoke coming out of her ears as her mind spins with possibilities. Let's hope she meets the man of her dreams through Darcy, so at least someone will have a happy ending when our farce is over.

"Wait," Elorie says. "Will you be quitting the supermarket job?"

I look at my beautifully painted nails. "Why would I do that?"

She shrugs. "Because he can use his connections to get you a better job, dum-dum."

Makes sense, but that's not why I'll quit. I'm going to give in my notice later this week because my contract with Darcy says so.

On page five.

We leave the salon and head to the nearby movie theater for some superhero action accompanied by popcorn and gummy bears.

"Hey, maybe he'll help you become a photographer for fashion magazines," Elorie says with enthusiasm as we slump into our armchairs in the back of the darkened room. “That would be so cool!”

Fashion photography *is* cool, except it isn’t my thing. But Elorie’s comment reminds me of another matter I wanted to discuss with her.

“I hope I can make it as a photographer on my own,” I say. “One of the depositories where I upload my pics asked me for a series of artful portraits in black and white.”

She mouths, “Ooh.”

“They want tasteful feminine nudes.” I hesitate before adding, “Will you pose for me?”

She chokes on her popcorn. “You serious?”

“Yes. You’re beautiful and fit, and so much more real than those anorexic fashion models... Not that I’m in a position to ask one to sit for me, anyway.”

It’s like a lungful of fresh air to be able to say something honest. I’m going to miss that feeling. I already do.

“I’m flattered,” Elorie says. “But I have to be careful about my image. Considering my plans.”

“Not to worry!” I lean in. “I’ll make sure nothing scandalous, such as a nipple, can be seen. The series will be more about the shapes, arches, skin, light, and shadow than about the body.”

Elorie chews her lip.

I give her a pleading look. “Please, pretty please?”

“Have you done it before?”

“No,” I say honestly. “You’ll be my first nude.”

“OK,” she says. “Why not. Could be fun.”

“Thank you, Elorie, you’re the best!” I give her a quick hug. “And, by the way, I’ll split my fee.”

She grins. “Why didn’t you start with that, dum-dum?”

Elorie, you rock.

When I get home after the movie, my thoughts return to my Greek weekend. Last night, when Darcy walked into our bedroom, I was already under the covers, pretending to sleep. I even produced a loud snore or two for good measure. Because I'm an ace at fake snoring.

And because *I have no class.*

In reality, it took me several hours to fall asleep. I was annoyed with my fruitless search, with Darcy's mean comment, and with the whole fake relationship thing. Suddenly, I was uncertain my plan would work. What if I don't find any incriminating evidence? Maybe Thibaud d'Arcy wasn't murdered. Maybe the family's closets have been purged of all skeletons. Maybe Parfums d'Arcy doesn't sneak carcinogenic components into its flavors and fragrances.

Maybe Sebastian Darcy is the only billionaire in the world who doesn't tuck his money away in offshore accounts.

Nah, I don't believe that.

What's more likely, though, is that the money is hidden too well for me to trace.

As our "relationship" is about to go public, some of the implications I've been ignoring hit me hard. Dad will be devastated. He'll be so disappointed he might even stop talking to me. I'll have to lie to him, lie to Mom, Chloe and all my friends. I'll spend the next four to six months pretending I love the man I hate.

And all I'll get out of this may be two hundred grand at best and fifty at worst. If my hidden agenda fails, I won't get any revenge or satisfaction out of this —just money.

It's a terrifying prospect.

PART III
CASTLE

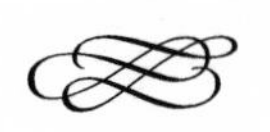

CHAPTER 9

SEBASTIAN

March is my least favorite month.

The weather is just as depressing in Paris as it is in Burgundy, London, Montreal, New York, and pretty much everywhere else in the northern hemisphere where I travel for work or leisure. Of course, there's always Tahiti and Australia, but those trips are notorious time eaters. Even Raph's paradisiac Ninossos gets too gray this time of year. Raph doesn't care—he's happy to go there rain or shine, but I'd rather brood in a big city than on a rock in the middle of the sea.

Notice that I haven't done much brooding lately. I've been working my tail off, consolidating the headway Parfums d'Arcy made last quarter and overseeing the launch of three new manufacturing facilities. Not to mention Le Big Ben. Raph and I purchased it last month, and it needs a loving hand to recover its old luster.

Thank God Octave is there—always in good health,

remarkably fit and imperturbable—to manage the town house! Because whenever I have a free moment, I spend it with Diane.

That woman makes it virtually impossible to brood even when you're determined to. Not that she makes a special effort to divert me, but she achieves that without meaning to. Sometimes, even despite herself.

Over the past few weeks, she's accompanied me to several society galas and soirées, where we've held hands and smiled for cameras. I've taken her to dinner at exclusive places such as La Tour d'Argent and Jules Verne and for drinks at Royal Monceau and Le Crillon. She didn't seem impressed. I bought a Cartier watch and Chopard earrings for her so she'd look more presentable. She gave me a signed note, saying she'd wear those items while working for me and return them as soon as we were done.

Strange woman.

Last week she mentioned she loved musicals, so I flew her to New York to see one on Broadway. She seemed to enjoy herself. But when we returned to Paris, she demanded that I slash the extravagance of my courtship from *overkill* to *gallant.*

Because, she said, she didn't want any perks.

The demand was made just as I was about to hire a personal shopper and a stylist for her. Not because the things she wears are ugly or cheap—which they are, by the way—but because they don't do her justice. Now that I've had ample opportunity to watch and hold her, I *know* she has a delectable figure underneath her sack-like gowns and baggy pants.

And I want to see that figure in a formfitting dress that stops well above the knee.

Beats me why I want that, but I do.

"Diane," I say as I offer my hand to help her out of the car. "You're quitting your job and moving in with me in less than two weeks. You *must* allow me to upgrade your outfits."

She takes my hand and puts a foot on the red carpet rolled out in front of the nightclub. Her delicate foot is shod in a clunky boot, which begs this question—is that all she can afford on her salary or is it what she actually likes? Above the boot, flaps the hem of an ample gown that reminds me of the traditional dress women wear in North Korea. I catch a glimpse of a slim ankle between the boot and the dress, and my fingers burn to touch it. I ignore that urge. It'll pass, eventually. It always does.

"Define *upgrade*," Diane says.

"Let me rephrase it—I'd like to buy you new clothes. And shoes."

"What's wrong with what I wear? Not *classy* enough?"

I hesitate, but only for a second. "Exactly."

Sometimes you have to be blunt to get your message across.

I close the car door behind her and instruct Greg to go home. He argues that he doesn't mind waiting, but I insist. Whether it's out of decency or to avoid Diane calling me a heartless exploiter is an open question.

She's quiet as we enter the club and join my friends partying in one of the larger booths. I decide to drop the subject of her wardrobe.

For now.

With the exception of Laurent, the rest of the company aren't really my *friends* in the original, pre-Facebook sense of the word. They're just people who entertain me enough to spend a couple of hours with them once in a while.

"Hey, look who's here!" Laurent stands to greet us.

The others follow suit, and a few minutes later, my *girlfriend* and I are cozying up to each other in one of the roomy armchairs, sipping our elaborate cocktails.

Unlike the last time I hung out with this group, the conversation is dull, dominated by Jean-François, who can't stop gushing about his new Ferrari. He's been droning on for at least fifteen minutes now, killing Laurent's and his date Yasmina's attempts to change the topic. The women study their nails, and even the men look bored.

"Let's dance," Yasmina says suddenly.

She grabs Laurent's hand and stands up.

"Great idea!" Laurent looks mighty pleased as he follows her to the dance floor.

One by one, the occupants of the booth follow Yasmina's example, and before we know it, it's just Diane, Jean-François, and me. I don't usually dance, but I've heard enough about Ferraris to last me a lifetime. As far as I can tell, so has Diane.

I stand and offer her my hand. "A dance, *chérie*?"

"With pleasure." She gives me a dazzling smile.

Considering the circumstances, she might mean it for once.

Diane isn't a very skilled dancer, but she has a good sense of rhythm, and the way she moves is nice to look at, despite her unfortunate outfit. Something else that's nice to look at are her eyes. Diane is the only person I know whose eyes always hold a private smile. As if she could see something amusing in everything and everyone, at all times. Even when she's angry or sulking, that little smile is still there, illuminating her lovely face and lifting my spirits in a most unexpected way.

A flash of light draws my attention away from Diane's eyes. Ah, paparazzi. I used to turn my back or walk away whenever I spotted one, but these days, their interests and mine are perfectly aligned. I put my hand on the small of Diane's back and draw her closer.

"There's a photo op at three o'clock," I whisper in her ear. "We need to kiss."

"Mild or medium?" she whispers back.

Diane has come up with a four-level Smooch Heat Index to help us navigate the murky waters of pretend affection. Her scale goes from *mild* to *extra hot*. The former is a peck that we use to greet each other and say good-bye in public. *Medium* involves a longer "docking" time and more pressure, but it's still just a brush and our lips remain sealed. I'm allowed to initiate it without asking, albeit a heads-up is always appreciated.

Hot corresponds to an openmouthed kiss, suggesting tongue play to an innocent onlooker.

That level requires a prior clearance and is reserved for special occasions. I presume our upcoming betrothal will qualify as such.

Finally, level number four—*extra hot*—is a passionate, shameless kiss, "tongues and all," which she included in her index as a point of reference rather than a workable option. Diane is adamant: *Extra hot* is and will remain out of bounds, unless warranted by exceptional circumstances such as an impending apocalypse or a real danger of exposure.

I cup her cheek and slide my hand to the back of her head. "Hot. We're in a nightclub."

I'm taking a risk here, well aware that a midnight dance can hardly be called a "special occasion." My request isn't justified, and I fully expect her to call my bluff and mouth "no way."

Diane arches an eyebrow as if to say she needs justification.

I just stare at her, holding my ground.

She gives me a small nod.

Before she can change her mind, I pull her into me with my hand at her nape and press my mouth to hers. Every time we kiss, it strikes me how much I enjoy it. My goals, my company, the whole world becomes unimportant as her delicious scent fills my nostrils and the softness of her lips overtakes my mind. So warm, so yielding. I've tried meditating with the best coaches in France and abroad to achieve the state of *mindful relaxation* wherein I empty my head and let go of all my worries.

I swear I have yet to find a shorter path to that coveted state than kissing Diane Petit.

She wraps her arms around my neck, melding her body to mine.

A camera clicks.

I graze her lips and tease them apart.

She lets me. Holding her tight, I stroke her back. My right hand slides to her glorious bottom and stays there, fingers splayed but not daring to squeeze. The temptation to slip my tongue between her soft lips and drink in the taste of her mouth is so strong I can barely resist it.

No tongues, I remind myself. She doesn't want tongues. She was very clear on that point.

Diane's hand runs up and down my nape, clutching the back of my neck as if she means it.

It's just for show. It's just for show. It's just for—

She removes her hand and draws away.

"We should go," she says.

I'm so drunk on her I need a moment to adjust.

And so does my erection.

She stands on tiptoes and whispers into my ear, "Now, Sebastian. If you grab my hand and we rush out, everyone will think we're running off to fuck."

CHAPTER 10

SEBASTIAN

I hail a cab.

"Rue Didot in the 14th," I say to the driver.

Our drill is that I accompany Diane to her place before going home. Sometimes I stay for an hour or so, checking emails on my phone and reading a paper while Diane does chores or edits photos.

She calls that a "quickie."

The few times we've gone to my town house after a date, I've insisted she stay the night, but she always has a good reason to return to her apartment.

As we drive across the city, I'm painfully aware of Diane's thigh next to mine.

Get a grip, man.

She isn't even my type. I'm sure I'm reacting this way because I haven't had sex in months, ever since Ingrid left me. That's it; this isn't about Diane, this is just about me having gone too long without a woman. It's decided—I'm getting laid as soon as Diane and I are done, and I won't be picky. The first pretty face who falls into my lap will do just to take the edge off.

Because, heaven help me, that *edge* will be the size of Everest by then.

I stare out the window, surprised to see we're passing by the imposing red gate of the Hôtel d'Hozier and other familiar buildings on rue Vieille du Temple. The taxi is taking us to the left bank through Le Marais. This itinerary is practicable only by night. By day, my neighborhood's mesh of one-way streets makes it a nightmare to drive through.

My town house is just a few blocks away, hidden from sight behind a walled garden, as a self-respecting Parisian *hôtel particulier* should be. It hasn't been in the family for very long—only half a century—but I hope it'll stay for generations to come.

Half an hour later, the cab pulls up outside Diane's building. I pay the driver and follow my intended upstairs.

~

"I'm not very good with cocktails," Diane says, opening one of her kitchen cabinets. "But I can fix us a gin and tonic."

I sit at the kitchen table. "Sure."

A Scotch is what I'd really like, but I already had two glasses of the best single malt at the nightclub, so I'm fine with a gin and tonic. Or anything, for that matter.

Diane hands me my drink and sits down across from me, nursing her own glass in her hands.

"When you walked me through the contract," she says, "you said something about waiting for 'a certain person to make his move.' "

"Did I?"

She nods. "Did he?"

"Make a move?"

"Uh-huh."

"Not yet."

"What kind of move are we talking about?"

I sigh and spend some time gulping down my drink. Diane is already halfway through her glass.

"My father worshipped my mother," I finally say. "Fifteen years ago, he made a terrible mistake and slept with another woman—a much younger woman, as it happened. She posted their sex tape online the next day."

"She didn't try to blackmail him first?"

"No, and that is additional proof her seduction of Papa was planned by someone who'd paid her."

"A *booty* trap."

I nod.

"Did your dad try to talk to her, find out more?"

"She disappeared."

"And your parents?"

"Maman said he'd broken the sacred vows of marriage and humiliated her. She packed up and left."

"To Nepal?" she asks.

"You're well informed."

She arches an eyebrow. "As your *significant other* and soon-to-be *better half*, it's my duty to be informed."

I guess she has a point. "The first year, she took an apartment in Versailles, and a year later, she moved to Nepal."

"What's she doing there, by the way?"

"Running a charitable foundation. She hasn't set foot in Paris in years."

"Really?"

I nod. "I was nineteen when she announced she was leaving the country, Raphael fifteen, and Noah only eleven. Raph and I chose to stay here with Papa. Noah went to Nepal with her."

"What happened?"

"Papa… he just… lost his way. Half the time he was depressed, and the other half he tried to *have fun*, often with the help of drugs. Ten years ago, he was found dead."

She nods sympathetically. "Suicide?"

"Overdose, more likely." I shrug. "The report was inconclusive."

"That's a very sad story."

I set my empty glass on the table next to Diane's.

She refills both. "So you believe someone orchestrated the affair that led to his downfall and will now try to do the same to you? Isn't that a bit farfetched?"

I can see how it would seem so.

"A year ago, I met a woman. I really liked her. She came from one of the country's most respectable and wealthiest families, and she was a rare beauty, to boot. We started dating, and things were going in the right direction. She moved in with me. I was thinking of proposing."

She nods as if she already knew this. Well, I guess she might if she reads gossip magazines.

I gulp down half the liquid in my glass and point at Diane's. "You have some catching up to do."

"Oh." She smiles and takes a good swig. "So what happened?"

"I suddenly became terribly popular with gorgeous women."

She cocks her head. "What do you mean by suddenly? You're rich, you're handsome—"

"Wait, did you just call me handsome?"

Diane brings her glass to her face, tips it toward her mouth, and mutters into it, "Did I?"

"I'm positive."

She sets her glass down and puts her chin up in defiance. "So what if I did? You *are* handsome. It doesn't make you a good person."

I suppress a smile, not sure why Diane's admission pleases me so much. "Fair enough."

"Finish your tale," she says.

"Where was I?"

"The Siege of Darcy by Hot Chicks."

"Right. So, all of a sudden, exquisite creatures were wooing me left and right. Naturally, I became suspicious. It was like somebody was trying to stage a remake of my dad's story."

"Or maybe you were just reading too much into someone's flirtation," she says with a wink.

I smirk. "You're right. I'm paranoid. Who would want to hurt me, the harmless do-gooder that I am?"

She doesn't look so amused anymore. I'm sure she's thinking of her father now and what I did to him. It bothers me. I wonder... Does she still hate me as much as she did before I hired her? Or have our conversations and kisses, no matter how fake, mellowed her? Is there a chance she actually enjoys my company?

And my kisses?

She stares at her hands, visibly peeved.

I shouldn't care. She's *not* my girlfriend, not even a friend. It doesn't matter what she thinks of me. It doesn't matter if she likes talking to me or kissing me. It's *strictly business* between us, and it'll stay that way.

"My gut feeling is very trustworthy," I say to break the silence. "And it tells me someone was pulling the strings behind both affairs, Papa's and mine."

"So how did the Siege end?"

"Ingrid grew jealous, and no matter how many assurances of my loyalty I gave her, her trust was broken. She kept saying there's no smoke without fire. It drove me mad."

"You should've told her about your suspicions."

"I did. But she was too far gone. She said I was grasping at straws and inventing ridiculous conspiracy theories to justify my frolicking."

"Because you didn't *frolic* at all, did you?"

"Of course not! I was merely being polite with the ladies." I give her a pointed look. "Anyway, Ingrid and I broke up a few weeks later."

"Who dumped whom?"

I shrug. "She told me she was leaving. I did nothing to stop her."

"I see."

"Miraculously, the lustful supermodels disappeared shortly afterward. Don't you find that strange?"

"Maybe…"

"Anyway, I got over the whole thing more easily than I'd expected. I just plunged into work and moved on."

She smiles. "Your imaginary nemesis must have been disappointed."

"I assure you he or she is very real. But yes, I believe, that person regretted putting things in motion too soon. I'm sure this time he'll wait until I'm married to launch the attack."

"Uh-huh." She looks like she's trying not to smile.

I rub my forehead. "Diane. I know how it sounds. Even Raphael, who witnessed Papa's debacle, isn't fully convinced… But I *know* I'm on to something."

Her expression becomes less amused and more sympathetic.

"Put yourself in my shoes," I continue, eager to capitalize on that seed of sympathy. "Can you imagine how hard it is to suspect everyone around you? And I mean *everyone*—family, friends, relations, help, competitors, subordinates… the whole damn world!"

She nods. "Must be tough."

"I've ruled out a bunch of people, but only Raphael —and now you—knows about my suspicions and my plan. Everyone else must remain in the dark to avoid leaks."

"Makes sense."

Opening up to Diane is a huge relief. Her natural intelligence and inquisitiveness were making it hard for her to play her part without having read the full script. Not that she didn't do a good job, but… let's just say I'm looking forward to having her hundred percent onboard with this.

"There's someone very dear to me," Diane says, "who's been… troubled for a long time—in a different way than you, but still. She's doing much better now."

Oh, great.

She thinks I'm crazy. *Hundred percent onboard*, my foot. Why did I tell her all this? Why didn't I keep my motives secret, as I'd intended? The gin and tonic must have loosened my tongue.

"I'm not *troubled*," I grate.

"OK." She stares into my eyes. "Whatever you say. I'm just here to do a job and collect my paycheck."

"That's right."

"When do you think your nemesis will make his move?"

"During our honeymoon."

"Why?"

"To be sure to strike while the iron is hot and to

maximize the devastating effect it would produce on me."

"What if he decides to wait?"

"He—or she or they—won't. He's running out of time and out of options. With my previous girlfriend, he didn't even wait for us to get engaged."

"And you're sure you'll catch him this time?"

"Oh, yeah. As soon as my new admirer makes an entrance, I'll have a private eye tail her 24-7. I'll be prepared."

She nods.

We finish our drinks in silence.

"You should go home now," Diane says.

She's right.

I pull out my phone and call a cab. I should get some shut-eye. Tomorrow morning, I'll be up at six thirty, as usual. I'll work out for an hour and head to the office. Sleeping in isn't an option. Even on weekends. There are simply too many things to take care of—new markets to conquer, old competitors to decimate, and a backstabbing Judas to unmask.

CHAPTER 11

DIANE

I gasp and forget to shut my mouth.

The view that opens up before me as Greg turns the car from the sinuous countryside road onto a gravel driveway lined with tall oak trees blows my mind. It's early April, and the ancient oaks have fully woken from their winter sleep, their branches spawning clusters of buds and pale green baby leaves. I scoot to the door and peep out the window. On either side of the driveway, green lawns stretch far and wide, smelling of freshly cut grass.

God, I love that smell!

We don't have nearly enough of it in Paris.

But it isn't the majestic oak trees or the vast expanses of grass that take my breath away. Set back at the end of the driveway is the Chateau d'Arcy du Grand-Thouars. A mixture of medieval and Renaissance, the castle reminds me of the Chateau des Milandes in Perigord that I visited with Mom, Dad, Lionel, and Chloe back when Lionel was still in good health. It's smaller, but just as elegant and romantic. As for its grand staircase leading up the main entrance, it totally deserves a red carpet sprinkled with movie stars.

I'm half aware I'm having a most ridiculous Elizabeth-at-the-sight-of-Pemberley moment, but I can't help it. The view is just too damn gorgeous.

And, yes, I'm still a convinced socialist.

And no, I don't think privilege is something people should be born into—it should be obtained based on merit.

And yes, again, I still think that aristocracy with their archaic titles, pompous names, and unwarranted sense of entitlement should be a thing of the past.

But right now, all those righteous thoughts scatter away into the deepest recesses of my brain, letting fascination and awe take center stage.

"What do you think of the castle, mademoiselle?" Greg asks, smiling in the rearview mirror.

I realize my mouth is gaping and quickly shut it, cheeks aflame.

He shifts his gaze to the chateau. "Beautiful, isn't it?"

"It certainly is."

"Monsieur Darcy landed at the Auxerre airport an hour ago. I'm not sure he's at the castle yet."

"He is," I say. "He just texted me. Raphael has been here since last night, and a few other people, too."

"You'll love it here," Greg says.

I'm not so sure.

Darcy insisted we spend a long weekend at his ancestral chateau in Burgundy, arguing it would be strange if he didn't bring his soon-to-be fiancée here. Incredible as it may seem, I've never visited this region. Well, now I'm going to get an insider tour of it.

Aren't I lucky?

On the program for the weekend is a tour of the

castle, its surrounding English-style park, and its wine cellars. We'll also drive through some of the nearby villages and towns and sample their best restaurants. But the highlight of our weekend will be the main local tourist attraction—the Darcy Grotto and its Ice Age rock art.

As soon as Greg stops the car, a youth with a shy smile opens the door for me, mumbling, "Hello, and welcome to the chateau."

Before I can introduce myself, he grabs my overnight bag and rushes inside.

I stare after him, blinking.

"Thank you, Roger," Darcy says to him as the two men pass each other on the staircase, one running up and the other down.

I take in my *boyfriend's* casual look—and quickly avert my gaze. His jeans and fine wool sweater hug his lean, muscular frame in a loose-fitting, conservatively masculine way.

I'm sure he hadn't meant it to be sexy.

Except it is.

He gives me a *mild* kiss. "Did you have a pleasant trip?"

"Oh, come on," I say. "It's just two hours' drive from Paris."

"Could've been an *unpleasant* two hours," he says, arching an eyebrow.

Did he just make a joke? I study his face. His mouth is unsmiling, and there are no laugh lines around his eyes or any other noticeable signs of humor.

Hmm… Hard to tell.

He's been doing this more and more lately—saying things which, coming from any other man, I would immediately recognize as jokes. But from Darcy… he's just not that kind of guy.

Can a man develop a sense of humor after thirty like some develop arthritis or a bald patch?

"Your chateau is awesome," I say.

"It's nothing special, really. There are dozens of similar castles here in Burgundy, and a few are more *awesome* this one. But there's one aspect of it that's unique."

"Which is?"

Darcy lifts a hand, palm up, as if to say, *hang on*. He turns to Greg, who has just parked the Prius between Raphael's flashy red Ferrari and another sports car and now bounds toward us.

"Madame Bruel will show you to your room," he says to Greg. "You're free until Sunday evening."

"*Merci*, Sebastian. I have some friends in Auxerre. It'll be great to see them."

"Take the Prius—I'll be driving the Lamborghini." Darcy turns back to me. "What's unique about this castle is that it's never changed hands. It was built by Chevalier Henri d'Arcy du Grand-Thouars at the end of the sixteenth century."

"Oh, my God!" I clap my hand to my mouth. "And he still owns it? Is he a ghost? Does he have chains? Can I meet him?"

Darcy's lips twitch and form that crooked, unpracticed smile of his that I hate because of what it does to my insides.

"What I meant," he says, "is that the castle has remained in the family. Its current owner is my brother Noah."

"Is he here? Am I finally going to meet him?"

"No. He—"

"Couldn't make it," I finish for Darcy.

Noah never makes it to any party or event organized by his older brothers—not even when said event is held at his own castle. Neither does Darcy's mother, by the way. But she, at least, has the excuse of living in Nepal.

Darcy's expression hardens.

"Let me get this straight," I say to lighten things up. "You don't own the island, you only co-own the jet and the club, and now you tell me the castle isn't yours, either."

"That's correct."

I arch an eyebrow. "And here I thought I was snatching a *real* billionaire."

"You are." He smiles again. "I inherited Parfums d'Arcy, which is worth well over a billion. It's one of Europe's largest individually owned businesses. Not to mention the trinkets such as the Paris town house and apartments in London and New York."

The expression of genuine pride on his face is the same as the one I saw on Liviu—Jeanne's friend's nine-year-old—last Wednesday. He'd dragged his mom to *La Bohème* so he could show everyone his new remote control drone.

As the saying goes, the only difference between men and boys is the price of their toys.

"Oh, good." I exhale in feigned relief. "I was almost about to call the whole marriage thingy off."

As we reach the top of the stairs and step inside, a skinny woman in her fifties holds her hand out. "I'm Jacqueline Bruel, the housekeeper."

I shake her hand. "Diane. Very pleased to meet you."

"The pleasure is all mine," she says with a sincere smile before pointing to a wide wooden staircase across the foyer. "My office is on the first floor, second door on the left. Knock if you need anything. Or give me a call."

She turns to Darcy, raising an eyebrow in half question.

"I'll make sure Diane has your number, Jacqueline," he says, leading me upstairs.

Unlike the sleek villa on Ninossos and the impeccably kept town house, the castle looks as if it has seen better days. Everything in here is authentic and beautiful—but also threatening to collapse at any moment.

The antique ceiling fixtures will be the first, I'm sure, followed by the creaky floorboards under our feet.

"Needs work, huh?" Darcy says, following my gaze.

I nod.

"I almost approached Chloe a month ago, seeing how tastefully and respectfully she rehabbed *La Bohème*, but…" He sighs. "This chateau is Noah's. He needs to at least confirm he wants it restored."

When we reach the second floor, Darcy opens a door, which groans and nearly unhinges itself in protest, to a spacious room.

"The lord and lady's chamber," he says. "Aka our bedroom. The bathroom is two doors to the right."

I step inside and take in the large four-poster, the exquisite Art Nouveau wardrobes and chests of drawers, and the mildew stains on the walls. The wood floor is covered with beautiful rugs, their blue flower patterns in perfect harmony with the rest of the decor.

I look around for the couch area like the one in the town house, but don't find one.

Darcy points to a small door between the wardrobes. "There's an adjacent room right there. Grandpapa Bernard and Grandmaman Colette, who were the last ones to refurbish the castle, slept in separate bedrooms."

"How clever of them," I say, my shoulders slacking with relief. "So, who's around? I saw Raphael's car outside. Anyone else I know?"

"Genevieve—you met her at his birthday party. We're also hosting Dr. Muller, the archeologist who manages the Grotto, and the mayor of the village with his spouse. You'll meet everyone at dinner tonight."

Ah, I see. The cream of the local society.

What a shame Elorie couldn't be here today! She had to stay in Paris for her dad's fiftieth birthday party. But she's coming over tomorrow morning, and Darcy and I will fetch her from the train station.

I can't wait.

"The dinner will be served at eight in the great hall, but at four, we all meet in the front yard to visit the cave." Darcy heads for the little door. "I'll let you freshen up."

"What's the dress code?"

The dos and don'ts of high society go over my head, so I always prefer to ask.

"Casual." He hesitates for a second and adds, "*My* casual."

Ha!

This is Darcy's way of admitting that what passes for casual in his circles, normal people call dolled up. *My* casual for midseason consists of well-worn baggy jeans and a roomy sweater. I wore the combo to a couple of *informal* outings with Darcy's friends. Only everyone else looked as if they'd read the wrong memo and had dressed for a job interview at *Vogue*.

When Darcy raised the matter of buying me clothes again a couple of weeks ago, I promised I'd make an effort. And I did. I bought a pair of jeans and two sweaters from a low-cost supermarket.

At least they were new.

In regards to the formal events that require gowns, I've found a solution that eliminates an extra expenditure from Darcy or me.

I borrow.

Elorie and I are the same size, and my initial idea was to ask for one or two of her little black dresses that would be perfect for any occasion. But something stopped me. It may have to do with the way Darcy looks at me, especially when I show some skin or wear pants that are a notch tighter than my norm.

It may also have to do with the way my stupid body reacts to those looks.

So instead of Elorie's sexy LBDs, I picked a few of Manon's formless gowns she's kept from her XL days as a reminder of what awaits her if she puts on weight again. Those gowns swallow me up, their thick material creating a shield-like barrier between me and Darcy. They're my chastity belts of sorts. And while it annoys and saddens me that I need one around Darcy, I'm not taking any risks. I haven't even moved in with him yet, for crying out loud.

Hmm, I wonder if there's an online shop that carries a high-tech twenty-first-century version of a *real* chastity belt... Perhaps I should order one.

Just in case.

CHAPTER 12

DIANE

Dr. Muller, whom I imagined to be an old gentleman with a white beard and a cane, is in fact a pretty woman in her early thirties. With a powerful flashlight in her hand, she gives us a private tour of the Darcy Grotto, a large complex of interconnected caves just a fifteen-minute walk from the castle.

Under normal circumstances, anyone can visit the Grotto even if, like most caves in France, it's on private land. We follow Dr. Muller through stalactite galleries and halls. Here and there, icicle-like stalactites meet with stalagmite mounds in passionate embraces. They're called columns, Dr. Muller explains.

We're headed to the Mammoth Hall, which hosts the oldest prehistoric rock paintings in France.

Dr. Muller says they're forty thousand years old.

As we trek behind her, I can't help thinking she looks like someone you'd expect to tread catwalks, rather than cave galleries, for a living. Her knee-length trench coat and snug little boots do a great job of drawing the eye to her slender and exceptionally well-shaped legs. I bet Darcy is ogling them right now.

Even I—a one hundred percent heterosexual woman—am ogling them right now.

There's no denying Dr. Muller is the bomb. She's smart, good-looking, and classy. Unlike the *perky* me, who doesn't have a *nanogram* of class, according to my future ex-husband.

Why didn't he ask *her* to be his fake girlfriend?

Maybe he's reserving her for when the coast is clear of his nemesis and he can have a real relationship with a suitable woman.

"*Et voilà*," Dr. Muller says, turning around. "We've reached the Mammoth Hall. I invite everyone to study the ceiling and the walls."

Striking images of mammoths, lions, and reindeer painted in ochre and charcoal adorn the cave. They're simple and yet perfectly drawn, the animals full of grace and easy to recognize despite minimal detail.

"I don't see any rabbits or foxes," Raphael says. "Why's that?"

Dr. Muller smiles. "The Paleolithic Man didn't draw the animals he hunted."

"So these paintings had a ritualistic function?" Genevieve asks.

"We believe so." Dr. Muller brushes a strand of hair from her face with the elegance of a ballerina. "But the truth is we don't really know."

I raise my hand. "Did you find any paintings of people?"

"We found a few representations of women. But no men. That is, no complete men."

"What do you mean?" Raphael asks.

"I mean this." She points her torchlight to a familiar-looking drawing on the ceiling.

I peer and realize it's an erect penis. Or, should I say in this context, a *phallus*.

I give Darcy a wink. "A forty-thousand-year-old cock and balls graffiti, huh? Some things never change."

Just before we climb out of the cave, I spot a distinctly Asian sculpture submerged up to its neck in a small pond formed by water dripping from the ceiling. It looks completely out of place in this prehistoric cave.

"Oh, it's a Buddha," Dr. Muller says matter-of-factly, following my gaze.

I stare into her eyes. "A Buddha."

She nods.

I clap my hand to my forehead. "But of course—stupid me! It's *the* famous Ice Age Bathing Buddha of Burgundy."

Darcy grins.

He actually stretches his lips and opens his mouth wide enough for this smile to qualify as a full-fledged grin, the first one I've ever seen on him.

It nukes me to a pile of rubble.

"I can explain," he says. "The Buddha is on loan from Le Louvre. The curators there wanted to see what the special variety of bacteria in this pool will do to him."

"He's been here for fifteen years now," Dr. Muller says.

I turn to her. "And?"

"Nothing." She spreads her hands. "No effect whatsoever."

"You need to have a word with your bacteria," I say to my *beau*. "Le Louvre counts on them."

"Oh, that reminds me!" Dr. Muller scurries over to Darcy. "I must discuss an urgent matter with you."

"Of course," he says. "We'll talk after dinner."

She adds something in a hushed voice, clearly unwilling for anyone to overhear. Must be business related, I tell myself. And confidential. Maybe she caught someone on the team cheating or she wants to negotiate an additional guide position.

Regardless, I'm rattled… and annoyed for being rattled.

But then I catch Genevieve watching me watch Dr. Muller talking with Darcy. Am I being prejudiced and way off the mark to read her expression as gloating?

Elorie can't come here soon enough.

CHAPTER 13

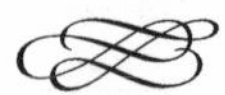

DIANE

At dinner, I meet the mayor, who's adorable with his seventies mustache and a polo shirt tucked into his old-fashioned jeans. His wife wears a pink tweed jacket and has an easy laugh. We get on immediately and chat away for most of the meal.

Just as I begin to tell myself this evening isn't as bad as I'd expected, Darcy invites the guests to move to the drawing room for a more relaxed second part of the soirée. Darcy and Dr. Muller walk over to the window and launch into a long conversation. Genevieve expertly maneuvers the mayor's wife away from me to the other sofa across a ginormous coffee table.

"Did you like the cave?" she asks.

Something tells me she doesn't really care. Her question is just an opener for something else.

"It was impressive," I say honestly. "I loved the paintings and I learned a lot."

She inches a little closer. "Isn't Penelope—that's Dr. Muller's first name—amazing?"

Et voilà. "She sure is."

"Such competence, such drive! You know, she comes from a long pedigree of writers and academics."

"Good for her."

"Penelope and I are very close," she says. "I have so much respect for her achievement. In my eyes, it's more important than money or titles."

She gives me a long, intense stare as if trying to gauge if the penny has dropped.

I'm itching to say, *Hey, I get it, despite my limited education. You're reminding me I have neither merit nor money, not to mention a title. You're suggesting I'm the odd one out in this room. But you know what? We're in agreement. I don't belong here, and I sure as hell don't want to belong. If I weren't bound by a contract, I'd be hanging out with Elorie and Manon at* La Bohème *instead of wasting precious minutes of my life listening to your aristocratic farts. They stink just the same as everyone else's.*

Unfortunately, I can't say any of it.

Damn that contract!

This is the hardest I've bitten my tongue in the past two months. There've been other temptations, but none of them this strong. Genevieve has been cold and indifferent, but not mean. Neither have any of Darcy's other acquaintances. Most of them just try to be friendly without realizing they're patronizing me. When we chat, they avoid long words. They find me "cute." In their eyes, I'm Darcy's long-overdue fling with a plebeian. They consider our *amourette* as his rite of passage, his brave—and brief—exploration of the world of commoners.

And I'm forced to put up with that shit.

If there's one reason I look forward to Darcy's announcement of our betrothal, it's to see the look on their faces at that moment. Especially on Genevieve's.

My peripheral vision catches Darcy's shape looming next to us.

"Can I steal my girlfriend for a moment?" he asks Genevieve.

"Of course." She gives him a canned smile. "You can sit here—I was going to go chat with Raphael, anyway."

Darcy puts his glass on the coffee table and sits next to me. "I hope you enjoyed your first day at the castle."

"I did," I say. "Up until ten minutes ago."

He doesn't ask why. Instead, he takes my hand and holds it with both his. I lift my gaze to his face. He's staring at me with an intensity that would've stopped my heart under different circumstances. *Wow.* Anyone looking at him right now would say he's crazy for me. Even I have to remind myself he's just playing a part.

And he's damn good at it, just like everything he does.

Hmm, let's see if I can match his skill. I peer into his dark brown eyes, remarking a hue in them I hadn't noticed before. It's amber gold. In fact, it's the exact color of the Scotch he was sipping before he sat down.

Will I taste it on his tongue if we kiss?

Right on cue, he leans in for a smooch, and I whisper "*extra hot*" before I can stop myself. Surprise flickers in his eyes. A split second later, he angles his head and slants his mouth over mine. His evening stubble grates against my chin in a most pleasant way. He runs his tongue over my lips and nips gently. I open up. His tongue penetrates deep inside between my teeth, against my palate and my cheeks, pushing against my own tongue.

He thrusts, strokes and suckles, giving my mouth the most sensual, shameless treatment it's ever had.

He's making love to it.

Desire shoots to my core in a lightning bolt of unspeakable sweetness. I find myself leaning into him, opening up more, asking for more. Me, who despises couples who can't restrain their ardor in public—I can't get enough of him at this moment, public opinion be damned.

He tastes of whisky and of something quintessentially male. That taste, combined with his head-turning scent, is nudging me into an unfamiliar territory that borders on total abandon. My breasts ache for his hand to cup and fondle them. As for his other hand, I want it between my legs.

I *need* it between my legs.

There's only one word to qualify the effect of this kiss—madness.

I'm losing my fucking mind.

And I don't even care.

Just as abruptly as he started the kiss, Darcy stops and draws away.

I gasp for air and open my eyes.

He's watching me. There's no more playfulness nor the slightest shade of amber left in his eyes. His gaze is dark, and his lips are red from our kiss.

He turns away and says something to the person on his right.

I blink to clear the haze from my eyes and focus on the man he's talking to.

It's Raphael.

My hearing returns next, and with it, a profound sense of embarrassment.

"I'll talk to him first thing Monday morning," Raphael says.

Darcy nods. "Be sure that you do."

Next to Raphael, Genevieve studies my face, barely pretending to listen to what her "very close" friend Penelope is saying to her.

Penelope glances at her watch and stands. "I should be going."

"You should stay," Darcy says. "It's late, and there are plenty of empty bedrooms in this castle."

She hesitates. "The village is only twenty minutes away. I'll be fine—I'm a big girl."

"Penelope." There's a bossy note in Darcy's voice. "I don't like the idea of you driving alone on dark countryside roads at this hour."

She stares at him, saying nothing.

"You'll sleep at the castle." He pulls out his phone. "I'll let Jacqueline know, so she can get you everything you need."

"That's very kind of you, Sebastian." Penelope smiles. "Thank you."

I approve of his thoughtful gesture, but I can't help wishing Penelope had refused. The thought of her sleeping in one of the guest chambers under the same roof as Darcy is unpleasant to say the least.

Is he going to join her later tonight, so that they could continue their *conversation*?

No, he won't. He'd never do anything that could blow our cover. This scheme of his matters too much to him.

Just as I sigh with relief, a thought strikes me.

I'm jealous.

Why else would I care if Darcy and Penelope spend the night together?

Chill out, woman.

What you're experiencing is a version of Stockholm syndrome, when hostages end up supporting the bad guy because they've spent too much time in close proximity with him. The difference between the classic version of the syndrome and mine is that instead of sympathizing with Darcy's cause, I've become sympathetic toward his body. Fervently sympathetic.

No, this won't do.

Repeat after me, Diane: *Darcy is an entitled jerk. He ruined and nearly killed Dad. It's sick to lust after him while plotting his downfall. My dream is to see him destroyed.*

Excellent.

And now the refrain.

I hate him.

I hate him.

I hate him.

CHAPTER 14

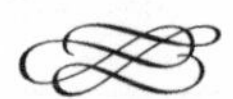

DIANE

Elorie's skin glows in the soft light filtering through the tall linen-draped window of this high-ceilinged room.

I fiddle with the controls of my camera. "Can you tip your head back a little?"

"Like this?" Elorie asks.

"Exactly." I release the shutter. "Don't move."

She's straddling a polished wood chair, her back toward me. The paleness of her skin is offset by the dark wood of the chair and the floorboards. I study the image on my preview screen. It's elegant and free of any vulgarity, yet there's a touch of delicious decadence you can't miss. It's perfect, thanks to this light and this space. If I could afford a professional studio for my portraits, I doubt I could find a better setting.

I click a few more times, gleeful.

This is going to be the best of the three shoots we've done so far. It has everything going for it. Especially three things—Elorie's lovely body, the shabby-chic charm of this room, and our mojo boosted by the best local Chablis from Darcy's wine cellar.

"More?" I ask, picking up the bottle.

She grabs her glass from the floor and holds it out. "Yes, please. When do you think you'll be done?"

"I *am* done, actually." I fill her glass and hand it to her. "I was going to take a few more pics, just in case. But if you're tired or cold, we can stop now."

Before she replies, the door behind me opens and Darcy walks in. Surprise flashes in his eyes as he takes in the scene. He looks ragged with ruffled hair, dark stubble, and a glass of Scotch in his hand. Combined with the jeans and a well-worn sweater, the look is so out of character I can't help wondering if he's OK.

Then I remember about Elorie and panic.

The poor thing must be mortified. Oh, and she'll kill me as soon as she gets over it. Our shoots were supposed to remain secret, and no one was supposed to know it was her in these photos.

"Get out!" I shout at Darcy.

"I didn't mean to intrude." He turns toward my model, his gaze trained on the floor next her feet. "Please forgive me, Elorie."

"It's OK," she says.

He glances at me again as he retreats toward the door. "I hope I didn't ruin your project. Please continue."

I glare at him.

And to my utter shock, my naked friend turns around, fully exposing to Darcy all her X-rated parts she's been so eager to hide from my camera. "Hi, Sebastian."

His lips quirk before he schools them into a polite smile. "Hello, Elorie."

She picks up her bathrobe and pulls it on. "We were done, actually and I was leaving. So no worries—you didn't ruin anything."

"I'm glad to hear it," he says.

"See you later, alligator." Elorie waves good-bye to me.

"I'll get you before the restaurant," I say as she makes a beeline to the door and shuts it behind her.

"You never told me you did nude portraits," Darcy says.

I shrug. "Our contract doesn't require that I tell you everything."

"Do they sell well?"

"Elorie and I are on our third series," I say with pride. "So yeah, my nudes seem to be appreciated."

He points at my camera. "Can I see one?"

My first impulse is to say no, but I remember Elorie's cavalier attitude and change my mind. Compared to the uncensored view she just presented him, my photos are PG-13.

I hand him the camera.

As he pulls up the pics, I survey him. What would he look like naked? I saw his biceps once when he wore a T-shirt. I've leered at the bulges of his pecs discernible through his shirts countless times. His stomach is flat, his shoulders are naturally broad, and his hips narrow. All evidence suggests he'd look very nice indeed. What I don't know is if his chest is hairy. I picture his bared forearms as an indicator. Hmm… it'll probably have some hair, but not too much. If I find the right aperture and exposure settings to accentuate the play of light and shadow on the planes of his chest, I could have some amazing photos.

"Will you sit for me?" I blurt.

He gives me a quizzical look.

"As in pose for a few pics... maybe?" I fully expect him to snort and say no.

He tilts his head to the side. "Are you serious?"

Am I? "Totally."

"Why? Are you having trouble finding male models?"

"I haven't tried. You'd be my first."

He glances at the preview screen once again.

I should stop holding my breath. He'll never agree to my brazen offer. No way.

"So you want me to pose for you," he says.

"Uh-huh."

"Naked?"

I nod. "I'll make them just as clean and artsy as Elorie's. And I'll hide your face by shooting from the side and the back only."

He hands me the camera, a smile crinkling his eyes. "Only for art's sake..."

Is he agreeing to my insane request? Is he actually, really, going to do it?

I clear my throat. "Is that a yes?"

He doesn't reply immediately, and I stare at him, a wave of shameful, giddy excitement shooting through my veins, filling my ears with a pleasant buzz and making me light-headed. Darcy is going to strip naked for me. He's going to position that gorgeous body of his however I instruct him to. I'm going to be able to feast my eyes on every inch of that taut, virile flesh with full impunity. Pretending to be just an extension of my camera and safe in the artist-model role-play, I'm going to lap up every line of that handsome face. It's shocking how badly I want him to say yes.

"One condition," he says. "I keep my pants on."

I do my best to hide my disappointment. "OK, but only the pants. I want your chest and your feet bare."

He nods.

"I'll prepare the backdrop while you undress." I try to sound businesslike. "We have to hurry—this light will be gone in twenty minutes or so."

He sets his glass on the windowsill and pulls his sweater over his head with the ease of a hunk who doesn't know what body-conscious means.

I don't budge, watching him.

He kicks off his sneakers, eyes riveted to mine.

I stare, mesmerized into a stupor.

He pulls his socks off and straightens his back. "Weren't you going to prep something?"

"What?" I wake up from my trance. "Oh. Crap. Yes, I was." I rush past him to move the chair out of the way and push the curtain a little to the side. My ears are aflame.

"Can you stand by the window?" I ask.

Without looking at him, I go back to my spot by the table and pick up my camera.

Darcy plants himself on the right of the window frame. His upper body is to die for. All lean muscle and tanned skin. Incredibly masculine. Totally camera worthy. Oh, and I was right about his chest, which has just the right amount of hair.

"Press your forehead to the frame," I say.

He executes.

Click, click, click.

"Now turn your back to me, lift your arms, and place your hands on either side of the frame."

He does as he's told.

"Higher. Yes, like that. Lean forward a bit. Perfect. Stay there."

I click frantically.

"Drop your head to your chest... Good... Now, straighten up again. Drop your right hand behind your neck and touch your back... Beautiful."

I order him to shift his body in a dozen more ways, each designed to highlight a particular group of muscles on his back and chest, the slant of his shoulders, the shape of his strong neck, his sculpted jawline, abs, hips, backside, and his unexpectedly sexy feet.

Male beauty is *so* underrated.

"How about a nude?" I ask on impulse. "Just one pic, to crown the series."

He stares at me, saying nothing.

His silence emboldens me. "I'll take it from the back, nothing indecent, and I'll render it in black and white. Please?"

His stare grows so intense it robs me of air. Literally. It somehow makes me unlearn the art of breathing, and I'm about to swoon when he nods and turns his back to me.

I take a few life-saving breaths.

He just nodded, right? He's going full monty for me.

Dear God, dear God, dear God.

Incredulous, I watch him unbuckle his belt and draw the zipper. In one smooth movement, he pulls his jeans and underwear down and steps out of them.

My gaze travels up his athletic calves and strong thighs and lingers on his derriere. A part of me registers that I'm staring at him directly without the intermediary of the camera.

Another part registers that I'm wet.

"So?" Darcy asks without turning to face me. "Are you taking that shot?"

I raise the camera and click, and click again, and again, and again.

"That's more than one pic," he says.

"It's just to have a few different angles to choose from."

And look at.

"We're done," I say a moment later. "It was very kind of you, Sebastian."

"Don't mention it." I hear the smile in his voice. "I'm glad I could be of help, Diane."

I turn to the door, hugging my camera. "I'll give you some privacy to get dressed."

"That would be nice. Thank you."

As I march out and pull the door closed, I already know I'm going to spend hour after hour pouring over the series, inventing new ways to edit the photos just to have an excuse to leer at them.

Especially, the last few.

CHAPTER 15

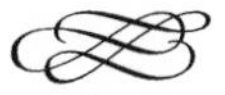

DIANE

Hating a man 24-7 drains your energy. Can you blame a woman for needing a break from it?

That's what this is—a break. Whenever I find myself enjoying Darcy's company, I tell myself that all it means is that I'm just taking a breather from constant hating. Neat, huh? In this light, there's no reason to panic every time I catch myself fancying Darcy's toothsome bod or admiring a trait of his character.

This theory is the *only* way to account for what happened in Burgundy. Prompting Darcy to give me an *extra hot* kiss was bad enough. I can tell myself I did it to spite Genevieve, who'd gotten under my skin, but how do I explain that I nearly disintegrated from it? And how in hell do I explain asking Darcy to strip and pose for me? A fit of madness? An attempt to sabotage my own plan? An admission of defeat?

I prefer to go with the *Everyone Needs a Breather* hypothesis.

Anyway, back to the here and now. I'm standing next

to Jeanne in the middle of the front room of *La Bohème*, staring at the long windowless wall opposite the entrance. At Jeanne's request, Chloe had fitted it with little hooks and strings so it could serve as a gallery to showcase local painters.

"Your photos of Parisian rooftops would be perfect for my first exhibit," Jeanne says.

"I'm flattered,"—and I truly am—"but I wouldn't want you to feel obligated to offer me this opportunity just because I'm Chloe's sis."

"I'm offering you this opportunity because I love those photos, period." Jeanne cocks her head and winks. "But don't expect me to pay for the prints."

"Are you insane? *You* should be charging me, not the other way around!"

We agree on the size and number of prints, and Jeanne returns behind the bar. I stare at the wall some more, brimming with excitement. Displaying my work outside the virtual world, printed and framed, is a big step toward becoming a real photographer. It doesn't matter how many photos I sell—this exhibit isn't about making a profit. It's my graduation from hobbyist to professional.

Manon zooms by with a loaded tray, mouthing, "Five minutes." This means she's about to take a coffee break and wants me to stick around. I pick a table by the window and engross myself in my current whodunit.

Manon's voice pulls me out of the story a few minutes later. "How can you enjoy that stuff?"

"What's wrong with detective stories?"

She sits down, placing a cappuccino and an espresso on the table. "All that violence and crime."

"To me, these books are more about the intrigue and

figuring out who the culprit is." I cock my head. "What *I* don't understand is how you can like romance."

"What's not to like?" She gives me a dreamy look. "I can never decide what I enjoy more—the thrill of the deepening love, the overcoming of obstacles, or the guaranteed happily ever after."

"There are no happily ever afters in real life."

"If you mean we all die in the end, I agree." She gives me a wink. "But romance books aren't about eternal life. They're about eternal love."

"Does it exist, your eternal love?" I sneer.

She stares at me, perplexed. "You just got engaged. Shouldn't you be a little more… optimistic?"

"I should—I mean, I am." I glance at the ridiculously big diamond on my finger. "It's just… People come together and split up. Or they stay together and hate each other's guts. That's real life—just look around you."

"OK." She nods, a sparkle of mischief in her eyes, and turns toward the bar. "Let's see… Oh, look, it's Jeanne!"

Manon turns back to me, beaming.

I know exactly what she's going to say.

"Last time I checked,"—she can hardly keep the glee from her voice—"Jeanne was still happily in love with Mat."

I shrug. "They're an exception to the rule."

"What about Chloe and Hugo?" Manon arches an eyebrow. "How long will you give those two?"

Hmm. Very long, actually. Until death do them part.

"My parents divorced," I say. "So did Sebastian's, and Elorie's, and plenty of other people I know."

"OK, I'll grant you that," Manon says. "Not *every*

couple gets their happily ever after. In real life, half of them split up."

"Ha! You see."

"But the other half stays together and continues loving each other, just like in romance books. And lots of divorcees remarry happily." She pats my shoulder. "It's one of those glass-half-full things—just a matter of perspective."

"Or a matter of dumb luck."

"Maybe." She rubs her chin. "Or maybe it's a matter of knowing yourself well enough to sense who's right for you."

"How can you ever sense that? It's not as if there's an alarm in your head that goes"—I cup my hands around my mouth—"weeeoooo-weeeoooo, all systems go! I have a visual. The individual at three o'clock is the perfect match. I repeat: Target at three o'clock. Go, go, go!"

"That's not how it works." She smiles and glances at fellow waiter Amar as he walks by eyeing Manon as if she were the Eighth Wonder of the World. "You don't always recognize it at once, but when you've spent some time with the right guy, you'll know it's him. Trust me."

Lucky her. I've never felt that confident about anyone.

I guess I don't know myself well enough.

CHAPTER 16

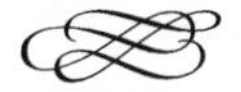

SEBASTIAN

Denying yourself someone you crave, and who happens to want you, too, drains your energy. Can you blame a man for wanting a break from it?

I'd been suspecting Diane had a thing for me since March, but the Burgundy trip killed the last of my doubts. I'll never forget our *extra hot* kiss, or the look on her face when she asked me to pose for her. Even harder to forget is the giddiness in her lovely eyes when I agreed. Not to mention the pent-up lust roughening her voice when she directed me, and the color of her cheeks when she began to take pictures.

How I managed not to knock on her door that night is beyond me.

I look out the car window as I drive to the 9th. I'm to join Diane and her gang at *La Bohème* tonight, where they're watching some show on the bistro's new TV screen. My original plan had been to take Diane to the opera, but she said she wouldn't miss that program for the world.

Why on earth did I buy those tickets without checking with her first? I suppose I was going for a surprise. As if I didn't already know Diane isn't the kind of woman who'd jump for joy at two center orchestra tickets for *La Traviata*.

I smirk and shake my head.

She's the exact opposite.

Setting aside the women who live in mud huts on under one dollar a day, Diane is as far from my interests and way of life as a Western female can be. And that's why I stayed away from her chamber in Burgundy. Just imagine the imbroglio of having sex with the woman I've hired to play my fiancée. *Hired* and *play* are the keywords here. Sleeping with her might give Diane the wrong idea. And if there's one thing a gentleman never does to a woman—regardless of her social background—is giving her the wrong idea.

Hang in there, man.

Just two more months of this charade and she'll be out of my life for good.

I park the Lambo on the corner of rue Lafayette and rue Bleue and climb out.

As I walk down rue Cadet, I notice an unusually large crowd blocking the sidewalk terrace of the bistro. It's early May, and mild enough to sip your *Kir cassis* outside, but that doesn't explain all those extra chairs, people standing in the aisles, and others sitting on their backpacks. And everyone—everyone—has their heads turned up, staring at the wall-mounted TV.

Diane, Elorie, Jeanne, and some of the waiters are among the crowd. My fiancée remains seated as I peck her on the forehead. She's wearing the perfume I gave her a few weeks ago, and this pleases me to no end. The delicate iris- and patchouli-based fragrance blends seamlessly with the alluring scent of her skin, highlighting her tomboyishness as well as her femininity.

I wish I could bottle it and keep it in my inside pocket at all times.

When my mind clears a few seconds later, I say hello to the others. They greet me without taking their eyes off the screen.

Is there some important match underway? Why didn't Octave or Greg tell me anything? They're both huge sports fans and between them, they have all major sports covered. So what is it—tennis, football, or rugby?

The screen displaying country names and points isn't helping.

"What are you watching?" I ask.

"The Eurovision Song Contest," Diane says before turning to her friends. "This can't be true! Belgium gave us *nul points*. How could they?"

Manon grits her teeth. "Traitors."

"So did the UK," Elorie says.

"Yeah, but that's normal." Diane looks at me. "It's a tradition. Brits always down vote France at *Eurovision*. We do the same to them, by the way."

I place my hand on her shoulder.

Diane gives me a sweet smile. "Will you stay and watch this with us?"

"I was hoping to take you to dinner—I haven't eaten yet. Besides,"—I look around—"there are no spare chairs."

"I can fix you a *croque-monsieur* or a hamburger," Jeanne offers.

Diane stands and pats her chair. "We can share this."

"OK." I sit down and turn to Jeanne. "A hamburger and a beer would be great."

She stands. "Don't let anyone steal my chair."

"I'll guard it with my life." Diane drops her purse on it.

"So, let's see what's this all is about," I say to Diane, as she lowers herself onto my lap.

This song contest is clearly something she enjoys. I'm not going to spoil her evening by insisting we go eat a proper dinner in a proper restaurant. And I wouldn't want to appear rude by leaving. So my reasons for staying are just gallantry and good manners. And perhaps curiosity about this European song contest I've heard about but never watched.

The prospect of having Diane's pert little ass on my lap and my arm wrapped around her slim waist for the next hour or so has nothing to do with anything.

"Who's the favorite?" I ask. "Are they good?"

Diane picks up her mojito. "Malta and Ukraine are number one and two, but it may change with the next country's vote."

"Everyone's equally awful in this contest," Elorie says.

"Then why watch it?"

"The point of watching the Eurovision Song Contest," Diane says, "isn't in discovering good songs or new talent—we have *The Voice* for that. It's in commenting."

"On what?"

Diane turns to me. "Everything. The contestants and their costumes, the hosts and their bad jokes, and, of course, the songs."

"You forgot the national commentators," Elorie says. "We comment on them, too." She turns to me. "This year it's your buddy, celebrity columnist Marie-Anne Blenn."

"She's not my buddy."

Elorie cocks her head. "But you've met her, haven't you?"

"Everyone with a 'de' particle in their name has met her."

Manon puts her index finger to her lips. "Shush! Australia is next."

"I thought this was a European contest," I can't help saying.

"Didn't you watch the news last night?" Jeanne puts my hamburger and beer on the table and takes her seat. "Australia was hauled across a couple of oceans and parked between Iceland and Scotland so they could take part in *Eurovision*."

"Shush!" Manon orders again.

We watch the song that's so resolutely and proudly tacky it deserves at least one point. To my surprise, it gets a lot more than one, including from France. Have my fellow citizens lost their famed good taste? A longtime opera buff, I forget that the vast majority of the seventy million people who are just as French as I am wouldn't set foot in an opera house even if I paid them.

The next performer has the left side of his skull shaven and the right side covered in long raven-black strands that drape his right eye like a little curtain.

"The Barber from Hell has struck again," Marie-Anne Blenn's voice-over informs the viewers.

"Wait till he starts singing," Manon says. "I've already watched his video on YouTube. His song is called 'Eagle.' "

Diane tilts her head back and looks up. "Lord, please make it so that he doesn't have wings attached to his back."

Manon purses her lips, struggling not to smile.

The singer opens his mouth—and spreads his eagle wings.

Diane drops her head to her chest. Manon giggles.

Next, a well-endowed female singer dressed in a long skirt and tight bodice steps out from behind a curtain. Ten seconds into her tear-jerking song, she raises her arms to the ceiling, clenches her fists and rips off her skirt.

"She has the male vote in her pocket," Elorie says.

Diane turns to her. "She doesn't have any pockets."

"Fine. Tucked into her bodice." Elorie pokes her tongue out. "Smartass."

And so it continues. Song after cheesy song gets points following a logic I fail to grasp. One thing is clear—it has nothing to do with their artistic quality.

At some point, I realize I'm staring at the screen without seeing anything. Nor am listening to Marie-Anne Blenn's and the girls' acerbic comments. My mind is completely overtaken by something a lot closer to home—Diane. More specifically her back against my chest, my left hand on her tummy, and my right hand, which has somehow made its way to her thigh.

I'm sporting wood. And I'm perfectly aware there's no way this development could've escaped Diane's notice. Right now, I'd give half of what I'm worth for everyone around us to be temporarily relocated to a parallel universe so I can do what I'm dying to do. Cup her breasts. Fondle them. Pinch her nipples gently between my index and thumb. Slip my hand into her panties and stroke her until she pants. And then stroke her more until she writhes and moans. All the way to her orgasm.

God, this isn't helping.

I must stop thinking these thoughts at once. What I should do is glance at my phone, look concerned, and say I have to go.

Diane shifts in my lap as she leans forward, peering at the screen.

Jesus. Christ.

My lids drop, and I forget what I intended to do. My breathing becomes shallow. All I can think of is my hand in her panties.

Would she be wet for me?

"My money's on yes," Jeanne says.

I open my eyes. *What the fuck?*

Jeanne passes a napkin with a two-column table drawn on it to Manon. Manon scribbles something in the first column and hands the napkin to Elorie.

"What's that?" I ask Diane.

She looks over her shoulder. "We're betting on the Greek contestant."

She points to the screen where a guy in a shiny white suit is wailing yet another heartrending ballad while playing a grand piano.

"And?"

"In roughly fifty percent of performances that feature a piano—especially when the contestant is playing it himself—the instrument is set on fire at the end of the song." She smiles. "So the bet is if the Greeks will burn their piano."

"I see."

I feel a little stupid for having panicked a few seconds ago.

"What's your bet—yes or no?" Diane asks, holding the napkin.

"No," I say.

She puts my name in the second column and hers in the first.

A minute later, the piano burns.

I hand Jeanne a fifty euro bill and a two euro coin. "I have to go now."

She starts to rummage through the pocket of her apron.

"Keep the change," I say. "Please."

"OK. Thanks!"

Diane stands up.

"Please stay," I say to her. "I don't want to be a spoilsport."

She shakes her head. "You aren't."

We stare into each other's eyes, and I'm sure she's asking herself the same question I am—are we going to have sex tonight?

We say good-bye to Diane's friends and get into my car.

"You know," she says, "I still don't understand why you hired me knowing I had a chip on my shoulder."

I hesitate. "I have a confession to make."

"Go on."

"Part of the reason I picked you was guilt. I'm not proud of what I did to Charles, and I guess I wanted to buy myself a good conscience by supporting him through you."

"I don't get it. Isn't driving competitors out of business what you do all the time, what all successful businessmen do as you keep telling me. Why the sudden guilt?"

"I may have gone further with Charles than I usually do."

"Explain."

"I had my R and D team clone his bestsellers." I pause, hesitating again.

The corners of her mouth drop. "And then?"

"My sales team pushed them at half of his price." I glance at her. "He didn't have a chance."

For the next fifteen minutes, Diane fidgets with the three-carat rock on her ring finger as if itching to take it off. She won't talk to me.

It doesn't look like we'll be having sex tonight, after all.

And that's a good thing, right?

PART IV
TOWN HOUSE

CHAPTER 17

DIANE

I'm staring at the prints of my rooftop photos spread out on the floor of my TV room. Only half of them—that is, twelve out of twenty-four—will be on display at *La Bohème* starting next Monday.

The question is which twelve. And I'll be damned if I have a clue.

Earlier this afternoon, Chloe stopped by to help me choose. She left an hour later, utterly frustrated with my inability to make up my mind.

"They aren't your babies," she said with her hand on the doorknob. "They're just photos."

I made a face. "I know."

"And they're all great, anyway."

Does she realize how totally counterproductive her last comment was?

I go over the prints again, remembering the exact location, circumstances, and weather conditions of each shoot. Some of them are colorful and happy, like the ones I took in Buttes Chaumont. Others are black and white and melancholy, just like Paris feels sometimes when it's drowning in smog and drizzle. I can handle that sort of weather all right for twenty-four hours. After forty-eight hours, my mind begins to crave a respite. After seventy-two hours, my body starts to zombify. After a week of fog, the only solution to avoid a total collapse is an immediate southbound evacuation of my person.

This photo was taken atop Notre Dame—the only spot in Paris with a view of the seven bridges across the Seine—in the middle of an epic downpour. And this one I shot by night in late December, from the top of the Arc de Triomphe. I wasn't allowed to take my tripod up there, so I had to get creative. But, man, it was worth it! I took my best night shot of the Champs-Elysées with its horse chestnut trees wrapped in sparkling garlands, snowflakes dancing in the air, and an unobstructed view of the boulevard all the way to Le Louvre.

Chloe has a point—in some ways, my photos *are* my babies.

Ask a mother of two to pick the child she likes better, and you'll know what I'm going through. Besides, now that I've resigned from the supermarket, as per my contract with Darcy, I have a lot more time for photography. This is great, but it has a flip side. I spend even longer on editorial decisions than before.

My doorbell rings.

I startle and glance at the clock on the wall. It's seven in the evening—too early for Darcy. Elorie is still at work. Chloe must be on her way to Montrouge to see the house she and Hugo will be refurbishing next. And, anyway, none of these people ever show up on my doorstep without calling first.

Turns out one of them does after all—Darcy.

"You don't have to let me in if you don't feel like it,"

he says from behind the door. "I realize I should've called or buzzed from downstairs." He doesn't sound quite like himself.

"It's OK," I say, deciding that my tee and leggings are presentable enough, and open the door.

He steps in, holding a gorgeous bouquet in one hand and a bottle of vodka in the other.

I put my hands on my hips.

"I bought these from the florist two blocks down the street," he says, handing me the flowers.

"What's the occasion?"

He shrugs. "Can a man give his fiancée flowers without needing an occasion?"

He's definitely acting weird.

I cock my head. "Is the man in question drunk?"

"Just a little."

Darcy smiles his crooked smile, provoking a mild quake in my knees.

I hate it when he does that.

"Have a seat." I motion him to the couch in the TV room. "Oh, and if you step on any of the prints on the floor, I'll strangle you with your own overpriced tie."

"Understood." He makes his way to the couch, slaloming between the prints.

I set the flowers in the vase that Chloe left behind when she moved out and fetch a bottle of Orangina and two glasses from the kitchen.

He points at the vodka. "We should drink this first. The Poles swore it's the best vodka in the world."

"Which Poles?"

"From Mleko, the biggest milk product company in eastern Europe. They're market leaders for yogurt and ice cream in over a dozen countries. My deputy and I, and most of my legal team, have been working on this since February. As of today, Parfums d'Arcy is Mleko's main flavor supplier. We signed a deal this afternoon."

I arch an eyebrow "While eating yogurts and washing them down with Polish vodka?"

"Exactly," he says. "And with French champagne. And without the yogurts."

I shake my head in disapproval. "So, you down a few shots and decide that now is a good time to go check on Diane."

He spreads his arms. "The alternative was spending the rest of the evening carousing with my new partners. I told them it was my fiancée's birthday today."

"And left the poor Poles to carouse in a foreign city all by themselves?" I tut-tut.

"My deputy's with them, bless his heart." He opens the vodka and pours a little in each glass. "It's called Zubrowka, and it's flavored with bison grass."

I sigh.

"Come on, *chérie*," he says. "Don't be a spoilsport. I want you to tell me if Zubrowka is the best vodka you've ever had."

"I've only tasted one other vodka before. A Swedish one, I think."

"Must've been Absolut. It's owned by Pernod Ricard now." He hands me a glass. "You'll tell me how it compares to Absolut."

I take a sip, keep the liquid in my mouth for a moment, and swallow.

"Can you feel the woodruff and almond notes on the nose?" Darcy leans in. "And the vanilla near the end?"

"Err… I'm not sure."

He drinks the content of his glass. "Definitely vanilla at the end."

I empty mine. "It does have a sweet aftertaste… I guess."

"Have you eaten yet?"

"Uh-huh. You?"

He nods. "The Poles came with pickles and sausage to go with the vodka."

He refills our glasses. "Try to drink this like a Pole, *to the bottom*."

I nod and we both empty our glasses in one gulp.

"Are these the photos that'll be displayed at *La Bohème*?" Darcy asks, pointing to the floor.

"I have to discard half of them." I give him a mournful look. "It's killing me."

He squats in the middle of my prints and spends a few moments studying them.

"You really can't choose?"

"Nope."

He picks up the photo I took from the terrace of l'Institut du Monde Arabe and sets it on his left. "Yes."

Next, he takes a pic from the series I shot in the 11th. "No."

He continues, taking one pic after the other and sorting them into his yes and no piles. I watch him until he grabs my Latin Quarter roofscape and places it with the rejects.

Crouching next to him, I lift the photo and transfer it to the "yes" pile.

He smiles. "Ah, so you do have some favorites?"

"I don't. It's just… I almost broke my neck taking this one. If you leave it out, it's as if my almost sacrifice was for nothing."

"I don't like the sound of this." Darcy frowns. "Where exactly did you go to take these pictures?"

"All kinds of places." I hesitate before admitting. "Rooftops, mostly."

His frown deepens. "Do you actually *walk* on roofs?"

"I don't when it can be helped. But, you see, my camera… it's a solid Nikon, perfect for portraits, but it doesn't have a full-frame sensor, so it's not ideal for landscape photography."

"Why don't you buy another one?"

I raise my eyes skyward and sigh. *Rich people.* "Anyway, the way around it is to take multiple shots and combine them in Photoshop. It just requires that I move around the roof a bit."

He stares at me for a moment and nods. "OK, your Latin Quarter's in."

"*Merci, monsieur.*" I put my hand to my heart. "You're very kind."

Thirty seconds later, he's done.

I look at the two piles and then at him. "May I know what criteria you used in your super-efficient selection process?"

"None." He screws up his face in a way that's so sexy I nearly drool. "When pros and cons are in a tie, the only way forward is to shuffle them together, push them aside, and let your gut guide your hand."

"Is that what you just did?"

He nods. "But I can see why you were having such a hard time. They're all amazing."

"They better be." I smirk. 'Considering that the photo lab's bill has put me in the red."

"Oh. I'm sorry to hear that."

I shrug. "The irony of it is that I could make better prints if I had the right equipment. And they'd be cheaper to produce."

"Really?"

"Oh, yeah."

"Wouldn't it be smarter to invest in the equipment instead of paying a lab to print your photos?"

"Sure," I say. "It would be much smarter."

"Then why—" He stops himself. "The cost. Listen, why don't I advance some of your fee so you can buy yourself a nice printer and a camera that's good for landscapes?"

I shake my head. "Your money goes to Dad. He'll need all of it to start over."

"In that case, I'd like to lend you some—"

"Thanks," I cut him off, "but no, thanks. I've managed fine so far with what I have, and I intend to go on until I save enough to afford what I want. There's no emergency."

He sucks his teeth, probably trying to come up with a counterargument.

"Hey, here's something you could do for me," I say to change the topic. "If you have any more tips on fast decision-making, I'll take them. I'm hopeless in that area."

His expression brightens. "It's certainly something you can improve with practice."

I set the photo piles on the coffee table and motion him to the couch.

"The first thing you can do," he says, "is narrow your field. In other words, discard all the options that aren't the best."

"OK. And then?"

"Remind yourself there's no perfect option, and that what you need is a decision that is fast and *roughly* right. That usually unblocks your gut instinct."

"Makes sense." I eye him up and down. "Have you always been so… decisive?"

He smirks. "No."

I wait for him to continue.

Instead he pours us two more vodka shots and raises his glass. "*Na zdrowie.*"

"Huh?"

"It means 'to your health' in Polish."

"*To the bottom*?" I ask.

He nods and empties his glass.

I do the same.

"Papa overdosed when I was twenty-three," he says. "I was *so* not prepared to fill his shoes. They seemed huge at the time…"

"Wasn't there someone else to run things for a while? A deputy or some experienced CEO?"

"We're a family business, and Papa had made sure it would be me who'd take charge if something happened to him."

"Did you *want* to take charge?"

He lets out a long breath. "In theory, yes. In practice, I wasn't ready. It's one thing to tell yourself that your future is in your hands. But realizing that the future of my younger brothers was in my hands, too—that came as a bit of a shock."

"How old were they?"

"Raph was nineteen and Noah only fifteen." He loosens his tie. "Do you mind if I remove this *overpriced* item?"

"Please."

He hangs it over the armrest and shrugs off his suit jacket. "My brothers had their trust funds, of course, and Maman was well taken care of, but most of the d'Arcy fortune was invested in the company."

"I see."

"Then I realized something else and it was even harder to stomach."

I give him a quizzical look.

"The livelihoods of hundreds of people employed by Parfums d'Arcy depended on me… When that realization hit me, it felt as if someone had loaded me up with a supersize backpack filled with rocks."

"How did you deal with it?"

"I created a persona." His lips curl. "I started acting as if I was the man Papa wanted me to be. Decisive. Unwavering. Someone who knows what he's doing."

"A real *homme d'affaires*."

He nods. "A man no one would dare call a greenhorn. A man his subordinates looked up to. I couldn't afford to show any sign of weakness or nonchalance." He smiles. "Not that I ever had any nonchalance to start with—that's Raphael's specialty."

"When my dad's business was going well," I say, "he hired someone to help him. It broke his heart when he had to let that person go a few years back. I can't imagine how it feels to know that hundreds of jobs hinge on your knowing what you're doing. That kind of responsibility would probably paralyze me into total inaction."

He leans toward me. "Let me tell you a secret. That's exactly how I felt, too, in the beginning. But I had no choice, so I began to… fake it. And I've been at it ever since."

"No way."

He nods and smiles. "I make my best guess and act on it with enough aplomb to convince everyone I *know* what I'm doing."

My head begins to turn as his charisma—yes, dammit, *charisma*—envelopes me in a soft, yummy-smelling cocoon and lifts me up. The sentinels I've stationed throughout my brain sway on their feet and fall one after the other, clutching their mortal wounds.

It's a bloodbath.

With my first line of defense decimated, I can't help inhaling the heady scent coming off Darcy. I have no clue what part of it is *him* and what part is cologne, but the mixture does nasty things to me on some primal, subatomic level. He's a fragrance man, I remind myself. He must've had his labs concoct a highly potent love potion for his personal use.

Hang in there, Diane!

The question is, onto what? The impenetrable Anti-Darcy Defense Shield around my heart is melting away faster than I can regenerate it.

That is, if I could be bothered to regenerate it right now.

In a last-ditch attempt to avoid inglorious defeat and capitulation, I peel my gaze away from his darkened eyes. Only instead of focusing on the wall or the ceiling, my traitorous peepers zoom in on the bulge in his pants.

And what a nice, *voluminous* bulge it is!

On a rugged breath, I dig my fingers into my thighs and force myself to look away.

Is it time to wave the white flag?

Darcy takes my hand and covers it with his large palm.

I stare at his hands holding mine and then plunge into his bottomless gaze.

Resistance is futile.

I'm done for.

CHAPTER 18

DIANE

"You never told me what you did with the portraits of me you took at the castle," Darcy says, stroking my hand.

"I sold them to *Voilà Paris* for five hundred euros." I give him a saucy smile. "Would you like a share?"

"What will *Voilà Paris* do with them?"

"They'll use them at their discretion to illustrate various articles in future issues."

"Including the nude ones?"

I nod. "But don't worry, no one will know it's you in any of the pics. I made sure of it."

"I'm relieved." He looks at me with a mischievous gleam in his eyes. "You asked if I wanted a share."

"I give Elorie fifty percent for her nudes, so it's only fair I offer you the same rate."

"How about you pay me in kind instead?"

My heart skips a beat. "What do you have in mind, Sebastian?"

"I want to take a photo of you naked." His gaze burns into mine.

Wow.

What happened to his aristocratic stuffiness? Has all that Zubrowka gone to his unaccustomed Scotch-lover's head?

Good thing it hasn't gone to mine yet. What I'm going to do is laugh in his face and say he can shove his brilliant idea where the sun never shines.

I really should do that.

Now.

"Why?" I ask instead. "Are you planning to sell it to a men's magazine?"

"Of course not." He hesitates. "I'll keep it for personal use."

Mmm. My subservient mind generates an image of him reclining on his pillow in the privacy of his town house bedroom. He's holding a sexy nude photo of me in one hand while his other hand slides under the blanket. His gaze is dark and deep—just as it is now.

"OK," I say. "But only one shot, facing away."

He nods, looking as if he just up and made another billion.

I fetch my camera, moving fast, determined to get it into his hands before I change my mind. Sitting next to him, I screw on the lens, adjust the settings, and show him the basic functions.

"Take your clothes off, please," he says.

I lift my T-shirt over my head.

"Now the bra."

I undo the front clasp, spread the cups apart and flash my tits.

He leers like a starving wolf.

I grin, satisfied with the effect, and remove the bra completely.

"Now take off the bottoms."

My stomach flips as I stand. Just as my hands slide to the waistband of my leggings, a bulb goes on in my head. This is not how it's done. I signed up to pose for him—not to strip for him. The deal was that he takes a nude photo. He was supposed to turn away while I undressed.

That's how it's done.

Fuck that.

I hook my thumbs under the elastic band and peel my leggings down. There's no denying how much I'm enjoying doing this shoot the wrong way.

"The panties," Darcy rasps. He isn't even trying to pretend this is about the photo anymore.

I shake my head.

He raises an eyebrow. "No?"

"Not until you lift the camera."

For a moment, he looks as if he has no idea what I'm talking about before his gaze lands on the device in his hands. "Oh."

He raises the camera in front of his face, and I let out a little sigh of relief.

"Will you take your panties off now?" he asks, still seated.

I turn around, push the lacy thing down my hips and wiggle until it hits the floor.

"Step out of it," Darcy says.

I do.

"Go to the wall."

I obey.

"Place your hands on it and spread your legs apart."

Done.

"Now lift your hands… higher… lean forward."

As I do what he's asking… er, *ordering* me to do, I realize he's repeating my instructions from the castle shoot almost word for word. The difference is that I'm sent to the wall, while he was directed to the window. And that he's forgotten about the camera again.

I can't help smiling.

"Bend down," Darcy says.

Oh. Monsieur is *improvising* now.

"Is that really necessary?" I ask.

"Yes, it is," he says. "It's *very* necessary."

I turn my head to look into his eyes, and suddenly I'm not smiling anymore. The desire in his eyes hits me like a shockwave, so hard I nearly stagger.

"Bend down," he repeats, his eyes drilling into mine. "Please."

I turn back to the wall and lower my upper body until my breasts touch the cold wall and my backside sticks out in the most shameless way imaginable. Arousal and discomfort wrestle inside me. My ears are open for the click of the camera—the single shot I promised Darcy—after which I'll straighten up and march out of the room.

But that click never comes.

Instead, I hear Darcy put the camera down and lurch toward me. He grabs my wrists, shackling them to the wall, pushing me up, and leaning both of us into its hard surface. His large body presses against mine. He trails his mouth along the side of my face, chest squeezing against my back, groin nestled against my backside.

It's as if he's trying to get as close to me as humanly possible.

His free hand fondles my breasts, slides down, and lingers on my tummy. Heat pools in my pelvis in anticipation of its next stop. But instead of going further down, he glides it over my hips to my derriere. Darcy caresses it with the flat of his hand, softly at first and then in a more demanding manner, digging his fingers into my flesh.

I arch my back with the pleasure of it.

When his hand travels over my hips again, back to the front and down, I'm so ready it's ridiculous. The second his fingers ascertain that fact, a guttural growl rises from his throat.

He bends his head to my ear. "I want you, Diane. I want you so much."

These are trivial, overused words that millions of men have said to millions of women in the past. A few men have said them to me in the past. They're nothing to write home about. They shouldn't impress me. My knees shouldn't wobble in response. I shouldn't have to press my lips together so that my mouth doesn't plead, *Yes, please, take me, any way you want, just do it now!*

Instead, I reach behind my back to palm him through his pants.

He moans and drops hot, toothy kisses to my neck and shoulders as I rub. Then he steps back. I hear the click of a belt being unbuckled, the crisp sound of a zipper, and a foil tearing. Had he planned for this to happen, or does he always have a condom on him? He steps closer, slides his knee between my legs and nudges them wider apart.

I stand on tiptoes to make his entry easier.

He wraps an arm around me and plunges in.

The sweetness of it almost unbearable.

My head falls back into the crook of his neck. I inhale him—that unique, masculine scent that's so quintessentially Sebastian I can't imagine him smelling any other way.

He stirs inside me.

I roll my hips to encourage him.

"Diane," he groans and begins to thrust, alternating sharp lunges with gentler strokes.

When his cadence picks up and we find a rhythm that's just perfect, I lean back into his torso and let go of the last shreds of restraint. My legs start to shake, and I find myself moaning and saying his name.

"Diane… come for me," he grates between his thrusts.

My inner muscles contract around him a few seconds later.

And as they do, long and hard, muddled words erupt from me that are half plea, half order. "Yes, Sebastian, don't stop. Oh God, please, don't stop. Don't you dare stop!"

CHAPTER 19

SEBASTIAN

A question has been eating at me since I woke up ten minutes ago and found my bearings—Diane's bed, her apartment, late Saturday morning. Following a short night. Short because we spent most of it fucking in the living room, in the hallway, and here in this bed.

I barely noticed that question when it arose as I was thinking of something else. But, for some reason, it stuck in my mind. It blitzed out all my morning routines and is now invading the areas of my brain normally reserved for strategic thinking and processing of financial data.

Diane stands by the window, gazing outside, completely oblivious to my turmoil. She's wearing my shirt in lieu of a dressing gown. I was still asleep when she got up and put in on.

This burning question is killing me. All my neurons are currently working on it, desperate to figure out the answer before it's too late. I wouldn't go so far as to say my life depends on it, but my emotional and physical well-being certainly do. Perhaps even my sanity.

What I'm so desperate to know is whether Diane is *commando* under my shirt.

I can discern her nipples, so I know she didn't put on her bra. But the cotton of my shirt is too opaque to see through. What's worse, its weave is too tight to permit an educated guess regarding the presence of panty lines across her butt cheeks. If only she would bend down to pick something up, it would give me a fighting chance. But as things stand, my guesswork is perfectly ineffectual, and I'm scorching my neurons for nothing.

Would it be too rude to dig into the heap of our clothes on the floor and hunt for evidence? Last night, we undressed in the living room, so she must've fetched our clothes when she woke up. I could always pretend I'm looking for my own underwear. Except my boxers are in full view on top of that heap.

Damn.

Will she tell me if I ask her politely? Will she be sympathetic if I beg her to put me out of my misery? Or I should try a different tack and I announce that I need my shirt back? Will she take it off?

One thing is certain: If I do nothing, she's going to pick up her clothes and head to the bathroom. That will mean I'll *never* know. And I'll have to live with that glaring gap in my knowledge for the rest of my life.

"Last night was a mistake," Diane says without looking at me just as I'm about to stand up and do something radical such as slip my hands under the hem of that stupid shirt and get my answer.

It takes me a few moments to process her meaning. "I had the impression you enjoyed yourself."

She still won't turn toward me, but I can see her ears and cheeks color.

Good.

"I did," she finally says. "And that's the problem."

"Why?"

She spins around. "We're in a fake relationship that's soon to become a fake marriage. That's hard enough to handle. But if we start having sex…"

My thoughts exactly.

Until last night.

"Won't it be easier?" I sit up and stare into her eyes. "It'll actually make our fake love look more natural."

"I can't." She shakes her head. "It'll be too fucked up, even for me."

I think I know what the *real* issue is here. "You're afraid you'll fall in love."

"With you?" Her face contorts into a grimace. "You're the last man in the world I could ever fall in love with."

The vehemence of her denial would've been suspicious if the horror on her face were less sincere. I know Diane well enough by now to conclude she's truly appalled at the notion of falling in love with me.

That rattles my ego somewhat.

But I remind myself that I, too, would find the prospect of falling in love with her unpalatable. Diane is a radical leftist and an undereducated *have-not.* When I identified and hired her, she was lower in the societal food chain than most every person in my employ. Her father tried to elevate his family to a better life. But he failed due to poor business skills.

And yes, I'm aware that part of the reason he failed was me—the highborn *have* who crushed him like an annoying bug. And who believes that the best social order is when the elites are at the helm and the masses are at the oars.

"Excellent," I say. "I have no intention of falling in

love with you, either. But I don't see why we can't have some fun while we're contractually bound to each other."

"My mind is made up." Diane gives me a hard stare. "I don't want this to happen again, and you have to respect that."

"Of course." I nod. "Not a problem."

An image of her face, flushed with arousal and pleasure as I stroke her core, pops into my head. Then another image of her moaning as I push into her. Ah, the sweetness of being inside her! I'm not prepared to give that up just yet. The desire will get stale, as it usually does, in just a few weeks. As for feelings, I'm perfectly safe from them. Even with Ingrid, whom I intended to marry, I never experienced that all-consuming emotion they call love. By the time my contract with Diane expires, I'll surely be through with her.

But not yet.

At this point in time, I want more of her sweet body, her pretty face and even her sharp tongue. She arouses me as much as she entertains me. And I know I arouse her as much as I repulse her.

Anyway, arguing now is pointless. She says she doesn't want to have sex with me again. Fine. So be it. I'm not going to beg her. Instead, I'm going to lie low and wait. Starting next Saturday and for the rest of the summer, Diane will live under my roof and sleep in my bedroom.

Who knows what will happen?

"When I move in with you," Diane says as if reading my mind, "do I absolutely have to share your bedroom?"

"It's in the contract."

"I know that. It's just... If I sneak out and sleep next door, no one will know." She gives me a pleading look.

"Let me ask you something. Have you ever slept in a house with live-in help?"

She shakes her head.

I sigh. "I thought so."

She smirks, and I realize my remark sounded more arrogant than I'd intended. But hey, Diane considers me an arrogant ass anyway, so I guess I'm just living up to her expectations. Anyway, I was trying to make a point.

"You see," I say. "You can fool your family—parents, children, siblings, cousins, grandparents... Grandmas can be perceptive, but even they can be duped. Who you can't fool is the people who serve you breakfast in the morning, make your bed, and clean your bathroom. They know everything."

"Do they?"

"Trust me, they do."

She turns away and stares out the window.

I'm sure she understands, but I want to make myself crystal clear.

"In addition to me," I say, "there are five other people living in my town house. Some of them you've met already, others you will the day you move in."

Diane gives me a sidelong glance, her expression wary.

"If we don't sleep in the same room," I say, "they'll know. I can't risk that."

"OK," she says. "Not a problem."

The next second, she picks up my boxers from the top of the pile and sets them on the bed. I watch, forgetting to breathe. She pulls my jeans from the bottom of the pile and places them next to my boxers. Then she grabs the rest of the pile, without sorting it, and heads to the bathroom.

"Sorry I borrowed your shirt," she calls from the hallway. "It won't happen again."

CHAPTER 20

DIANE

The *majordome* opens the door and bows his head. "Welcome to Darcy House, mademoiselle. Everyone is thrilled about your arrival."

"Thank you, Octave." I clench my fists to stop myself from giving him a hug and a cheek kiss. "I'm thrilled to be here."

On my first couple of visits, I cheek kissed him. Then Darcy explained to me it was inappropriate and it made them uncomfortable. So, I've learned to keep my body language in check, hoping that my friendliness shows in the smile and the tone of my voice.

And that's how I greet the rest of the inhabitants of the mansion on rue Vieille du Temple—Lynette, a dynamic woman in her late fifties who helps Octave run the house; Michel, the cook with a proud beer belly that he calls his professional deformation; the shy maid, Lou; and Samir, the smiley gardener/handyman.

Samir carries my suitcases inside.

"Mademoiselle. Monsieur." Lynette hands Darcy and me a glass of bubbly. "This calls for a celebration."

Darcy touches his glass to mine. "It certainly does. Welcome to your future home, my dear."

I produce a saccharine smile. Someone, give me a *Légion d'Honneur* medal for not rolling my eyes.

We spend a few minutes in the foyer, sipping champagne and chatting with the staff. I insist that they call me by my first name. Lynette, Lou, Michel, and Samir promise they will. Octave says he can't. He'll call me *mademoiselle* and, once Darcy and I are married, he'll switch to *madame*. He apologizes profusely for his refusal to comply with my request, but he's just old-fashioned like that. It can't be helped.

When our glasses are empty and Lynette carries them away, Darcy takes my hand. "Let me show you around properly."

As we tour the airy *hôtel particulier*, Darcy explains that it was built almost four hundred years ago for a royal paramour. It changed hands many times and fell into disrepair in the nineteenth century when the aristocracy abandoned Le Marais. But his smart grandfather Bernard bought the mansion from a Swiss couple in the sixties, just before the neighborhood became hip again, and had it restored to combine the original grandeur with modern comforts.

"Have you always lived here?" I ask.

We've finished the tour, had a light dinner, and are now lounging in wicker armchairs in the most secluded and romantic spot in Darcy's picture-perfect back garden. The air is filled with the incomparable sweetness of a summer evening, enhanced by the climbing roses that lace the vintage cast-iron gazebo we're chilling in.

Top marks, Samir!

Darcy smiles.

I forget all about the roses.

Dammit, he's becoming an ace at this formerly so un-Darcy-like facial expression. Must be thanks to all the practice he's been getting lately, to my utter dismay. I'm determined not to slip again. Darcy hasn't made any intentional attempts to derail me—I'll grant him that. But he's been in the best of moods all week, laughing at my witticisms and even attempting a few of his own.

Imagine that!

He stopped by *La Bohème* every night—just as I did—to watch customers look at my photos, and he celebrated with me every print I sold.

The problem is Darcy being sweet, supportive, and funny is just as bad as deliberate seduction. No, it's worse. Much worse.

Give me the biblical serpent and his juicy apple any day over this.

"Yes," he says. "I've lived in this house since I was born, with a hiatus of five years in my late teens and early twenties."

"Don't tell me you lived in a student dormitory during your *hiatus*."

He shakes his head. "But I assure you, my accommodations were modest."

"What made you return home?"

"It's a long story."

I stretch out my legs, cross my ankles, and lift the glass of homemade lemonade in my hand. "Do I look like I'm in a hurry?"

"OK," Darcy says after a short hesitation. "I moved back here sometime after Maman left and before Papa passed."

He sips his lemonade in silence, his expression somber. Whatever thoughts he's thinking they aren't happy.

Darcy sets his glass on the metal table and turns to me. "Both of my parents entered a delayed and severe midlife crisis when I was about nineteen. Papa turned into a compulsive *bon vivant*. When he wasn't gambling in Monaco, he sailed in the Mediterranean or raced his Lamborghini around Tuscany. He'd come home only to see his boys and then be off again on his next adventure."

"You and your brothers lived with your dad?"

He shakes his head. "I was renting an apartment in the 6th, and my brothers lived with Maman."

"Who ran the company?"

"No one, really. It kind of ran itself—those were the good old days before the subprime mortgage crisis. Only at some point, the company started running *downhill*."

"What about your mom?"

He sighs. "Papa tried really hard to win her back and persuade her to join him on his fun-in-the-sun trips, but she despised all of it. Her own midlife crisis led her in the opposite direction."

"To the North Pole?"

He snorts. "Maman became very religious and passionate about charity work."

"If you were nineteen, your brothers were…" I close my eyes, computing.

"Raphael was about fifteen and Noah eleven." A shadow passes over his face. "They needed their parents. An older brother, a butler, tutors, cooks, maids, and extravagant amounts of pocket money can't stand in for mom and dad."

"I guess not."

"One day I stopped by the house and caught Raph smoking pot with a couple of other kids like him."

Darcy's lips compress into a hard line. "With too much money and too little supervision."

"Did you tell your parents?"

He shakes his head. "There was no point. Papa would've freaked out and overreacted, and Maman… let's just say we weren't close."

"What did you do?"

"I took measures." He shrugs. "Someone had to."

"Did your measures work?"

"Oh, yeah." He gives me a smug smile. "And I didn't stop there. Someone also had to convince the company's employees and the staff here and in Burgundy that the d'Arcys weren't on a path to self-destruction."

"But you were only nineteen!"

"It's not as if we had other candidates for the task." He chews on his lip. "Besides, I was already twenty-one by the time Papa involved me in the business."

It's funny how his voice, tone, and eyes are neutral when he says *Maman* and filled with warmth when he says *Papa*.

"You loved him, didn't you?" I ask.

He smiles. "Papa was the best. A great guy—kind, generous, incredibly charismatic—despite his poor judgement and mistakes. Yes, I loved him, even when he went through his personality yo-yo… I loved him more than I've ever loved anyone."

That's how I feel about my dad, too.

I tuck a strand of hair behind my ear. "You wanted to help him any way you could, didn't you?"

"Yes, I did. But, as it turned out, I couldn't save him from himself." He shrugs. "So I resolved to at least save his name and his life's work. His legacy."

"I thought you didn't care much for the family

name." I wink at him. "You did shorten it to Darcy, after all."

"It's just to make the conduct of business easier. I didn't want to put a certain type of people off with my long name and my title."

People like me?

I narrow my eyes. "Fess up, Sebastian—you're actually proud to be Count d'Arcy and so forth, aren't you? You burn the midnight oil drawing your family's coat of arms and reading up about the lives and deeds of your illustrious ancestors all the way back to Charlemagne."

"We don't descend from Charlemagne. The first recorded d'Arcy du Grand-Thouars de Saint-Maurice was a knight of Irish descent ennobled in the sixteenth century."

He smiles.

Slowly, his smile stretches into a grin. A grin of the panty-dropping variety.

I focus on my lemonade.

"I suppose I *am* proud of my ancestry and *most* of their deeds," Darcy says. "That pride was one of the things that kept me going all those times I was a hair from saying screw it all."

I gaze at the white roses over my head. What I just heard explains a lot about Darcy. But not all. It doesn't explain why he had to be so hard on my dad. The man was no threat to him. Dad's artisanal workshop was a little mosquito to Darcy's King Kong.

Couldn't he just live and let live?

Why hadn't he at least attempted to buy Dad's fragrances before he "cloned" them and drove the man out of business?

I'll never forgive myself if I forgive him for what he did.

"Why exactly did your mom leave your dad?" Darcy asks out of the blue.

"I'm not sure I want to talk about it."

"I answered your questions," he says. "Now it's your turn."

"Fine."

"So?"

"Several reasons," I say. "His drinking, of course. Dad can't hold his liquor, and he'd sworn to quit when they got married. He kept his promise until… until you ruined him."

"I see."

"She tried to help him, she really did. She got a waitressing job and urged him to do the same."

"Wait tables?"

"Get a job. Move on." I shrug. "But he was stuck on saving his company—his baby—at any price. When Mom discovered he'd secretly taken a mortgage on the house, she went ballistic."

"I can imagine."

"He faked her signature!" I shake my head. "I think it was the last straw."

Darcy nods. "She couldn't forgive his lie."

"Not just that. She loves that house. They bought it shortly after they married, and completely rebuilt it over the years. It's where they raised Lionel, Chloe, and me. We still have our rooms there, always ready for an impromptu visit."

His gives me a sympathetic look. "She kept Lionel's room?"

"Yes." I rake my hand through my hair. "I used to tell

her she should empty it out, but now I'm glad she never did. When I go in there, I remember him and my childhood… It's always bittersweet, but it's more sweet than bitter."

He reaches over and takes my hand. I tell myself it's just to say he's sorry for my loss. He's trying to convey that he, too, knows what it feels like to lose a dear one.

He'll let go of it in a moment.

Lynette comes out of the house, carrying a fragrant candle in an ancient chandelier. She sets it on the table between our armchairs.

I realize it's dark. A quick glance at my watch confirms the lateness of the hour—a quarter past eleven.

"I'm off to bed, children," she says, smiling. "Remember to blow out the candle when you go in."

"Will do," Darcy says.

He's still holding my hand.

I'm still deluding myself he'll release it any moment now.

Instead, he gives it a gentle squeeze and strokes the inside of my palm with his thumb.

Lynette's steps fade away and a door clicks shut.

Darcy tugs on my arm. "Come here."

In the candlelight, his eyes are two bottomless black wells, the pull from their depths almost irresistible.

I tip my head back and peer at the stars through the holes in the foliage. Dear Lord, I'm weak, so freaking weak. I'm about to let Darcy pull me toward him and have his way with me. My libido is taking control of my brain in a way I hadn't anticipated. My lust has become the enemy within—a traitor only too happy to do the rival power's bidding to the detriment of his homeland.

Darcy gives me another gentle tug, and I go to him, a slave to my baser needs. Without standing up, he leans toward me and runs his hands over my hips and thighs. He strokes them, down to my knees and up to my bottom, sliding his hands under the hem of my sundress.

I move closer and sit on his lap, facing him, my legs on either side of his. He nudges the straps of my dress and bra down my shoulders. Dying for the feel of his hands on my breasts, I pass my arms through the straps. The material slithers down and pools at my waist.

Sebastian reaches behind my back, unclasps my bra, and finally cups my breasts with his big hands. His touch is warm and snug and necessary.

Wait a sec!

Did I just call him "Sebastian"? Not because I had to, but of my own free will, inside my head where there are no witnesses?

Yes, I did.

This is *so* messed up.

I inch closer to his hard-on, debating if I should free it now or wait. When he puts his mouth to one of my breasts and begins to suckle, I forget what it was I couldn't make up my mind about. The softness of his lips, the tightness of his latch around my areola and the sweet intimacy of his tongue on my nipple make me arch and whimper.

He grips the back of my neck, raking his fingers through my hair, and pulls me to him. When his kiss arrives, openmouthed and hot, I revel in every exquisite moment of it, in his heady taste. It occurs to me that *extra hot* has become our new normal when we're alone. It also hits me that he no longer asks for permission to kiss me like that.

Thank God.

Who knew I'd love spice so much?

As we kiss, I begin to feel the ache and the emptiness

in my core, exactly the way I did before our first time a week ago.

I hope he has protection because I really don't see how I can make it to the bedroom.

The urge to touch him overwhelms me. I undo his belt and zipper, draw his boxer-briefs down, and wrap my fingers around him.

He makes a noise deep in his throat and pulls a condom out of his pocket.

My famished body cheers and pops champagne.

"When we get to the bedroom," he says, sheathing himself, "I'm going to kiss and lick you absolutely everywhere."

"Including the toes?"

"Oh, yes."

I sigh theatrically. "Do your worst."

"Trust me, I will."

"If you're trying to impress me," I say, raising my chin in defiance, "it isn't working."

It's working just fine—I'm soaking wet.

He smiles. "I'm not trying to impress you. I'm just giving you a heads-up."

I zoom in on his erection, proud and unapologetic, like the rest of him. "What if I walked away now and left you hanging… er, getting it up?"

He stares at me. "You wouldn't."

"I could."

Gripping my hips, he pulls me close enough for our sexes to brush. "But you won't."

As he says those words, Sebastian tugs the crotch of my panties to the side and drives in.

You're right—I won't.

CHAPTER 21

DIANE

"Another cappuccino?" Lynette asks.

I smile at her. "Thank you, but two is enough this early in the day."

Actually, it isn't *that* early.

The others have been up for at least a couple of hours. Three, in Sebastian's case. Lynette and I are the only late risers, so we've gotten into the habit of taking our breakfast together. Besides, everyone else favors the minimalistic French breakfast of coffee, orange juice, and croissant. Lynette and I like *real* breakfasts.

And real breakfasts require prep work.

So, it goes like this: Lynette makes pancakes or porridge, fries eggs, and brews coffee that's second only to Manon's. I pick and wash a handful of strawberries from the garden and then toast some bread. When everything's ready and we sit down, Lynette opens the paper Sebastian has left for her, and I check the newsfeed on my phone. Sometimes we chat, but mostly we just enjoy our big, fat, and infinitely rewarding breakfast in companionable silence.

I help Lynette clear the table and head upstairs.

Today Octave is out of town visiting his mother's grave and taking care of some private matters. I'll be using this opportunity to snoop around his quarters. He's Sebastian's most trusted staff member, so I figure maybe I'll find something.

But the moment I open the door to Octave's office, the knot in my stomach doubles in size, forcing me to stop and take a few fortifying breaths.

I inspect my palms.

Clean.

Funny, I would've bet they were smeared with sticky mud.

What I'm about to do feels so wrong I'm a hair from backpedaling. It's one thing to nose into Sebastian's life, but intruding on an innocent man's—a *good* man's—private space isn't something I can easily justify.

However, considering I still haven't found any dirt whatsoever on my betrothed, I have no choice.

How naive I was to imagine that once I lived here, I'd gain access to his financial information or the inner workings of his business! The documents he keeps in his home office are as innocuous as a document could be. He may as well publish them online. He never discusses sensitive matters with me or when I'm around. Or when anyone is around.

Sebastian's life is so perfectly and hermetically compartmentalized it should be used as a case study in management books.

When working, he's a steely business shark. In his private life, he's a loyal friend and brother, and a respected master of the house. He's also the most gallant of men with yours truly… on camera. At night, his alpha side comes out again, only in a different way. He forgets his good manners and becomes demanding and greedy.

It seems duplicity is his second nature.

As for me, I've taken a page from his book, forcing myself to compartmentalize, too.

I crave his brand of sex. I enjoy his conversation. I have a hard time keeping my eyes or hands off him.

All true, all undeniable.

But deep inside, I'm still the person who attacked him with a cream cake last October. I'm not impressed by his riches. Well, maybe just a little. It would take a saint not to be. And I'm no saint—not even close.

What Sebastian will never have is my forgiveness.

Even if I'm soon to become Madame d'Arcy du Grand-Thouars de Saint-Maurice, I'm still *me*. And I still care more about justice than I do about money.

On that thought, I force myself to step in and look around.

The first thing I notice is a black-and-white portrait of a smiling young woman on Octave's desk. Her hair is huge, its ends curled and flipped up, and she wears more eyeliner than Sophia Loren and Aimee Winehouse combined. The portrait screams "the sixties" in all their rock 'n' roll glory.

This must be Octave's mom.

I note there's no portrait of his dad anywhere. From what I gather, the man is still alive, even if Octave never talks about him. Maybe they don't get along.

But I should stop distracting myself—it isn't Octave I'm after.

I spend the next hour going through the perfectly organized and labelled files on the wall shelves. They contain nothing but bills, contracts, bank statements, and administrative correspondence.

A roomy cabinet next to Octave's desk hosts an unusual-looking audio device and headphones. Maybe he's an amateur radio broadcaster or something in that vein.

Next up, his desk.

When I realize that some of the drawers are locked, I'm relieved. This means I'll get out of here sooner.

The guilt is killing me.

I open the unlocked ones. Pens, scissors, staplers, paper… One drawer contains Octave's passport and his birth certificate.

Octave Bernard Rossi, born March 14, 1958.

Ha! I didn't know his middle name was Bernard, like Sebastian's grandfather's. But let's face it, if my middle name was Bernard, I'd keep mum about it, too. It's undeservedly but irrevocably *démodé* and even mossier than Octave, which, at least, is original and even appears to be making a comeback.

As I close the last drawer and tiptoe out the door, I beg Heaven to forgive me this particular trespass.

And then I beg for a memory wipe so my tongue will never slip and call poor Octave by his unfortunate middle name.

CHAPTER 22

DIANE

"Welcome back, madame." Octave performs his signature head bow and takes a suitcase from Sebastian. "Monsieur, it's good to see you smiling and tanned. I hope everything went as planned."

"Better than planned," Sebastian says, heading upstairs with the rest of our baggage. "It was a *perfect* wedding."

And in many ways, it was.

Now that I've faked a marriage to the man, I find it hard to believe it's been only a month since I moved in with him in mid-May. This has been the speediest month of my life. Almost every night, we've gone out or hosted a dinner at home. Sebastian has been acting as a man utterly and completely smitten with his fiancée. When I took him to Nîmes, he charmed the bejesus out of Mom and all my childhood friends.

I didn't dare to take him to Marseilles.

In fact, I didn't even have the courage to tell Dad about him. Chloe did that for me.

As expected, first he was shocked. And then he was mad.

I hope he'll forgive me one day after I've completed my mission and he's put two and two together.

If that day ever comes, that is.

Because so far, the muddiest, stinkiest dirt I've found on my fiancé is a speeding ticket.

Our wedding was an "intimate" affair, held in the privacy and extreme luxury of a paradisiac Bahamian island. My fiancé told everyone we couldn't wait for the chateau wedding scheduled for next May, to which everyone and their cat will be invited. This gave rise to rumors that I'm pregnant, which both of us denied so vehemently that a lot of people decided they were true.

The ceremony took place on a pristine sand beach with only the minister, Sebastian, a handful of guests, and me to stain its unspoiled purity. I wore a bespoke wedding dress of hand-embroidered silk and exquisite *Alençon* lace. It hugged my body like a glove, pushing my breasts up and flaring out at the hem.

Now that Sebastian and I are on shagging terms, wearing sacks is kind of pointless.

Our handpicked guest list included Raphael and his bestie Genevieve, Sebastian's aunt and uncle, and a few of his closest friends including Laurent, who arrived alone, and Mat, who came with Jeanne.

Sebastian's mother and his youngest brother Noah were "unable"—read "unwilling"—to attend.

My side consisted of Mom, Chloe and Hugo, two childhood friends from Nîmes, and Elorie. Manon couldn't make it.

Unsurprisingly, neither could Dad.

A couple of weeks before the wedding, Sebastian published the banns, which made me jittery.

"Are you sure our marriage is truly fake?" I asked him for the umpteenth time.

"Better than that," he said. "It's *genuinely* fake. Everything is real and legit, in case anyone wants to check."

Color drained from my face.

"Don't look so terrified!" He laughed. "I *forgot* to submit a crucial piece of paperwork to the closest French consulate in Miami. I'll be sure to keep forgetting for three more months, after which our marriage will be null."

I exhaled in relief.

"My dearest, Diane." He patted my hand. "I have just as little desire to marry you for real as you do. So relax and enjoy your fake wedding and honeymoon."

And so I did.

We both did, judging by my new husband's insatiable appetite throughout the week. We fooled around at the hotel, on the beach, up against a palm tree, in the sea, in the pool, in the Jacuzzi, in the shower, on the bed, on the couch, on the floor, and against the wall in our palatial suite.

Against every wall in our suite.

The whole week was a nonstop sexfest, leaving certain parts of my body a little sore, but also pleasured beyond my wildest fantasies.

On the way home, I sat next to Chloe for a good part of the endless flight. We talked about her physical and emotional recovery, and how she was beginning to see life in a different light. She said it felt like putting on Technicolor lenses after years of gray scale. Happiness still scares the shit out of her, but she's learned to breathe through her fear and carry on.

"I'm grateful for every day with Hugo," Chloe said,

staring at the blue expanse above the clouds. "It took me a while to recognize that he's the love of my life. But now that I have…" She paused, her expression dreamy.

"What has changed, now that you have?" I asked.

"I keep falling in love." She smiled. "Every day, I tell myself it isn't possible to love a man more than I love Hugo, and yet the next day I find myself loving him more."

"Your fiancé is a wonderful man," I said.

And I meant it.

"And you"—Chloe gave me a wink—"still haven't told me how you went from hating Sebastian Darcy to marrying him six months later."

"It's a long story," I said, borrowing his favorite excuse.

Fortunately, Chloe didn't point out that we were stuck on a plane with nothing to do for a few more hours.

Good girl.

CHAPTER 23

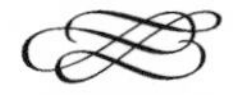

DIANE

Finally in the quiet and comfort of the master bedroom at Darcy House, I stretch out on the bed and catch a quick nap while Sebastian showers.

Lucky bastard—he had no problem sleeping on the plane.

"I'm off to the office," he says, emerging from the bathroom all crisp and kissworthy. "Lots of catching up to do."

"Go catch them all up, *darling*!" I produce a nauseatingly saccharine smile. "What's a little jet lag to a captain of industry?"

He laughs. "What about you?"

"Bath. Pajamas. Sleep."

"It's only four in the afternoon."

I give him a "so what" shrug.

As soon as Sebastian is gone, I take a long bath and put on my PJs. The problem is I can't sleep. With no industry to captain and no catching up to do, I should've dropped off the moment I shut my eyes. But my wayward brain has decided otherwise. After thirty minutes of vain attempts to cop some z's, I give up and get dressed.

Too tired to read, I decide to explore the last unchartered area of Darcy House—the attic. Vast and high-ceilinged, it's used for storage—an unpardonable waste of space in any *normal* person's point of view. As I climb the wooden staircase and step into the loft, I remember Sebastian telling me his father wanted to install an indoor swimming pool in here. But the city of Paris denied him the permit, what with the mansion being classified as a historic building.

Poor rich man, he must've been heartbroken!

I wander around, running my hand over mismatched pieces of furniture and unveiling old paintings stacked against the walls. Specks of dust dance in the light coming in through dormer windows. The place smells of old wood and the lavender hanging from the ceiling beams in little dried bunches. The attic has so much character and charm that if I were the *real* mistress of this house, I would've wiped the dust, washed the windows, and set up my workspace here.

But as things stand, I'm the *fake* mistress of this house, and my goal is to find dirt on my fake husband.

Get to work, Diane.

I begin with the massive chest of drawers in front of me and work my way through the loft, leaving no object unturned. Two hours later, just as I begin to tell myself this is pointless, I pull out the middle drawer of an unpretentious little desk that's hiding behind a gigantic throne-like armchair and stacks of old magazines.

Weird… The drawer looks shallower than its siblings.

Using my tiny Swiss army knife—Lionel drilled into

me to always have it handy—I hook the false bottom of the drawer and lift.

Bingo!

Concealed underneath is a secret compartment that holds a bundle of four letters. I open the first one. It's from Sebastian's mom, accusing her ex-husband of having turned their older sons against her and insisting Raphael would be much better off living with her in Nepal than with him in Paris. Why only Raphael, I wonder before remembering that Noah was already with her and Sebastian must've been around twenty by then.

The second letter is more or less the same as the first with the addition of a few choice adjectives I wouldn't've expected from a high-society lady.

The third letter, again from her and again on the same topic, ends with this passage:

> *I was hoping it would never come to this, but your blatant refusal to meet me halfway leaves me no choice. So here goes. Do you remember how I was already pregnant with Sebastian when we married? I'm sure you do. What you don't know is that I wasn't pregnant by you. That's right—Sebastian, your adored firstborn, your rock and your heir, is not your son. He's Emmanuel's. If you don't believe me, you're welcome to steal a few hairs from Sebastian's comb and have them tested. Once you've done that, it's up to you to wait until I tell him the truth or to send Raphael to live with me.*
>
> *Marguerite*

I reread the passage twice more and then open the fourth—and last—letter and read the following:

> *Thibaud,*
>
> *I'm glad you did the paternity test. Now that you have*

proof that I wasn't bluffing, will you please send Raphael to me? I promise that if you do, I'll never tell Sebastian the truth. It would break his heart. But I'm prepared to do that if you leave me no choice. It is my duty to shelter Raphael, who lacks his older brother's sense of purpose and moral rectitude, from your debauched lifestyle. I hope you understand my motives and will do the right thing.

Marguerite

The letter is dated a month before Darcy senior overdosed.

This revelation must've been the straw that broke his back. He'd already lost his wife, his good name, and his youngest son. He was being blackmailed and pressured to send his middle son to a faraway country. But, perhaps worst of all, he'd been robbed of his oldest and favorite boy. Not in the literal sense, but on that fundamental *fruit-of-my-loins* level, which means more to us than it should.

With shaking hands, I fold the letters and stick them in the back pocket of my jeans.

That's it.

My mission is accomplished. I've found the muddy, stinky dirt that I've been looking for.

The dirt that could destroy Sebastian Darcy.

CHAPTER 24

DIANE

The round-faced pastry shop assistant gives me a bright smile. "What can I get for you, mesdemoiselles?"

"A small bag of *coucougnettes*, please," I say politely.

Elorie snorts. "Did you just ask for testicles?"

"I did." I pay and offer a soft pink sweet from my bag to Elorie. "I promise you'll like it."

She studies the almond paste "ball" spiced with ginger and candied in sugar and pulls a face. "Really?"

I nod to encourage her. "They're a Southwest specialty, but I discovered them only a month ago here in Le Marais."

Elorie puts the *coucougnette* in her mouth and chews it slowly.

"So?" I ask.

"Tastes better than it sounds."

I grin. "Told ya."

We step out and amble along the cobblestone streets of this medieval *quartier* until our next stop—the European House of Photography. The exhibition space is located in an eighteenth-century *hôtel particulier* at 5 rue de Fourcy. Impressive as it is, the building can't hold a candle to the splendor of Darcy House.

It's just an impartial observation, that's all.

The plan is to split up for a while. While I check out the new exhibit at the photography museum, Elorie will explore the best vintage clothes shop in the capital just around the corner on rue de Rivoli.

An hour later, I leave the museum and head to the "falafel street"—rue des Rosiers. When I arrive, Elorie is already standing in the long line in front of L'As du Fallafel.

She holds up a big plastic bag filled with clothes. "Your new neighborhood rocks."

"I know!" I grin. "Where else in Paris can you have so much fun on a Sunday afternoon?"

"Unfortunately, being so cool has a flip side." She sighs and points at all the people ahead of us in line. "I hope you aren't too hungry."

"Fear not, my friend." I pull the *coucougnettes* bag from my purse and wave it in front of her nose. "We have balls."

Fifteen minutes later, the line has barely moved.

"You know," Elorie says, helping herself to a pink bonbon, "sometimes I hate this country."

"Why's that?"

"It's all about *égalité*, but when you scratch below the surface, there's no real equality. What we have is a sky-high fence between the rich and the poor."

"I agree," I say. "But I would argue it isn't as tall as it seems."

Elorie shakes her head. "Your Cinderella story, *ma cocotte*, is so improbable it's suspicious. A man like

Sebastian Darcy falling in love with a cashier? Marrying her? You have to admit it sounds fishy."

Of course it does.

Because it is.

"Hey, what about your 'marry-a-billionaire' plan?" I ask. "If you don't believe in Cinderella stories, aren't you wasting your time plotting to snatch a prince?"

"Maybe I am." Elorie bites her nails, her expression morose. "I haven't had much success, even with all the opportunities you're throwing my way."

I give her hand a squeeze.

Suddenly, she perks up. "I know what I have to do! I need to adjust my strategy and focus on the *nouveau-riche* billionaires. The *new* money, not the old."

"Athletes? Start-up wonder kids?"

"Yes, but also mafia bosses." She winks. "They'll be less picky."

What can I say to that?

If anything, my fake Cinderella story only proves she's right.

Best to change the topic. "Remember I told you about Belle Auxbois and how she didn't want to credit Dad for his work?"

She nods.

"You won't believe it, but she changed her mind."

Elorie holds her thumbs up while chewing another *coucougnette*.

"Dad sent me a link to the talk show that aired on TF1 last Saturday."

Elorie widens her eyes. "She went on TV with it?"

"Yup." I beam. "Prime time. The show host asked her about the perfume, which is selling really well, and she said she hadn't done it alone. She admitted she'd had precious help from Charles Petit, one of the country's best *parfumiers*."

"She said that?"

"Uh-huh." I can't wipe the grin off my face. "Isn't it fantabulous? I have no idea what triggered her sudden confession, though. Maybe she just woke up one morning and realized that acknowledging Dad's work was the right thing to do."

At last, we enter the eatery. Just as I'm about to order a falafel plate with a side of grilled eggplant, Elorie claps her hand to her forehead. "I know why she caved in."

I stare at her expectantly.

"It's your husband."

"What?"

"When I stayed over at the castle, I overheard him talking on the phone with someone. He sounded stern, even a little scary."

"What did he say?"

"He mentioned the perfume, some other stuff I didn't understand, and said things like 'I have proof' and 'it's in your best interest to announce it yourself.' "

"Anything else?"

Elorie furrows her brow, trying to recall. "Oh yeah, he also said 'I'm giving you a month, and then I'm suing the pants off you.' "

I can't believe what I'm hearing. "Why didn't you say anything before?"

"I didn't make the connection." She gives me an apologetic look. "It's only now that everything clicked into place."

I can't think of much else for the rest of our girls' day about town.

We say good-bye at *République*, and I take the *métro* to

my apartment in the 14th, which Sebastian has been paying for since I chucked the supermarket job.

My head throbs as I struggle to adjust to Elorie's revelation about Sebastian.

And to how I can possibly reconcile it with what I intend to do.

CHAPTER 25

DIANE

Two hours later, after I get to my apartment and frame the rest of my rooftop prints for Jeanne's gallery, my thoughts are still in a jumble of epic proportions.

So, Sebastian worked behind the scenes to help Dad, and hid it from me. Clearly, he didn't do it to improve my opinion of him. Does this mean he's sorry for what he's done to Dad? Is this his way of making amends?

Am I prepared to forgive him?

After all, he can truly be held responsible only for Dad's bankruptcy. My parents' divorce and Dad's stroke were the consequences of that but they weren't, strictly speaking, Sebastian's fault.

There's another question that's been growing in the back of my mind for weeks now. It started as a tiny seed that I could ignore, but it's exploded inside my head, deafening me.

Could our fake relationship ever turn into something real?

I lean my forehead against the window and stare outside.

Don't be daft, woman.

Sebastian and me, it'll never work. We're like fire and ice, matter and antimatter. We're wired for mutual destruction. Whatever it is that's sprouted between us, it's doomed.

I read *Libération*, vote for socialists, and believe in strong government. He gripes about France's "archaic" labor laws that "overprotect" employees and discourage entrepreneurial initiative. Even though in public he supports the Greens, I'm sure it's only because his PR people told him it's good for the company's image. Deep inside, he's as conservative as it gets.

He's a billionaire, for Christ's sake.

And he reads *Le Figaro*.

I hate that kind of people. They have no civic sense, no notion of solidarity. Their only concern is how to make more money and pay less in taxes. And while these glorified crooks succeed in dissimulating their income in Swiss banks and offshore companies, people like Dad—hardworking, honest people—go belly up.

I rack my brain for additional arguments.

What I'm trying to do here is to wind myself up into a righteous anger against Sebastian. Only a couple of months ago, I had no difficulty doing it.

It used to come naturally.

But now, all my valiant attempts hit a brick wall and fly into pieces. That wall is the belief—a conviction, really—that Sebastian is nothing like the rotten, self-absorbed golden boy that I've been painting him to be. His arrogance is superficial. It's just a mask he wears to hide his insecurities from the world. And to project an image of someone who "knows what he's doing."

Underneath the veneer, Sebastian Darcy is an honorable man in every single way that matters.

I take my head in my hands, wishing I was on a deserted island so I could bawl my confusion to the four winds.

My door buzzer sounds.

It's Sebastian.

I let him in, wondering what's so urgent it couldn't wait 'til I get to the town house later tonight.

He steps in, a huge cardboard box in his hands.

"What is this?" I ask as he sets it on my desk.

"A top-notch professional-quality printer," he says. "So you can make your own prints. And a landscape camera."

I sit down, flabbergasted.

He opens the box and unpacks the printer first. Unable to resist, I jump up and take a closer look. He's right—it's top-notch equipment. To think of all the stuff I could do with it…

"I hope this is what you were talking about." He hands me a camera.

Not just any camera—a Seitz 6x17 Panoramic.

I've read articles about it. I've dreamed about it. This baby takes the world's largest digital photos. The quality is so good I can make a wall-sized print of the Chateau d'Arcy and still be able to see the little spider swinging under one of the third-floor windows.

It's the best of the best of the best.

I push it back toward him. "This thing costs a small fortune. More than what I make in a year."

"It's nothing," he says.

"I can't accept it."

"And I can't have you walking on roofs so that you can take enough shots with your portrait camera to assemble them into a landscape."

"Why…" I look away, trying to form my question. "Why are you being so nice to me?"

"Do you want the conveniently honest answer or the brutally honest one?"

"Give me both."

He places the camera on the table, takes my chin between his index and thumb, and turns my face toward him.

I stare into his somber eyes.

"The conveniently honest answer is that I'm *nice* to you because I like your photos and want to help."

"And the brutally honest one?"

"I'm being *nice* because I want to continue seeing you after our contract expires and you *leave* me."

"You want a real relationship?"

"I'm not sure that's exactly what I'd call it." He hesitates. "Diane, I don't want to mislead you or give you false hopes. You're *not* the kind of woman I'd ever pick as a real wife."

I square my shoulders, trying not to show how much his words hurt me.

"You despise what I stand for," he says. "You have no interest in my world, in being my *partner* in every aspect of life." He pauses before adding, "My mother had the same distaste for the things that mattered to Papa… And look where it got them."

He lets go of my chin.

We're both silent for a long moment, gazing out the window, at our shoes, at the equipment on the table—everywhere except each other.

I'm the first to break the silence. "Thank you for your honesty."

His gaze burns into my eyes as he waits for me to continue.

"I think it would be best if we stopped seeing each other after the contract expires," I say.

His face hardens. "If that's what you want."

I nod.

Dammit, this conversation is hard.

"Tell me something," I say to get us out of the minefield. "Why are you so sure your nemesis will use the same method on you as he did on your father? Maybe this time he'll do something different, something more drastic."

"Like what?"

"I don't know… poison you?"

He laughs. "I don't think so."

"Why not?"

"It's just not his MO. You see, the guy—or the gal—hates me, but he won't take unnecessary risks. He's super careful."

"If you say so."

"From what I've observed, he seeks to inflict pain—not to kill. What he wants is to punch me where it hurts most. If I wither and die as a consequence, he probably won't complain. But his goal isn't my quick death. I'm sure of it."

Punch me where it hurts most.

Isn't that what I'll do to him if I make those letters public?

He doesn't need his nemesis to give him pain and suffering—he has me.

"Ready to go home?" he asks after our conversation returns to the equipment I've agreed to keep.

"You go ahead," I say. "I still have some stuff to do."

"Need help?"

I shake my head. "Need privacy."

He nods and walks out.

I place his mother's letters into the kitchen sink and put a match to them. As they burn to ashes, I tell myself that now nobody—not Sebastian's nemesis, not even me in a moment of anger—will be able to punch him where it hurts most.

CHAPTER 26

DIANE

We're in the home stretch.

If Sebastian's nemesis doesn't make his move *really* soon, my fake husband of one month and I will go on a break, separate and divorce, pretexting irreconcilable differences.

Sebastian is getting a little nervous about the success of his plan.

I would be, too, in his place.

All his efforts of the past six months, the elaborate deception of family and friends, the marriage to a woman he'd never consider wife material, the luxury wedding, extravagant parties, and lavish receptions—it's all been for naught. To say nothing of the money he's still to fork over when my payday arrives.

If nothing out of the ordinary happens this week, I'll pocket my fee and leave next week. Sebastian will go back to his normal life, none the wiser. And his enemy will thank his lucky stars for having stayed under the radar.

No wonder my still-husband is cramming as many

opportunities for his enemy as he can into this last week. The first one is underway right now, and it's a happy event, regardless of our hidden agenda.

Jeanne's hubby, Mat, was elected Member of the European Parliament, as the *Top-of-the-List* for the Greens.

Sebastian had backed his party's campaign, so he's doubly pleased.

To celebrate Mat's achievement, we're hosting a big reception at Raphael and Sebastian's gentlemen's club. Mat wanted to do it at *La Bohème*, but the bistro was too small for the occasion. Everyone who's anyone in Paris and from Mat's home base in Normandy is here, schmoozing, drinking, and stuffing themselves with caviar canapés.

Sebastian steers the event with his usual efficiency, making sure Mat meets all the movers and shakers and opinion leaders.

I play the perfect hostess—at least, my idea of the perfect hostess. Dressed in a shimmery gown that feels and looks as if it was poured on me, I welcome and make small talk with as many guests as I can manage without appearing rushed.

As I do my rounds, I notice Sebastian chatting with a creature who should totally represent France at the next Miss Universe. They smile at each other, the distance between them considerably smaller than what's expected of two people holding a polite conversation. She plays with her earlobe as she speaks. Sebastian beckons to a server and picks up two champagne flutes.

A needle of jealousy pricks me somewhere in the upper left quadrant of my chest, but I will myself to ignore it and carry on.

One of the uniformed waitresses carrying a tray

with food and drinks keeps glancing at Raphael. The depth of her gaze is intriguing. Every time she steals a glance at him, something flashes in her pretty eyes—something bigger than just *OMG-what-a-studmuffin*. Her furtive looks have an undeniable gravitas that goes beyond flirtation. It suggests a history. And a *complicated* one, at that.

When I spot Manon, I rush to her side for a chat that I'll actually enjoy.

"Where's Amar, by the way?" I ask after we've covered her recent raise and the encouraging sales of my new prints at *La Bohème*. "I haven't seen him yet."

She looks down, visibly distressed.

"What's wrong? Is he OK?"

"I don't know."

I give her a quizzical look.

"He's disappeared."

"What do you mean?"

"He's gone," she says. "It's been three days now. He hasn't showed up for work, and he won't return my calls."

"Are you going to report his disappearance to the police?"

She shakes her head. "I managed to get hold of his mom. She says Amar left the country."

"Why?"

"I couldn't get anything else out of her." There's a tremor in her voice. "I'm at my wit's end."

I give her a hug. "He'll come back. He loves you."

"I'm not… I'm not so sure anymore."

Someone taps my shoulder. "Here she is, the beautiful hostess of this great celebration!"

I turn around—it's Sebastian's pal, Laurent.

"Thank you for the 'beautiful,' " I say as we cheek kiss. "I hope you're enjoying yourself."

"Absolutely." He tilts his head toward Manon. "Will you introduce me to your equally beautiful friend?"

I do and leave them to it. God knows, Manon could do with a distraction right now.

Besides, I really need to pee.

Just as I'm opening the door to the ladies' room, Raphael and the glancing waitress come out of the gents' toilet. He's tucking his shirt into his pants. She's smoothing her uniform. Both are rumpled and flushed, leaving no doubt about what they were doing in the men's bathroom.

Or about the nature of their "history."

When I return to the front room, there are daggers flying around. Not material ones, of course, but the looks Genevieve is giving the waitress. They're so sharp it's a miracle her victim isn't screaming in pain and collapsing to the floor.

I smirk.

Raphael may believe that Genevieve is only a friend, but the truth is she may as well be wearing a T-shirt that reads, *Hands off the middle Darcy brother—HE'S MINE.*

Men can be so selectively blind!

Sebastian comes over to me. "Did you see the woman I've been talking to for the past thirty minutes?"

"I did."

"We've already *bumped* into each other at the Chanel luncheon I attended for work last week." His eyes are bright with excitement.

"Do you think…" I search his face. "Do you think she's it?"

"I just texted the PI to stand by outside."

"What happens next?"

He looks at his watch. "In an hour or so, people will start leaving. You'll say you're tired and go home."

"And you?"

"If all goes well, I'll leave with my temptress."

I'm itching to ask if he'll do more than just "leave" with her. For his scheme to work, I guess he'll need to. The question is how far he'll go. Will he just drive her home, kiss her, and let his private eye shadow her until she contacts her employer, or will he actually go all the way and sleep with her?

He's never been very specific on that part of the plan.

I nod and force myself to smile. "Fingers crossed."

"Don't wait up for me tonight," he says.

That needle I'd felt earlier morphs into a dirty bomb and blows up inside my chest just as Sebastian turns and walks away.

PART V
HOVEL

CHAPTER 27

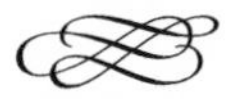

DIANE

How hard can it be to open a pair of healthy, well-functioning eyes? Right now, extremely hard. Almost impossible. It's not just the eyes. My head is pounding. Nausea reigns supreme in my stomach, threatening to advance through my throat and erupt at any moment.

How much exactly did I drink last night? Barely a glass. I was too busy playing hostess. So why am I having the hangover of my life? I try to rub my eyes, but my hands won't come up. A few more failed attempts later and it hits me. My wrists are bound behind my back. My ankles are tied, too.

What the hell?

With a superhuman effort, I peel my eyes open and take in my surroundings. I'm lying on top of a mattress in a dark, moldy-smelling room. Probably a cellar. I writhe and buck, testing the strength of the tape at my wrists and ankles. It's impossible to untie or even loosen a little. After some more wriggling, I manage to sit up, lean back against the wall, and look around.

It *is* a cellar. It's small, so I doubt I'm in the mansion, where I've thoroughly explored the huge basement. There's a minuscule opening just below the ceiling. That's where the air and light come through. A suitcase sits in one corner of the room. My suitcase. The wall opposite me has a door with no handle. I don't like that door any more than I like the window covered with a solid metal screen.

Clearly, at some point between the moment Greg dropped me off in front of Darcy House and now, I passed out and was brought down here.

Did someone hit me over the head? Drug me? Hypnotize me?

The thing is I have no memory of it.

I call for help, scream, call for help again, and then scream some more.

Nothing happens.

I call for help a few more times.

The door opens. A sturdy man steps in and locks the door behind him. He pauses for a moment by the door and then walks slowly toward me.

Recognition slaps me on the face like a bucket of icy water.

"I hope *madame* slept well," Octave says, mockery palpable in his voice. "I hope you weren't too cold and your restraints not too tight."

He halts in front of me.

I give him a long, hard stare. "It's been you—all this time, pretending to be a friend and sharpening your knife behind Sebastian's back."

"I was never his *friend*," Octave hisses. "I'm his *majordome*, remember?"

"What do you want?" I ask.

"I'm not sure yet." He gives me the smile of a deranged man. "I'm considering different scenarios."

"What about Miss France at the bash last night? Wasn't she supposed to seduce Sebastian? Wasn't that your plan?"

He throws his head back and roars with an uncontrollable laugher, tears and all. "Is that what you both thought? I was hoping you would."

Octave pulls a hanky from his pocket and wipes his eyes. "She was just a diversion."

I blink, processing that piece of information.

"You see," he says. "I had to adapt my initial plan after you moved in."

"Why?"

"Because I heard Sebastian and you talking one night, between humping sessions, about outing his nemesis."

"You—what? How?"

"I bugged your bedroom."

Dear Lord.

That explains the device and headphones in his closet.

I'm toast.

Unless… The bugging might be good news. It means he's discovered the truth about us.

"In that case," I say, "you know our marriage is a sham."

"What?" He looks genuinely surprised.

"If you've bugged our bedroom, you must've figured out from our conversations that we're not for real. Sebastian hired me to help him unmask you."

He sneers. "Nice try."

"It's the truth."

"You really expect me to believe your bullshit?"

I close my eyes and try to concentrate. Could it be that neither Sebastian nor I ever said anything in that bedroom that would give away the real nature of our relationship? We've had a lot of sex, many laughs, and a few serious conversations, but… is it possible that we never mentioned our contract?

But of course, we did—as recently as two weeks ago. Only we weren't in Darcy House. We were in my apartment.

Octave squats and checks the tape at my wrists and ankles.

"I may be just a manservant, but I'm not stupid," he says. "I've seen the way you look at him—like he's the only man on the whole fucking planet. I've seen the way he looks at you—like he wants to nosh you for breakfast, lunch, and dinner every fucking day."

I take a ragged breath and look away.

"And don't get me started on the way he touches you." Octave stands up, smirking. "These things can't be faked."

I lick my dry lips, realizing how parched I am.

Octave turns around and heads to the door.

"Wait," I call after him.

He halts and looks over his shoulder at me.

I point my chin to the suitcase. "What's that for?"

"To buy me a few days. He'll think you got jealous and left him."

In a few days, I'll be dead from dehydration. That is if he doesn't kill me before.

"Will you please bring me some water next time you come down?" I ask.

"No," he says. "I'm not your servant anymore, sweetheart."

CHAPTER 28

SEBASTIAN

I get home in the wee hours of the morning.

Valeria—that's my temptress's name… fake, no doubt—wanted to go to her favorite nightclub. She *loooooves* dancing. After that she asked me to take her for a ride around the Boulogne Forest, driving my Lamborghini as fast as it would go. She *adoooooores* speed.

When I took her back to her hotel, she invited me upstairs for a "cup of coffee." That's when I went off script and declined her invitation.

"Wife?" She gave me a sympathetic look.

I nodded.

Valeria pointed at her watch. "It's three in the morning. She won't believe you anyway."

"I'll try my luck." I planted a quick smooch on her lips and promised I'd make arrangements so we could meet again soon without raising anyone's suspicions.

She gave me her number and told me to use it anytime.

I drove off, praying she wouldn't wait too long before contacting her employer. Despite her striking beauty, I really don't care for the prospect of "meeting her again soon."

Right now, what I long for is sleep. Next to Diane. I picture myself performing what's become my favorite bedtime ritual. It consists of spooning Diane to my chest, wrapping an arm around her, and breathing in the skin at her nape.

It occurs to me as I climb the stairs to the second floor that I haven't had a single sleepless night since she's been sharing my bed.

I also realize that what I told her the other day about not wanting a relationship with her was, as she'd say, a big pile of shit.

Treading as lightly as possible so I don't wake her up, I enter the bedroom—and know at once that she's gone. I turn on the light and look around. The bed hasn't been turned down. Her nightstand is free of her baubles. I rush to the walk-in closet. One of her suitcases and some of her clothes are missing.

She's left me.

Why? Up until now, she'd stuck to our deal remarkably well. Why quit now before we have proof that my plan has worked, before our contract has expired, and before we've had a chance to discuss this new development?

Was it jealousy?

I've suspected for some time now that Diane has feelings for me, but I didn't think they were strong. And I certainly didn't think she'd let them cloud her judgement.

I sit down on the bed and drop my head into my hands, disappointment washing through me in cold, sticky waves. The funny thing is I'm more upset about Diane's walking out on me than jeopardizing my plan.

Her departure makes the prospect of a future without her real for the first time.

That future holds no witty commentary on everything under the sun, no adorable goofiness, and no refreshing disregard for my money and status.

Nor does it hold lovemaking that's been growing sweeter every night, instead of palling.

I'd believed a future without Diane Petit was what I wanted.

But all I can see in it now is bleakness.

Depressing, morbid, unbearable bleakness.

What have I done?

In the quiet of the house, the sound of a door unlocking and gently closing comes from the foyer. I jump up and run down the stairs, tripping on the carpet, getting up, and running again. Is it Diane? Has she changed her mind? Did she reconsider the wisdom of her actions?

Let it be her. Please, let it be her.

But it's only Octave—the last person in this household I expected to come home at this hour.

He smiles apologetically. "I hope I didn't wake monsieur up."

"No, I was awake." I hesitate. "Have you seen Diane?"

He shakes his head. "Didn't she come home with you?"

"No," I say drily. "She didn't."

I wish Octave good night and return to my bedroom, which feels awfully empty without my lover.

When I crawl into bed fifteen minutes later, I lie on her side and bury my nose in her pillow.

I'm a fool.

Blinded by Diane's charm, I was beginning to

convince myself she could be the right woman for me—a partner for life, my anchor, my rock. Drunk on her body, I was beginning to see her as the woman who'd stay by my side through good times and bad, sickness and health, society obligations and job demands, babies to be raised and mistakes to be forgiven.

I'm such a pathetic fool.

CHAPTER 29

DIANE

It's my second day in Octave's cellar.

I shift my position to sit a little more comfortably and close my eyes. My mouth and lips are on fire. I'm dizzy and so tired I can barely think.

Tyrion's words from *Game of Thrones* come to my mind: "Death is so terribly final, while life is full of possibilities."

With the prospect of death a lot closer to home than when I watched the series with Chloe, I've been thinking a lot about possibilities. My favorite one is code named *Clean Slate.* It goes like this: Sebastian Darcy isn't the filthy-rich fragrance mogul who ruined Dad. It was his main competitor, David Bauer, who did it.

Dreaming here, remember?

Actually, no one has ruined Dad. His business is doing well, he didn't suffer a stroke, and he and Mom are still together. Sebastian exposes Octave, thanks to his formidable powers of deduction. This means he doesn't need to hire me—or anyone—to be his fake wife.

We meet in the most conventional way at Jeanne and Mat's, and we fall in love. Just like that—*Bam!*—at first sight. It doesn't matter that he reads *Le Figaro* and is worth more than the GDP of a small country.

Nobody's perfect.

We date, kiss, make love, make babies, and live happily ever after.

I open my eyes and stare at the door.

He'll find me.

Just as he found me after the cake incident, which now seems like a lifetime ago. If there's something I've learned about him, it's that Sebastian Darcy won't just shrug at my sudden departure and move on. He'll want to know why I left. He'll call. He'll poke around, talk to Mom, Chloe, and Elorie.

And he'll end up figuring it out.

I must believe it.

The alternative is to give up and stop struggling to stay alive even before Octave turns up to finish me off.

The door opens and Octave comes in.

"Have you made up your mind about me?" I ask, my voice coarse.

"I had last night," he says. "I was going to come here and strangle you. But then I lost my nerve."

I look into his eyes. "Bummer."

"You're funny, you know?" He lets out a sigh. "It *is* a bummer."

"Tell me something, Octave—just so I don't die stupid—why?"

"Why what?"

"Why are you doing this? Why are you going to such pains to punish the person who thinks the world of you?"

"Does he now?" Octave smirks. "He *is* less full of

himself than his legendary Grandpa Bernard, and his adored papa. I'll grant you that."

An image flashes in my head when he mentions Sebastian's grandfather—that of Octave's birth certificate.

"Your middle name is Bernard," I say.

The side of his face twitches. "So what?"

"It isn't a coincidence, is it? Your hatred of the d'Arcy men… it has something to do with your middle name, I'm sure."

"Not only are you funny," he says. "You're also perceptive."

I wait for him to continue.

Because he will. The man is clearly burning to tell his story to *someone*. He's been burning for years, decades maybe. And now he has an ideal audience: captive, genuinely interested, and expendable.

He'd have to be made of steel to resist that.

"Bernard d'Arcy had a fling with my mother when they were both young," he says.

I knew it!

"It was more than a fling, actually. They were together for over a year until he ditched her and married the fancy-schmancy Colette."

"What did your mother do?"

"She up and married a good-for-nothing from her hometown. And then she had me."

"Are you Bernard's son?" I ask.

He sighs. "I don't know. My mother always denied it, but she never got over Bernard and she did give me that middle name. Besides, she wrote to him when I turned eighteen, asking if he could offer me a job at Parfums d'Arcy."

"Did he?"

"He offered me a job at Darcy House instead." Octave runs his hand through his thinning hair, his expression melancholy. "I was over the moon. I thought it was a sign that the Count was willing to take me under his wing, maybe even acknowledge me one day… I was so naive."

"I take it he didn't acknowledge you?"

Octave shakes his head. "Worse. He never even bothered to get to know me, let alone groom me for bigger things. He groomed Thibaud, all right, and then Sebastian. But never me."

"Did you ever talk to him about your mother?"

"I didn't dare. He was so distant, so much above me… We weren't equals. He was Count d'Arcy du Grand-Thouars de Saint-Maurice. I was the help."

"Why didn't you walk away?" I ask. "Once you knew Bernard would never treat you like a son, why didn't you just leave?"

My mouth and throat hurt from talking, and I'm extremely tired but still lucid enough to remember that as long as Octave is telling his story, he isn't strangling me.

"At first, I had hope," he says. "I thought if I proved myself to him, if I showed him how good and loyal I could be, he'd let me in. I tried so hard, for so long… And then, when I accepted that I'd never earn his love, it was too late. I'd become too appreciative of the grandeur of Darcy House and the comforts of my life to quit everything and start over."

"So instead you chose to stay and poison their lives," I say.

"Exactly." Octave puts his chin up. "My mother died around the same time, and I made a promise on her grave. I vowed I'd make the lives of Bernard, Thibaud, and Sebastian miserable without risking my freedom or my job."

"My hat's off to you," I say. "You succeeded."

He gives me a smug smile. "Yes, I did."

For a moment, we're both silent. Then Octave's eyes dart to my neck. *Oh no.* I must get him to start talking again—and presto!

"Have you done a DNA test to find out who your father is?" I ask.

He shakes his head. "I can't."

"Why not?"

He hesitates and then shrugs as if to say, *What the hell, I might as well be honest with the soon-to-be-dead woman.* "I'm too scared. What if the test says I'm not related to the d'Arcys? Do you realize the implications?" He points at me. "Your… end, Thibaud's disgrace, Sebastian's grief—it would all be for nothing. Meaningless. I wouldn't be able to handle it."

"And you think you'll be able to handle *murdering* me?" I ask.

He opens his mouth to say something when the door bursts open and a bunch of police officers in bulletproof vests storm in. Two of them slam Octave to the floor and cuff him. The others rush to me and cut my restraints.

It all seems surreal. A few moments later, I'm wrapped in a blanket and carried up the stairs into the daylight.

Sebastian runs to me and takes me in his arms. He's crying.

"You're alive," he says, raining kisses on my cheeks, eyes, nose, and forehead. "You're alive!"

I start crying, too.

"Shush, *mon amour*," he says in a hot whisper, kissing away my tears. "You're safe now. It's over. I'm here. You're safe."

CHAPTER 30

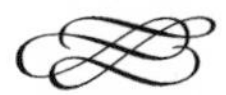

DIANE

"I signed up for meditation and yoga." Mom turns to Chloe. "And I might call your therapist as well."

Chloe smiles. "It won't hurt."

Mom takes my hand. "First Chloe in October, now you… Please—both of you—don't scare me like that ever again."

I nudge her lemonade glass across the garden table. "You should taste it. Michel makes it from a medieval recipe he guards with his life."

She takes a sip and swishes it around in her mouth before swallowing. "Mine is better."

An hour later, they're gone and I recline on the deck chair for a nap. I've been sleeping a lot over the past two days, which is weird because I hadn't been exactly *active* during the preceding forty-eight hours.

When I wake up, I find Sebastian sitting on the grass at my feet.

"It's Wednesday," I say. "Shouldn't you be at the office, bossing people around?"

He kisses my ankles. "I'd rather be here."

"I need to stretch my legs," I say.

He jumps to his feet and helps me up.

As we stroll through the garden, I brush my hand over tree branches and shrubbery, caressing the leaves. Everything smells so good, looks so beautiful, feels so pleasant to touch… God, I'm happy I made it.

"Mom told me you went on TV, offering a ransom," I say.

He nods.

"She says you didn't specify an amount—you just said, 'Name your price, I'll pay it.' "

He nods again.

I give him a sidelong look. "Don't you think that was a little presumptuous?"

He shakes his head.

I'm itching to ask whether he'd have paid up if Octave had demanded a billion euros.

"I would've given everything I have," he says. "Don't you ever doubt that."

I stop and hug him, burying my face against his chest. He puts his arms around me and kisses the top of my head. There are so many things I want to say to him, but they're all too sentimental for my cynical mouth. So I hug him tighter instead, hoping he'll understand.

Praying that he knows.

"When did you first suspect foul play?" I ask after a long moment.

"Sunday morning. I called you a dozen times. I called Elorie, Chloe, and your Mom. When your Mom said she hadn't seen or heard from you, I knew you hadn't just upped and left."

"Thank God you didn't call Dad, and thank God he doesn't own a TV," I say.

"Chloe was very helpful. She called him for a chat and ascertained that you weren't with him."

We walk in silence for a few minutes. I listen to the birds in the trees and insects humming around us. But I have too many questions to fully enjoy the peaceful magic of this place.

"When did you start suspecting Octave?"

"Sometime Sunday night. I tossed and turned, and then I remembered him coming in at four a.m. the night you disappeared."

"Powers of deduction," I say under my breath.

"Pardon me?"

"Nothing." I wave my hand dismissively. "Just a side effect of having only me to entertain myself for two days straight."

He puts his hand around my shoulders.

"What did you do once you had your suspicions?" I ask.

"I texted my PI to forget Valeria and start tailing Octave ASAP. Then I dressed and drove to the nearest *commissariat.*"

"Thank goodness you didn't call the police or your PI from home. Octave had the bedroom bugged."

Sebastian stops in his tracks, his jaw clenched in anger.

"Finish your story," I ask.

"Things went pretty fast from there," he says. "On Monday morning, the police figured out Octave had inherited a hovel in Yvelines, an hour's drive from Paris. That's when the PI texted me that he was driving behind my *majordome* in that same direction."

Sebastian trails off, his gaze suddenly unfocused.

"You OK?" I ask.

"Yes, of course. It just hit me how, at one point

or another, I've suspected everyone—my competitors, my aunt and uncle, Greg, Lynette… even Laurent! But I never doubted Octave." His nostrils flare. "How could I be so blind? It almost cost you your life."

"But it didn't." I give him a bright smile. "You got there on time. You found me."

"I love you, Diane," he says. "With all my heart."

I sort of figured that out but, dear Lord, it's good to hear him say those words!

"I love you, too, Sebastian."

He takes my left hand and strokes my ring finger. "You're still wearing your engagement ring and your wedding band."

"Oh." I pull my hand away and begin to remove the jewelry. "Silly me! We don't need them anymore now that—"

"Don't!" He takes hold of my hand again and pushes the rings back to the base of my finger. "Will you do me the honor of remaining my wife?"

My jaw drops.

He smiles. "Your spontaneity is priceless. Please don't ever change."

I keep silent, still digesting his words.

"Say yes," he pleads.

"I don't understand," I say instead. "What do you mean by 'remaining your wife'? Our marriage is fake."

He shakes his head. "Not if I send the missing document to the consulate in Miami. We still have two weeks until the deadline."

"I can't." I say. "It would be against what I profess, against my principles."

"Which are…?"

I focus on my feet. "I hate rich people. They're all

exploiters and crooks. I don't believe it's possible to amass a fortune by being a good person."

"Diane." He takes my chin between his index finger and thumb, nudging me gently to look at him. "I don't care what you think of 'rich people' as a class. However, I do care what you think of me. Do you believe I'm an exploiter and a crook?"

"No," I say without a second's hesitation. "I don't. Ludicrous as it is, I think you're a good person."

The corners of his mouth curl up. "You sure?"

"Yes. And I have proof."

"You do?"

I nod. "It was you who 'persuaded' Belle Auxbois to go on prime-time TV and credit Dad for her perfume. Now he has so many offers he's raised his fee and established a waiting list." I grip Sebastian's hand and give it a squeeze. "Thank you."

"How did you—"

"It doesn't matter." I bring his hand to my lips and kiss it. "And there's something else. When I told him who was behind Belle's sudden generosity, he admitted you'd offered to buy his company before you crushed it."

"I thought you knew about it," he says.

I shake my head.

He strokes my hands and touches my engagement ring. "Do you like it? Or shall I get you a new one, something *you* would choose? We could go to Place Vendôme tomorrow—"

"No!" I cut him off. "I mean, I wouldn't mind something less ritzy, but that's not what I… It's just… How…"

He tilts his head to the side, waiting for me to form my question.

"What would be the terms?" I finally manage.

"Let's see." He opens the thumb of his left hand. "You'll have to kiss me. A lot." He extends his index finger. "You'll have to sleep in my bed, and you'll be expected to have sex with me—both in and out of that bed."

I smile and roll my eyes skyward.

He uncurls his middle finger. "You'll call me 'my beloved spouse' in public and 'my stallion' in private."

I stick my finger in my mouth and pretend to gag.

"It was a joke," he says.

"You sure?"

He nods vigorously.

I pretend to wipe my brow. "Phew."

"But this one isn't." He unfolds his ring finger. "I'll expect you to be my teammate. I'll need you to stand by my side through everything and support me in running the company and the house, regardless of your leftist ideology."

I draw in a deep breath.

"And this one isn't a joke, either." Sebastian opens his little finger, eyes burning into mine. "I'll be the happiest of men if you give me a child. A few, if possible."

I swallow and hold his gaze.

He smiles again. "That's it. Those are the terms. Do you think you can do those things for me?"

"I think I can," I say. "And then some."

His smile grows into a huge grin.

"But," I say, taking his hand. "What I meant by 'terms' was actually of a more… *financial* nature. You and I are too unequal in that regard."

He says nothing.

"Do you have a prenup contract drafted?" I ask.

He shakes his head. "We don't need one."

"You've lost your mind."

"Quite the contrary." He lifts my hand to his lips and plants a hot kiss to my palm. "I've found it."

I look down, thinking.

"Say yes, Diane." He gives my hand a squeeze.

I lift my eyes. "On one condition."

"Anything."

"You'll pose for me naked again. Every time I ask you to."

He arches an eyebrow.

I put my hand to my heart. "For strictly personal use, I promise."

"OK," he says. "But I'll be your *only* male model."

"Deal."

He nods. "Deal."

"Then it's a yes." I throw my arms around his neck and add in a husky voice, "My stallion."

AUTHOR'S NOTE

The chateau and the cave in this book are fictional.

The Chateau d'Arcy is inspired by several castles I've visited in the Loire Valley, Normandy and Burgundy. A real Chateau d'Arcy exists in Burgundy. Previously home to viscounts and barons, it is now the property of the French State.

The Darcy Grotto in this book is fictional, but it is inspired by three amazing rock-art caves in France.

My main inspiration is the cave complex near the village of Arcy-sur-Cure in Burgundy. Just like the Darcy Grotto, the real *Grotte d'Arcy* is located on private land, which is currently owned by Gabriel de la Varende. The paintings and engravings in the *Grotte d'Arcy* are "only" 28,000 years old.

My second inspiration is the world-famous Lascaux

complex in Dordogne. The age of its spectacular paintings is a measly 18,000 years.

My third inspiration is the Chauvet cave in the Ardèche region whose 32,000-year-old cave art is the most magnificent and oldest in France.

The Chauvet and Lascaux caves have been closed to the public, to protect the art inside from the damaging mold and bacteria caused by thousands of daily visitors. So, what you'll see if you go there will be copies, or *replicas*, not the actual caves.

The Grotte d'Arcy, on the other hand, is still accessible (only until they build a replica, no doubt), so grab your chance to see the real thing while you can!

RAPHAEL'S FLING

THE DARCY BROTHERS BOOK 2

PART I

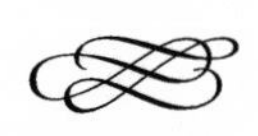

CHAPTER 1

How did I come to this?

I sigh, smooth my clothes one last time, and head for the cream, leather-padded door.

"Mia, wait!" Raphael calls after me.

I halt and turn around.

He opens his chiseled mouth as if to say something, then shuts it, and gives me a tight smile. The smile of a person having second thoughts on the advisability of what he was going to say.

Well, I'm not waiting around for the result of his inner deliberation. There are two bulky reports on my desk and a few dozen emails I need to go through before I can leave tonight.

Ergo, time is of the essence.

I resume my hike across Raphael's vast office until I reach the door. It unlocks smoothly and without a sound, bless its high-tech heart. After a sneak peek in the hall to check if the coast is clear, I slip away without saying good-bye to Raphael or Anne-Marie, his faithful PA.

Just like a lawbreaker.

Well, maybe not a lawbreaker, but definitely a reoffending violator of the *Workplace Code of Honor.* In particular, of Rule #1, which says: "Workers shall not have sexual intercourse with their hierarchical superiors, inferiors, or posteriors."

While there's some controversy over the exact meaning of "inferiors" and "posteriors," everyone knows that a "superior" is more than just your immediate boss. The concept also covers your boss's boss, your boss's boss's boss's boss, and the Boss of Them All—the CEO.

It's a very sensible provision, by the way, and one I totally approve of and adhere to.

As I rush down the hallway, my heels clicking on the marble floor, I realize I should've put my observation in the past tense. As in, "I *used* to adhere to."

Having repeatedly broken the Code's first rule since March makes me a rogue and a hypocrite of the worst kind.

How did I fall so low?

Here's a clue: it's Rudolph the Reindeer's fault.

God knows I hadn't planned on this when I landed the world's most unexceptional job as assistant to the daily bulletin editor at DCA Paris. DCA stands for "D'Arcy Consulting and Audit." Yup, the same "d'Arcy" that's sandwiched between "Raphael" and the rest of his fancy name on my lover's official letterhead.

Having sexual intercourse with Raphael d'Arcy du Grand-Thouars de Saint-Maurice, a gentleman and a libertine, was the last thing on my mind when I started at DCA. In fact, it was nowhere *near* my mind.

Despite my murky past, that's not who I am. Nor does my life need more complications right now.

Trust me.

Pauline Cordier's familiar silhouette takes shape at the end of the hallway just as I reach the elevator and push the button. My heart skips a beat. If my direct supervisor sees me on this floor, she'll assume one of the following two things: (a) my presence here is work-related, meaning I'm going over her head; or (b) my presence here has nothing to do with work, meaning I'm sleeping with one of the senior managers.

Needless to say, both alternatives are equally conducive to me getting sidelined, ostracized, and ultimately fired.

I take a deep breath and give the approaching figure a furtive glance.

It isn't Pauline.

The woman doesn't even look like her, now that she's closer.

Phew.

You may not believe me, but I wasn't sure what Raphael d'Arcy looked like when DCA hired me. Having scanned his official bio in preparation for my job interview, I had formed a vague image that boiled down to "young, well-born, and well-dressed." The specifics of the founding CEO's background and appearance hadn't lingered in my mind. I doubt they'd even entered it.

Because they were not important.

All I wanted from Monsieur d'Arcy was a job at his firm that gave me a monthly paycheck to complement the pittance my school calls a scholarship. That way, I could finish my doctoral program without having to sleep under bridges or borrow money.

Parisian bridges can be drafty, you see. And damp. As for the stench, courtesy of well-groomed dogs and ill-groomed humans, don't even get me started! On top of all that, bridges offer no suitable storage space for research notes, photocopies, and books.

In short, they suck as accommodations.

As for the borrowing, my parents taught Eva and me that debt must be avoided at all costs. Their "debt is bad" precept proved stronger than the knowledge that everyone lives on credit in Western societies today.

Except my parents, that is.

Then again, they live in rural Alsace. Life's a lot cheaper there than in *la capitale*, so they were able to make it into their fifties without a single loan to cloud their horizon.

I step off the elevator on the second floor, relieved that no one saw me in Top Management's Heavenly Quarters, and my phone rings. Considering that I've been sneaking out like this for two months already, the probability that someone *will* see me and that it'll reach Pauline's ears is growing by the day.

It freaks me out more than I care to admit.

As I answer the phone, Raphael's deep, sexy timbre breaks me from my worries.

"You left your panties here," he says, sounding amused and smug at the same time. In short, his usual self.

"No, I didn't—"

Oh crap. I did.

"I've got five minutes before the managerial," he says, "so if you want to come back and collect—"

"No!" I look around and lower my voice. "It's OK. I'm sure I can make it through the afternoon without them."

"Oh, I don't doubt that. The question is whether *I* can make it through the afternoon *with* the knowledge you're *without* them." He pauses, as if pondering the question, and then adds, "And *with* them in my pocket."

My stomach flips.

Something achingly—yet delightfully—heavy gathers low in my abdomen, reminding me of what Raphael and I had been up to a mere half hour ago. Suddenly, every step I take makes me aware of my pantyless condition. The friction of my skirt's silky lining against my bare skin makes it prickle. My breathing becomes strained, and my heart thumps in my chest.

As I struggle to calm myself before entering the office I share with two other assistants, I picture myself in Strasbourg in our family physician's immaculate office.

"What's my diagnosis, doctor?" I'd ask after he's examined me.

"Not to worry, *mon enfant!* You'll live." He'd push his regular glasses to his forehead and put on his reading glasses. "You have a textbook case of *lustium irresistiblum.*"

"Please, can you make it go away?"

He'd smile and shake his head, updating my file on his computer. "It's like a viral cold. It'll clear up on its own, eventually."

And that, my friends, is the second clue to the mystery of how I got here.

It appears I've caught a virulent strain of *lustium irresistiblum* for lady-killer Raphael d'Arcy. And with my luck, we'll likely get caught before it clears.

"Got to go," I whisper into the phone and hang up.

I take a few long breaths to chase my arousal away before I enter the office.

Easier said than done.

The things Raphael says, the things he does to me… They don't just *excite*—they break into my brain and muddle it up on a deep, molecular level. Throwing ethical norms against that kind of invasion has been as effective as attempting to shoot down the Death Star with foam darts.

But I'll keep on trying.

Till the bitter end.

CHAPTER 2

I spent the first month at DCA Paris without a single sighting of *Le Big Boss*, as the assistants in my department call him. This is not surprising, considering the six floors and about as many layers of hierarchy that separate us. If we had ever bumped into each other in a hallway, he wouldn't have known me from a bar of soap and I wouldn't have recognized him.

Then the traditional Christmas party arrived. The organizing committee decreed it would be a costume event, and anyone who dared to turn up without a proper disguise would be sent home.

By a stroke of luck or misfortune, I happened to own an old costume just perfect for a Christmas party—Rudolph the Red-Nosed Reindeer. It was a fluffy onesie that came with a set of antlers adorning its roomy hood that covered the top half of my face and an elastic-band red nose. The costume had been in my parents' attic since I'd graduated high school. It begged to be worn again.

I shouldn't have listened to its pleas!

Had I known where that brown faux-fur onesie would land me, I would've never worn it to the office Christmas party. Heck, I would've never gone to that party to start with! But in the absence of a crystal ball to foresee the future, Rudolph had seemed like a great idea.

When I entered the meeting room, which had been transformed into a dance floor complete with a disco ball, it looked anything but Christmassy. Scantily clad Santa babes, provocative elves, and seductive angels—to say nothing of Playboy Bunnies—were gulping down champagne and undulating their lithe bodies to the beat of "I Know You Want Me." Many of them were also singing along and winking at their dance partners, *I know you want me, You know I want cha.*

Their male coworkers weren't far behind. They sported costumes representing an assortment of shoulder-padded Marvel superheroes with an occasional bare-chested Santa thrown in. Nearly every one of them drank, danced, and flirted with the ferocity of someone determined to get lucky.

In other words, much fun was being had.

"The name of the game is *Locate Le Big Boss*," my office mate Delphine said, handing me a glass of bubbly.

A champagne cork shot through the air, a little too close for comfort to my face. I ducked, spilling the contents of my flute and making Delphine chuckle.

Straightening up, I looked around. "Maybe he isn't even here."

"Word on the street says he is." Delphine winked, refilling my flute. "Barb and I have been trying to figure out which Iron Man he is, based on stature and voice."

"Personally, I think he's neither," a tutu-clad black swan said, planting herself next to us.

Upon closer examination, the swan was Tanya, a junior auditor famous for her illustrious conquests.

"Personally, I think he's Père Noël over there." Tanya pointed at the tall, fully dressed Father Christmas stroking his white beard and chatting with two Playboy Bunnies in the corner of the room.

"You may be right," Delphine said, contemplating the group. "I've heard Raphael's latest fling was one of those ménage à trois deals that every man dreams about."

I smirked. "So you think he's trying for an encore?"

"The hell he is." Tanya put her chin up and pulled down her areola-revealing top. "His next fling will be *me*."

With that, she strode toward Père Noël, her head high and her step bouncy. I couldn't help picturing her firing at will from her jutting boobs, decimating the bunnies, and snagging *Le Big Boss.*

At least for the night.

"Have fun, *ma cocotte,*" Delphine said to me, moving away to greet a newcomer.

I marched away from the champagne cork crossfire and imminent Bunny Massacre. Since I hadn't the slightest intention of locating Raphael d'Arcy, I stayed away from superheroes and Santas the entire evening, gravitating toward the older and more conservatively dressed colleagues. At some point, I danced with a fellow onesie-clad snowman who had an oversized carrot for a nose. But mostly, I sipped champagne and talked politics with the over-fifty crowd.

The problem was said crowd thinned quickly after midnight. By one in the morning, it became hard to find someone more interested in having a conversation than in making out. Not that anyone—male or female—

would want to make out with Rudolph the Red-Nosed Reindeer.

My second problem was that I was growing increasingly warm and uncomfortable in my faux-fur costume. I would've left—*I should've left!*—then and there, but Delphine and I had agreed to share a cab ride home, seeing as we live in the same arrondissement.

Unfortunately, by the time I was ready to leave, Delphine was engrossed in an advanced flirtation with The Hulk, who looked a lot like her longtime crush, Alberto.

There was no way she was leaving now.

I sighed, refilled my flute, and stepped out onto the dark balcony. Removing my red nose, I turned my face up to let the fresh December air cool it. Five minutes later, I was having a blast all by myself on the balcony, which was more of a terrace, as far as I could make out in the dark. My body temperature had dropped, and my champagne-soaked brain had cleared enough to realize that the random balcony I'd escaped to offered the best view of Paris I'd ever seen.

My night was beginning to look up.

Looking out over the parapet, I downed my champagne and admired the brightly lit city when someone stumbled out and came to stand next to me.

It was the snowman I'd danced with earlier.

He gave me a nod and touched his beer bottle to my flute. "To your good health."

"And to yours," I said, trying to figure out how drunk he was.

And if I was peeved or pleased at his arrival.

Peeved, I decided. *Definitely*.

Unlike us staid reindeer, snowmen were fickle creatures.

They could melt down on you any time.

CHAPTER 3

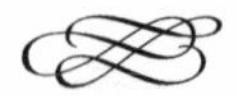

"Rudolph, buddy, I feel for you," Snowman said, turning to me. "It's a fucking sauna in there. Is it always that hot in our offices?"

I shook my head. "It's the fairies' fault."

"Er…?"

"Linda and Cat," I explained. "They were too cold in their filmy numbers, so they turned up the heat about an hour ago."

"I see."

Snowman drew a little closer and placed his beer on the parapet. His face was still completely hidden by his headpiece, but judging by his voice, he was at least twenty years younger than I'd thought when we danced briefly. He hadn't opened his mouth then, so I'd assumed he was older based on his funny costume and wacky dancing style. It reminded me of the snowman in *Frozen* and demonstrated a level of self-mockery uncommon in men under forty.

My fellow workplace-warming victim held out his hand. "I'm Olaf the Snowman. You can call me Olly."

Ah, so I'd been right about *Frozen*.

"I'm Rudolph the Red-Nosed Reindeer," I said. "And you absolutely cannot call me Rudy."

We shook hands, my brown mitten against his white one.

Olaf removed his mittens and took a swig of his beer. "Ooh, this is good. I was melting in there."

I gave him a sympathetic smile.

"I dare not ask how *you* felt." He pointed an unexpectedly attractive hand at me. "What with all that fur on your chest."

I shrugged. "Like a Laplandic reindeer parachuted to Africa."

"You're new at DCA, right?" he suddenly asked.

"Uh-huh. You?"

"Not anymore." He tilted his head to the side. "Auditor?"

"God forbid. I'm terrible with numbers."

"What then?"

"Editorial assistant."

He didn't offer a comment, but I could almost hear his brain hum as he tried to figure out my purpose at DCA.

"The news bulletin," I prompted.

He lifted his chin in comprehension. "Of course! Stupid me. I read it every day!"

"And so you should," I said primly. "Especially the global politics section compiled by this reindeer."

He fake tipped his hat off to me.

"What is it you do for a living, Olly?" I asked.

"I audit."

"Smart career choice."

"I guess." He shrugged slightly. "What did you study?"

"History."

"I see," he said.

"Do you?"

"It's one of those fun subjects that won't fetch you a well-paying job."

I sighed. "And yet I persist on my path to economic marginalization."

"What do you mean?"

"I'm enrolled in a doctoral program."

"What's your topic?"

"Prostitutes in medieval Paris."

"Wow," he said. "Can you give me some fun facts?"

"Prostitution isn't exactly a *fun* topic…"

"Oh, come on!" He gave me a small nudge. "Don't go all priggish on me. I'm sure you've dug up things that are at least a little bit entertaining."

"OK, let me think."

I racked my brain for a piece of information that would qualify as entertaining. *OK, here goes.* "Harlots were required by law to wear special clothing to distinguish them from honest women."

He propped one elbow on the parapet and turned to me completely. "Like miniskirts?"

"Yeah, right." I curled my lip. "It could be a cloak, a belt of a specific color, or a certain type of headdress."

"What else?"

"Hmm…" I pinched my chin. "OK, here's one more. Decisions on which neighborhoods should host the *maisons closes* were sometimes made at the highest level. In Paris, for instance, it was Louis IX who chose to put them in the Beaubourg neighborhood."

"That makes sense."

"Why?"

"There's a street off rue de Rivoli named after *bad boys*—rue des Mauvais-Garçons."

"Actually, the name of that street has nothing to do with harlots."

"How disappointing."

"But that of rue Petit-Musc does! The original name was rue Pute-y-Musse. A whore hides here."

"How fascinating." His gaze lingered on the uncovered lower half of my face. "One more?"

"All right," I said. "Last one."

"It better be good, then."

"Olly." I arched an eyebrow. "Don't you go all *cocky* on me. It doesn't work when you're dressed as a snowman."

"Good point, Rudolph." He tugged at his carrot nose so it pointed downward. "I stand humbled."

I tucked my bottom lip in with my teeth to hide my smile. "So, by popular request, here's one more *fun fact*: foreign guests of state were taken to luxurious brothels for a special treat as late as the nineteenth century."

"Oh, I can *so* imagine their official program," he said, hilarity tinting his voice. "Three p.m.: briefing at the Foreign Ministry; Seven p.m.: dinner at the Elysée Palace; Eleven p.m.: French-kissing in Beaubourg."

I chuckled, noting how deep and velvety Olaf's voice was. Actually, it was really handsome, his voice.

For a snowman, that is.

"Sorry to disappoint you," I said, "but the official program didn't mention any kissing. Those outings were usually marked down as 'a visit with the president of the Senate.' "

He threw his head back and whooped with laughter.

For the next five minutes or so, Olly and I watched the festive lights of Paris in companionable silence.

When the Eiffel Tower launched into its hourly dancing-lights show, I found myself growing disturbingly aware of Olly's physical presence. He still looked just as comical in his incongruous costume as I did in mine. But his sexy baritone and beautiful hands had made me notice other things about him, such as his tall frame and broad chest.

It was very disconcerting.

"Who knew being a climate refugee was fun," he said, breaking the silence.

"In my case, it's climate *and* crossfire."

"How so?"

"Champagne."

He furrowed his brow.

"Whenever someone pops a bottle," I said, "I expect the cork to hit me in the eye."

"Even when the bottle is directed at the opposite wall?"

I nodded. "I expect the cork to ricochet off that wall and hit me in the eye."

"Has that happened before?"

"No," I admitted. "Which increases the statistical probability it would." Guilt kicked in before I'd finished that sentence, making me regret the inappropriate analogy.

How dare I compare myself to real refugees fleeing armed conflict?

Then I heard Olly's soft chuckle, and something weird happened. The shame and guilt withdrew into some faraway recess of my brain, leaving me wonderfully giddy. Soon enough, those feelings would come back with a vengeance in all their sticky glory. The Poison Duo never left me alone too long, not since the *calamity*. But right there on that enchanted terrace, the

Duo was offering me a Christmas gift—a rare moment of genuine, unmarred fun.

And I was taking it, no questions asked.

"Is it just me, or is it getting warmer out here, too?" Olly asked.

It *wasn't* just him. I was definitely feeling it.

Was it because of the costume? If that was the case, I should ditch my useless wool blend coat and wear Rudolph all winter. Or maybe we were experiencing a bout of real global warming that had nothing to do with fairies, heaters, or faux fur.

"You're right," I said. "The air *is* abnormally warm for late December. If you were a real snowman, you'd be a puddle at my feet by now."

"If you were a real reindeer," he retorted, "you would've said 'at my hoofs.' "

Oops.

He cocked his head. "Actually, if you were a real reindeer, you wouldn't have said anything at all. You would've lapped me up and noshed on my carrot."

Was there a sexual innuendo in his words, or was it just my dirty mind?

I couldn't see Olly's expression, but I could feel his eyes boring into me.

That's when I realized how much I itched to see his face.

"Aren't you too hot with your headpiece on?" I asked.

He snorted. "You'd like me to go headless, Rudy?"

"I'm just concerned about your comfort." I put my hands on my hips. "And it's Rudolph to you."

Am I flirting? How unlike me.

"Nah, you're Rudy," he said, making "Rudy" sound

like a super-sexy endearment… unless it was my dirty mind again.

And then he removed the headpiece.

In the dark, I couldn't make out his precise features or the color of his eyes, but I could discern his wavy hair, high cheekbones, firm jawline, and the shape of his nose. All of that suggested Olly's face was as handsome as his voice.

Besides, he looked vaguely familiar, even if I couldn't place him. On the other hand, we were colleagues. I might have ridden the elevator with him several times over the past few months.

"Your turn," he said, taking a step toward me.

He flashed his teeth in a sweetly innocent smile, but his voice and posture communicated something a lot less innocent. I half expected him to grow fangs and sink them into my neck.

God help me, I craved that bite.

"And what big mouth you have, Grandma!" I said, widening my eyes for effect.

He blinked and then laughed.

I loved his chuckle.

Kudos, Mia, on saving yourself from a wolf!

Then why the frustration?

I tugged on my hood, baring the upper half of my face to him.

He stopped laughing and drew closer.

"Your eyes are green," he said, leaning toward me.

His mouth was so close.

It *was* big, but in a clean, masculine, super attractive kind of way. And did I mention he smelled as if sex appeal were his middle name?

"Does the color of my eyes matter?" I asked.

Why had my voice gone so raspy all of a sudden?

Oh, Mia. You know very well why.

"No," he said, inching closer still.

We were almost touching now.

"Can you keep a secret?" he asked.

I nodded.

"I'm a *lesbian* snowman."

I raised my eyebrows.

"There are so many hunky Santas in there,"—he pointed to the meeting room—"and yet it's the female reindeer I want to kiss."

I swallowed.

"In fact," he said, angling his head, "I've been dying to kiss her for several hours now, ever since she danced with me."

And then he pressed his lips to mine.

I gasped as his heady scent invaded my nostrils. He slid his tongue between my lips. It tasted like heaven. Behind the faint smack of the beer he'd been drinking and the hint of minty toothpaste, there was the essence of Olly.

And it was scrumptious.

His tongue explored my mouth with confident, sweeping strokes, and I couldn't help kissing him back. With enthusiasm. He pulled me closer while he removed my scrunchy and tangled his hand in my hair.

Oh oui.

Suddenly, he let go of me and drew back.

I stood there, panting, drunk on his taste and completely disoriented.

"You're Mia, right?" he asked, putting his headpiece back on and adjusting his nose.

"How do you—"

"Someone's calling for you. They've been hollering your name a good five minutes now."

With an effort, I focused on my surroundings. Someone—more specifically, Delphine—was, indeed, calling my name.

"I should go to her," I said.

He nodded and pulled the door open.

As I tumbled into the room, I collided with Delphine, who was about to venture onto the terrace and look for me.

"There you are!" She grinned with relief. "Ready to go home?"

"What about Alberto?"

She shrugged with an exaggerated nonchalance. "Turns out he's married."

"Aww. I'm so sorry." I gave her arm a sympathetic squeeze.

"It's OK." Delphine pulled out her phone and began to scroll. "How long have you been out there freezing your reindeer ass off?"

I glanced at my watch. *More than an hour.* It had seemed like fifteen minutes to me.

Delphine narrowed her eyes. "And what exactly were you doing alone with a snowman?"

I looked around only to discover Olly was gone.

Luckily, Delphine found what she was looking for on her phone. She tapped, brought it to her ear, and then gave the cab service operator our details.

By the time she hung up, I'd come up with a reply. "What do you think a reindeer and a snowman do when they find themselves alone?"

"No idea."

I smiled triumphantly. "Bitch about their boss, Santa, of course."

Delphine rolled her eyes but didn't press further.

Five minutes later, we climbed into our cab. As we

rode home, both of us lost in our thoughts, I realized Olly hadn't given me his real name. Maybe our chemistry had been one-sided and he hadn't enjoyed our kiss like I had.

Getting involved with a coworker isn't a good idea, I remember telling myself as a consolation.

How I wish I'd recognized him back then!

If I had, I wouldn't have ended up with acute *lustium irresistiblum* for Raphael d'Arcy four months later. My Alsatian common sense would've warned me that getting involved with my company's womanizing CEO wasn't just a bad idea.

It was the mother of all bad ideas.

CHAPTER 4

"How did we, as a nation, come to this?"

Màma's green gaze sweeps the room, touching every single person in the congregation with a mixture of fondness and authority only this woman is capable of.

She drinks from the tall glass on her pulpit and lets her question sink in and foment in our minds. Whenever my mother pauses her sermons to do this, I have the impression everyone can feel her firm hand on their shoulder.

I, for one, always do.

When I manage to get to Estheim early enough, or stay long enough, I do my best to attend Màma's Sunday sermon. "You know you don't have to," she always says to Pàpa, Eva, and me. But we insist. Pàpa, because he's a devout Christian who supports his pastor wife in everything she does. Eva, because she actually enjoys Màma's sermons. And me… To be honest, I'm not sure why I come along.

I'm not really a Protestant, like the rest of the family.

I'm not a Catholic, either, or any other denomination, for that matter.

I'm a Darwinist.

Considering how close humans are to monkeys—especially on the *métro* during rush hour—how can anyone believe in anything other than survival of the fittest?

"What twisted path," Màma continues, "led us to believe we *must* use images of naked women to sell chocolate ice cream? And why has it become our new *normal* to have sexual relationships and even babies out of sacred matrimony?"

Today's sermon is called *On Purity*. It's a recurrent theme with my mother.

Eva and I have debated hundreds of times if Màma thinks her grown daughters—I'm twenty-six and Eva twenty-eight—are still virgins. Our conclusion is that she does. Because that's what she expects of us. And because we have yet to muster the courage to tell her the truth.

"*For this is the will of God, that ye should abstain from fornication*," Màma reads from her Bible.

Pàpa nods.

Eva and I focus on our feet.

Màma ends the sermon with Jesus's forgiving a fallen woman, followed by a passionate appeal to all lost souls to repent and keep their bodies clean of immoral sex.

It's all very sweet of her to promise Jesus will forgive me, but the question is will *she* forgive me? Will Pàpa forgive me? Not just for fornicating with Raphael, but for the bigger, dirtier sin I committed five years ago?

Judging by what I know of their past actions, I'd wager they won't. Because actions, as my parents like to say, speak louder than words.

"If you could miraculously have your virginity back,

hymen and all," I whisper in Eva's ear as we leave the church, "would you do it?"

"No way."

I raise my eyebrows. "I thought you were a believer."

"I am. But not in physical abstinence."

"If I didn't know better, I'd assume you were getting laid."

Eva lets out a sigh. "I wish."

Wrapping an arm around her shoulders, I give her a tiny squeeze. I know about her hopeless crush on Adam.

"And you?" she asks. "A new boyfriend, maybe?"

I look away.

Eva puts her hand over mine and gives me a gentle pat. She knows about my doomed affair with Raphael.

Last time she came over to Paris to spend a weekend with me, I swore to her I'd pull myself out of it. I promised myself the same thing at least three times already since January.

It's April.

I stopped promising.

Eva nudges me with her elbow. "Did you at least try to break up?"

I shake my head.

"Has he changed?" she asks hopefully. "Is there a chance he has feelings for you? Would it help if you quit your job?"

"I don't want to talk about Raphael," I say, still avoiding Eva's eyes.

He hasn't changed.

And I very much doubt sacrificing my job would help.

Eva shrugs and catches up with our parents.

"I loved your sermon," she says to Màma.

She always tells her that, and most of the time, she

means it. But this time, her fingers are crossed behind her back. I guess the disconnect between this sermon's high standards and the reality of our lives was too big even for Eva's indulgent heart.

At home, Pàpa sets out to cook lunch while Màma takes care of administrative stuff. Pàpa is a retired policeman with a passion for cooking, which is fortunate, seeing as Màma couldn't fry an egg to save her life.

Neither can I, by the way. My single culinary competence is pasta, which is not so bad since I happen to love it, as I do all Italian food. To vary my dinners, I stock up on Bolognese, pesto and whatever pasta sauce I find at my local supermarket, and then I rotate them.

Works fine for me.

When Eva visits me in Paris, she arrives with a huge tub of homemade pesto sauce, which she then portions out into small containers and sticks them in my freezer. My sister has inherited Pàpa's talent. *Man, she can cook.* The dinners she used to whip up for us as teenagers were better than the three or four Michelin-starred restaurant meals my parents offered us on special occasions.

Eva studied at Le Cordon Bleu, one of the best culinary schools in the country, and worked as an undercook with some hotshot chef whose name I forget.

Two years later she quit, trained as a secretary, and after a year of temping, landed a "well-paying and stable" admin assistant job at the European Space Agency.

Màma was very proud of her.

Pàpa was very upset.

I was both, but mostly perplexed. Eva didn't comment on her radical change of career except for a casual remark that cooking wasn't her thing, after all.

Màma took it at face value. With no love lost between her and the stove, she could easily relate to that justification. My theory is that Eva was pushed a little too hard by her celebrity boss or bullied by her fellow undercooks. A less sensitive person would've grown a thicker skin and carried on. But Eva, as usual, took the path of least resistance and convinced herself the career of a chef wasn't for her.

All of this goes through my mind as Eva and I stretch out in our favorite hammocks under Pàpa's gorgeous apple trees. My life may be screwed up beyond redemption, but Eva has options.

It's a crime to turn her back on them.

"Remind me again how a promising chef ends up as admin assistant?" I ask.

She fake-yawns. "Please, not again!"

"Humor me. I just want to understand."

"Your fixation with what I do for a living is unhealthy. Do you realize that?"

"You're skirting my question," I say.

"What's wrong with being an admin assistant?"

"Nothing." I hesitate and then shake my head. "Everything."

"Speak for yourself."

"My current job is just a temporary means to an end, while you seem bent on ignoring your true vocation."

She shrugs. "I'm perfectly happy where I am."

"That's because you're crazy about Adam."

She glares at me.

I glare back. "You've been pining for him for how long? A year?"

Eva says nothing.

"He's never asked you out."

Silence.

"Has he ever done anything to suggest he likes you?"

She shakes her head.

"He's had a girlfriend during this time, right?"

She nods.

"You haven't."

"I'm not into women."

"Very funny." I give her a sympathetic look. "Let me rephrase my question: Have you had a boyfriend or even a one-night stand ever since you laid eyes on Adam?"

She sighs and shakes her head.

"On top of it all, he's your boss," I say. "Don't repeat my mistakes, Evie."

She pushes her glasses up to the bridge of her nose. "Adam is my hierarchical superior, but he's *not* my direct boss."

"To-may-to, to-mah-to."

"And he isn't a womanizer like yours."

I feel a sharp pang somewhere in the upper left quadrant of my chest. Must be the truth hurting.

"Let's change the topic," Eva says, giving me an apologetic look.

"Good idea."

I stare at the delicate blooms over my head, then shut my eyes, and spend the next half hour pretending to nap before Pàpa summons us inside.

CHAPTER 5

"Since we rarely get to see both of you at the same time," Pàpa says, handing Eva and me plates with huge slices of onion pie, "I thought I'd make something traditional."

"Yay!" Eva digs into her slice. "Love *flammkuche*."

"I know." Pàpa watches her chew her first bite. "Verdict?"

Eva swallows and raises her wine glass. "Three yummy stars."

Pàpa grins, mighty pleased.

"The Riesling could've been better, though," my sister declares with her nose in her glass.

"Really?" Pàpa takes a sip from his own glass and nods. "Next time you'll pick it, OK?"

Eva bows theatrically. "It'll be an honor, sir."

Those two have always had a special bond, cemented by their positivity and love of good food. Màma and I have a less cheerful disposition. Which doesn't automatically mean we enjoy the same bond Eva and Pàpa do.

Come to think of it, I don't really enjoy a "bond" with anyone.

Once, when we were in our teens, Eva made a remark that stayed with me.

"Why are you so aloof all the time?" she asked.

I disagreed with that characterization, of course, but I did wonder—why, indeed? And it was only a couple of years ago that I figured out, after many an hour of soul-searching, what keeps me from confiding in Màma and Pàpa the way Eva does.

It isn't a lack of affection.

God knows, I love them. Together with Eva, they're my favorite people in the world, and my most ardent wish is that they be as healthy and happy as humanly possible.

What holds me back is fear. I'm scared that if I let them closer, they'll see me for who I really am and they won't like it.

I tune out of Eva and Pàpa's lively chat while an old memory returns as vivid as ever.

I'm thirteen.

I wake up in the middle of the night to my parents' unusually loud voices coming from the kitchen. They're engaged in an animated conversation with a third person, a woman I can't identify. My curiosity piqued, I tiptoe down the hallway, sit down at the top of the staircase, and listen.

"So, if you could lend me the five grand," the strange woman says, "I'll be able to repay my debt in full."

"And you're sure your pimp will let you go?" Pàpa asks.

I clap my hand to my mouth in shock. I've seen

enough forbidden movies to know exactly what a pimp is.

"Oh, he will," the woman says. "I'm not some helpless Eastern girl who doesn't know her rights and is scared shitless. I'm a French national, and I've covered my back."

"Smart girl," Màma says.

"His only leverage is the money I owe him," the woman says.

There is a moment of silence, and then the woman speaks again. "I asked my family, and I asked my banker, but those were dead ends. Believe me, I wouldn't have come to you if I had other options."

"You've come to the right place," Màma says.

"I heard your sermon last Sunday when you talked about fresh starts." The woman pauses before adding, "It inspired me."

"Give us a couple of days to reflect and look into our finances, OK?" Pàpa says.

I have no doubt what the outcome of their thinking will be. They'll help her. On top of being professional helpers—a pastor and a policeman—my parents send monthly checks to the Red Cross, Doctors Without Borders, and Amnesty International. They also sponsor four little girls on different continents by paying their school fees. When they receive handwritten letters from those girls, they take the time to read them and to write long, thoughtful replies.

In short, helping people is what my parents do, both for a living and for fun.

"Thank you from the bottom of my heart," the woman says, emotion palpable in her voice.

I hear chairs move and scramble away from the staircase.

"We'll call you before the weekend," Màma says, opening the door. "And remember, you're not alone, Suzelle."

Suzelle.

For the next two days all I can think of is Suzelle the Repentant Sinner. How I wish I'd caught a glimpse of her! I'm filled with a mix of fascination and awe for the fallen woman determined to walk away from her unholy life. In the hopes to see her if she returns—*when* she returns—I keep myself awake reading with a flashlight under my blanket.

And then, on Friday night, I hear my parents discuss the subject in the kitchen—only without Suzelle this time.

"I'll report it to the *Commissaire*," Pàpa says, his voice devoid of its usual warmth. "It's my duty."

"We promised we'd call her," Màma says.

"We're not bound by that promise, Petra. We owe her nothing."

There's a long pause, then Màma says, "You're right."

They turn off the light in the kitchen after that, so I pad to my bed and crawl under the covers, taking care not to wake Eva up.

Needless to say, I didn't sleep that night.

Rather than quietly helping Suzelle, my parents were going to set the police on her pimp. They'd opted to do what was *right* rather than what was *kind*. Even if it put Suzelle at risk.

Maybe their charity had its limits, after all.

And it didn't extend to fallen women.

CHAPTER 6

Everyone barring Eva does stupid things in college.

Some of us are stupider than others—real *doddele*, as we say in Alsace. A select few make sure the stupid thing they do in college is of the time bomb variety set to go off years later.

I'm among the latter group.

On the desk in front of me is a letter that arrived by snail mail this morning in a simple envelope stamped *Sydney, Australia*. How different it is from the naughty missives Raphael sometimes sends me from his business trips. The letter I'm staring at doesn't open with a hello or end with a good-bye. No name, date, or signature anywhere. Not much text, either. Just three short words written in large block letters.

I HAVE PROOF.

My hands shake as I crumple up the note into a tight

ball and shove it in my pocket. This is the second compactly ominous message I've received from Australia in six months. The first one had even fewer words. It said, *I KNOW.*

"You OK?" Delphine asks, peeking from behind her computer. "You're super pale this morning."

"I noticed it, too." My second office mate, Barbara, chimes in without shifting her eyes from her screen.

I shrug. "No makeup. Coupled with too little coffee."

"And too little sleep?" Delphine gives me a meaningful wink.

"That, too."

"When will you tell us who your mystery lover is?"

"Never."

Delphine narrows her eyes. "I bet he works at DCA."

"No, he doesn't."

"Then why the secrecy?" Suddenly, Delphine's expression softens. "Is he married? Is that why you sometimes sneak out at five and return around seven?"

"He isn't married," I say.

Delphine doesn't look convinced. Neither does Barbara. And I can totally see why. An affair with a married man is exactly what my fling—or whatever it is I'm having with Raphael—must look like.

The infamous *cinq à sept.*

It stands to reason that the man I'm seeing is married. That's what I'd figured, too, when I showed up for our second rendezvous out on the terrace.

On a crispy morning in early January, I had found a handwritten note on my keyboard.

9 p.m., eighth-floor terrace (the very same, access through the meeting room). If you don't turn up, I won't bother you again and I won't hold it against you. If you do, you might want to put in your office calendar: "A visit with the President of DCA."

Olly

My first reaction was giddy joy.

The funny-guy-turned-great-kisser who'd been on my mind throughout the Christmas break had reached out. *Woot woot!* In just a few hours I was going to see him. And kiss him.

Indignation came as an afterthought. But once there, it took root and doubled in size with every passing minute.

The cheek of him!

By hinting at the ribald "visits with the president of the Senate" I had told him about, Olly was making his intentions crystal clear. Which was sort of rude. And too freaking self-assured.

It was also inconsiderate and ungallant.

He was basically inviting me for some hanky-panky out in the cold, right under our colleagues' noses, and on our second date.

Or, should I say, our second *meeting* because neither occasion qualified as a date.

The bastard!

Why couldn't he invite me for a drink first, like *normal* men would do, even when their ulterior motive is to get laid? I don't expect a full-blown courtship, but there's a certain way of doing things. There's a set order, which prescribes that a couple have drinks and dinner together before scaling up to more intimate encounters. That dinner or three isn't a pointless formality—it's an opportunity to get to know each other and to establish trust.

I sighed in frustration, which was when it hit me: Olly must be married, just like Delphine's Alberto.

So I decided I wasn't going.

That was about four in the afternoon.

At seven-thirty, I was still in my office, finishing up perfectly non-urgent work and filing completely unimportant emails.

By eight-thirty, I stopped pretending I was't going to the terrace and swapped that lie out for a more plausible but still ego-friendly justification. I *was* going, but *only* to give the cocky bastard a piece of my mind.

The moment I entered the meeting room, I spotted Olly on the other side of the sliding glass doors leaning over the parapet. Unlike the night of the Christmas party, the terrace was well lit now.

He slid one of the doors open and peeked in. "Lock the door behind you. We'll want privacy."

Seriously?

I did lock the meeting room door, though.

Under the bright neon light, Olaf the Snowman, whom I suspected to be good-looking, turned out to be a real hunk. And a dandy. He wore a well-cut dark wool coat and a scarf that was the quintessence of masculine elegance. Wind played with his floppy dark hair. As for his dimpled chin and mischievous smile… let's just say I've never seen a sexier man in my whole life.

Chris Pine included.

As I crossed the room to the terrace, excitement and anxiety launched into a boxing match in my head, making me dizzy.

"Wow, you're even prettier than I remember," Olly said when I stood next to him. "Those eyes…"

He surveyed me appreciatively.

Anxiety won the match. "How about you give me your real name before I leave in…"—I looked at my watch—"exactly one minute."

He cocked his head to the side. "Why would I do that if you're leaving anyway?"

"To satisfy my curiosity."

"What's wrong with Olly?"

I glanced at my watch. "Fifty seconds."

"Raphael d'Arcy du Grand-Thouars de Saint-Maurice," he said. "I thought you knew."

Oh, please. "Is that a joke?"

"No."

He whipped out his phone, tapped, and then held it out for me. On the screen was the "Who's Who" page of DCA's website. I enlarged the photograph at the top of the list. The one that was captioned *Founding CEO and Owner*.

It was Olly, all right.

I mean, Raphael d'Arcy. *Le Big Boss.* The worst Casanova in town.

Fuck.

I glared at him. "Why didn't you say anything when we first met? I feel like an idiot now."

"In my defense, I was going to, but then you suddenly had to leave."

Should I believe him?

"Besides," he added, "My note did mention you were going to visit with the president of DCA."

"I thought you were just being funny."

"That, too." His smile widened. "But I was also being truthful. Which means your accusation is unfounded, and you don't have a good reason for leaving."

Considering who this man was and what I knew about him, I had at least ten good reasons for leaving.

But not just yet.

"I'll give you ten more minutes," I said. "Provided you don't attempt physical contact."

He gave me a sad puppy look. "But I'm dying to kiss you."

"That's *so* not happening."

"Why not?"

"First, because I have no interest in joining your army of conquests. Second, I don't think it's appropriate to make out in the workplace."

"You're right," he agreed unexpectedly. "It isn't."

I searched his face for signs of sarcasm, but his expression was earnest.

I smirked. "Are you saying you've never *visited* with a subordinate?"

"I didn't say that." His face grew even more serious. "Despite what you must have heard about me, I've never… harassed anyone. The very notion is abhorrent to me."

I hadn't heard anything specific about him—apart from his playboy fame—so I was a little puzzled at his reaction.

"Rudy," he said. "I want you to know I'm breaking one of my big rules just by talking to you here. But there's something about you that's too intriguing to resist."

I kept silent.

"What I said in my note still holds." Raphael adjusted his watch strap. "If you walk away right now, I'll never bother you again, and there'll be no reprisal whatsoever. You can be absolutely sure of it."

Why, oh why didn't I get out as fast as I could?

I have no rational explanation for that. Zero. Zilch. None whatsoever.

The irrational one is that my legs refused to take me away from the man I fancied so much.

More than I'd ever fancied anyone.

CHAPTER 7

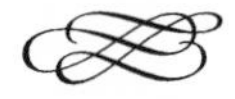

Raphael's smile returned. "Next time, I'll take you to a more suitable location."

"Define suitable," I said before adding, "and, please, don't take it as a yes."

He gave me a small shrug. "My place, for instance."

I rolled my eyes.

"What's wrong with that?"

"Call me old-fashioned," I said, "but I believe people should meet socially before they… ahem… visit the Senate. It's called *dating.*"

"Would it count if I took you to dinner and *then* to my place?"

I shook my head.

"Three dinners?"

"No."

"Five dinners and a concert at *L'Olympia*?"

"Stop bargaining—it's useless."

"Do you realize what you're saying no to?" He cocked his head. "I've never taken anyone to five dinners plus a concert *before* taking them to bed."

"I'm flattered, but no, thanks."

He arched an eyebrow. "I can see what you're doing here. You're playing hard to get."

"Honestly—no."

"Am I so distasteful to you?"

That sad doggy expression again. He didn't believe for a second he could be distasteful to anyone.

I held his gaze.

"Come on, Rudy," he said. "I want to hear you say it. Tell me you don't like me and you didn't enjoy our kiss."

"Olly," I said. "I like you, and I enjoyed our kiss. Very much. I'd totally date you."

He grinned.

"Raphael," I said. "There's no way I'm having casual sex with you, not tonight, not ever."

He looked a little taken aback by my determination. "I wasn't planning on us having sex tonight, anyway."

"No? What was your plan then?"

"Just talking. Getting to know you better." He gave me a small shrug. "Maybe a bit of cuddling and kissing those yummy lips of yours."

He zeroed in on my mouth.

I stared at his, remembering our first kiss. Without asking permission, my tongue darted out and licked my lips.

Traitor!

"The closest to a *visit* I envisioned," he said, "was to bare your chest for a sec and see if your breasts are shaped as I imagined them. I've done *a lot* of imagining after the Christmas party."

So had I. About the shape of his… *thing.*

"You're blushing. It's sweet." He brushed my cheek with the tips of his fingers. "Did I scandalize you?"

No, I did that myself, thank you.

"You make me sound like an ingenue." I sneered for more effect, even as my cheeks flamed under his touch, which now involved more than just the tips of his fingers.

"Because you're not," he said, stifling a smile.

"No, Raphael, I'm not."

And someone has proof of it.

I removed his hand from my cheek. "Your ten minutes are up. I'm leaving."

"Wait!" He blocked my way. "Now that I know you like me and that you enjoyed our first kiss, I must kiss you one more time."

"Not happening."

"One *last* time."

We stood so close to each other we were almost touching. His masculine scent invaded me, making my toes curl in my boots. Summoning what was left of my willpower to push desire back into the shadows where it belonged, I shook my head.

"Please?" His dark eyes held a genuine plea. "One kiss, and then I'll be out of your hair. Forever."

Just one kiss.

One delicious, hot, Olly-tasting kiss…

As if my body was detached from my brain, I leaned forward ever so slightly. Suddenly, his hands were in my hair and he was kissing me. There was nothing tentative about this kiss. Crushing his mouth against mine, Raphael held me tight and pushed his tongue between my lips.

He devoured me, his touch raw and blistering hot.

I kissed him back, hard, desperate to savor his taste. Closing my eyes, I tangled my tongue with his in a frenzied *pas de deux*. Blood pounded in my brain.

Raphael's tongue stroked against my palate, my tongue, the insides of my cheeks. He pulled it out to caress my lips and teeth and then penetrated my mouth again, making me moan with pleasure.

I was on fire, ravenous.

His mouth roamed my face and my throat, his lips searing my skin. I arched my neck, desire licking through me as I became aware of his bulge pressed against my tummy.

My breaths grew shallow.

Raphael's were just as ragged when he backed me against the strip of wall between the two glass doors. I didn't resist when he slid a hand under my coat and cupped one of my breasts. My vision blurred as I let him fondle and stroke it through the thin layers of my shirt and bra. When he rubbed my nipple with the pad of his thumb, I whimpered.

"The other one, too," I begged.

He obliged.

When, long moments later, he grabbed my wrists and shackled them above my head, my core tightened, heavy with need.

He pressed the full length of his body against me, and I reveled in the heat coming off him, in his hardness, his strength. I quivered and groaned into his mouth when he took my lips again in a savage kiss.

But it wasn't until his knee nudged my legs apart and I rubbed myself against his thigh, wild with lust, that I knew I couldn't walk away from his offerings.

This wouldn't be our last kiss.

Womanizer Raphael d'Arcy would add another trophy to his collection, and that trophy would be me.

Game over, Mia. You lost.

CHAPTER 8

I stare at the ten-page Middle East article I need to summarize for today's bulletin and wonder what marked the point of no return in my fall under Raphael d'Arcy's spell.

A bird twitters something incomprehensible but resolutely upbeat outside the window.

You're not helping, little friend.

The obvious culprit for my undoing was the "last" kiss Raphael sweet-talked me into back in January. More specifically, my unexpected passion for it.

But it's also possible that my fate had been sealed in December, when a snowman who went by Olly made my heart flutter. His banter made me laugh, and his sweet kiss made me giddy. I hadn't felt that way in a very long time.

Not since the *calamity*.

In fact, it doesn't really matter which of Raphael's kisses did me in. What matters is that I couldn't resist him then and I can't resist him now.

Once a wench, always a wench, as medievals would say.

"What is your opinion, Mia?" Delphine asks, interrupting my musings.

"About the Middle East?"

"No, silly, about beauty."

"Er…"

"She wasn't listening to us," Barbara says to Delphine. "She was focused on her work."

Ahem.

"Barbara was saying beauty is useless in this day and age," Delphine recaps for me.

"Not exactly." Barbara raises her index finger. "What I was saying is that beauty was more important back when women had no rights."

"Do you agree with that as a historian?" Delphine asks.

I smile. "Archival records and troubadour poetry would support that hypothesis."

Barbara pushes her hair back and gives Delphine a smug little shrug. "Ha!"

"Fine," Delphine says. "Maybe beauty is less important these days than it used to be, but it's still great to have."

"Sure," Barbara concedes magnanimously.

"True beauty is like a Chanel bag," Delphine says. "Very few own the real thing. Most of us can only afford counterfeits."

"What do you mean by counterfeits?" I ask.

Delphine makes a sweeping you-name-it gesture with her hand. "Bleached hair. Contouring. Nose jobs. Breast implants."

"Which only proves my point," Barbara says.

"Beauty is a nonessential luxury item. Like you said—a Chanel bag."

"Except some women would die for it," Delphine says with a wink.

Barbara shrugs a perhaps. "But I'm sure more women would die for a career or a legacy."

"Pff." Delphine waves dismissively. "Nobody's willing to die to leave a good name, *ma cocotte*."

I just might.

There's little I wouldn't I do if I could turn back the clock and make sure a certain drunken gang bang never happened. Or that it could be erased from my real-life timeline. And from the memory of everyone involved.

That fateful night had started innocently enough with some college kids drinking (OK, binge drinking), smoking pot, and having a good time. We'd finished our second year and were celebrating the achievement in a huge shared apartment in central Strasbourg. As the hour grew late and the bottles emptied, most people—including all of my friends—either left or dropped off in one of the bedrooms.

I was sleepy, too, and plastered under the combined effect of wine and weed in a way I'd never been before.

Why didn't I just conk out like the others?

But no, I stayed awake, albeit teetering on the edge of consciousness. I didn't even puke until after three young men undressed me and had sex with me on the couch. *Consensual sex*. Wasted as I was, I did participate—or, should I say, made pathetic attempts at participating—in the "fun."

That I remember.

What I don't remember is who those men were, if there were other people present, and whether anyone filmed our antics.

It would appear someone did after all, judging by the letter I received last week.

It's no biggie, I tell myself. We're not in the Middle Ages or in Taliban-controlled Afghanistan. Even if some a-hole posted my foursome online for everyone to see, there'd be no Morality Police bursting in to arrest me and no outraged mob to stone me for slutty behavior. *We're in France, Toto.* A country where women may get fined by *gendarmes* for showing *too little* skin on a public beach.

I must stay calm and carry on.

It's the only sensible thing to do.

Rationalizing like this helps… somewhat, until notions like shame, public humiliation, and ruined academic career pop into my head. They attack on a level that's too base for logical arguments.

But even those I can deal with.

What unravels me beyond the salutary reach of reason is the image of Màma and Pàpa receiving a tape from a "well-wisher." Watching it. Recognizing their daughter. Taking the measure of the abyss between what they thought of her and what she is.

I plunge both hands into my hair and muss it, trying to reshuffle my thoughts.

Middle East, Mia. Concentrate on the Middle East!

That's what pays my rent and makes sure I can stay in my PhD program and still be able to afford best quality Bolognese and carbonara for my spaghetti.

Raphael's attention span in regards to women is about as long as Dory's in *Finding Nemo*. He'll get tired of me any day now. If, in the meantime, my work becomes sloppy, I'll lose my job on top of losing my lover.

And, *bam*, no more enchanted nights and no more carbonara.

Speaking of carbonara, I had the best one ever the other day in a discreet Italian restaurant close to Raphael's place. That sauce had the perfect ratio of parmesan, bacon, and pepper. As if that wasn't enough, the fettuccine it accompanied was so good I would've enjoyed it with no sauce at all.

Eva will never hear this from me, but the carbonara they make in that place is better than hers.

I can make that affirmation because it's the third time I've had it since the original epiphany back when Raphael and I were "dating."

True to his word, he had taken me to dinner five times and then to a Daft Punk concert at *L'Olympia*. Only after that was I invited to "visit with the President of DCA" in his spacious penthouse apartment near Odéon.

That was on January 30th.

In February and March, I "visited" with Raphael in his humble abode some more. A lot more, in fact. But whenever I suggested we go to my place for a change, his answer was a polite no. Instead, one Friday night in February he whisked me off to a charming hotel in London. Another Friday in March, he flew me to Venice. And this month, he drove me to Deauville and to Tours in his flashy Ferrari.

Those trips were lovely, and I'm truly grateful for them. But I can't help wishing we'd gone to Ninossos instead. Raphael owns an unspoiled little island south of Crete in the Mediterranean Sea. It's rocky with a narrow strip of sand, an unusual-looking villa up on a hill, and a plantation of magnificent olive trees.

I know all that from the large prints that adorn nearly every wall in Raphael's apartment, showing the island in every season and time of day.

Looks like that place is really special to him.

Maybe that's why he's never offered to take me there.

CHAPTER 9

I sit back in my roomy armchair and survey the cabin. It's flooded with soft light, all milky leather, pearl-gray carpets, and pale wood panels. The epitome of luxury.

I smile, recalling the disappointment I felt when I first set foot in this jet that Raphael co-owns with his older brother Sebastian.

It seemed small.

Not that I'd had any personal experience with private jets before. In fact, my point of reference had been movies like *Air Force One* and TV shows like *House of Cards,* both featuring the designated aircraft of the president of the United States.

No less.

Now that I know what a regular private jet looks like, I find this twelve seater perfectly sized. Big enough to be able to stretch your legs, yet small enough to feel comfortable.

We're flying back to Paris from a lazy weekend in Costa Brava. Well, *relatively* lazy because whenever we weren't in the pool, restaurant or bed, we worked in the luxury spa's outdoor cafe, enjoying the perfect early May weather. When he wasn't on the phone with his aides, Raphael studied some highly sensitive file, and I toiled on my thesis.

My inner nerd loved the quiet companionship during those studious hours just as much as my inner strumpet enjoyed kissing him on the beach.

But everything good comes to an end.

This flight included.

Reminding myself it'll be over before we can say "Paris," I get started on my mouth-watering breakfast of poached eggs, stir-fried mushrooms, smoked salmon rolls, and maple syrup pancakes. Next to me, Raphael skims a report and types an email while sipping his double espresso.

Who says men can't multitask?

"Eat while it's warm," I say.

"Oui, maman." He puts his tablet aside.

I pick up a bowl of mixed berries. "Just because you can have this kind of breakfast any time you want isn't a reason not to enjoy it."

"True." He digs in. "It's going to be a hell of a week."

"Work?"

"Uh-huh." He gives me sideways look. "I won't see you much."

I fold my napkin and arrange the remains of the food on the tray, avoiding eye contact. He doesn't need to know how dismayed I am at the prospect.

Raphael turns away from me and begins to fumble with the controls on his armrest. Suddenly, we are shut off from the rest of the aircraft by a felt partition. *Neat.*

He presses another button, and my seat slides into a reclining position. A second later, so does his.

He leans over me. "We could put the next twenty minutes to good use."

Except I can't. My period started this morning. The problem is my upbringing won't allow me to say this to a man. Even a man that's intimately familiar with every inch of my body.

"That trick you did with the seats," I say instead, "was cheesy."

He nods. "And cheap."

"Exactly."

"And childish," he adds.

"That, too."

"And Chinese."

I frown. "Why Chinese?"

"Because… I ran out of pertinent ch-words."

I burst out laughing.

He unbuttons my shirt and pushes the cups of my bra under my breasts. The feel of his hand against my skin is too pleasant to resist, so I let him caress me from the waist up.

He begins to stroke my left breast, his palm scooping and kneading it. At the same time, his mouth descends on my right breast, and, after swirling his tongue around my nipple, he captures it between his lips. A shiver runs through me. His eyes on my face, Raphael draws the nipple into his mouth and sucks on it. I moan and arch my back as he rolls my other nipple between his fingers, pinching it gently.

This is so damn good.

I mean, *not good.*

Because he clearly doesn't intend on stopping at my

waistline. He's just unbuttoned my jeans and is drawing the zipper down.

"I should've warned you to wear a skirt," he says, sliding his hand under the lacy front of my panties.

I grab his wrist. "What if the attendant comes in to collect the trays?"

"She won't," he says, halting nonetheless, "as long as the partition is up."

"What if there's an emergency? What if we're crashing and the pilots need to let us know?"

"If we're crashing, we'll *know*."

As I look for another reason why we should stop, he moves his hand between my legs.

I jerk his wrist. "Stop!"

"Why? What's wrong, baby?"

OK, to hell with good manners. "I'm on my period."

"Oh." He looks a little confused. "Do you need to use the bathroom?"

"No, I'm good. But I don't want you to… you know."

He puts his hands on my lower abdomen. "Cramps?"

"A little."

"Poor sweetie."

Before I can catch his wrist, his long fingers slip inside my panties and find the string of my tampon. "Wonderful invention, isn't it?"

"Yeah. Can you just… return to my breasts?"

"Here's a deal." He gives me a crooked smile. "My mouth returns to your lovely tits, but my hand stays where it is."

"I don't think—"

"Without moving."

"You're such a… *dickkopt*," I say.

He widens his eyes. "Did Mia Stoll just use a swear word?!"

"It means 'pigheaded' in Alsatian."

"Phew." He drops his head to his chest in fake relief. "For a moment there, I thought the end of the world was upon us."

I smile, and Raphael gives me a tiny stroke down there, his touch featherlight.

I squeeze my thighs. "Your hand stays only if you can control it."

"I promise I'll do my best," he says. "If I fail, slap me."

"Oh, I will."

He blows air across my nipples and resumes his ministrations. But I find it impossible to relax, too aware of his hand between my legs. In particular, of his fingers that begin to stir again. When he presses them against my bud, I open my mouth to cry foul, except the pleasure turns out to be stronger than my inhibitions and taboos.

Encouraged by my permissiveness, he starts to rub in earnest.

My lids grow heavy.

He applies more pressure, and soon I'm writhing under his touch. I forget I'm menstruating. I disremember I have cramps. My brain doesn't even know what cramps are anymore.

Raphael rubs faster, whispering against my lips, "Mia, baby, you're so beautiful."

I peak the moment his tongue pushes into my mouth. As he kisses me hard and deep, wave after wave of sweet pleasure washes over me.

I abandon myself to it.

When I come down from the high, I realize my fingernails have dug into his back, hard.

"I'm sorry," I say, letting go of him. "Did I hurt you?"

"A little." That panty-dropping smile again. "But I loved it."

I grin back. "Well, that makes two of us with self-control issues."

"Isn't it weird," he says and blows softly against my stiff nipples, "how I have no problem exercising control in every sphere of my life, except this?"

"It *is* weird."

"I can go days, sometimes weeks without thinking about women, until I see something that tempts me. And then I'm toast."

"Some-*thing*?"

"On a woman," he explains. "Like your eyes. And lips. And neck, and boobs… Actually, every part of you."

As he names the various parts he touches his lips to them, a little clumsy at times. What with his right hand still in my panties and his left hand splayed against my seat propping him up, the poor man is forced to use his head.

Literally.

"It's like with Q-tips," Raphael says.

"Pardon me?"

"Haven't you ever caught sight of Q-tips in a bathroom drawer, and suddenly your ears felt itchy?"

I smile and nod. Just hearing the word makes my ears itchy.

He trails his tongue up my neck and over my chin. "It's like once you see them, you simply *must* grab one to scratch your itch! You know?"

"Yeeeah…" I draw it out.

The truth is I don't know if I *know*. The real Q-tip situation is something I can definitely relate to, but we're no longer talking about Q-tips, are we? Raphael is describing his relationship with the opposite sex.

Scratch the itch, huh?

I'm struck by how insensitive his comparison is. And even more by the fact that he doesn't realize it.

Or doesn't care.

For heaven's sake, Mia, walk away from this man!

He'll get you addicted to his lovemaking and rakish charm and then discard you like a used Q-tip.

"Baby, is something wrong?" he asks.

I shake my head. "All's well."

"I doubt it." He searches my face. "Did I bite your lip too hard, or is it what I just said?"

How can a man be so blunt and so sensitive at the same time? He says the most outrageous things without caring about their effect, yet he's capable of noticing the slightest change in the way my body reacts to him. Why isn't he just a regular entitled jerk? Things would have been so much easier!

I would've dumped him by now.

No, scratch that, I would've never hooked up with him in the first place.

"It's not something you did," I say.

He nods. "It's what I said about Q-tips, right?"

"Not a very flattering comparison."

"I'm sorry," he says. "I didn't mean it that way."

I tug at his wrist, and he pulls his hand out of my panties.

"At least it was honest," I say, sitting up. "I'll get over it."

He pulls himself up, too, and then puts the backs of our seats into an upright position.

I sort myself out and decide this is a good time to talk about my colleague Sandro, whom my lover is about to sack.

"You're letting Sandro Marnier go," I say.

Raphael gives me a slightly surprised look. "I am, indeed."

"Is he bad at his job?"

"Why do you care?" His expression hardens. "Is he a friend of yours? Or more than a friend?"

"He's a friend of Barbara's," I say. "We sometimes eat lunch together."

Raphael nods, his jaw relaxing.

"So, is he bad?" I ask again.

"No. But he showed up to work drunk three times over two weeks."

"His boyfriend of three years dumped him out of the blue."

"Not my problem." Raphael's lips flatten.

My jaw clenches.

"I must act before his probationary period ends," Raphael explains. "If I don't, he'll get an open-ended contract, join the staff union, and continue drinking. And then it'll definitely be *my* problem."

"He won't continue drinking," I say. "I can vouch for him. He loves his job, and he needs to work. It was just a glitch."

Raphael shakes his head. "If things are the way you describe them, he would've never allowed the glitch to happen in the first place."

"Haven't you ever lost your way?" I ask. "Haven't you made misguided decisions and done stupid things you regretted bitterly later?"

He surveys my face.

"Please, will you give Sandro a chance?"

He stares out the window for a long moment. "Yes, there was a time when I lost my way," he says, turning to me. "Many years ago, back in my teens."

"But you got your act together, and I'm sure you didn't do it alone. Someone—your parents, most likely—was there to help you."

He gives me a humorless smile. "Someone was, indeed, only it wasn't my parents. Maman was running her charity in Nepal, and Papa… Anyway, the person who had my back was Seb. I may have never cleaned up my act if it weren't for him."

I gaze into his eyes.

He stares back. "I'll take another look at Sandro's file."

"Thank you."

The corners of Raphael's mouth curl up. "You should apply for sainthood with that heart of yours."

Ha! The irony of it.

I'm not championing Sandro out of the goodness of my heart. My motives are more complex and somewhat less altruistic. The main one is a ludicrous wish. I hope that if my sex tape ever hits the Internet, the universe will return the favor. I hope the people who know me won't see it, or if they do, they won't judge me too harshly.

And, above all, I hope the people who matter most won't cast me off.

CHAPTER 10

I'm stretching my legs in the airy foyer of the Pompidou Center, fighting the temptation to check out its Dadaism exhibit. But the purpose of my being here isn't art. It's work.

My *main* work, that is.

I'm at the Pompidou Center tonight—just as I was last night and I will be tomorrow night—because its well-provisioned library is open until ten p.m. That means I can come here straight from the office and toil on my thesis for full three hours.

Tonight, I've been particularly inspired. Not only did I manage to track down an elusive thirteenth-century source, I also did quite a bit of writing. Oh, to hell with false modesty. I did a *huge* amount of writing and—wait for it—finished Part II of my thesis.

Go Mia!

As of today, exactly half of my dissertation is done, ready to be shown to my supervisor, and used for conference papers and journal articles. On top of that,

I'm a whole month ahead of the deadline Professor Guyot and I had agreed on.

What can I say?

Mia Stoll rocks.

Some day she'll be a recognized authority on the harlots of medieval Paris. No, think bigger! She'll be the world's biggest expert on women in medieval France.

I turn around to head back to the library and collide with someone's broad chest.

A very familiar chest.

"Hey, Rudy," Raphael says, putting his arms around me and planting a kiss on my mouth.

My lids fall as I savor the scent of him and the feel of his lips against mine.

Wait… what is he doing here?

I draw away. "Weren't you supposed to be in Rio?"

"I came back two days early." He shrugs. "The work was done so there was no point in lingering."

"No point in lingering in *Rio*?" *Man, he's jaded.* "Didn't you say you wanted to explore the city?"

"I did. And I was planning to… but then…" He gives me a crooked smile. "I realized I missed my Ferrari."

I stare at him in incredulity. "Let me get this straight. You left Rio two days early because you missed your car."

He nods.

"Poor lovesick man." I give his upper arm a sympathetic squeeze. "Does your Ferrari feel the same way about you?"

"She won't say—seeing as she can't talk—but she lit up when she saw me earlier." He beams.

I beam back. "That's a good sign."

"So, how's the study coming along?"

"I just finished part two."

"Madame Stoll." He takes an imaginary hat off. "That deserves a celebratory dinner."

I just grin, feeling ridiculously proud of myself.

"Speaking of dinner, have you eaten yet?" Raphael asks. "I'm starving—came here straight from the airport."

"I grabbed a sandwich on the way from the office."

Hang on a sec…

Did he just say he came here straight from the airport? I thought he'd gone home first to check on his Ferrari, which "lit up" for him?

Raphael pulls a face. "A sandwich doesn't count as dinner. How about that place on rue Rambuteau we went to last week?"

The place that serves Kobe steaks for the price of my monthly rent and swarms with movie stars, some of whom greet Raphael with a "Hi, baby, we should get together sometime."?

No, thanks.

"You go ahead," I say. "I'm in this crazy productive flow tonight. I want to write some more."

"Not even George's at the top floor of this building?"

I shake my head.

He looks around and takes a step toward the escalator. "Follow me."

Intrigued, I do as requested.

Turns out he's leading me to the mezzanine café.

"Unless you have serious and well-justified objections," he says, motioning me to a table by the balustrade, "I'll order your favorite brownie and chai latte and something more substantial for myself."

He spins around and heads to the counter before I get a chance to utter my objections.

Honestly. Men.

When he returns with an overflowing tray and I sink my teeth into the brownie, I feel a lot less peeved at his unceremonious ways.

"Do you have your laptop?" he asks.

"Of course." I point at my backpack on the floor. "I'm not crazy enough to leave it in a public library unattended."

"Will you show me an interesting passage from your new chapters?"

Every time he asks me to do that, I get inexplicably excited.

So I pretend to be miffed. "Are you suggesting my thesis has passages that are *boring*?"

"Yes," he says, unfazed. "If it didn't have any, it would be a Stephen King novel."

He does have a point.

I open my laptop and scroll through my new chapters.

Hmm.... All of it looks interesting to me.... OK, how about this one?

I turn my screen toward him and point. "Read this bit."

> In the twelfth and thirteenth centuries, the sex worker had no legal status and wasn't even allowed to speak for herself in court. But her right to be paid for her services was firmly established and protected in Norman laws. The influential English canonist Thomas of Chobham, who had studied in Paris in the 1180s, wrote: "It is wrong for a woman to be a prostitute, but if she is such, it is not wrong for her to

> receive a wage. But if she prostitutes herself for pleasure and hires out her body for this purpose, then the wage is as evil as the act itself."

"Ha!" he says, looking up at me. "So this Thomas is basically saying it's a mild sin if a woman has sex for money, but it's a really nasty sin if she does it for pleasure. Right?"

"That's not exactly what he says, but you aren't far off the mark."

"Well, I'm glad medieval *canons* are dead and buried now, at least in this part of the world."

"I'm not so sure." I narrow my eyes. "What do you pay an average male auditor versus an average female auditor?"

"At DCA," he says with visible pride, "male and female auditors get equal pay for equal work."

"OK, then how about male and female staff, all categories included?"

He runs his hand through his hair. "That wouldn't be a fair comparison."

"No? Why?"

"Because…" He hesitates for a second. "OK, I'm going to be blunt about this. We don't have any women in the top management. And we don't have many male assistants."

I nod. "Still a long way to go even for this part of the world, huh?"

He chews his sandwich in silence.

I study his serious face. "You're suspiciously thoughtful."

"I'm trying to picture myself living in medieval France where all pretty young things who don't sell their bodies are chaste."

"And?"

"It's terrifying." He widens his eyes in mock despair. "As a man who's not interested in marriage, I'd have to either grin and bear it or pay for sex."

"Something tells me you'd go with the second option."

He smirks. "I'd probably have loyalty cards from brothels all over the country."

"What if you were a medieval woman and you weren't interested in marriage?"

"I'd become a harlot," he says without hesitation.

Of course.

"What about you?" he asks.

I don't hesitate either. "I'd become a nun."

"Really? I didn't realize you shared your mother's passion for Jesus."

"I don't, even though I do think he was an admirable individual."

"Then why a nun?"

"Well, for starters, taking the vows was the best escape route for a woman who didn't want to marry the man her parents had chosen for her—or any man at all."

He nods. "I see."

"But it isn't just that. Career options that were open to a nerdy medieval woman—even wealthy ladies of the manor—were extremely limited."

He slaps his forehead. "Of course. Why didn't I think of that? A woman wasn't supposed to be smart, right?"

"Right, unless she became a *religieuse*."

I pick up the last crumbs of my brownie and then lick my fingers.

He opens his water bottle.

"A *religieuse*," I continue, "could read philosophical treatises to her heart's content. She could have opinions, and write, and engage in intellectual debates."

"I get it, really," Raphael says. "What I don't get is that you'd forego sex for intellectual debates."

"No pain, no gain," I say.

"Your life credo?"

"Not a credo, more like a rule of thumb."

"My life is ruled by a finger, too," he says. "But it's not a thumb."

I screw up my face, expecting the worst.

True to form, he holds up his middle finger. "It's this one."

"Prick," I say.

"And proud," he says with a grin.

CHAPTER 11

Raphael locks the door of his office behind me. "Should I have a word with Pauline?"

"What for?"

"So she'd let her assistants take credit for the sections they compile."

I stare at him as I process his suggestion.

"I checked your contract," he says. "Your pay grade requires only proofreading and formatting."

"I'm *happy* Pauline gives me more challenging tasks," I say.

"Yes, but the bulletin still has your name only next to *layout*."

"And that's perfectly fine by me."

He looks taken aback. "I'll be very diplomatic if you're worried about raising her suspicions—"

"It isn't just the suspicions," I say. "Honestly, I don't care how I'm credited in the bulletin. I'm here only until I get my PhD and find a job in the academia."

"I know that." He frowns. "Still, it isn't right that someone should take credit for your work."

"Your concern for your foot soldier is commendable." I give him a wink. "How about you extend it to the ones you aren't sleeping with?"

"I discussed Sandro Marnier's case with my aides," he says. "I might give him a second chance."

I beam.

He smiles back and pulls me into his embrace. "We have two hours before I head out of town."

His hands begin to stroke my back. Palms flat and fingers splayed, they travel up to my nape, slide down my shoulder blades, press against the small of my back, and cup my ass. While his hands roam at will, leaving no inch untouched, his lips brush my face, hungry and demanding.

I love this part.

That is not to say I don't love what follows more, but there's something about Raphael's touch that hits all the right spots. Even the ones I didn't know I had. It's as if his hands have the exact size, warmth, and strength that my nerve endings require. And it always feels as though he has more than two—like a Hindu deity—when he caresses me like this.

As he backs me toward his massive oakwood desk, I feel him harden against my tummy.

My eyes close. "Will I see you this weekend?"

"I'm afraid not." He trails hot kisses along my neck. "I'll be away all weekend and all of next week."

I dare not ask where he's traveling to.

Or with whom.

Is it because I'm awed by this man? Bearing in mind he's only twenty-nine, it's hard not to be impressed by what he's achieved. It's hard not to be affected by his status and wealth, not to mention his blue blood and crazy good looks.

But it isn't those awe-inspiring features that got me stuck on him. Whenever I forget to be wonderstruck, *Le Big Boss* disappears and a sweet, carrot-nosed snowman takes his place.

Lovemaking achieves that every time.

Raphael hooks an arm around my waist as he pushes the files on his desk to the side. I expect him to lift me and sit me facing him as we've done before, but he turns me around instead. Before I realize what he's up to, he has me bent over the desk. Placing a hand between my shoulder blades, he nudges me lower until my cheek is pressed against the polished wood.

He holds me firmly in place, pushing my hem up with his other hand. I'm wearing a tight pencil skirt today, so Raphael's task isn't as easy as it sounds, especially when performed single-handedly.

But he keeps at it until, finally, my skirt is bunched at my waist and my panties are around my right ankle.

He groans as he strokes my bared flesh.

I feel exposed and vulnerable, with my ass sticking out like this.

We have, of course, done it doggy style before. But we were in bed and it was different. The room was much darker, and I was completely relaxed and uninhibited after the exquisite wine and even more exquisite tonguing he'd treated me to.

I'd had none of that today.

And this office is flooded in light.

Raphael glosses the back of my thighs and my derriere. Murmuring encouragements, he grasps my hips and pushes my butt higher while his knee nudges my legs wider apart. I let him. His right hand reaches around me and his fingers rub, then delve inside. Just as I begin to moan with need, he takes a step back.

The ticking of the clock on the wall and his ragged breathing are all I hear. And I don't need to look at his face to know what he's staring at.

"You're a joy to behold, Mia," he says.

I flush.

Part of it is gratification.

His compliment is my reward for the dreadful Brazilian waxing appointments I've been putting myself through since January.

I hear him unbuckle his belt and draw down the zipper of his pants. By the time the sound of a condom foil being ripped reaches my ears, I'm not just ready for what's coming—I crave it.

He grasps my hips once again and plunges into me.

The sweetness of it wrings a low-pitched, raspy *aah* from somewhere deep in my chest.

Raphael begins to pound into me.

I push back to meet his thrusts and help him penetrate me even deeper. My breasts are crushed against the warm surface of the desk, and my mind is wonderfully empty. My body is so drunk on what he's doing to it, I find myself wishing he could go even deeper, fill me even more completely.

I'm wild with lust.

"*Oh oui,*" I breathe out with every push. *"Oh oui. Oh oui. Oh oui."*

"Sounds like you like it," he grunts, leaning forward.

Like it? I think I might die with pleasure.

He straightens up, and then a sharp smack lands on my backside.

"What about this, Mia?" he asks. "Do you like that, too?"

Actually, I don't.

But there's a lump in my throat preventing me from uttering those words.

He smacks me once more.

I stiffen.

He stops thrusting.

A few seconds later, he's sitting on the floor with his back against the desk and me ensconced on his lap.

"Mia, baby, are you OK?" He strokes my face, holding me to his chest. "You didn't enjoy the spanking, did you? Was I too heavy-handed?"

He wasn't. His taps were light and playful. They were certainly not meant to hurt. They *didn't* hurt.

So, why did they kill my arousal?

And why do I feel so… cheap?

Maybe it's because of the *calamity*, coupled with my being his subordinate, bent over his desk, and clueless as to with whom he's going to spend next week…

Raphael tips my chin up so that I'm forced to meet his eyes. "Please, Mia, I need to know. Was it the spanking?"

I nod. It's easier to say yes than to try to explain what I don't really understand myself.

His expression becomes solemn. "Hit me."

I blink at his strange offer.

"Kick me anywhere you want, twice," he says.

"Don't be silly."

"Please." He gives me a pleading look. "We'll be even, and we'll both feel better."

Will we?

Oh, what the hell.

I draw back and slap his face.

"Ouch." He rubs his cheek.

"Give me your arm," I say archly.

He holds his left arm up.

I run my hand over his bulging biceps—any pretext to touch his biceps is always welcome—and then pinch as hard as I can.

He winces.

I let go of his arm. "I'm done."

"Do you feel better?"

"Surprisingly, I do."

"Good. Me, too." He delves his fingers into my hair and strokes. "Next time I wanna try something kinky, I'll be sure to ask if you're into it first."

"Do you enjoy kink?"

"No," he says before adding, "Thing is, I've never been with a woman this long."

"We've hardly been together five months."

"As I said, I've never been with a woman this long."

"How is that related to kink?"

"I thought I'd spice things up a bit."

My heart sinks. "Are you getting tired of me?"

"Not at all." He searches my face. "I had the impression *you* were getting tired of me."

What? "Why would you think that?"

He shrugs. "You've been reserved and… a little distant lately. I thought you were cooling off."

I sigh. *If only he knew how far that is from the truth!*

My being reserved is the result of the growing preoccupation with the Australian letters. I can't help it. Every time I open my mailbox or check my office pigeonhole, I expect to find a new letter. What will it say? Will my "secret admirer" state what he wants from me? Will he ask for money? How much? Will I be able to afford it?

I wish I could tell Raphael about my looming blackmail. But that would require explaining the grounds for it.

And I can't.

Telling him about the *calamity* would push me even lower than I already am on the social food chain. I'd plummet from the "little assistant with academic ambitions" whom he bangs when he has a spare moment straight to the *slutzone.* And not just your average garden-variety slut, but an advanced one with a gang bang and a sex tape under her belt.

That sort of confession won't just widen the gap between us. It'll turn that gap into a chasm.

"Don't worry," I say, forcing a smile. "You're still as attractive to me as when I first saw you in your fleece onesie."

He smiles back, but the crease between his eyebrows doesn't go away. "Then what is it? What's bothering you?"

Maybe I can give him *a part* of the truth. "It's my finances," I say. "I need to find a second job."

"I can lend you—"

I clamp my hand over his mouth. "No way."

"All right." He nods, sucking his teeth. "How about I offer you that second job?"

I wrinkle my nose. "As what?"

"Waitress." He gives me a bright smile. "Seb and I own a bar in central Paris, Le Big Ben. It's an English-style gentlemen's club."

I smirk. "How chic."

And how *revealing* that he's never mentioned it before. Or taken me there.

"The manager said the other day he was looking to hire another server for the evening shift."

"So you plan to go nepotist on the poor man and impose me?"

"Have you waitressed before?" he asks.

"Plenty."

"Then, yes, I'm going to go nepotist on him."

I open my mouth to say he shouldn't when we hear loud voices right outside the door.

It's Anne-Marie and a man.

They're arguing.

CHAPTER 12

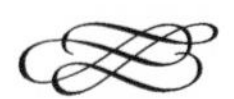

"I'm sorry, Monsieur d'Arcy, but Monsieur d'Arcy isn't there," Anne-Marie says from behind the door.

I give Raphael a puzzled look.

"It's Seb," he explains.

Woah.

Standing behind the door is Count Sebastian d'Arcy himself. Arrogant. Antisocial. Ruthless. A man whose bad side you don't even want to imagine, let alone *be on.*

At least, that's what I've heard.

A commanding bass rumbles, "Oh, I think he *is* in there."

"You're mistaken, monsieur. He isn't," Anne-Marie persists, but there's a quiver in her high-pitched voice.

"Then why don't you open this door and let me see for myself?"

Sebastian's tone is so icy it sends a chill down my spine. I don't envy Anne-Marie right now.

"I cannot do that, monsieur."

She sounds like she's about to burst into tears.

"Poor thing." Raphael screws up his face in sympathy. "I'm not sure how much longer she can hold down the fort."

I begin to panic. "You think she's going to let him in?"

"Seb can be intimidating at times." He pauses before adding, "Frequently." He sighs. "Always."

I jump to my feet and begin neatening myself as fast as I can.

"I'm going to open the door," Raphael says, standing up, "before Anne-Marie has a heart attack."

"Is there a back door or something so I can sneak out?"

He shakes his head, tucking his shirt into his pants.

I adjust his tie. "I don't want your brother to see me here."

"Why do you care? He doesn't even know you."

I smirk, decoding the message between the lines: *Don't worry—to Sebastian, you'll be just another faceless conquest of mine he won't even try to commit to memory.*

To be honest, I'm not sure why Sebastian's seeing me here matters. Maybe it's the remains of my dignity thrashing about in final spasms.

"OK, I have an idea." Raphael points to the floor-to-ceiling closet running along one of the walls. "Why don't you go hide in there, and I'll get rid of Sebastian as fast as I can?"

I nod and scurry to the closet.

Raphael opens the office door.

"You're alone." Sebastian sounds surprised.

"I was doing some strategic thinking," Raphael says. "Which is why I had instructed Anne-Marie not to let anyone in."

"You locked your door to do strategic thinking,"

Sebastian parrots with a tangible note of mockery in his voice.

"Nobody's perfect," Raphael says.

"OK, whatever." Sebastian's tone becomes conciliatory. "I didn't come here to fight with you."

"Why *did* you come here?"

"I need your legal training again to help me with my nuptial arrangement."

"So you're moving forward with your crazy scheme."

"Yes, I am," Sebastian says drily.

There's a brief silence before Raphael asks, "How's my future sister-in-law doing, by the way? Haven't seen her since the dinner at Genevieve's."

"She's fine. How is Genevieve?"

Who is Genevieve?

Is she a longtime fiancée waiting patiently for Raphael to let off steam? Or a crazy wife he keeps locked up in the attic of his house in the country like Mr. Rochester in *Jane Eyre*?

I gasp as a light bulb goes off in my head. What if Genevieve is his child? How little I know about the man whose body I've explored so completely over the past few months!

"Her usual indomitable self," Raphael says. "She just started a new project."

"Another documentary?"

"No, this time she's producing fiction. A remake of a forties noir."

"You think she'll manage to sell it?" Sebastian asks.

"Who knows? They say third time's the charm."

There's another short pause.

"Here's the paperwork," Sebastian says. "I'd appreciate if you could take a look."

"Will do. So… um… see you around?"

"Any headway with Noah?" Sebastian asks.

"Nope."

"Me neither."

"He'll come around," Raphael says. "He just needs time."

"It's all Maman's fault."

"Will you leave our mother out of this?"

"Why?" The permafrost is back in Sebastian's voice. "It's the truth."

"Yeah, sure." Raphael sounds peeved. "Just like your theory that she's somehow responsible for what happened to Papa."

Silence.

"The man dug his own grave," Raphael says.

"I've never blamed her for it."

"Oh yes, you have. You still do."

"Do I? I don't know…" Sebastian hesitates. "Maybe you're right. Maybe I'm too hard on her."

They're both silent for a long moment, and then Sebastian says, "But you can't deny she's responsible for setting Noah against us."

"I don't know about that—"

"Oh, come on! We find out *by accident* that our little brother left Nepal and has been living here in Paris for six months now."

Raphael doesn't offer a comment.

"He won't answer or return our calls," Sebastian says.

No reaction from Raphael.

"He goes by Maman's maiden name."

"Not everyone is as proud to be a d'Arcy as you are, bro. We'd better accept that Noah would rather be a Masson."

Sebastian doesn't respond to that, and I almost give in to the temptation to sneak a peek at his face. But I resist. I don't want to risk being caught.

The brothers say good-bye shortly afterward.

Raphael locks the office door and lets me out. "I'm sorry you had to listen to that. I shouldn't have let Sebastian in."

"No, it's OK. I learned more about your family in those ten short minutes than over the past five months."

He gives me a humorless smile.

"Besides," I say, "your conversation was interesting from a scientific perspective."

"How so?"

"It proved my theory that blue bloods produce just as much dirty laundry as everyone else."

"We certainly do." His smile becomes genuine. "Is that a good thing?"

I shrug. "It makes you my equal in dirty laundry, at least."

"I still have twenty minutes," he says taking hold of my hand. "How about we finish what we started?"

I frown.

"Minus the spanking," he adds quickly.

"How about we finish it after you're back?" My eyes dart to the door. "And preferably, someplace where we won't get interrupted."

He nods.

We kiss good-bye, and a few minutes later I'm back in my office to finish up the day's work.

Delphine gives me a meaningful look as she applies her lipstick before heading out. "He *is* from the office."

"Who? I was just—"

"Fine, don't tell me," she says. "But when I figure out who he—or she—is, you'll have to be more forthcoming, *ma cocotte,* like I was with you about Alberto."

"Or else?" I ask, trying to sound playful.

"Or else I might not be able to keep the scoop to myself, regardless of his—or her—marital status." She gives me a consider-yourself-warned look and sashays out the door.

Threatening me is becoming *à la mode* these days.

Somehow, I manage to focus on my work and finish it a little after nine.

As I step out of the building, the air is so pleasant it's hard to believe I'm in Paris. With the rush hour over, the smell of gas and diesel is replaced by the springy scents of flowers and buds. The temperature is as perfect as it gets in this country—somewhere between mild and warm—with winter's chill gone without a trace and summer's sticky heat still far away.

According to to the weather forecast, it'll be like this all week and through the weekend, which I'd been hoping to spend with Raphael.

What a shame he chose to spend it with someone else! Probably Genevieve, whoever she is.

As I walk toward the *métro* station, jealousy and bile team up in my head to ruin the beautiful evening. For the umpteenth time, I promise to try harder to end my affair with Raphael.

And to never, ever have sex in his office again.

The first couple of months, we religiously kept our trysts out of the DCA premises. Raphael seemed as keen on it as I was. The downside was that we'd go days without seeing each other, even when he was in Paris. Raphael d'Arcy is an important man. His calendar has weeks where every single evening is taken up by a social event he can't bow out of.

I suspect some of those social evenings spill over into his nights.

But I'd rather not ask.

We broke our no-sex-at-work rule for the first time about a month ago after ten days apart. Considering that Raphael was in town only for a day, we "visited" in his office under the protection of his loyal gatekeeper, Anne-Marie.

Then we relapsed after he returned from his business trip the following week before leaving again later that day.

And then we slipped anew this afternoon.

Each of those "quickies" left my body sated—and my soul a little dirtier than before.

Because despite his unwavering interest in my person, I am *not* Raphael's girlfriend.

I'm his sex mate.

We are two single people having a secret affair. Our relationship doesn't move forward. I wouldn't even call it a relationship. It's a one-night stand on a loop. It's as if we were reenacting a porn spoof of *Groundhog Day.*

It's called *Groundhog Lay.*

Raphael seems happy with his part in it.

I'm not.

But then I'm not the one in the director's chair.

CHAPTER 13

As I enter my apartment, I'm struck by how clean and tidy it is. My hands itch to grab my phone and immortalize this rare condition. When Màma and Eva are gone and my place returns to its usual "creative mess," I'll look at those pictures and the urge to clean will consume me.

Or not.

But it won't hurt to try.

"Dinner will be ready in twenty minutes," Eva calls from the kitchen.

"What is she cooking?" I ask Màma, who's fluffing the cushions on the couch.

"Lasagna."

I close my eyes and smile beatifically. "Yum."

"She thought you'd be pleased."

Màma unfolds the ironing board and dumps a pile of colorful clothes onto a chair next to it. Looks like she did my laundry while I was at work.

Again.

She leaves me no choice but to carry out my threat

to lock up my dirty laundry inside a suitcase before her visits.

"How are you, Mia?" she asks.

"Great."

She picks up a white blouse and lays it on the board. "Can you be more specific?"

"Sure." I start unfolding my fingers. "The thesis is on track, the job doesn't suck too much, and summer is coming. As I said, everything's great."

She shakes her head. "Why is it that when I ask Eva the same question, she always has a lot more to say?"

"She's chatty." I shrug. "It's her nature."

"And your nature is to be secretive, isn't it?"

"That's ridiculous." I wave my hand dismissively. "I'm just… introverted, that's all."

She arranges the blouse over a hanger. "*Herzele*, do you think you could make an effort to tell me more?"

Herzele. My little heart. I love it when she calls me that.

"Like what?" I ask.

She hesitates. "Are you dating someone?"

As in *fornicating*?

I give her a wide-eyed stare. "Seriously, Màma?"

"You *know* what I mean." She tilts her head to the side in admonishment. "Is there a young man you like who likes you back?"

I shake my head.

"I wonder if it's my fault," she says.

"What are you talking about?"

Màma draws a heavy breath and picks up the next item from the pile. "Eva has a crush on a man who's great but inaccessible," she says. "You seem to stay away from all men as if they were dangerous beasts. Is it because of how strict Pàpa and I have been with you?

And because of how I always insisted on no intimate relations before marriage?"

Oh God.

She sighs again and places my panties on the board.

"Not the underwear!" I snatch them from her. "Please, it isn't meant to be ironed."

She gives me a forbearing look. "Of course it is."

I moan and pretend to pull my hair out.

"You didn't answer my question," Màma says, staring into my eyes.

"OK, I'll answer it." I hold her gaze. "Don't worry, Ma, your high standards and your sermons about chastity are *not* responsible for my single status."

"It's perfectly OK to date a man, you know," she says. "Pàpa and I should've stressed that point more. As long as you can abstain—and I'm sure strong-willed women like you and Eva can—you *should* date. I *encourage* you to date."

I show Màma my palms. "Need to wash these before dinner."

As I walk… er, *run* to the bathroom, a thought strikes me. The affair with Raphael aside, I haven't actually dated anyone since college. More specifically, since the *calamity*.

Just a coincidence, no doubt.

"How's Pàpa?" I ask my mother when we sit down to dinner.

I'm determined to steer the conversation away from Eva's and my private lives and to keep it there.

"His usual self," Màma says. "Volunteering as much as he can, gardening a lot, and trying out recipes from around the world. Right now we're eating our way through Cambodian cuisine."

Eva serves the lasagna.

I almost drool looking at the dish.

"Is he still involved in that refugee support project?" Eva asks.

"The one with the educational NGO?" Màma's eyes the lasagna on her plate. "Where they teach refugee women basic French and help them find jobs?"

"Yes, that one." Eva sits down and nods in a *please-eat* gesture.

Màma digs in. "Actually, I'm involved in that project, too. You know how we're both keen on helping women in need."

You certainly are.

As long as those women have good morals.

I focus on my lasagna, which is as delicious as everything Eva cooks, and let my sister and mother do the talking. At some point, I tune out, my mind wandering to the topic that's become a bit of an obsession for me recently. Raphael's *other* women.

He's never mentioned anyone, and I've never actually seen him with anyone. But every time I pick up *Voici* or another gossip magazine, there's a picture of him chatting with this model or that heiress at some posh event or other. Does he do more than chat when off camera? The man has a *reputation,* after all, and he seems eager to uphold it.

Besides, he's always made it clear he's not a "relationship" type of guy.

I asked him once if he remembered all the names and faces of the women he'd slept with.

He shook his head.

I looked askance. "What about those you saw more than once?"

He stroked his chin, thinking.

"Or do we all look the same?" I asked. "A blurred image with boobs and girlie bits?"

"That's mean." He tut-tutted.

I shrugged.

"To answer your question, yes I do." He arched an eyebrow. "Regardless of what you think of me, I love women. I believe they're the most amazing of God's creations, vastly superior to men in every way."

"Maybe that's your problem," I said. "You love women too much. And… in the plural."

He gave me a strange look, but didn't say anything.

"Your gal pals," I plowed on, unable to drop the subject. "Are they usually OK with your sleeping around?"

"The few times I stuck around long enough to ask, the answer was yes."

"Thank God for condoms," I said.

"My thoughts exactly."

"What about your lady friends having a lover on the side? Are *you* OK with that?"

He clicked his tongue on the roof of his mouth. "Good question."

"So?"

"Well, there's no reason why they shouldn't enjoy the same freedom I do. It's only fair."

I winced at his branding promiscuity as freedom. Then again, what right does a gang bang girl have to be prudish?

"That said, I doubt my partners have a need for a supplementary lover while I'm with them." Raphael gave me a smug little smile.

I rolled my eyes.

"It's just an observation," he said. "But we could do

a random test. You, for instance—do you have a lover on the side?"

"No."

"Do you feel you need one?"

I shook my head.

"See?" He grinned. "I'm enough."

I don't remember what I said to that. What I do remember is that I was too chicken to ask the question that had been gnawing at me since January.

Do you *have a supplementary lover, Raphael?*

Or am I enough?

CHAPTER 14

I stare out the floor-to-ceiling windows at Raphael's professionally landscaped rooftop terrace. Even in the dark, the effect is breathtaking, with tiny lights spattered over the plants, twinkling softly. I can hear the steady drone and the rut-rut-rut of assorted vehicles, the wail of a police car in the distance, and the laughter of diners enjoying a late meal on the sidewalk terrace beneath us.

Here on the Boulevard Saint Germain, we're smack in the throbbing heart of Paris, just a stone's throw from the Notre-Dame Cathedral. But we're also above the city inside a giant fish tank loft surrounded by a breezy oasis of green.

Raphael is making some fancy cocktails behind the slick granite bar of his open-plan kitchen.

"You sure you're not hungry?" he asks.

"Absolutely sure."

He must find that hard to believe because I'm usually famished at the end of a workday. But tonight, after my first double shift, I'm exhausted beyond hunger.

I left DCA at six, causing raised eyebrows in my office, and headed to Raphael's gentlemen's club where I managed to survive my first night as a front-of-the-house waitress.

"Survive" is a bit of an exaggeration, because—objectively speaking—the work itself wasn't hard, and the staff were friendly. Including the manager, who'd been *kindly requested* to hire me.

The real reason I'm feeling so drained is because I received my third Australian letter this morning. It was a little wordier than the first two.

I'LL BE IN FRANCE ALL JULY. GET READY.

For what?

That question has been on my mind all day. Is my mystery pen pal going to blackmail me, or is he going to post his proof all over the Internet and watch my life fall to pieces?

I let out a heavy sigh.

It was a mistake to come over to Raphael's tonight. Instead of getting into his car, I should've headed straight home and avoided a potentially unpleasant situation.

Because I won't be of any use to Raphael tonight. For the first time since January, I'm feeling too down to want sex with him. And I'm about to tell him as much.

Hearing his step behind me, I turn around. Raphael comes nearer, a tray with two tall glasses in one hand and a small object in the other. He places the tray on a side table next to the window and hands me the mysterious object.

It's a palm-sized orange box with Hermès written on it in block letters.

"For you," he says. "I hope you like it, but if you don't, it's totally fine."

"Perfume?"

He nods.

The cursive line above Hermès reads *24 Faubourg Extrait.*

I have no idea what *24 Faubourg Extrait* smells like, but I'd wager it's expensive.

I narrow my eyes. "Is this your way of saying you hate the fragrance I wear?"

He chuckles. "Quite the contrary. I love your fragrance. But since you won't tell me what it is, I tried to find something that was close."

The reason I won't tell Raphael—or anyone—the name of my perfume is that it's as far from Hermès, Baccarat, and the like as any scented liquid sold in a pretty little bottle can be.

I buy it at at my local supermarket.

Sue me.

It's cheap, fresh and flowery, and that's good enough for me. I've been wearing it for a couple of years now. And I must admit I'm tickled pink that my upper-crust lover likes it, too.

I push the box back.

"Oh, come on, Mia!" He looks flustered. "You never accept anything from me."

"Not true," I say. "I let you pay for all the drinks, meals, and getaways. I dread to imagine how much I'd owe you by now if I wasn't *accepting* that you foot those bills."

"You should see it as a form of patronage," he says. "I do it for science."

I give him a *yeah right* look.

"I mean it. The world needs your book, Mia. It

needs to learn the truth about medieval harlots."

The corners of my mouth turn up despite my best efforts to remain serious.

"They've been hiding it from us too long," Raphael adds, encouraged by my smile.

"Who?"

"You know—*they*."

"No, I don't know."

"Do I have to spell it out?"

I nod.

He stage-whispers, "The government. CIA. Wikipedia."

My sense of the ridiculous gets the better of me and I giggle.

"Finally," Raphael says. "It's becoming harder and harder to make you laugh. I must be losing my touch."

And I must be turning into a bore…

He thrusts the perfume back into my hand. "Will you at least open it and tell me if you like the scent?"

"If I open it, you won't be able to ask for a refund."

He arches an eyebrow. "Do I strike you as someone who'd bother asking for a refund?"

"Well, maybe not a refund, but you could give it to someone else."

He tut-tuts.

"Who's Genevieve?" I blurt out.

Raphael blinks, surprised by my question.

"Your brother asked you about her when I was hiding in the closet," I explain.

"I see."

"So?"

"I'll tell you if you open the perfume and tell me in all honesty if you like it."

I glare at him and remove the plastic wrapper from

the box. Opening the beautiful bottle, I spray a bit of its contents onto my wrist. Then I lift my wrist to my nose and sniff.

Mmm.

"You like it!" Raphael sounds triumphant. "Don't even try to deny it—I can see it on your face."

"I love it," I admit.

He gives me a smile that's so adorably proud I can't help smiling back.

After a few moments of grinning at each other like idiots, I set the perfume on the side table and fold my arms across my chest. "So who's Genevieve?"

"My oldest friend."

"With benefits?"

"No, it isn't like that between us. Just friendship."

"Do you fancy her?"

"No."

"Does she fancy you?"

"As I said, it isn't like that. I don't think I'm her type, anyway." He gives me a small shrug. "What's relevant here is that she's an heiress to one of France's richest families, so my money isn't what attracts her to me."

I smirk. "Because it's your money that draws women to you."

"That and the looks." He gives me a Mr. Bean-like eyebrow wiggle that cracks me up. "Certainly not my good husband potential."

"Oh yes, I almost forgot," I say. "You'll never marry."

"What's wrong with that?" He counts on his fingers. "The world is overpopulated, babies are a pain, and the future of the d'Arcy line is secured now that Seb found his match. Why on earth would I want to get yoked?"

I give him a noncommittal shrug.

"Oh, and on top of that," he says. "I take after Papa. He was a dedicated pleasure-seeker, and marriage didn't change that. If anything, it made it worse. A man like that is unqualified to be a husband and unworthy of being a father."

I look him up and down and, all of a sudden, I'm ready to raise the matter of our exclusivity.

Why now?

I don't have the foggiest, but I do know that I'm not going to *ask* for it. I'm going to demand it as a condition for our continued "visits." For the first time in months, I'm all systems go, consequences be damned. If Raphael says no, which he most likely will, I'm prepared to walk away.

"There's something I need to talk to you about," I say.

"Sandro?" He cups my cheek. "I'm extending his contract by three months. If he can pull himself together, he'll stay."

I give his cheek a loud smooch. "So there *is* a heart in that broad chest of yours!"

Raphael puts his arms around me and grins.

I take a fortifying breath. "The thing I wanted to discuss… It wasn't about Sandro."

"Someone else I'm letting go of? Mia, my *heart* won't stretch for two—"

"I want us to be exclusive for as long as we're *visiting*."

"Are you worried about catching a nasty disease?" He narrows his eyes. "May I remind you I never *visit* without protection."

"It's not just that," I say, racking my brain for a reason that won't sound too pathetic.

"Then what?"

"You see, I'm not a *sharing* kind of person."

His eyes crinkle with a smile.

I give him an *it's-the-way-it-is* shrug.

"OK," he says.

My jaw slackens. "Really?"

"Uh-huh. It won't be hard."

Now I'm not only astonished, I'm confused.

"As much as I hate tarnishing my Casanova image," he says, "the truth is I've been exclusive with you for a while. *Not* by design, mind you. It just… happened."

"Since when?"

He rubs his chin. "Christmas."

"What?"

He gives me the stupefied look of a man who just realized he's a ghost. "I know. Wow."

"That can't be true."

"And yet it is." Raphael spreads his arms apologetically. "I'm just as shocked as you are."

I put my hands on my hips. "I don't believe you."

"I'm not saying I haven't *spent time* with other women since December," he says. "But I didn't sleep with them."

I peer into his chocolate eyes, incredulous.

"I didn't feel the need for a supplementary lover," he says, giving me the funny look I've seen a couple of times before.

Unlike all his other facial expressions that I know like the back of my hand, this particular look is a mystery to me.

I simply cannot read it.

CHAPTER 15

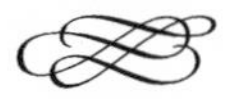

"You're a hamster," Jean-Pierre says to Delphine.

Her face falls. "Why?"

The consultant gives her an are-you-dumb look. "Based on your responses to my questionnaire."

"Are you certain?" Delphine asks.

"This test was developed by trained psychologists," Jean-Pierre says, impervious to her distress. "Don't blame the messenger."

Delphine purses her lips. "All right, I'm a hamster. What does that mean, exactly?"

"You bustle about too much. Don't work harder—work smarter." He gives her a cheerful smile and moves on to the next victim.

I hate this man.

I hate this whole ego-crushing corporate retreat imposed on everyone by the newly appointed head of HR.

It was announced to us as a "fun break from the routine," which would make the DCA staff happier, more relaxed, and more effective. Participation was mandatory, though.

Now I see why.

So far our "break from the routine" has been a modern form of the medieval pillory with lots of public humiliation and no fun at all.

We're into the late afternoon of day one—thank heaven there's only one more day to endure—and many of us are considering acute diarrhea as an exit strategy.

As soon as we'd gotten off the buses this morning and dropped our luggage in the log cabins of this exclusive facility, the fun began. Jean-Pierre stuck a name tag with a celebrity's name on it to everyone's forehead and ordered us to mingle over coffee while asking indirect questions to figure out who we are. Those who asked, "What's written on my forehead?" were subjected to torture by cookie deprivation.

That was the *icebreaker.*

After that, we did other exciting stuff such as egg catching, tree hugging, standing in a circle holding hands, and fly-fishing. But that's duck soup compared to the highlight of the retreat, which is tomorrow afternoon. In what Jean-Pierre has described as the latest inter-rank bonding trend from Japan, subordinates will share a Jacuzzi tub with their supervisors and converse.

Naked.

Thankfully, same-sex only.

And *after* taking a solo shower.

I've decided my acute diarrhea will happen tomorrow right after lunchtime.

Oh, and by the way, I'm a mole.

Not in the sense of "spy," as our Master Executioner Jean-Pierre pointed out after returning my verdict, but as in "a small burrowing mammal." That's because my test has revealed I'm too introverted and unforthcoming. According to our guru, one cannot be a good team player unless one adopts an open-door policy, including to one's private life.

"Did you notice," I whisper into Delphine's ear, "how the size of everyone's totem animal is directly proportional to their position in the DCA hierarchy?"

She considers my observation for a moment, and then her eyes light up. "Oh my God, you're right!"

She beckons Barbara and shares my finding with her.

Barbara—who, incidentally, is a mouse—gives me a thrilled look. "But of course! Why didn't I think of it? The three of us are rodents, Susanne is a zebra, Sandro is a giraffe and every manager is some kind of a large predator."

"This test was rigged," Delphine says loudly.

Several people turn around.

She folds her arms across her chest and puts her chin up in defiance.

I pull her to the side before someone from HR notices her rebellion. "Hang in there, Delph! Another half hour and we can go vent in the Chalet Bar."

"I'm so getting drunk tonight," she declares.

Barbara pats her shoulder. "Me, too."

"Me, three," I say.

At least a dozen people yell, "Amen to that!" and "Oh, yeah."

Sounds like we *will* have some team building, after all. Especially because most of the booze served at the Chalet Bar is free, courtesy of *Le Big Boss*. The food and snacks are complimentary, too. The cocktails are the only thing not complimentary. Except no one in my pay grade is stupid enough to order a cuba libre when they could gulp some free rum and wash it down with a free Coke.

"Does anyone know if the CEO is here today?" Sandro asks, refilling Barbara's wine glass.

"Haven't seen him all day," she says.

"Me neither." Delphine holds her empty glass out. "Same as Barb's, please."

"What about you?" Sandro points at my empty glass.

"I've reached my limit," I say.

Delphine claps demonstratively. "How very disciplined of you."

"It's a matter of habit," I say.

And of patently disastrous ramifications.

Sandro sets the Bordeaux bottle on the table and pours both me and himself some Coke.

That's my boy.

"I know *Le Big Boss* is in town," Barbara says. "Which makes his skipping the team-building retreat weird."

What *I* know is that he didn't want it in the first place. Raphael doesn't believe in forcing his subordinates to spend their weekends in the countryside playing stupid games with colleagues in the hopes of conjuring up *team spirit.* He believes in giving them bonuses so they can take weekend trips and choose where they go and with whom.

Or stay home and watch TV.

All of us had one such bonus last Christmas, then again in April, and we're hoping for two more this year. The collective torture inflicted on us this weekend was the brainchild of the new head of HR. The man was so convinced it would allow us to better ourselves and allow him to "figure out the team dynamic" that Raphael ended up caving on the condition he wouldn't have to participate.

He doesn't know what he's missing.

Lucky bastard.

"Maybe he's staying away to avoid getting trapped by another gold digger," Delphine says.

Barbara's eyes bulge out. "Do tell!"

"You didn't know?" Delphine frowns. "I thought it was common knowledge. That's what every new recruit used to be told—unofficially—during the orientation week."

"I heard nothing of the sort," Barbara says.

"Me neither," Sandro chimes in.

Neither did I.

"OK, listen up, children." Delphine shifts on her barstool. "Once upon a time about five years ago, Raphael d'Arcy was famous for being the twenty-five-year-old prodigy who started an innovative little audit firm and grew it into a serious company two years later."

"*That* I learned during my orientation week," Sandro says.

Delphine arches an eyebrow. "Patience, young man. The part they didn't tell you is that our whiz kid had another talent—getting any woman to sleep with him."

"That's no secret," Barbara says.

"What's wrong with young people today?" Delphine asks me.

Rhetorically, I'm sure.

Barbara rolls her eyes. "Why don't you ditch the 'old wise woman' crap and cut to the chase? You're only ten years older than us."

"What counts is that I'm old *in the company*,"

Delphine says. "Anyway, I'll give you the short of it if that's what you want."

Sandro nods. "Yes, please. The shortest short."

"Five years ago," Barbara says, "Raphael had a fling with an auditor at DCA. A month after he dumped her, she told everyone she was pregnant with his baby."

Delphine pauses and studies our faces as if to survey the effect of her scoop.

Barbara's mouth forms a perfect O.

Sandro winces. "Ouch."

I clench my fists and do my best to keep a poker face.

"Raphael said he doubted it," Delphine continues. "He asked her to do a prenatal paternity test. She refused, claiming the tests could be dangerous to the fetus."

"Did she do it after the baby was born?" Barbara asks.

Delphine shakes her head. "It never got to that. She miscarried in her fifth month."

My nails dig into my palms, slicing my skin.

"That's when things got really ugly," Delphine says. "Adele—that was the woman's name—started hinting that her miscarriage had been caused by foul play."

"Like what?" Sandro asks.

"She said she suspected a poisoned drink."

I force myself to open my mouth. "What did Raphael say?"

"He denied it, obviously, and insisted she should get full blood work and every possible test that could prove her accusations. He said he'd cover all the expenses."

"Did she do it?" I ask, trying to contain the quiver in my voice.

"Not as far as I know," Delphine says. "Instead, she

launched a new smear campaign. She told everyone at DCA she'd gotten pregnant after the CEO raped her."

"Bullshit," I blurt before I can stop myself.

"That's what most people thought," Delphine says. "It was just so over the top. Anyway, she never pressed any charges, and a month later she resigned from DCA."

Barbara leans in. "He must've paid her a lot of money to shut up."

"Maybe. Maybe not." Delphine shrugs. "But the whole thing certainly shook him."

"How do you know?" Sandro asks.

"You should've seen him then." Delphine makes a sullen pout. "That's what he looked like. Green face, sunken cheeks, no smiling. No jokes. He barely spoke to anyone."

"Well, looks like he's over it now, judging by his constant good mood these days," Barbara says.

"I think so, too." Delphine empties her glass. "But the whole thing does seem to have taught him a lesson. He hasn't banged anyone from work ever since."

Sandro gives her a surprised look. "Really? Not once in five years?"

"Not once," Delphine confirms. "I know at least a dozen women in various departments who went out of their way to get into his bed. Nothing doing." She yawns.

"So we shouldn't even bother, eh? " Barbara says.

My ears start to burn.

"That's a shame." Sandro lets out a sigh. "Given his will-bang-everything-that-moves reputation, I was hoping he'd ask me to teach him the *gay ways* as a thank-you for giving me a second chance."

Barbara giggles.

Delphine climbs down from her stool and yawns again. "Night night, children."

Thank God, she's too wasted to pay attention.

Sober, she would've never missed the bright red radish that's sprouted where my head used to be.

CHAPTER 16

"A mojito and a single malt for table two," I instruct Karim, omitting that the drinks are for the co-owner of our establishment and his fiancée.

I don't say it because I'm not sure.

When the stern-looking man in his midthirties ordered the drinks, his voice was very similar to Sebastian d'Arcy's, at least, the way he had sounded through closet doors. He resembled Raphael, too—dark haired, dark eyed and well built. Except where Raphael always looks as if he's about to crack up, this man looks graver than a news anchor announcing an earthquake.

To my surprise, he isn't so serious anymore when I return to his table with the drinks.

His fiancée, Diane—assuming that's her—has just finished saying something. And it has amused her companion. A lot. His smile grows wider by the second until it's a full-blown grin. And then it turns into rumbling, wholehearted laughter.

It *is* Sebastian. He laughs the same way Raphael does.

He leans forward and takes Diane's hand. She gazes into his eyes with unabashed affection. His face has I-love-you written all over it.

I set their drinks on the table and scurry away.

Delphine, who knows everything about everyone, told me Sebastian's fiancée used to be a checkout clerk at Franprix before he snagged her. Soon she'll be the rolling-in-money Countess d'Arcy du Grand-Thouars de Saint-Maurice.

Miracles do happen.

Maybe—just once—a small miracle could happen to me, too? Maybe the Sword of Damocles that's gotten so close to my neck I can feel its blade against my skin would vanish as if by magic. And never ever come back.

A loud sneeze distracts me from my daydream. It's Marcus, the night shift bartender, who has just come in and is heading toward the bar.

"Hi, Mia," he says before sneezing again.

I say hi and follow him to the bar area.

He doesn't look good.

"You should've called in sick," I say, putting my elbow on the counter.

"I did," he says. "But Karim couldn't fill in for me tonight."

"Sorry, *mon pote*." Karim emerges from the staff room, already changed out of his uniform. "I'm in the early days of a relationship. Can't risk her thinking I'm blowing her off."

Marcus nods. "I understand."

"But I called Raphael," Karim says. "He'll be here in half an hour or so."

Marcus blows his nose. "To do what?"

"Give you a hand, *mon pote*. You look like you'll need it."

I'm about to add that our customers will need it, too, unless they like germs in their drinks, but I bite my tongue. Poor Marcus is feeling bad enough as it is.

Exactly half an hour later, Raphael shows up in all his perky, masculine glory. He smiles, positively thrilled as he removes his jacket and tie and rolls up his sleeves. How can anyone look like that after a fourteen-hour workday is beyond me.

But, evidently, not beyond him.

He says hi to Sebastian and Diane, shakes hands with a few other patrons, and then swaggers behind the counter.

"Hello, Mia," he says before giving the pasty-faced bartender a nod. "Marcus."

"Hi, boss," Marcus and I say in unison.

"Why don't you come sit over here?" Raphael sets a chair under the wall-mounted wine rack and motions Marcus to it. "That way, you can be my prompter without scaring off our customers."

Marcus slumps down onto the chair and lets out a relieved sigh.

The next few hours are a sharp learning curve for Raphael, who discovers how limited his cocktail-making skills really are. But he puts on a brave face and does his best to follow Marcus's achoo-punctuated instructions. What he lacks in experience he makes up for in creative shaking techniques and humor.

It also helps that whenever Marcus moans "Nooo, that's too much rum (vodka, tequila, wine, syrup, sugar, lime, ice), Raphael just puts that cocktail on the counter next to a napkin that reads "Experimental / On the House."

A line of eager patrons has sprung up by that napkin, growing fast as the news of free cocktails spreads through the bar.

Sebastian and Diane leave a little after midnight. By two a.m., the bar is finally empty and we can go home.

Raphael calls two cabs—one for Marcus and the other for him and me. The poor rich man is without his car tonight. His Ferrari is at the mechanic's and his company driver was sent home with the company car several hours ago.

In the cab, I put my head on Raphael's shoulder and doze off. It's Thursday night, which means I have to be at the office at nine tomorrow morning. Any shut-eye I can catch between now and then is welcome.

A gentle rub of my shoulder wakes me.

"We're in front of your building," Raphael says.

I sit up and try to peel my lids open.

He pays the cabby, climbs out, and slides his arms under my thighs and back.

"Grab your purse," he says.

Before I realize what's going on, I'm out of the cab and in Raphael's arms.

I snuggle to his chest as he halts in front of the intercom. "Can you key in the code?"

I do.

"Which floor?" he asks, carrying me into the foyer.

"Second." I smile. "You can put me down."

He ignores me and heads to the staircase.

I try again. "I'm fully awake now."

Even if this does feel like a dream.

"I know." Raphael kisses the tip of my nose. "And I will… as soon as we're in front of your door."

When he does and I begin to fumble with the wonky lock, an inkling I've had since he lifted me up grows into a certitude. A bubbly, singing-to-forest-animals-and-dancing kind of certitude.

For the first time ever, Raphael is going to walk into my apartment.

And he's going to stay the night.

CHAPTER 17

"Shoes off," I say, switching on the light. "The floor is squeaky clean, so you can walk around in socks or barefoot."

I sit on the tiny bench by the door and remove my sandals.

Ooh, the relief.

Raphael pulls off his shoes and socks. Then he moves to the center of the room and surveys my studio apartment.

"How much are you paying for this?" he asks.

"Seven hundred euros."

"It's a rip-off."

I arch an eyebrow. "It's the market price for this neighborhood. When was the last time you paid rent in Paris?"

He gives me an apologetic look. "Never."

"Thought so."

He points to the small desk with tall piles of books and printed pages on it. "Is this where you write about the respectable and less respectable women of the Middle Ages?"

"Yep."

"Did you finish the new chapter? Can I read it?"

I nod. "Once I've cleaned it up."

Raphael turns the handle on the door next to my desk. "This must be the bedroom."

It's a broom closet.

"Seven hundred? Really?" He shuts the door. "The whole place is smaller than my kitchen. And I don't have a very big kitchen."

I shrug.

"No wonder you need a second job." He nods in sympathy. "So, where's the bedroom?"

"Right here." I march to the wall bed and pull it down. "*Et voilà!*"

"Wow. It must be black magic!" Raphael drops to his knees and stretches himself out the floor. "Madam, you must be a powerful sorceress."

I throw two pillows onto the bed and go over to my prostrating boss. "And what are you, my good sir?"

"A frog prince." He sits on his heels and puts his hands on my hips. "How do you feel about frog princes?"

"Not sure."

"Is my being green and slippery an issue?" He pulls me closer.

"It's the least of your issues."

"You're too harsh, sorceress."

He slides his hands to the front of my Le Big Ben uniform shirt, which I'd been too tired to change. With a rush of sweet anticipation, I let him undo one button after another.

"I'm not as slippery as people think," he says, tugging on the sleeves.

I help him remove the shirt. My lacy bra comes off next.

He presses his face against my tummy and spends some time kissing and licking every inch of it. I give a small "oh" when he dips his tongue into my navel.

His hands glide along my sides, gripping and rubbing. Then they move on to my back and then my ass, which they knead and squeeze with utter dedication.

I love what he's doing to me.

Careful, Mia.

Using the L-word in relation to Raphael is a no-no, even when it isn't about feelings. I must not forget who he is. My lover isn't a frog prince as he claims to be. He's a fuck prince. As everyone knows, when a fair maiden—or a sorceress, as the case may be—kisses a fuck prince, the act doesn't turn him into a real prince and her into his princess.

It turns both of them into fuck buddies.

And yet…

When this gorgeous male kneels before me, presses hot kisses to my stomach, and worships me like this, all caution flies to the wind. I run my hands through his hair as my gaze caresses the perfect lines of his strong neck, shoulders, and arms wrapped around me.

Throwing my head back, I close my eyes to savor the feel of his lips on me. My breathing becomes uneven as he slips his hands under my skirt and grips the backs of my thighs.

"Soon, my beautiful sorceress," Raphael murmurs, his voice husky, "you'll be the slippery one here."

Oh, I think I already am.

A few long moments later, he brings his hands to my

left hip and unzips my skirt. He tugs the waistband, pulling it and my panties down over my hips. I open my eyes and look at him. Raphael's gaze is riveted to my mound. It's hot with lust, dark and hungry with need.

Beware, Mia—it will scorch your soul.

When my skirt and panties pool around my ankles, I step out of them. He pulls me back to him immediately and brings his mouth down on my *very slippery* flesh. His tongue explores and strokes me, while his fingers spread me open.

I clutch his shoulders because my legs are suddenly too weak.

The orgasm that follows isn't the deepest or most intense I've ever had, but it's incredibly sweet. It's as if my loins had grown tastebuds and savored honey.

When I return to reality, Raphael is gripping my hips, arms stretched. Sitting back, his lips glistening from what he'd been doing a moment ago, he watches me.

All of me.

I stare into his eyes.

What I see in their depths makes my heart quicken. They hold lust—tons of it—but also admiration. And tenderness. So much of it that my knees wobble and I sway forward.

He props me up and levels his gaze with mine.

I gasp.

That "funny" look I'd noticed before is back, amplified a hundred times. Do I dare name it? Could it be that the admiration and tenderness in his eyes weren't just for my body, but also for my person? Is it possible that the country's most notorious womanizer has a crush on a girl from work? A girl with quirks, ragged edges, and a bluestocking level of nerdiness.

I must be imagining it.

Those double shifts must be taking their toll, making me delusional. I should know better than to let myself think Raphael d'Arcy has feelings for me. Because he doesn't. He can't. That's not how he's built. A twenty-nine-year-old unapologetic bad boy can't change his tiger stripes for someone like me.

Or can he?

CHAPTER 18

I wake up surrounded by Raphael.

His chest is pressed to my back, his left arm is under my head, and his right arm is wrapped around me. I don't dare budge for fear of disrupting the sweetness of this moment. As I lie in his arms with my eyes wide open but my body still gooey and listen to his steady breathing, a realization begins to form in my mind.

For a while, I pretend everything's fine, but my inaction allows the epiphany to take shape and grow. By the time I start shooing it away, it's too late. The bastard has made itself comfortable at the forefront of my consciousness and is opening its mouth to say something.

I begin to sing in my head, *La la la la la la. Can't hear you, can't hear you, can't hear you—*

Except I can. Loud and clear, every murmured word.

I'm in love.

Carefully, I lift Raphael's arm, roll out of bed and head to the shower. I'm going to take it cold. And long.

When I return to the bedroom, wrapped into a bathrobe, Raphael is sitting on the bed, his feet on the floor and his phone in his hands.

"Bruno just texted me. He's on standby," he says.

Bruno is his driver.

I sit down next to him. "What does that mean, exactly?"

"That he's having a coffee in the nearest bistro, waiting for my signal."

"I see."

"When do you think you'll be ready?" he asks.

"Why?"

"So I can give Bruno a heads-up."

"I'm going to walk," I say.

"Don't be silly. DCA is at least an hour's hike from here."

"Actually, it's only forty minutes of brisk walking. And it's the only exercise I get these days, soooo…"

"All right." He taps something on his phone before looking up at me. "I just told Bruno to take his time and then drive to the office without me."

I frown, confused.

"I'll walk with you," Raphael says.

"What if someone sees us?"

"They won't. We'll split where I usually let you off when we go to work from my place."

It's a great spot, actually, in the middle of a roundabout a few blocks from DCA. It swarms with office people and cars. If you're dressed for work, you immediately melt into the crowd like an ant stepping into an anthill. You're no longer a person—you're just a suit among suits.

"I don't know this neighborhood well," Raphael says as we emerge from the bistro on the corner of my street, steaming paper cups in our hands. "Will you give me a guided tour?"

I shrug. "It's super ordinary compared to yours. No sites or historical monuments to speak of."

"I'm not interested in those. What I want you to tell me about is *Mia's* Ménilmontant quarter."

"OK. Sure." I give him a bright smile. "Welcome to Mia's hood! I'll try to make your tour as exciting as it can be."

"Thank you."

"On your left"—I point to the bakery across the street—"you see one of the many wheat temples of our capital."

"So we're a nation of wheat worshippers?"

"Of course."

He lowers his brows, unconvinced.

"Picture a freshly baked, warm baguette," I say.

He shuts his eyes for a second. "Done."

"What do you want to do with it?"

"Break off a piece, smell it, and sink my teeth into it."

I smile.

"Or, if I make it home," Raphael adds, "I'll cut my baguette in half lengthwise, butter one half, layer sliced goat cheese and dried tomatoes onto it, top it with the second half, and wolf it down."

He sighs dreamily and swallows.

My lips quirk. "Now picture a rice cracker."

Raphael stares at me for a moment and then throws his hands up in surrender. "You win. I'm a wheat worshipper."

"On your right," I say, pointing to a colorful building, "is our local *médiathèque*."

"Is that a fancy multimedia library?"

"Correct."

We walk in silence for about five minutes until we reach a crossing with traffic lights.

"And this is the fateful intersection," I say.

"Why is it fateful?"

I point ahead of us. "That way is an early arrival at the office. And that way"—I point at the corner to our left—"has the best chai latte in Paris."

Raphael grins. "I can see your dilemma."

"You have no idea what I go through every morning as I wait for the green light here."

"The call of duty versus instant gratification, eh?"

I nod.

"Which one carries the day?"

I give him an apologetic look. "I'm only human."

He chuckles softly.

"Now, look at that building," I say.

Raphael looks at the classic nineteenth-century limestone façade with cast-iron balconies and wooden shutters.

"Follow my finger." I point.

"Are those…" He peers at the mosaic above the main door, blinks, and then peers again. "Space Invaders from the video game?"

"Oui, Monsieur d'Arcy."

"How? Why?"

"It's pixel street art. We owe it to an artist who goes by Invader and to his copycats."

"I love it." Raphael snaps a picture with his phone.

"Invader claims he's placed a thousand installations all over the city."

"Really?"

"I read it online," I say.

"Must be true, then."

When we reach the next intersection, I spot a bright yellow postal van and stop in my tracks.

"What is it?" Raphael asks.

"You see that *La Poste* van?"

He nods.

"It's almost *always* at this crossing when I get here."

Raphael surveys the van, looking amused.

"What's worse," I say, "it *always* stops to let me cross."

"Why is it so bad?"

"Because it feels wrong. You know how even the most polite Parisian turns into an a-hole behind the wheel? Not this guy, not once. And that gives me a creepy *Truman Show* feeling." I give him a comically panicked look. "What if my life isn't real? What if it's the *Mia Stoll Show*?"

"It's real," he says.

"Of course," I say, going around a pile of dog poo. "I know that. But here's the thing… I can't prove it."

"I can."

"How?"

He puts his hand on his chest. "I'm real."

I look at him expecting a grin but his expression is earnest. Way too earnest for the conversation we're having.

"And so is my cock," he adds, the anticipated smile finally curling his lips. "I promise it hasn't been enlarged, elongated, stiffened, or otherwise tampered with surgically or chemically."

I roll my eyes.

"And here"—he points to the postal depot on our

right—"is the explanation for the mystery of your ever-present van."

"I *have* considered it," I say. "What do you think? The depot may explain the van, but it doesn't explain the driver's unflagging courteousness."

"You know you're weird, right?" Raphael asks.

I sigh. "I'll work harder on suppressing my weirdness."

"Please don't," he says. "I love it."

I look at my feet, grinning.

A pair of fairy wings sprouts on my back, and I have to stay very focused for the rest of the walk so I don't fly.

When I get into the office and fire up my computer, there's an unread email at the top of my Inbox. Its subject line draws my attention immediately. "The day of reckoning." My hand trembles when I click it open.

> MEET ME AT THE SANDWICH PLACE OUTSIDE YOUR OFFICE AT NOON. IF YOU DON'T SHOW UP, I'LL POST SOMETHING ON THE INTERNET THAT YOU WON'T LIKE. I'LL ALSO EMAIL IT TO YOUR PARENTS.
>
> SEE YOU AT NOON.

CHAPTER 19

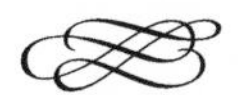

I close the email and stare out the window. My heart beats so fast my chest hurts. The inevitable has happened. Today is the first of July, and after six months of virtual threats, my blackmailer is about to show his face. It could be *her* face, too, but I have a hunch it's a man.

Will I recognize him? What will he want in exchange for his silence?

Last time I checked my bank account, I had twenty-five hundred euros. It's the richest I've ever been, but will it be enough to get him to destroy whatever "proof" he claims to have? I doubt it. I can only hope it'll be enough to keep him from posting it until his next visit.

Thankfully, today is quiet at work, so I can get away with just staring at my screen for the next three hours. Even more auspicious, Delphine and Barbara are super busy, which means no coffee-and-chat break this morning. I couldn't chat right now. And I don't think I could swallow anything without throwing up.

At five to noon I leave the DCA offices and enter the

sandwich place. It's still empty, given that the Parisian lunch break starts around one. The only customer in the eatery is a man wearing a bright green T-shirt and nursing a beer in the back of the room. He gives me a hard stare and then beckons ominously.

I plod to his table and sit across from him. "Who are you?"

"You don't remember me, do you?"

"I wouldn't've asked if I did."

"We started the same year at the *Ecole des Sciences Sociales,*" he says.

"So you were at that party?"

He nods.

"And you filmed it."

He nods again.

"Prove it."

"Sure." He pulls out his phone, taps the screen, and turns it toward me.

What I see on the screen is what I've been trying to forget for five years.

I peer at him, my mouth a hard line and my hands clammy.

"I zoomed in on your face in this sequence," he says. "See?"

I take a glance at the screen and then turn away. "You've made your point. What do you want from me?"

"Take a wild guess."

"I have two thousand five hundred euros," I say.

He sneers. "I don't need your money, Mia. I want you to be my plaything, my personal… *petite pute.*"

My little whore.

Suddenly, a light bulb goes off in my head. "I remember you! You're Gaspard—the creep who followed me everywhere in my freshman year in Strasbourg!"

His nostrils flare. "I *worshipped* you."

"No kidding."

"I thought you were an angel, with that elfin face of yours and those eyes…" He sneers. "And then I overheard you calling me exactly *that*—a creep—in front of your girlfriends."

"You deserved it! You snuck up on me everywhere, and you *stared*." I search his face. "Can't you see how an eighteen-year-old girl would feel in that situation? Put yourself in my shoes. You stalked me in the canteen, in lecture halls, in the dorm… I even spotted you in the ladies' room a couple of times!"

"Big deal." He shrugs. "I didn't touch you, did I? I just looked."

So much for getting him to relate.

"You disappeared in the second year," I say. "I thought you'd dropped out or transferred. I forgot all about you."

"Of course you did." He purses his lips. "But I didn't go anywhere. I just made myself more discreet after you ratted me out to the administration."

I survey him for a long moment.

He holds my gaze, his eyes filled with lechery so revolting it makes me gag. Just like it used to eight years ago, every time I caught him leering at me from behind a tree or a pillar.

"So, Mia," he says at length. "Do we have a deal?"

"No, we don't."

"You're being stupid."

"Why come forward now?" I ask. "You sat on this video for six years. What pushed you to take action?"

He smirks. "I went to Sydney for my third year,

graduated, landed a job, and a girlfriend—Sandy. A genuinely good girl, unlike *some*."

I ignore his meaningful glance, keeping my expression as impenetrable as I can.

"But you ruined my relationship," he says.

"*Me*? How?"

"That video… I couldn't stay away from it, couldn't stop watching you getting banged." He shakes his head, his expression bemused. "I had the wildest fantasies about you, Mia. The things we did in them!"

Panic fills my chest, but I do my damnedest not to show it.

Gaspard leans forward. "It became a bit of an obsession."

"You don't say."

He glares. "I tried to get Sandy to be more like you… I asked her to dye her hair auburn. Then I bought her green-tinted contact lenses. And then I began to push her sexually where she didn't want to go."

"Let me guess—she ditched you."

I shouldn't have said that! But I couldn't help myself.

He nods. "I could've made her stay if I had leverage. But I didn't—unlike with you."

The gleam in his eyes is borderline deranged.

Oh God.

Gaspard sits back. "After Sandy left, I wasted some time hooking up with prostitutes and all kinds of trash. They did everything I asked them to do, no problem, but… I felt shortchanged. You know?"

He bares his teeth in a sickening smile.

I turn away.

"That's when I realized I didn't have to use cheap substitutes. I could have *you*. Mia Stoll, my fantasy, the haughty slut of my dreams, was within my reach if I played my cards right. All I had to do was to find you and—"

"Blackmail me," I cut in.

"Exactly," he says without a hint of discomfort. "It took me a while to locate you, though, seeing as you're not on social media or in the phone directory."

"But you managed."

"Yeah, I did."

I force myself to look him in the eye. "I won't be your plaything."

"Listen," he says, his tone conciliatory. "It won't be as bad as you think. I won't humiliate you in public. I'm a reasonable man."

"Reasonable?" I choke back a bitter laugh. "You're a raving lunatic."

He glares. "Why don't you drop the innocent act? I *was* at that party. I *filmed* it, remember?"

"People change," I say.

"Oh please." He makes a face. "Do yourself a favor and accept my terms."

"No."

"Mia, darling," His tone becomes softer again, and even creepier than before. "All I'm asking is that you put your sweet little body at my disposal, just like you did for *three* other men at that party, once or twice a year when I'm in France. The rest of the time, you're free to fuck whomever you want."

"No," I say again.

He frowns. "You'll risk your academic career? Your job? Your pastor mom cutting you off?"

Those prospects are terrifying, indeed. Especially, the last one.

"Tell you what," he says with a saccharine smile. "Why don't you sleep on it? Actually, take the entire weekend. I'll be visiting with some family in the countryside, and then I'll be back on Monday."

It's tempting to tell him he can go to hell, but I bite my tongue.

"I can totally see how my offer may seem daunting at first." His smile grows increasingly sickening. "Especially since you expected to just pay your way out of this."

I refuse to look at him.

"But you're a big girl. You'll survive." He stands up. "Until Monday, *chérie*."

And then he marches out.

CHAPTER 20

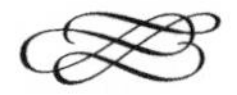

I return to the office and format the news bulletin with my brain functioning on autopilot. When I'm done, I email Pauline that I'm unwell and won't be able to compile the international politics section today.

Then I shut down my computer and leave.

As I walk home, barely aware of my surroundings, I collide with a woman who stopped suddenly in front of the *médiathèque*. I apologize. She smiles, pats my arm, and tells me it was her fault.

She's very pregnant.

A chill runs down my spine as I take in her rounded belly and realize I missed my period in June.

That means I haven't had it for almost two months.

It could be nothing.

It has to be *nothing.*

I repeat those words in my head as I purchase two pregnancy tests at the pharmacy on the corner. I keep repeating them until I pee on the white stick and it gives me a smiley face.

I do the second test, and the stick smiles at me once more.

So, it *isn't* nothing.

I wash my hands and pick up the tweezers on the little shelf under my bathroom mirror.

How is this possible?

Raphael and I never had sex without protection. Not once.

Absently, I study my face in the mirror and tell myself my eyebrows could do with some trimming.

I pull out a hair.

Ouch.

This is almost as painful as Brazilian wax. How can women do this daily?

It's common knowledge that condoms only work ninety percent of the time. Given how much sex we've had since January, I should've asked my OB-GYN to put me on the pill.

I pluck more hairs on each side.

If I'm really pregnant, I could just go to a hospital and get an abortion. Thankfully, you can do that in France without a problem.

I study my thinned eyebrows in the mirror. They're uneven.

Man, I'm crap at this.

I have another go at the left eyebrow.

Raphael never wanted this to happen. He doesn't want a baby or a family. He doesn't even want a regular girlfriend. What's happening to me isn't his fault, and it won't be fair to make it his problem.

My left eyebrow is a thin line now, the way women wore their brows in the seventies. I'd better fix the right one so they match.

I'll have an abortion.

And then I'll become creepy Gaspard's long-distance sex slave to make sure my dirty secret stays under wraps and Màma and Pàpa never see that video.

Or, I'll take a chance on Raphael and tell him the truth. All of it—the gang bang, the blackmail, the pregnancy. *The whole enchilada.* He'll probably think I'm just like that auditor, Adele. A gold digger out to trap and use him.

I'd rather die than have him think that of me.

Alternatively, I could just carry on and do nothing.

My brows now have holes in them and look like dotted lines. I pluck some more until I'm staring at a woman with no eyebrows.

I bare my teeth at her and wave.

Hello, everyone. I'm Mia Stoll, the slutty freak.

Here's what will happen if I do nothing. The fetus inside me will grow and become a baby. Raphael will despise me. Gaspard will email the video to my parents. They'll be devastated. They won't want to see me again.

I put the tweezers back on the shelf and walk out of the bathroom.

Actually, there's one more thing I could do.

Disappear.

PART II

CHAPTER 21

From: Eva Stoll

To: Mia Stoll

Subject: What's up?

Hey Little Sis,

So how's life in sunny Martinique? Are my friends taking good care of you? Did you get the job? Did your thesis supervisor agree to the long-distance thing?

I went over to Alsace last weekend. Màma and Pàpa had received your postcard. They must have read it so many times they'd learned it by heart before putting it in the center of the family-room mantelpiece. They're a bit puzzled by your "quarter-life crisis," as you described it, but they say they're happy if you're happy.

Most importantly, they haven't received any emails from Gaspard. I'd wager he hasn't posted the video on the Internet, either. He was bluffing, Mia. He's a cheap, sad, pathetic loser who tried to play smart and failed. Now he knows you're gone, and he doesn't have your postal or email address. No more *leverage*. In a week or so, he'll return to Australia with his tail between his legs. I hope he understands that the Stolls don't negotiate with blackmailers!

Hugs,

Eva

~

From: Mia Stoll

To: Eva Stoll

Subject: Martinique

Hi Evie,

Life is good here, as good as it gets under the circumstances. It rains a lot, but the showers are warm, and they don't last long. I love the sun, the sea, the beaches—all the stuff that makes me feel like I'm on an extended vacation somewhere in the Caribbean. Oh wait, I *am* in the Caribbean! And yet I'm still in France. Everyone speaks French, all the signs are in French, the TV is in French, not to mention all the familiar restaurant chains and shops. I love it.

Sandrine and Henrik have been so very kind to me. I don't know how I'll ever pay them back. You're lucky to have friends like that, and I'm lucky to have a sister like you.

And now, drumroll please… I got the job! I can't believe how easy the whole thing was. Starting next Monday, your fugitive sister will be a substitute history teacher at one of the Fort-de-France junior highs. The other great news is that Professor Guyot agreed to the "distance thing," even if it wasn't quite kosher. We'll do our tutorials over Skype. This means I'm still enrolled in my PhD program and still on track to defend my thesis in a year.

You have no idea how happy I am to hear that Gaspard hasn't carried out his threats—at least, not yet. It's a load off my shoulders.

xoxo,

Mia

~

From: Eva Stoll

To: Mia Stoll

Subject: News

Congrats on your new job and on Professor Guyot's leniency! Well done, baby sis.

You won't believe who called me the other day. Sebastian d'Arcy. He introduced himself, apologized for bothering me, and then inquired after you. I had no idea he knew about your existence. Or mine, for that matter. Anyway, as per our script, I gave him the yada yada about your impossible-to-refuse job offer in Quebec. Then I went off script and asked if he was calling because his brother was "heartbroken."

I'm sorry but I couldn't help myself.

Sebastian said he doesn't seem to be and added that, in fact, Raphael is in such high spirits one might think he was consuming if one didn't know him better.

I asked him why he called. He was silent for such a long time I almost hung up, but then he said never mind and something about his wife being right about him worrying too much. After that, he said good-bye and hung up.

Wasn't that *weird*?

That's a rhetorical question, by the way. What I really want to know is if being far away is helping you forget Raphael. I hope it does. Maybe I should do the same to get over Adam…

And now for the most important question. Are you still pregnant or did you go through with the abortion plan?

Love,

Eva

~

From: Mia Stoll

To: Eva Stoll

Subject: RE: news

Hi Eva,

I'll answer your rhetorical question first. :-) Sebastian d'Arcy's call *is* weird. But it's good to know Raphael is doing great. When I texted him that I was moving to Canada, he replied, "Good for you! Appreciate the heads-up." I thought he was being sarcastic.

But now it looks looks like he meant it.

As for my getting over him, it's a work in progress. To speed it up, I read self-help books. It's called bibliotherapy, and you should definitely try it to help you get over Adam.

Another trick I've found is buying tabloids, where I almost always find photos of him in the company of dazzling creatures. I put a finger on his face and focus on the women, trying to guess which ones he has or will sleep with. And if I catch my finger caressing the paper, I bite it really hard.

It's brutal, but it's necessary.

To answer your most important question—yes, I'm still pregnant. I don't think I can go through with the abortion. Not because I suddenly feel Raphael should have a say or anything like that.

I'm not too eager to be a mom, either.

If I miscarry, it would be a relief. A *huge* relief. But I'm almost three months along now, and the amalgamation of cells in my womb already has a heart. A tiny little beating heart, Evie. Blame it on our family background and education or my stupidity, but that means something to me. The critter is a product of *lovemaking*, not of mindless drunken sex or rape. I just can't go to the hospital, have doctors silence its heartbeat, and then carry on with my life as if everything was fine.

It's one of those "damned if you do and damned if you don't" situations, and it looks like I'm going to go with a "don't."

xoxo,

Mia

CHAPTER 22

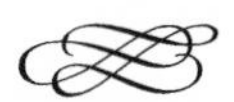

FOURTEEN MONTHS LATER

If I'd known how much being back in Paris would mess with my supposedly healed heart, I would've prepared better. I would've obtained a homeopathic prescription in Martinique and made sure I was on the highest permissible dose throughout my stay. Then, maybe, I wouldn't be seeing Raphael on every corner, and I wouldn't be thinking about him as a fellow scholar tells me about his work.

I force myself to tune in.

"It took as long as *six months* for the uprising to blow over," Xavier says.

"Really?" I do my damnedest to figure out what uprising he's talking about and why.

Xavier nods. "I couldn't return to Mali and finish my fieldwork until last October."

"Bummer."

He spreads his arms. "That's what happens when your study subjects live in an unstable country."

I smile. "My subjects have been dead for centuries. Which is great for keeping my work on schedule."

Xavier chuckles.

He has a shrill, almost girlie laugh you wouldn't expect from a tall man wearing chunky boots and a lumberjack shirt.

"So what class are you teaching, *maître*?" I emphasize the last word, hinting at his official title, *maître de conférences*—associate professor.

My teasing is a little hypocritical, though. I'd be thrilled to land a *maître de conférences* contract once I have my PhD.

"I hope to teach my own class soon," he says. "But for now, I conduct seminars for Professor Bosc's Introduction to Sociology."

"It's a great course. I took it in my third year."

I steal a glance at my chest to check for wet stains around my nipples.

So far so good.

"So you did your undergrad studies here in Paris?" Xavier asks.

I nod. "First two years in Strasbourg, then I transferred to Paris."

"How long did you stay in Martinique?"

"A year. The plan is to return there after the defense." I glance at my chest again.

Still dry, but not for much longer, I'm afraid.

"Listen, I need to dash to the bathroom." I give Xavier an apologetic smile. "Will you stall Professor Guyot if he comes out during my absence?"

"You bet."

"Thanks! I'll be right back."

I bolt, scolding myself all the way to the bathroom for my absent-mindedness. In my rush to get to the *école* this morning, I forgot to slip nursing pads inside my bra. That means the milk oozing from my boobs might seep through my underwear and stain my blouse any moment now.

I hate this part of breastfeeding.

What I don't hate is the act itself. Watching my *herzele* latch onto my breast, close her eyes in bliss, and derive nourishment from me is pure joy. We started solids recently—Lily is six months old now, and the doc said it was time—but I plan to breastfeed her twice a day for a few more months. It's good for her well-being.

And for mine, too.

I wipe my nipples and line the cups of my bra with toilet paper. This should tide me over. Professor Guyot should finish his class anytime now, and when he does, we'll talk. Then I can go pick up Lily from the day nursery.

Fingers crossed he has good news for me.

I've been in Paris three weeks now, and I still don't have a date for my defense. It was supposed to take place last Wednesday. But then one of my two rapporteurs lost her father, and the whole thing had to be postponed.

"He's still inside," Xavier says when I return, almost running, and sit down next to him on the bench.

"Phew. Good."

"You must be bummed about your defense last week," he says.

"I am."

"Mine had to be rescheduled earlier this year. My supervisor broke his leg."

"How long did you have to wait?"

"Two months."

I drop my head into my hands. "Oh no."

"You may be luckier," he says before adding, "even though I hope you won't be. Selfishly, I hope you'll stay in Paris as long as possible."

I look up at him, surprised.

He holds my gaze as if to say, *yes it* is *like you think.*

What the what?

We met two weeks ago through Professor Guyot. Xavier is a sociologist. I'm a historian. Our mentor is both, and he involved us in his new seminar on "Research Methods in Sociological History." The seminar is for PhD students and postdocs only, so participating in it is a great learning opportunity. And great fun. Our group is small enough to fit around the long table in the café across the street where we end up after each session to finish our debates around a drink.

I had no idea Xavier had taken a more than academic interest in me.

"I have a baby," I blurt my new anti-pickup line of choice.

He looks at my ringless hands. "Are you still with the father?"

I shake my head.

"Then there's no issue. Babies don't bother me at all." He smiles. "In fact, I love them."

Right.

Thankfully, the door to the lecture hall opens and Professor Guyot steps out.

"Hello, Mia, sorry I made you wait." He nods to Xavier before turning back to me. "Every single student had a burning question to ask after today's lecture."

Xavier and I say good-bye, and I follow Professor Guyot down the hallway.

"Can you walk with me to the Raspail Annex?" he asks. "I don't want to be late for the faculty meeting."

"No problem."

Please let it be good news!

My current arrangement is so precarious I won't be

able to keep it up much longer. I'm renting an Airbnb studio in the twelfth. It's cheaper than a hotel room, but it's still double my rent back in Martinique. I was lucky to get a place for Lily at the nursery just two blocks down the street. Like this, I can take care of all the administrative stuff and attend seminars. But the cost of the studio and nursery is burning through my meager savings like a swarm of locusts through a field of corn.

Staying in Paris beyond October is out of the question.

"I have two pieces of good news for you and one bad," Professor Guyot says as we leave the building. "Which one do you want to hear first?"

"Why don't you sandwich the bad news between the two good ones?" I suggest.

He nods. "OK, good news number one. I arranged for you to co-moderate one of my grad-level workshops. You'll get a small contract for the rest of September and all of October."

My eyes widen. "Really?"

"It isn't much," he says, smirking, "but it'll see you and and your baby through until your defense."

"Do we have a date for it?" I ask.

"We do—and that's the bad news."

He stops at a traffic light, turns, and gives me an apologetic look. "The only time Mathilde, myself, and the rest of your committee are all available again is the third week of November."

"That's in two months."

The light turns green, and we start walking again.

"I know," he says. "And that brings me to the second bit of good news. The history department will have a *maître de conférences* opening next month."

"But…" I mumble as we turn onto the Boulevard

Raspail. "I won't have my doctorate until November. Assuming everything goes well."

"It will, I'm sure."

We reach the Annex and climb the steps to the entrance.

"You did a fantastic job with your dissertation," he says as we halt in front of the revolving door. "Everyone on the committee loves it. Even Mathilde loves it—and you know how hard it is to impress her."

It's near impossible to impress Mathilde.

I was obliged to ask her to be on my committee because she's a top expert in my field. But I was fully prepared to have her rip up her copy of my thesis during the public defense and announce it's the only fate this kind of BS deserves.

She's done it to other candidates before me.

Professor Guyot smiles. "I talked to the administration, and they're willing to sit on the vacancy announcement until mid-November."

"This is…" I search for words. "It's too good to be true."

He shakes his head. "No it isn't. You still have to apply and do well at the interview, which I have no doubt you will."

"Thank you so much, Professor—"

"Please. Off you go." He glances at his watch. "I'm already five minutes late."

"I… I *really* appreciate everything you're doing for me!"

"It's no trouble at all." He sighs. "After the faculty meeting, I'm seeing another doctoral student of mine, and that conversation is going to be a lot less gratifying than this one."

He flashes his card to the security man and marches inside.

I run down the stairs, eager to get back to Lily, cozy up with her at home, and call Eva with the good news.

Could my life finally be getting on track?

CHAPTER 23

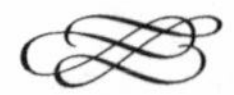

"Mia? Hey, Mia!" someone calls just before I descend the stairs to the *métro* station.

I turn around.

Sandro looks me over and then throws his arms around me. "*Ça alors!* What are you doing here? Why didn't you write you were coming to France?"

"I… I was going to," I mumble.

And I really was. During my stint at DCA, Barbara, Delphine, and Sandro had become more than colleagues. When a year ago I announced my imminent departure, they insisted on a going-away dinner at Delphine's and made me promise to stay in touch.

Toward the end of the evening, Delphine cornered me as I was exiting the bathroom. "Are you OK?"

"Yes, why?"

"I heard you barf in there."

"I'm bulimic," I lied.

"*Mais bien sûr.*" She tilted her head to the left. "And I was born yesterday."

I held my chin up, refusing to say more.

Thankfully, she didn't insist—she just shook her head and stepped aside to let me return to the dining table.

In her first two or three emails after I left Paris, she reminded me she wasn't buying my story, but then dropped the subject.

Sandro and Barbara never questioned my irresistible job offer tale.

I look at my watch and then at Sandro. The day nursery closes in forty-five minutes.

"Are you in a hurry?" he asks.

I smile apologetically.

"No problem," he says. "Are you free to join your former colleagues for lunch on Friday? Barb, Delphine, and I are having a special one to celebrate my promotion."

I high-five him. "Go Sandro! I'm so happy for you!"

"So you'll come?"

"What's the venue?" I ask, hoping it isn't the the canteen.

Not that Raphael eats there often, but I'm not taking any chances.

"We're venturing to La Coupole," Sandro says.

Phew.

La Coupole is spicy, but it's far from DCA.

I give him a big smile. "I'll be happy to join in the celebration."

We say good-bye, and I rush down the stairs.

When Lily and I get home and I call Eva, she's over the moon about my news.

"That means you're staying in Paris," she shouts. "And I'll be able to see my little niece every weekend if I want!"

I hold the phone away from my ear while she hollers

in French, English, and German. "*Youppi*! Woohoo! *Techtelmectel*!"

That's international civil servants for you. After three years at the European Space Agency, Eva feels compelled to repeat her French interjections in the other two working languages of her organization.

"Is Raphael still in the dark about her?" she asks all of a sudden.

I clear my throat. "He has no clue about her existence, and it's better this way."

"If you think so."

"I *know* so."

"I take it you haven't told him you're in Paris, either?"

"No. And I'll kill you if you do."

"Are you going to try and cook for me again?" she asks. "The dinner you made when I visited you in Fort-de-France almost killed me."

"No, I'll tickle you this time. I'll start with your neck, then move to your armpits and finish with your feet."

"Mercy," Eva squeaks. "Not the feet! I'll do anything you want me to, just don't tickle my feet."

"I want your silence."

"Don't worry, I'll keep your secret." Her voice is back to normal. "But you'll have to tell Màma and Pàpa about Lily sometime soon, real soon."

"I know."

"How about you take her to Alsace next weekend?"

"I'm not ready."

"OK," she says. "I understand. But the longer you wait, the harder it'll be for them to forgive you for hiding her."

"What makes you think they'll forgive me for *having* her in the first place?"

Eva scoffs. "Don't be silly."

"I'm being realistic. You know what Màma thinks about having sex and making babies outside of wedlock."

"She'll change her mind the moment she sees Lily."

"I don't think so." I let out a sigh. "And what about Pàpa?"

"What about him?"

"You know what *he* thinks about… women like me."

"No, actually, I don't."

Shit.

Of course she doesn't. How would she? She had slept like a baby through both chapters of the Suzelle the Sinner Affair.

"Never mind," I say.

"No, tell me. I insist."

"Lily just woke up," I lie. "Can we talk about this later?"

"OK." There's a brief silence before Eva speaks again, "Anyway, I'm really happy you're staying in Paris. Martinique may be lovely, but it's so damn far away."

We hang up, and I tiptoe to the kitchen. As I start peeling potatoes for our dinner, I take care to make as little noise as possible so I don't wake up Lily, who's napping in the main room behind a folding screen.

My *herzele* is a light sleeper just like me.

Which is probably the only feature she and I have in common at this point. She hasn't inherited my auburn hair or green eyes. Neither does she have Raphael's darker coloring. Lily is a blue-eyed, curly-haired blonde with a skin like porcelain.

I bet she's going to turn heads, which may be the only thing she and her dad will have in common.

How many heads has Raphael turned since I left? Is

he still a committed *bad boy* or did he meet someone special? Does he think of me sometimes?

Damn!

I can't believe I'm doing this again. Were all those self-help books and auto-suggestion drills for nothing? *Moving On* was the title of the first one I bought. *Wipe Him Out of Your Memory* was the second. *How to Get Over Your Ex in Three Months* (with a Money Back Guarantee) was the third and most expensive one I read.

It's been fourteen months, for Christ's sake.

Maybe I should ask for a refund.

Except I won't get it because even though I did everything the books recommended, I failed to implement the number one strategy all three insisted on. Dating someone new. I'd been planning to, and there had been opportunities, but I always had an excuse to put it off.

At the beginning, I told myself I'd just gotten there and was busy settling in. Then my belly started to show, and it completely killed the mood. Once Lily was born, I put everything else on hold and spent three months being her appendage.

When she became a little more autonomous, I had to finish my dissertation and make arrangements for the defense.

And then I travelled to Paris.

Wait—I could date here.

I slap my forehead. It's a brilliant idea!

A new man in my life is what I need to free me from the "Raphael Syndrome" once and for all. And that new man could be Xavier. Why not give him a chance? We have so much in common that it would be hard to find a more suitable man.

It's decided, then.

For the sake of my sanity and, by extension, for Lily's sake, the dating strategy deserves a try.

No, it deserves my best shot. I nod with determination as if to seal the deal and start dicing the zucchini.

And then someone knocks on the door.

CHAPTER 24

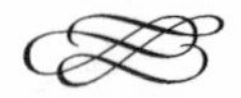

I freeze.

Breathe, Mia.

It could a neighbor. Or the postman. Or the landlady who realized she had something urgent to tell me, just after her phone battery died.

The school administration has this address, too.

Except no administration goes knocking on people's doors at seven in the evening. It doesn't go knocking at any time of the day, for that matter. It *summons* you instead, preferably at eight a.m., just for the pleasure of making you wait outside a locked door.

"Who is it?" I ask.

If only this stupid door had a peephole and this stupid building, an intercom!

"It's Raphael," a familiar voice comes from the other side.

My knees wobble.

Several physiological processes kick off in my body, making me lightheaded, queasy, burning hot, chilled to the bone, scared, and thrilled beyond words—all at the same time.

"Mia?" he says. "I'm sorry I didn't call first. Will you let me in?"

I bite my nails. "You should've called."

"Oh, I would've, but you changed your number," he says. "And you didn't give me the new one, remember?"

The familiar note of humor in his tone makes me smile. For some strange reason, it makes me want to cry, too.

"Listen," Raphael says. "I have no bones to pick with you. I'm sure you had your reasons for preferring the beaches of a tropical island to the drizzle of Paris. I'd live on an island, too, if I didn't have a company to run."

I smile, remembering the rocky island pictures on the walls in his loft.

Then I realize he knows I wasn't in Quebec.

"Why are you here?" I ask.

"Just for a chat… as a friend. For old times' sake."

This is the perfect opportunity to say, *Sorry, Raphael, but I've really moved on,* and wish him all the best.

"How did you find me?" I ask instead, opening the door.

Momentary madness is the only explanation for it.

Over the past fourteen months, I'd gotten so used to putting the words "far away" and "long ago" next to "Raphael" that I tricked myself into believing he lived in a parallel universe. Raphael d'Arcy became a hunky humanlike life-form I'd met in a time-space loophole. But then the loophole got fixed, and I returned to reality with Lily as proof that the whole thing hadn't been just a dream.

And now here he is—the hunky life-form.

My ex-boss and ex-lover.

My baby's dad.

The man I ran from.

The man I would die for.

I take in his tall, lean, hard-bodied frame. He looks exactly like he did a year ago and yet a little different. I'm not sure what that difference is. Is he taller? That's an impossibility. Brawnier? I don't think so. Scruffier? Nah. Must be just in my head.

"Wow," he says, stepping in. "You've changed."

I raise my eyebrows.

"Your hair is shorter," he says. "*Way shorter.*"

He reaches over and rakes his fingers through my pixie cut.

"It's convenient to wear it short," I say, drawing back.

He pulls his hand away and surveys me some more.

"Anything else?" I ask with as much sarcasm as I can manage.

"Your eyes are greener than I remembered." He strokes his chin, looking me up and down. "It's little things… I can't even put a finger on anything specific right off the bat."

I shrug. "Keep me posted if you do."

He nods.

For a few seconds we just stand by the door and stare at each other.

It dawns on me that this moment right now is my second—and probably last—chance to say, "Listen, it was good to see you, but I really need to run, so bye and take good care of yourself."

Only who am I kidding?

All the willpower and resolve I possess are barely enough to keep myself from throwing my arms around his neck, closing my eyes, and tipping my head up for a kiss.

I spin around and head for the kitchen.

He follows me.

"How did you find me?" I ask.

"Through your school."

I turn around and give him a quizzical look.

"I've been following your progress over the past year," he says. "Just out of curiosity and because it's so easy with the Internet. You published three articles, which I read."

My brows go up.

"Quiz me if you don't believe me," he offers.

"Maybe later." I narrow my eyes. "But the *Internet* doesn't know my current address."

"Your school does, though. I was looking you up last night—you know, just to see if you'd published something new for me to read, and I saw you were moderating a workshop in Paris."

"Co-moderating."

"Right." He nods. "With your supervisor. Anyway, once I knew you were in Paris, finding your home address was a matter of ruse and money."

"You didn't try to find me while I was in Ma—Canada," I say.

"Actually, I did," he says. "And that's how I knew you were in Martinique. I almost flew there in February, but then I reminded myself you'd dumped me."

Dumped him?!

"You weren't my *boyfriend* to dump," I say.

He looks taken aback, but then his expression softens. "You're right, of course. 'Dump' wouldn't apply to our case. What about this: You notified me via a text message that our exclusive arrangement was terminated with immediate effect due to your delocalization?"

I smile. "Sounds about right."

Raphael looks around the kitchen. "You were cooking."

"Uh-huh."

I am *not* going to ask if he'd like to stay for dinner. Anyway, a dinner of steamed veggies and mashed potatoes isn't something Raphael would enjoy.

"Tell me something." He steps closer. "I'm just curious. One moment you were saying you wanted us to be exclusive, and the next moment you were gone. That doesn't compute."

I shrug. "Breakups rarely do from the perspective of the ditched party."

"Touché." He smiles. "Mind if I steal that line for my next splitsville?"

"Knock yourself out."

"Can I ask for something to drink?"

"There's a can of Coke in the fridge," I say, tossing the diced veggies into the steamer. "Maybe even a beer, hiding in the back."

He pulls out the Coke and the beer. "Bingo!"

"I don't have a clean glass," I say. "But I can offer you a teacup."

He shakes his head. "I'll drink from the can. Which one do you prefer?"

"The Coke."

"Good." He hands me the can. "At least some things have remained the same."

I set the can on the table.

He raises his beer. "Cheers."

"Hang on a sec."

I move to the half-sized dishwasher and fill it. Given

the limited amount of tableware in this kitchen, I have to wash the dishes all the time.

"Done!" I press a button on the front of the machine and keep an ear out for its starting noise.

The dishwasher ignores me.

"Not again, you *beerflaschebrunzer*!"

"Another one of your select Alsatian epithets?" Raphael asks. "What does it mean?"

"The one who pisses into the beer bottle," I say, opening the machine and retrieving the dirty dishes.

"That's very… apt." He squints at me. "Can I help you do the dishes?"

"You can help me fix this bastard," I say. "The landlady showed me what to do when this happens."

"I await your orders, ma'am," Raphael says.

I point at the dishwasher bottom. "Can you unscrew and remove that plastic filter?"

He squats in front of the dishwasher and unfastens the filter.

I begin to rinse it. "Now look for chunks."

"Where?"

"In the drain."

He gives me a quizzical look.

"It'll be tricky because you'll be searching blind. But fear not, there are no piranhas in there. Just dip a finger in and wiggle."

His face crinkles up with amusement.

I smile condescendingly. "You've never done this sort of thing before, have you?"

Raphael clears his throat. "Dip a finger in the hole," he comments, as he plunges his index finger into the pipe. "Wiggle blind."

Why are his lips twitching?

He tilts his head to the side and gives me a mischievous look as if to say, *can't you see how this is funny?*

"What?" I ask.

"I do believe I've done this sort of thing before," he says. "And I believe you were there, too."

"Oh," I breathe out.

That.

Just as heat starts creeping up my cheeks, Raphael shouts, "Yes!" and pulls a small chunk out of the drain.

It could be an apple heart, I note before he tosses it into the trash can.

I reload the dishwasher and press Start.

The machine is silent for a second and then it begins to grind.

I let out a sigh of relief. "Ah. Music to my ears."

"I know what's different about you," Raphael says. "Apart from the diminished hair and the enhanced eye greenness."

I put my hands on my hips. "What?"

"That." He points at my hands. "Your posture. It's different. And you're more muscled."

That's from carrying Lily in my arms half the night when she had colic.

"It's from swimming," I say.

I've done that, too… a couple of times.

"I love your new posture and your muscles," Raphael says.

Lily chooses that precise moment to wake up and wail.

I rush to her cradle.

"Mommy's here; everything's fine," I say, fumbling for her pacifier.

Raphael tiptoes in and halts behind me.

I turn my head to see his expression. He looks stunned.

"You have a baby?" he asks, frowning as if something doesn't add up.

"It would appear so."

"Who..." His voice cracks. "Who's the father?"

Lily is still crying, so I pick her up. "I wish I could tell you he's a Klingon from Kronos, but he's just a man."

Raphael's fists are clenched and his breathing is visibly strained as he studies my little girl. He must be computing in his head and dreading the possibility that the baby might be his. *Poor man!* If I tell him the truth, he'll feel he'd been used again, tricked into parenthood by an unscrupulous sex partner.

It would mean *I* am that unscrupulous sex partner just like Adele.

"Relax," I say. "Lily's dad is back in Martinique."

"Lily," he repeats, staring at my baby.

"I named her after my favorite grandma."

"So you jilted the father?"

"We broke up by mutual agreement."

He nods. "How old is she?"

"Four months," I lie.

"I don't know much about babies, but I would've given her six. At least."

"Her father is very tall," I say. "She's his spitting image."

He nods again, visibly calmer.

"Can I hold her?" He attempts a smile.

I turn Lily around and sniff. "Maybe some other time. I think she's done a poo."

He studies her diaper-clad posterior. "Are you sure

it's poop? Maybe her diaper just slid down and... bunched under her butt."

I lift her closer to his face. "Smell it."

"Ugh." He grimaces and turns away.

"Told ya."

"It could also be gas," he says.

"Here's a rule of thumb with babies." I set Lily down on the floor to get her change mat. "If it looks like poop and smells like poop, then it's poop."

"Ah," he says. "Mia and her rules of thumb. You haven't changed that much, after all."

"Raphael and his rule of the middle finger," I say. "You haven't changed at all."

CHAPTER 25

As a uniformed maître d' leads me to Sandro's table at La Coupole, I admire the art deco murals of this legendary brasserie where Joséphine Baker once came with a lion cub and Marc Chagall celebrated his last birthday.

I also take the full measure of how nervous I am about today.

First, because the DCA gang—especially the perceptive Delphine—is bound to ask me questions I'll have to skirt. Second, because Xavier, whom I'm seeing later this afternoon, might attempt hand-holding or other forms of physical contact for which I'm not ready yet.

Barbara throws herself at me with such force I sway. "Mia, you bastard, how long were you going to keep your return from us?"

She gives me a bear hug and then moves away to make room for Delphine.

"I'm sorry, guys, I really am," I say as I embrace Delphine and then then Sandro.

Delphine arches an eyebrow. "We might forgive you if you tell us *everything*."

And that's exactly what I do over the next hour. I fill them in about my life in Martinique, my upcoming defense, and the co-moderated workshop. I also tell them about Lily, feeding them the same version of her origins I gave Raphael. Who knows, if I repeat it often enough, maybe I'll start believing it myself.

"So her dad stayed back in Martinique?" Sandro asks. "Is it really over between you two?"

I nod.

"I had a romance like that, too, a couple of years back," Barb says, her eyes dreamy. "It took just three or four weeks before my rose-colored glasses fell off. But while it lasted, I was crazy about the guy."

"Sounds like your glasses were colored by horniness more than roses," Sandro says.

Barbara shrugs a perhaps.

I glance at Delphine, who's been suspiciously quiet.

She's eyeing me with an impish look in her eyes, and I know exactly what she's trying to communicate.

You can fool those two, ma cocotte, *but not me.*

Thankfully, she doesn't say it out loud.

We say good-bye at two-thirty on a promise to do this again in a couple of weeks and that I'll bring Lily along so they can meet her.

At a quarter to three, I'm in front of the main entrance of the Montparnasse tower for my rendezvous with Xavier, who hasn't arrived yet. Fifteen minutes later, he climbs off his bicycle, secures it with a U-lock, and heads toward me. He's right on time. It's me who got here early, having almost run the short distance from La Coupole. I suspect I'm too eager to get this dating thing started… and over with.

Argh!

I shouldn't think that way. What's the point in trying to date someone if I'm already looking forward to the end of the experiment?

Xavier seems to be such a great guy.

He says he loves children. He volunteers for several humanitarian organizations. Whenever he can, he participates in antiwar rallies, and he has recently purchased an indoor worm composter. It's a container filled with worms that eat organic waste, and it's perfect for apartments as an alternative to outdoor composting. Xavier claims the worms stay inside the container. He told me everything there is to know about it in minute detail after Professor Guyot's workshop last Monday.

A man like that deserves my best effort.

And I'll be damned if don't give it to him. Raphael's impromptu visit two days ago won't make me change my mind.

"So what's the plan?" I ask after we cheek kiss. "I have two hours."

Annoyance flickers in his eyes. "Why so little?"

"Lily," I say. "The nursery closes at six, and I need an hour to get there, factoring in the usual *métro* suspects like suspicious packages on the platform, electricity outages, and personnel strikes."

He smiles. "The trade unions haven't announced any strikes for today."

"Did they also promise no abandoned backpacks?" I ask, smiling back.

"Unfortunately not."

"Then we have two hours."

"OK," he says. "Let me think. I wanted to take you to one of the charities where I volunteer, then to the recycling cooperative, and then to a café."

"Pick one."

"Let's do the cooperative." He gives me a determined nod. "Maybe you'll find something nice to buy in their shop."

I wish he'd picked the café.

Shame on me.

A recycling cooperative is of course a much better choice.

Fifteen minutes later, Xavier opens the door to a folksy-looking shop, and we walk in. Introductions and handshakes ensue, after which Xavier gives me a tour of the premises.

"These are made in Senegal from recycled plastic bags." He points at a selection of god-awful pocketbooks that cost a fortune.

"Nice," I say.

He picks up a wallet with a splashy yellow-green pattern reminiscent of vomit. "Would you like to buy one? It's Fair Trade Certified, like everything here."

"Um…" I give him an apologetic look. "I don't need a wallet."

He puts the item back on the shelf.

I wonder why I felt compelled to apologize. Why didn't I just say the wallet was ugly as hell and not worth a quarter of the price the cooperative charges for it? Out of politeness, no doubt. I don't know Xavier well enough to be frank. It'll come.

As we continue the tour, he shows me more objects that are as hideous as they are useless. I say "nice" every time, itching to ask if the shop ever manages to sell anything. But I bite my tongue. The cooperative must be one of those outfits that exist as long as they're funded and dissolve as soon as the grant dries up. Purchasing their products is an act of solidarity with workers in developing countries rather than regular shopping.

I should be ashamed of myself.

"This key ring is lovely." I point to the cheapest object, which is as "lovely" as a pack of hyenas feasting on a carcass.

He follows my gaze. "It was made in Somalia."

"I'll buy it."

Xavier's expression brightens.

Phew.

I can't get out of the shop quickly enough.

"We still have forty-five minutes," Xavier says after we wave good-bye to his buddies. "How about a coffee?"

I beam. "Good idea."

A few minutes later, we're seated in the back of a dimly lit bistro. "I hope you enjoyed the excursion," Xavier says. "Next time I'll show you the homeless shelter I volunteer for."

"I'd like that."

Liar.

"And maybe another time," he says, "we could hang out with your baby so you won't need to rush home?"

"Sure," I say.

And I almost mean it.

We order two espressos.

"Did I tell you I practice tantric yoga?" he asks.

"Sounds impressive."

"You don't know what that means, do you?"

"Nope," I admit.

"It means I have such control over my body I can last forever during sex."

"Oh." I stare at my hands on the table. "That's... nice."

I've said "nice" at least a hundred times today.

Xavier covers one of my hands with his and strokes his thumb across my palm, slowly and deliberately. I let him, trying to figure out if I like it. There's no reason why I shouldn't. Xavier is attractive, and *good*, and I haven't been touched by a man in over a year.

There's a pattern to his stroking… It's a spiral… Clockwise expanding, then a straight line, then counterclockwise shrinking.

Must be a tantric thing.

He lets go of my hand, bounds around the table, and sits on the bench next to me.

I wonder what he'll do next.

He lowers his head and begins to tongue my earlobe.

I stiffen.

He continues with a redoubled zeal.

That makes me think of my early days with Raphael, when we were still learning each other. My freezing like this would've stopped him short. Unlike all the other men I've kissed, made out with, or had sex with, Raphael pays attention to nonverbal feedback.

Maybe he's a freak.

I draw back and give verbal feedback to Xavier. "I don't like ear licking."

He looks stung, as if I said something mean.

That's a shame.

I wish he'd just say, "Note taken, I won't do that again," and move on, like Raphael would've done. I wish he weren't so heavy going and earnest.

I wish Raphael hadn't ruined me for everyone else.

CHAPTER 26

It's nine on a Saturday morning and Lily is still asleep, bless her sweet little heart. Me, I'm wide awake. It's been a long night. The few short bouts of sleep I managed to catch where filled with weird dreams. In one of them I kissed Raphael who turned into Xavier who turned into a pixelated space invader.

Gah.

My first date with Xavier had been a total flop.

Before we said good-bye, he insisted on meeting Lily and that we take her to the Jardin du Luxembourg or Tuileries on Sunday.

I said this Sunday wouldn't work.

Not that I had any plans. It just felt too soon. Or maybe it was the image of Xavier, me, and Lily strolling in the park together like a family. That just felt… wrong.

We *should* try that sometime—he's totally right about it—but I guess I'm not ready yet.

Anyway, there's no rush. I have other, more important matters to take care of.

The positive outcome of my sleepless night was that I made up my mind. Next time I call Màma and Pàpa, I'm going to tell them about Lily, consequences be damned.

Eva is right—I can't put it off much longer. The excuse that I'm too busy to go to Estheim is old, seeing as I've been back in continental France over a month now. Last time we talked, Màma hinted she and Pàpa were planning a little Parisian vacation in October. My confession had better happen *before* that vacation.

It will *happen before that vacation.*

I rub my eyes and drag myself out of bed.

Someone knocks on the door.

Raphael.

Please, let it be him!

"A little early for a second courtesy visit," I say as I open the door and stare at his sexy, clean-shaven face.

I hope my enthusiasm doesn't show.

"Are you referring to the time of day or the time of year?"

"Both."

He nods and steps inside. "With all the excitement from fixing your dishwasher, I forgot to get your number last time."

"Why would you need my number?"

"So I could invite you and Lily to come with me on a little weekend trip."

I blink.

"This weekend," he says.

I blink again.

"It wasn't planned."

I fold my arms across my chest.

He screws up his face, eyebrows roof-shaped, sexy as hell. "Will you come?"

"No."

"Please?"

"I have other plans."

He unleashes his ultimate weapon—the sad-puppy look. "Can your other plans be postponed?"

"Why is it so important?"

"Because…" He hesitates. "I managed to get my closest friends *and* Sebastian and his wife to clear their schedules."

I shake my head in disbelief. "Why? And… where to?"

"So they can meet you… on a Greek island south of Crete."

"The one in the photos in your apartment?"

"Ninossos," he says with a nod. "It's even more beautiful in real life. I hope you'll like it."

I rub my forehead as if trying to prevent my thoughts from scattering all over the place. "I don't know what to say."

"Say yes." He smiles. "I promise there's no hidden agenda, no expectations, no strings." He gives me a wink. "I'm a conscientious objector to strings, as you know."

I do.

God, this is tempting.

"All I want is for you to have a bit of fun," he says.

"Why do you care?"

"Honestly?" He shrugs. "No idea."

"OK," I say, hardly believing my own words. "Why not? Lily and I will tag along."

He plants a kiss on my forehead, then turns around, and heads to the door. "I'll pick you up at ten thirty"

And then he's gone.

~

He was right—Ninossos *is* even more gorgeous in reality than in those beautiful prints on the walls of his penthouse.

I take in a deep breath of air that smells of seawater and several other delicious things I can't identify and put Lily back in her stroller. She was agitated earlier, so I left Raphael and his friends to finish their lunch on the patio of his villa and took Lily for a calming walk. I had to promise him we'd stay in the vicinity of the house and be back in fifteen minutes.

You'd think the island was swarming with wild beasts.

The wildest creature we've met so far was a sea gull.

The flight to Ninossos was quick and easy, Lily's incessant crying notwithstanding.

"This is Mia and Lily" was how Raphael had introduced us to everyone before we boarded the jet. No other qualifier or explanation—just "Mia and Lily." The responses to that laconic presentation ranged from Sebastian's nod to Diane's bear hug. When she let go of me, she asked if I'd let her hold Lily, and as she gently took her from me, I realized she was pregnant.

Between those two extremes were the firm handshake from Raphael's buddy Cedric and the contactless cheek kiss from his bestie, Genevieve.

Yes, *that* Genevieve.

Finally, I had the honor of meeting Raphael's oldest friend, who turned out to be a refined creature in her late twenties. Clearly, his equal in both status and money. Also, probably the only woman in his life he's been faithful to, if not in flesh then in spirit.

She looked vaguely familiar. Maybe I'd seen her before in Raphael's bar without knowing who she was.

Despite their different greetings, all four guests had one reaction in common. They stared at Lily longer and with more intensity than a regular person would look at a baby. The expression on their faces was that of a person trying to solve a puzzle. I knew exactly what that puzzle was.

Is this baby Raphael's?

As I push the stroller, I wonder what conclusion each of them had arrived at.

By the time I'm back at the patio, Lily is fast asleep.

I set the stroller in the shade and return to my place around the table. The catering service Raphael has hired so we could "just chill" brings out coffee and dessert.

He apologizes to Genevieve, with whom he was chatting, and comes to sit next to me.

She glances at me with so much hatred it feels like a sharp punch to my face. I gasp, incredulous, and take a second look at her. Genevieve lifts her teacup to her lips without the slightest hint of emotion on her serene face.

I must have imagined it.

"I saw Noah yesterday," Genevieve says.

"Where?" Sebastian and Raphael ask in unison.

"At the Tintin exhibit in Grand Palais. A friend of mine dragged me there." She picks up a *canelé* and bites off half of the miniature pastry. "Mmm."

"Noah's always been a huge fan of Tintin," Raphael says with a smile.

Sebastian's gaze is hard when he turns to Genevieve. "Did you talk to him?"

"First, I wasn't sure it was him," she says. "Last time

I saw him, he was a child. But I thought I'd try my luck, so I asked him if he was Noah d'Arcy."

Raphael's expression is now as grave as Sebastian's. "And?"

"He said, 'Noah Masson, why?'."

"He uses Maman's maiden name these days," Raphael says.

Genevieve nods. "I knew that, so I introduced myself."

She puts the second half of her *canelé* in her mouth and chews slowly.

"Come on, Vivie," Raphael urges. "Don't keep us hanging."

"Sorry." She smiles. "I told Noah his brothers were hoping he'd return their calls. He said he was hoping you'd gotten the message by now. And then he said good-bye."

Raphael and Sebastian exchange a look full of frustration and disappointment.

"Fine," Sebastian says, wiping his mouth. "I'll stop reaching out. He can continue living like a bum, renting a shitty rathole in a shitty neighborhood while his trust fund is collecting dust and his castle in Burgundy is falling into disrepair. Not my problem."

Raphael lets out a sigh.

"My theory is he doesn't want any part of the d'Arcy fortune for ideological reasons," Genevieve says. "Maybe he's become a left-wing radical like Diane—except he actually lives by his principles."

Ouch.

I feel bad for Diane, whom I like. I've been trying to like Genevieve, too, despite the pangs of unwarranted jealousy, but that's finished now.

Diane stares at her, poker-faced.

"My wife has never been a radical," Sebastian says, giving Genevieve a smoldering look. "And trust me, she *does* live by her principles."

"I have another theory," Cedric says. "Noah's behavior isn't political. It's religious. He's joined a sect which believes the meek shall inherit the earth."

"I believe the *mice* shall inherit the earth," Raphael says. "Or rather, the rats."

Everyone smiles, looking relieved. The conversation had been turning way too serious for a weekend lunch.

We chat for another half hour about this and that, until all the *canelés* and macarons are gone and the coffee pots are empty.

Right on cue, the caterers return to clear the table.

One of them is a pretty young woman whose skirt is much shorter and tighter than her colleague's. Her shirt is unbuttoned far enough to show the front clasp of her bra. She plants herself across from Raphael and sets her tray on the table. As she loads it with empty cups and plates, she bends down so that her breasts are practically in his face.

I steal a glance at him, fully expecting him to be enjoying the view.

But he isn't even looking in that direction. He's turned toward Cedric on his left, talking investments and financial markets.

This is weird.

The Raphael I used to know wouldn't necessarily flirt with every woman who hit on him, but he would definitely acknowledge her.

There's one possible explanation for this. Something is wrong with him. So wrong, it's changed his personality.

Maybe he's dying.

Raphael shifts closer to me, and I feel his hand on my knee.

OK, he *isn't* dying.

Without interrupting his conversation with Cedric, he slips his hand under the hem of my skirt and trails it up my inner thigh, fingers splayed. As he progresses, hidden from sight by the tablecloth, the hairs on my body stand on end and my pulse quickens. By the time he reaches the edge of my panties and cups me, I'm soaked.

This is my undoing, and I know he knows it.

When I agreed to "tag along," I suspected how today might end. How Raphael might want it to end. With the two of us in bed together.

The shameful truth is I want it, too.

Worse, I need it.

So badly I wonder how I'm going to make it through the afternoon.

OK. Fine. Bring it on.

At least I'm sure of one thing—there's no way I'm relapsing into a dead-end affair with Raphael. I won't let it happen—for Lily's sake, if not for mine.

But selfish as it may be, I can't… I *won't* deny myself a night with the man I still love.

The man I never stopped loving.

A whole night to kiss and be kissed. To feel him enter me, move inside me. My stomach clenches just thinking about it. My body is so hungry for him it's hard to sit still and not push against his hand.

Patience, Mia. Tonight.

He'll make love to me tonight. I'll kiss him, touch him everywhere, bite him, and lick him to my heart's content. After I come, I'll run my hand through his thick, wavy hair the way I used to do. And then I'll fall asleep against his naked body.

The best part?

Sunday morning, I'll wake up in his arms.

On this gorgeous island.

Outside of time.

CHAPTER 27

Looks like we aren't going to make it through the afternoon.

As soon as everyone leaves the patio and disperses around the island, Raphael goes to the still-sleeping Lily and begins to push her stroller toward the house. I follow. He carries it up the stairs and down a hallway before entering a room where he parks it by the wall. Then he takes my hand and leads me to the adjacent bedroom.

The window is open, and even though the sea is hidden from view by the linen curtain, I can smell it.

"We'll hear her if she wakes up," Raphael says, gathering me into his arms.

God, it's good to be in his arms again!

So freaking good.

He takes my chin between his thumb and forefinger and tips it up.

For a few moments, I stare into his eyes, spellbound.

"I want you so much, Mia," he whispers. "In every possible way."

I put my arms around his neck and stroke his nape. "What are those ways, *cher monsieur*?"

"You want me to list them?" He trails the pad of his thumb over my lips. "For starters, I want you in bed on your back."

"How old-school."

He smiles. "Old-school is the best way to get you where I want you. It's your favorite position, if memory serves me right."

"It is," I admit.

He kisses my forehead. "After that I want you to ride me."

"I'd like that," I say, feeling decadent and safe at the same time.

The way I always feel with Raphael.

His hands roam my body. "And then I'll take you standing, your palms on the wall and my hands on your tits."

Yes, please.

He begins to rain kisses on my nose and cheeks. "I want you in the hot tub, too. And on the rooftop of the villa on your hands and knees. Also on the beach, spread open like a starfish."

"That's *a lot* of ways, *cher monsieur*," I say with a sassy smile.

"That doesn't even scratch the surface." He kisses my lips. "I want the entire fucking Kama Sutra with you, Mia."

I sigh in fake resignation. "Do your worst."

You have until Monday.

We undress faster than ever before, tearing off each other's clothes as if they were contaminated. A few moments later, we're completely naked, staring at each other shamelessly in broad daylight.

"Your breasts are bigger," he says, eyeing them appreciatively.

"They'll deflate to normal once I stop breastfeeding."

"I see." His gaze zeroes in on my mound and he touches his fingers to it. "You used to be waxed here. Smooth and silky."

"And now I'm—"

"Bushy," he butts in.

"*Au naturel*," I finish my sentence.

"Letting yourself go, huh?"

"No." I arch an eyebrow. "I just prefer myself this way."

He flashes me a saucy smile. "But *I* prefer you smooth."

"Tough shit," I say. "I'm done with waxing. All that pain and hassle—just not worth it."

"Are you serious?"

"Absolutely." I touch my fingertips to his lower abdomen, just above his jutting manhood. "Here's the scoop—grown women have pubic hair just like men. Regardless of what porn movies would have you think."

"I know, but—"

"I'm done with Brazilians."

He gives me a pretty-please look.

"Raphael, darling, you're a grown man… sort of." I pat his cheek. "Deal with it."

He leans his head into my palm. "You've become very authoritative."

"Have I?" I shrug. "Motherhood does that to you."

A moment later, he lifts me in his arms and takes me to the bed where he lays me down on my back as promised. His eyes are riveted to me as he climbs onto the bed and begins to caress his way down my body. I revel in the sight of the muscles on his arms and chest. When he bends down to place hot kisses on my tummy, I feast my eyes on the shape of his back.

Oh, how I missed that!

How I missed *him*.

Raphael stretches out next to me, his body touching mine, and I tremble with want. I stroke a hand across his broad chest, remembering his skin, his smell, the bulges of his pecs, and the tiny buds of his nipples. When my hand slides to his heart, I rest there for a while, absorbing his pulse.

"Mia," he murmurs.

As I caress his hard stomach, my fingers skim the tip of his erection. He lifts his hips to goad me on. But, even though I'm a wet mess of need, I don't want to rush this. Every moment of this afternoon is precious, and I intend to cherish it.

So I press a kiss to his neck and start gliding my hand back up to his chest.

He catches my wrist over his belly button.

My heart ratchets up as he grips it and holds my hand still.

For a moment, we stare into each other's eyes, and then he pushes my hand back down.

"Touch me," he gasps. "I'm dying for your touch."

I wrap my fingers around his thickness.

He moans.

I startle at the intensity of the tug deep within my own groin, wondering how much longer I can bear not having him inside me.

And then suddenly, within what seems like a second, he sheathes himself, nudges my thighs apart, and enters me.

I arch underneath him with the joy of it.

"Let's get the first one out of the way," he says, bracing himself on outstretched arms. "Then I can go as slow as you want for the rest of the Kama Sutra."

I nod.

He looms over me for another moment, as his smile fades and his gaze grows dark. And then he slams into me.

I groan with pleasure.

Soon, our bodies move in synch, just like they used to, finding their perfect rhythm. We cling together as he drives into me, and I rock my hips to meet his thrusts.

When Raphael seeks my mouth and pushes his tongue between my teeth, I begin to spiral toward my climax. My vision grows hazy, but I force myself to keep my eyes open so I can watch his beautiful body toiling and sweating as he pounds into me without holding back.

I clench the sheets in my fists.

My body writhes and my heels press into his buttocks, spurring him on.

When I spasm around him, my legs shake uncontrollably.

He groans and collapses on top of me.

I welcome his weight.

I need it.

A few moments later, he presses a kiss to my cheek and moves to roll away. But I'm not ready to let him go yet.

"Stay a little longer," I murmur.

He finds my hands and laces his fingers with mine. "I'll stay as long as you want."

CHAPTER 28

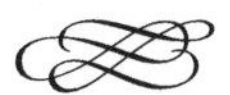

Raphael is a morning person, so I kind of knew the part of my fantasy where I wake up in his arms might not happen. Based on prior experience, it occurred no more than twenty percent of the time.

The thing is I'm a hopeless night owl. Especially these days, when I get up for Lily once or twice during the night.

Last night was no exception.

Her whimpers woke me up at around three. She wanted her pacifier and my company. I know that the right thing to do is to let her cry herself back to sleep. It's the only way to tell her mommy won't be getting up for her in the middle of the night anymore. I've read several clever articles and a whole book on the subject. All of them guarantee that baby stops waking up at night after a couple of weeks of such treatment.

I'm definitely planning to try it… some day.

The truth is I love those cuddle sessions as much as I hate being woken up in the middle of the night.

I glance at the clock on the wall. It's ten.

As I begin to envisage getting up, the door to the en suite bathroom opens and Raphael ambles in naked except for a towel wrapped around his hips. His dark hair is combed back and damp from his shower. I take all of that in as I arch my back and stretch my limbs. He halts by the bed. With an appreciative smile, I clasp my hands under my head and survey him.

Yummy.

I eye his handsome face, lingering on his lips and breathtaking jawline. Then my gaze travels to his broad shoulders and sculpted chest and further down to his hard abs. A fine line of black hair runs from his belly button down into the towel. My breathing grows shallow. I expect him to unwrap the towel and lie next to me, but when I level my gaze with his, he's grinning.

He opens his right hand to show me something.

It's tiny, fluffy, and pink.

And it's a pair.

Lily's socks.

"I stopped next door to check on Lily and found these on the floor," he says. "What a ridiculous size."

"You should've seen her newborn socks six months ago."

He arches an eyebrow. "You mean four, right? Seeing as she was born only four months ago."

Crap.

"Yes," I say. "Of course. I mean four."

He doesn't press the matter further.

I wonder if he believes me. Probably not. But whatever suspicions he might harbor on Lily's account, he's choosing to respect my choice and keep them to himself.

Unless it isn't from respect but from his preference to remain childless and family-less. A preference he's voiced clearly and repeatedly many times.

Raphael pulls one little sock over his left ear and the other over his right ear. "Do I look good?"

"Perfectly silly," I say.

"You're being socksist."

I raise my brows.

"Haven't you heard about sockers?" he asks. "I converted while you were in Martinique. My religion prescribes that I wear pink socks on my ears at least ten minutes every day."

I roll my eyes.

He sits down next to me, his expression growing sober. "We're gonna go exclusive, like the first time around, right?"

I look away, my mouth refusing to tell him there won't be a second time.

"No," I finally say.

His mouth gapes, then flattens in comprehension. "You're seeing someone."

I nod.

"Is it serious?"

"I don't know yet," I say honestly. "We're sort of colleagues, and I've only had one date with him."

He gives me a forced smile. "OK, then. I hope you choose *me* before you reach the five-date threshold with him. Assuming you still adhere to *that* rule of thumb."

"I do."

He shakes his head, incredulous. "I never dreamed Mia Stoll would agree to a non-exclusive arrangement, let alone *ask* for it."

"There won't be any arrangement between us this

time around," I say. "What happened here was a one-off."

He gives me a long, hard stare. "You can't resist me, Mia. We both know that."

"Then don't put me in a position where I have to resist," I say, my voice cracking with emotion.

"Why are you so hell-bent on driving me away when you want me so much?"

"Because you're toxic."

He flinches at my epithet.

"That came out meaner than I intended." I sit up and cup his cheek gently. "What I wanted to say is that I'll never be able to fall for another man if you stick around."

His eyes bore into mine. "When you say you won't be able to fall for another man, does that mean you've fallen for me?"

I study a speck on the sheet.

"Does that mean you're in love with me, Mia?" he asks.

I nod, my gaze still on the sheet.

"Then let me ask you this: Why are you so hell-bent on falling for another man if you're in love with me?"

"Because…" I give him a pleading look. "Don't you see how we're after completely different things? All you want from a relationship is a fun time. You won't even call it a relationship, for Christ's sake. You call it an *arrangement*."

I lift up my chin, daring him to say I'm wrong.

He doesn't.

"I want more than that," I say. "A lot more. I want something solid and long-term. And that means I need to find a man who wants the same thing."

A part of me hopes against hope he'll say, "That's my wish, too, Mia. I've changed. I want to be there for you and Lily."

When he opens his mouth, my muscles are so tense with apprehension it's surprising they don't snap.

"I see," he says.

I hang onto a glimmer of hope a little longer, but he doesn't add anything to his "I see."

Slowly, I breathe out, hiding my disappointment the best I can.

That's when my handbag beeps on the floor at the foot of the bed.

Saved by the gong.

I rush to it and fish out my phone.

"I'm expecting an important email," I lie and click on the notification on the screen without reading it.

The message that opens up makes me forget my letdown. It makes me forget to breathe. I read it once, then once more, and then a third time in a crazy hope it will melt away before my eyes. But it doesn't. If anything, its words appear bigger and their lowercase letters scream louder than the caps of Gaspard's one-sentence notes a year ago.

Hello, Mia.

You thought you could just change your phone and email to make this go away, didn't you? You should've changed your name.

I'll be in Paris next week. I know you have your defense coming up, so you won't run again.

Meet me next Saturday at noon, in the same diner. If you don't show, the tape hits the Internet, and I mail it to your parents the same day.

You will not get a third chance.

So, choose wisely this time.

Gaspard

CHAPTER 29

After breakfast, Cedric pulls Raphael aside to pick his brains about some business-related matter. I use the opportunity to head to the beach with Lily and a book. My plan is to play with my baby, read, and try to relax. I'm aware it's a shaky plan, given the distressing effect of Gaspard's email, but I'm determined to do my best to enjoy this beautiful island a little more before we fly back to Paris.

A half hour into "reading" without registering a word, I shut my book and sit up.

Diane sits down next to me. She picks up Lily's Sophie the Giraffe teether and plays with her for a while, making my little girl giggle.

Then she turns to me and smiles. "You know, I recognized you the moment I saw you at the airport. I'd seen you a year go at Le Big Ben."

"I recognized you, too," I say, smiling back and pointing at her rounded belly. "Five months?"

"Six."

"Boy or girl?"

"Wait and see." She gives me a wink before adding. "I'm so glad *you* are the woman who tamed Raphael! I feared he'd end up with—oh, never mind. It doesn't matter now."

"I've tamed no one," I say. "As for Raphael, he's untamable."

"He was. Before you."

I smirk. "You want to know the truth? A year ago, Raphael and I had a fling. Then I went away. Now that I'm back, he wants more of the same. An 'arrangement,' as he called it. That's all."

"Is Lily his?" she asks.

I blink. "You're… direct."

"I'm sorry." She gives me a pleading look. "Please disregard my question! My curiosity will be the death of me."

"She is," I surprise myself by saying. "But that's not what I told him."

"Your secret's safe with me," she says.

Inexplicably, I believe her.

She runs her hand through Lily's feathery curls. "Do you think he believes whatever it is you told him?"

"He didn't say anything to the contrary."

"It doesn't matter what he said." Diane smiles as Lily grips her thumb and pulls it into her mouth. "What matters is what he did. He brought you and Lily here, to his sanctuary, so you could meet his brother and his closest friends."

I dig my hands into the sand, processing her words.

Diane gives Lily a soft kiss and sets her on the towel.

"Don't judge Raphael by his words," she says, standing up. "He uses them to disguise his feelings. Judge him by his actions."

And with that, she saunters away.

As I ponder her advice, Genevieve turns up by my side and points to where Diane sat a few minutes ago. "May I?"

"Please."

Did I unwittingly occupy everyone's favorite spot on this beach?

"Nice weather, isn't it?" Genevieve asks, leaning back and stretching her slender legs.

I nod. "Just perfect."

"I looked you up," she says, turning to me. "You're a medievalist."

"Yep."

"I remember you from a year ago."

"I waitressed at Le Big Ben for a few weeks." I smile. "Didn't realize I'd made such an impression on Raphael's friends."

"He dumped you like he dumps everyone," she says. "But then he took you back. Why?"

My smile begins to slip.

"What's your agenda?" she asks.

I stare at her, too unsettled to respond.

She stares back. "Actually, you don't need to answer that. Your plan is transparent enough."

"Is it?"

"You're hoping to snag him, like so many before you." She shrugs. "And you're using your baby as bait."

On impulse, I pick Lily up and wrap my arms around her in a protective gesture.

"Listen to me carefully, Mia." Genevieve leans toward me. "Raphael may charm the hell out of you, but he'll never marry you."

We're in agreement on that point.

"Do you realize he's so much more than just a rich and handsome playboy?" she asks.

As it happens, I do.

Raphael is bright and great at what he does. Despite his breezy persona, he cares for his company and works his tail off to grow it. He's hilarious, but never at the expense of others. He's a Casanova all right, but he doesn't cheat or lie to the women he sleeps with. Come to think of it, he's one of the most honest people I know.

"He's nobility," Genevieve says. "And so am I, for your information."

"For your information, this is the twenty-first century."

"*Et alors?*" She lowers her eyelids in contempt. "The world is still run by a select few. Raphael is an heir to one the country's oldest and wealthiest aristocratic families. Do you know his full name? You *must* know it, seeing as you worked for him."

I look away.

"Besides, he and I have a pact," she continues. "If we haven't fallen in love by thirty-one, we'll get married."

I glance at her face to check if she's serious.

"And that day is fast approaching," Genevieve says, deadpan.

I shrug. "So what's the problem? You'll have him all to yourself soon enough, if your pact means anything to him."

"It does." Her left eye begins to twitch. "We're perfect for each other, and he knows it. We're both rich, influential, and cynical. There's a reason I'm his best friend and his *only* female friend."

"Good for you," I say.

"He despises the women he sleeps with."

I say nothing.

"We'll be *the* French power couple of the century

once we're married," she says, pushing her hair back.

I lift my chin up. "Then why do I get the feeling you're scared of me?"

She points at Lily. "Is she his?"

"That's none of your business."

"Even if she is, your plan won't work," she snarls. "I'll make sure he sees you for what you are. You're a cheap gold digger like that woman Adele, who went around claiming he got her pregnant."

I wrap my arms tighter around Lily.

"I'm positive the baby wasn't Raph's," Genevieve says. "Regardless, I was happy the bitch miscarried."

Did you help her miscarry?

"But then she started saying he'd raped her." Genevieve rolls her eyes. "Pathetic fool."

I stroke Lily's hand. "I've heard she suddenly up and left."

"She left because I gave her a good incentive." Genevieve's eyes light up. "I could pay you, too. Name your price."

"You can keep your money," I say.

She glowers at me. "Oh, I see. You think you're smarter than Adele. You think you'll get more from him than from me."

My mouth contorts with disgust.

"OK, then." Genevieve stands up and folds her towel. "I'll keep my money, but I'll give you a free tip. Take your bastard and disappear."

"And if I don't?"

"Then I'll do what it takes to protect Raphael from garbage like you."

With that, she picks up her designer beach bag and heads toward the villa.

I stay on the beach, entertaining Lily with her

favorite buzzing bee game and hoping to compose myself before I go back to Raphael and his nearest and dearest. *Easier said than done.* I lay Lily down on the towel, and stretch out by her side. There isn't a hint of a cloud in the sky, and the breeze is so gentle it makes the Mediterranean Sea sound as docile as the pond in the Jardin du Luxembourg.

What a contrast to the turmoil inside my head!

Twenty minutes later, I admit that composure is beyond reach, even on this island. Why, oh why didn't I stay put in Martinique? My ambition to get the darn PhD brought me right back to the two men I'd run from a year ago. And now it feels like I'm living a déjà vu, wondering which one of them will hurt me more: Gaspard, on purpose, or Raphael, without meaning to?

I collect my things, buckle Lily up in the front carrier, and trudge in the direction of the house. Just as I reach the hedge around the patio, Geneviève's polished voice reaches my ears. Her words are less polished than her accent.

"Bullshit," she says.

There's a brief silence, and then she speaks again. "But what about our pact?"

"What pact?" Raphael's voice is soft.

"To get married when we turn thirty-one." Genevieve's voice cracks. "When we talked about it a few months ago, you failed to notify me you'd unilaterally rescinded it."

"We *joked* about it a few months ago! Oh come on, Vivie, we were kids when we made that pact."

"We were eighteen."

"Exactly—kids," Raphael says placatingly. "I always thought of it as a standing joke between us, and I was sure you saw it the same way."

"Well, I didn't."

"I don't get it," he says. "You *know* I'm not a marrying man. The whole world knows that."

"Yes, but I thought… I thought our bond was special. We're cut from the same cloth, Raph. You always agreed with that."

He says nothing.

"Don't you see how much sense it makes for us to get married?" Genevieve asks.

"No, I don't. We haven't even dated, for Christ's sake!"

"We could."

"We won't."

There's another silence.

"Jeez," Raphael says. "Vivie, I had no idea…"

"Then you're stupid," Genevieve clips. "But cheer up. Your Mia is smarter than than the two of us together. She's definitely going places."

"What does that mean?"

I hold my breath.

"We just had a nice long chat, she and I," Genevieve says. "I offered to pay her to fuck off—"

"You—*what*?"

"You heard me right. I offered her money." Genevieve's voice trembles with repressed fury. "And you know she said?"

"What?" Raphael asks coldly.

"She said, 'Keep your money. You'll never be able to offer me more than I can squeeze out of Raphael.' "

Lily chooses that precise moment to sneeze loudly.

When I reach the end of the hedge and step onto the patio deck, Genevieve is gone, and Raphael gives me an unreadable look before turning on his heel and marching inside the house.

CHAPTER 30

Having made it through today's seminar without falling asleep is a small miracle, given that I didn't sleep last night. At all.

We landed in Paris late in the evening after a bumpy flight that kept Lily wailing nonstop.

Raphael drove us home.

We barely spoke.

When he parked the car and helped Lily and me out of it, I was a hairbreadth from telling him that Genevieve's words were a shameless lie. But I didn't. Nor did I invite him to come upstairs.

He drove off without asking when he could see me again.

How ironic.

I'm making sure it's really over between us, which is just what Genevieve wants. Granted, I'm doing it for my own selfish—and less selfish—reasons.

The idea of watching the man I love hook up with other women is unbearable. Regardless of the mistakes of my youth, I deserve better than that. My baby deserves better than that.

Raphael deserves better, too.

Neither of us had wanted a child, but once pregnant, I changed my mind. I *chose* to become a parent, and I neglected to ask Raphael's opinion. So now, it isn't fair to rob him of his choice *not* to have a family. And if he ever changes his mind about it, shouldn't he have the option to pick a wife with a past to be proud of, and a future unmarred by public disgrace?

Honestly, I don't know if these are good reasons to deny myself the love of my life and to deprive Lily of her birth father.

But in the end, reasons don't matter.

Just like it doesn't matter how much I regret having taken part in that gang bang years ago. What matters is that someone taped it and is blackmailing me once again with his tape. While I'll never give him what he wants, there's nothing I can do to stop him from punishing me for my lack of cooperation.

"You look preoccupied," Xavier says, touching my hand. "I'm blabbering on about my conference paper while your mind is somewhere else. Is something wrong?"

He had implored me to stay for a chat after the post-seminar coffee with Professor Guyot. I agreed. He chatted. I nodded without registering a word of what he was saying.

And now I'm ashamed of myself.

Xavier is a good person. Aside from Pàpa, he's the most ethically conscious and morally solid man I've ever met. And while my stupid heart refuses to transform that appreciation into attraction, I hope we can enjoy a true friendship. The kind that could, one day, turn into something more.

And to lay the foundation of that friendship, I'm going to tell him about the blackmail.

Besides, this thing will drive me crazy if I don't confide in someone I can trust. Normally, I'd call Eva. But she's in Florida until next Monday where she's organizing a big international conference on manned flights. These types of trips are always crazy busy for her. She works around the clock, starting at six in the morning and dropping dead after midnight. There isn't a worse time to burden my sister with my problems than now.

The thing is I need to burden *someone*. And who better than Xavier to share the weight?

I draw a long breath and give him the lowdown.

"Have you seen the video?" he asks after I'm done.

I nod.

"So it's real—not something he's invented so he can sleep with you?"

"It's real."

"Can I see it?"

I need a moment to process his unexpected request. "Why?"

"So that I can… you know…" Xavier shifts in his seat. "See how bad it is."

"What for?"

"To… er… assess the potential damage."

"It has closeups of my face and other parts, if that's what you want to know."

Is that *keenness* I discern in his eyes? No, it cannot be.

"Anyway," I say. "I don't have a copy."

"Are you sure?"

I tilt my head to the side. "Let's say I did have a

copy. Let's say you viewed it and ascertained it was as bad as I said it was. Then what?"

"I don't know." He sits back. "I won't turn my back on you, if that's what you're worried about. But I might… be less understanding of your desire not to rush things."

What?

"Let me get this straight," I say. "Are you saying you expect to have sex with me now that you know what kind of woman I am?"

He averts his gaze. "No! Of course not."

I gulp down my coffee.

"What are you going to do about the video?" he asks.

"Not sure yet."

"It's a really bad situation." He gives me a sympathetic nod. "If you give him what he wants and he deletes the video in front of you, you can never be sure he doesn't have other copies."

You're right—I can't.

"If you…" He hesitates. "If you agree to do his bidding, how far would you let him go?"

I purse my lips and begin to rummage in my purse for my wallet.

"Would you deepthroat him?" He leans in. "What if he asks for backdoor action? Would you do plugs?"

I put a fiver on the table and stand up.

"Mia, wait!" He grabs my wrist. "I'm so sorry. I got carried away."

I yank my hand from his grip.

"Put yourself in my shoes," he says. "Only half an hour ago, you were this beautiful Virgin Mary type. I almost believed your baby was the result of Immaculate Conception! And then it turns out you're a… a…"

His lips move silently as he censors himself, searching for a euphemism.

"A slut," I say. "Is that the word you're trying to substitute?"

"Yes."

I whirl around and march to the exit.

"No!" he shouts. "Shit! Mia, wait!"

He continues yelling something when I'm already at the door and even as I pull it behind me.

Well done, Mia, I tell myself as I rush to the *métro* station.

It had been a genius idea to share your burden with your friend and good man Xavier.

Now you're one day closer to Gaspard's deadline.

And one fuckup richer.

CHAPTER 31

"There *must* be a better way of dealing with this mess," Delphine says. "We just need to think harder."

She called me for a chat an hour ago, and I ended up telling her everything. Well, almost. My sharp-witted friend knew I'd been pregnant when I left Paris a year ago. She'd also figured out Lily's dad worked at DCA. When I refused to give her his name, she said, "As you wish. I'll work it out on my own soon enough."

Considering her street smarts and tenacity, she just might.

The blackmail part had come as a total surprise to her, though. I gave her the whole story—the gang bang, the video, Gaspard's cryptic notes a year ago, my brief meeting with him in the diner, and his latest email.

While Delphine mulled over my mess, I went to Lily, who needed a change of diaper. Then I called her back, and we brainstormed my options. But, unfortunately, none of the courses of action Delphine came up with bettered mine.

In three days, Lily and I are boarding a plane that will take us back to Martinique.

"Come visit when it's winter here," I say to her, trying to sound light.

"You don't have to go away, you know. That moronic Gaspard, didn't he say he'd post the video if you didn't show up?"

"He did."

"You think he's bluffing like last time?" she asks.

"I'm afraid not. I think he means it this time around."

"But then why run? The damage will be done anyway."

I rub my forehead. "I just can't… I'm not strong enough to face the music in Paris. It will be easier in Martinique. Everything is easier in Martinique. Like in that song by Aznavour, *Emmenez-moi.*"

"Misery is less gruesome in the sun," Delphine quotes.

"Exactly."

"And your parents? What if they open Gaspard's email and watch the video?"

"I'm going to Alsace tomorrow morning to come clean and warn them about the video."

"Oh dear. I wouldn't want to be in your shoes right now."

I smirk. "Nor would I, if I had a choice."

"What about your academic career?" she asks. "You're so close, you can't quit now!"

"Yes I can, even if it breaks my heart to disappoint my supervisor like this. He's been a fantastic mentor to me."

"Then don't!"

I let out a heavy sigh. "Can I ask you a favor?"

"Sure! Anything I can do to help."

"I need you to write down a note and hand it to Gaspard on Saturday. I know it's a lot to ask—"

"Are you kidding? I'll be happy to do it! Hang on." I hear a noise that sounds like a drawer being pulled. "OK, I have a pen and paper. Talk."

"Write in block letters, please," I say and dictate the short note.

Delphine writes it down. "Shall I read it to you to be sure?"

"Yes, please."

She clears her throat. "I *know* you're a scumbag. I *have proof* you're a creep. If you post that video, I'll report you to the police. Burn in hell."

"Thank you," I say. "I owe you one."

"No, *I* owe *you* for the opportunity to see the look on his face when he reads your note."

We say good-bye, and I sit down at the kitchen table, which doubles as a desk. My measly belongings are all packed up. I'll call Eva as soon as she's back from Florida to give her the news.

She'll be mad at me at first, but I hope she'll understand.

There's just one more thing left to do before Lily and I catch our train to Alsace. I rip a blank page out of my notebook and write.

Raphael,

I don't want to leave without saying good-bye, or to say it via a text message like last time.

So here goes. Good-bye, my favorite snowman. Lily and I are going back to Martinique. We'll be happier there.

Please don't believe Genevieve's mudslinging.

It makes me feel petty and contemptible asking you this, but I must.

Have a good one,

Mia

I fold the sheet, stick it in a small envelope and address it to Raphael's Parisian home. With the letter in my purse, I grab Lily and head out to the post office.

If Raphael receives my letter within the next forty-eight hours, I'll be in Alsace, where I've booked a room in a bed-and-breakfast outside Estheim. If he gets it over the weekend, I'll be in Martinique.

It hasn't escaped my notice that I'm denying him the chance to persuade me to stay. But given how we parted after Ninossos, I doubt he'll even try. As for the guilt trip over taking Lily so far away from him, it's completely unjustified. He doesn't want her.

So there you go—I'm actually doing him a favor.

I'm doing what's best for all of us.

CHAPTER 32

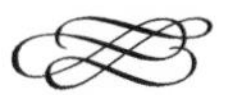

Màma and Pàpa are already at the designated spot by the merry-go-round when I get off the bus with Lily in a front carrier against my chest.

The reason I chose this location is that there's a discreet bench hidden from sight by shrubbery. It's always vacant because people forget it's there.

My parents might need it in a few moments.

Lily and I arrived in Alsace last night and went straight to the hotel. I called my parents this morning. Màma answered the phone. I asked if she and Pàpa could meet me later today in the town hall park. Màma had a hard time accepting I'd stopped at a nearby hotel. I told her it was because I'd come to Estheim with someone they were about to meet. She was silent for a long moment, processing my declaration. Then she informed me, her voice tight, that *he* could sleep in the guest bedroom in the house.

I didn't dare scandalize her further by saying it was a *she*.

As I get nearer, I can see my parents squint in my direction, bewilderment written all over their faces.

This isn't going to be easy.

"Meet Lily," I say after Pàpa greets me with a tight embrace and Màma with her customary forehead kiss.

They pet her.

"She's adorable," Màma says. "Are you babysitting for someone?"

I shake my head. "Lily is mine."

They blink, take a step back and plonk themselves down on the bench.

"Is that a joke?" Pàpa asks.

"No," I say. "I had her in Martinique, and I've been too chicken to tell you."

For several endless moments, they just stare at Lily and me without saying a word.

Then Màma takes a sharp breath. "Who's the father?"

"It doesn't matter."

"What do you mean it doesn't matter?" Pàpa yells.

Wow.

I had to reach my late twenties to have my father yell at me.

Màma looks so shocked and confused as she peers at Lily that my heart goes to her.

"I wanted you to meet her before we return to Martinique," I say.

She levels her gaze with mine. "What? Why?"

There's a tightness in my chest threatening to transform into waterworks any minute. I must say my piece before it does.

"There's something else you need to know about me," I blurt out.

Pàpa drops his head into his hands.

"When I was in college," I say, "I did something stupid, really stupid, and now there's a video out there… and someone is going to post it on the Internet… and also email it to you."

They survey me, wide-eyed, as though they were wondering if the woman in front of them was indeed their daughter.

"Please don't open it," I say, my voice on the verge of cracking. "Please don't watch that video."

They say nothing.

I clench my fists, digging my nails into my palms to delay the tears.

"How could you—," Pàpa begins.

"I'm so sorry," I butt in. "I'm sorry I turned out to be such a disappointment. Please don't blame yourselves, and please know I don't expect you to forgive me. I just wanted to say… I love you."

I spin around, nearly choking on the pent-up tears, and scoot to the bus stop.

CHAPTER 33

My phone rings as I'm blowing my nose between two muffled sobs and Lily is whimpering in the travel cot provided by the hotel.

The caller ID says "Raphael."

My heart swells with joy before I tell myself I better not answer this. I have nothing to add to what I've put in my letter. Which he must have received. Which is why he's calling.

Problem is Raphael is right—I can't resist him.

"I'm in the lobby of your hotel," he says when I finally answer the phone.

"What? How did you find me?"

"I went to see Delphine after I got your letter this morning, hoping you'd confided in her. And you had."

Damn. "What exactly did she tell you?"

"Only where I could find you. She said the rest wasn't her secret to tell."

I exhale in relief.

"Can I come upstairs?" he asks.

"Will you go back to Paris if I say no?"

"Take a guess."

"Room 210," I say and go to the door.

Thirty seconds later, he's inside.

"How could you think I'd believe Genevieve's preposterous accusation?" he asks, frowning. "I'm not as shallow as I seem."

I give him a tiny smile. "I know that. I hoped you wouldn't believe her."

He rolls his eyes before drawing his brows in concern. "You were crying. What gives?"

"Nothing." I point to the wooden chair. "Please have a seat."

Instead, he steps closer and takes my hand.

"Something is obviously very wrong, Mia. Please tell me what it is."

"I'm fine." I look down at his hands clutching mine. "And I'll be even finer in Martinique."

He tips my head up, forcing me to look at him. "What about your defense? The seminar? The job offer you got?"

"I… I can't stay."

He lets go of my hand and sits down. "So here's the deal. I won't budge from this chair until you tell me what's going on."

With a defiant look, he folds his hands across his chest and crosses his legs.

Motionless, I watch him.

A few long moments later, he shifts, uncrosses his legs, crosses them again, and screws up his handsome face into a comical expression.

My lips curl up, despite my misery.

"Is there a more comfortable chair in this room?" he asks.

I shake my head, struggling to remain serious.

"Then I'm transferring my sit-in to the bed," he says.

"Sissy."

"Not a sissy—a result-oriented person." He stands up and flashes me a sexy smile. "I'll last longer on the bed."

I grab his hand to stop him from going to the bed. "Lily is cranky. She needs quiet to fall asleep."

He cups my cheek, his gaze boring into mine. "What are you running from, Mia?"

"A video," I say, surprising myself.

His brows go up.

"Someone has a compromising video of me from my college days…" I begin.

Oh, what the hell.

I'm going to tell it like it is. Unembellished. *The whole freaking enchilada.*

"Someone has a drunken gang bang video with me in it," I blurt out before I lose the nerve. "If I don't meet him tomorrow and do what he wants me to do, he'll make it public."

Raphael stares at me for a long moment. "Is that why you disappeared a year ago?"

I nod.

"Why didn't you tell me?" A deep crease appears between his brows. "Why didn't you ask for my help?"

"This… situation is the result of my mistake. So it's my problem to deal with."

"You're wrong. It's mine, too."

"It shouldn't be," I say. "It's not fair."

"Fair is not how life works." He pulls me to his chest.

"You're about to bolt—again—because some jerk is blackmailing you. Baby, it *is* my problem."

I peer into his eyes.

"Let me handle it," he says. "Where and at what time tomorrow were you supposed to meet him?"

"What will you do?"

"Whatever it takes."

"He doesn't want money—I've already offered." I wring my hands. "He wants… sexual favors every time he's in France."

Raphael's body tenses against mine.

"I wasn't going to pay him," he says. "That's a short-term solution."

"Then what? Beat him up?"

He smirks. "For starters."

"And after that?"

"Impress upon him that if he makes his move, I'll unleash a pack of top-notch lawyers who'll eat him alive. It's illegal to post nudes without a person's consent."

"I know that, but what if he posts the video anyway?" I sigh. "He isn't a *reasonable* person."

Raphael shrugs. "OK, let's say he's a suicidal nutcase and he posts it. So what?"

"What do you mean, *so what*?"

"Your little sex tape will join millions of other sex tapes the Internet is teeming with. Who cares?"

I chew my lip. "You don't?"

He shakes his head.

"Will you watch it if he posts it?"

"Absolutely not." He gives me a stern look. "What kind of douchebag do you think I am?"

Clearly, not the kind Xavier turned out to be.

"It might ruin my academic career," I say.

He quirks an eyebrow. "Really? You're concerned

about your academic career? Is that why you're quitting it?"

I look down, flushing.

"Why don't you tell me what it is you're *really* worried about?" he asks.

"He's going to send the video to my parents."

"He can't force them to watch it."

"He can trick them into watching it."

Raphael encases my face with his hands. "You have to come clean before they get it."

"I just did."

"And?"

"It was too much for them—the gang bang, the video, Lily…"

"They didn't know about her?"

I shake my head. "I'm not sure they'll want to see me again."

"Of course they will. They're religious people—they'll find it in themselves to forgive you."

I shake my head again and let out a sob.

He draws back and stares me in the eye. "Mia?"

"I hate myself for how much I've hurt and disappointed them," I say. "And it breaks my heart that they'll stop loving me."

"They won't," he says.

"You don't know them! You have no idea how high their moral standards are. Things like virtue and uprightness mean everything to them."

He lowers his brows. "Oh come on."

I draw away, march to the door, and open it wide. "Please go. You're making this whole thing harder than it already is."

Not to mention that I'm about to lose it again, and I don't want to lose it in front of him.

"Mia, please."

"Just go."

He walks out.

I grab a pillow from the bed, press it to my face, and wail into it.

CHAPTER 34

Barely five minutes into my crying jag, Raphael knocks on my door again.

"Did you forget something?" I ask as I open it.

He steps inside. "You're right about me not knowing your parents. Maybe they *are* the kind of people who'd stop loving you."

I stare at him, a little woozy from the crying.

"But I won't, Mia." He draws closer and wipes my cheeks with the pads of his fingers. "I won't stop loving you."

The enormity of his words stuns me.

My mouth falls open, and I eye him as if he just confessed to being an android sent from the future to save the human race.

"You look *slightly* surprised," he says with a soft chuckle.

"Last weekend on Ninossos," I say once I find my bearings, "you were talking about our new *arrangement*. And now you… love me?"

He nods.

"You haven't loved anyone before," I say. "How do you know what that feels like?"

"I love my brothers," he counters. "I love my mother. I even loved my good-for-nothing father. How's that for a yardstick?"

"It's different. They're your family."

He smiles. "Not that different, actually. Just like with them, I want to give you *everything*. I want to give you *me*."

I snort at his total lack of false modesty.

"Gee, that sounded pompous," he says. "Let me try again. I want to put an end to 'Mia versus the world' and replace it with 'Mia and Raphael versus the world.' "

It's scary how much I like the sound of it.

"I've lost my appetite for food," he says. "Seriously. That has *never* happened before. I can't focus on work, I think about you all the time. It's like paragliding. There's this crazy lightness and joy in every bone and muscle of my body."

My head begins to spin as I soak up his words, and I'm getting drowsier by the second.

"What do these symptoms tell you, Doctor Stoll?"

"I'm not a doctor yet," I say, feeling incongruously playful. "Even if I stay and get my PhD, I won't be a *medical* doctor. So I'm afraid I can't diagnose you."

"Then assess my state from an objective historical perspective."

"Hmm." I bunch my eyebrows. "I'd say your condition has aggravated since our office fling. But… won't you miss being with other women?"

"No," he says without a moment's hesitation.

"Are you sure?"

"As sure as I am of how much I need you in my life." He looks the most sober I've ever seen him. "You see, I used to think I was just like Papa, even though Seb kept telling me I wasn't. But he was right. I'm not."

"What are you saying?"

"My womanizing… I've figured it out. I didn't do it because I couldn't help it, or because I was insecure. I did it because…" He hesitates. "You're going to laugh."

"Try me."

"Without admitting it to myself, I was looking for a… soulmate."

That word is so incongruous coming from Raphael that I can't help smiling.

"Ludicrous but true." His mouth curls up. "When you fled to Martinique… er, correction—when you *dumped me* and fled to Martinique, I had three one-night stands in two weeks."

My smile fades a little. "That's a lot."

"It was pathetic. I felt pathetic. So I went to Nepal for a month. Officially, it was to visit Maman, but in truth, I was hoping for some kind of miraculous healing."

I hang on his every word.

He shrugs. "At the end of that month, I still missed you so much my chest hurt."

So did mine.

"After I returned to Paris," he continues, "I met a woman. She was pretty, kind, and smart."

I give him a quizzical look.

"It lasted a week." He stares at me.

I stare back.

Raphael encases my face with his hands. "You're the only woman with whom the longer it lasts, the longer I want it to last. Please, say you'll stay."

I open my mouth then close it again.

God, it's tempting to say yes.

"I'm not offering marriage, OK?" He runs his hands over my face and through my cropped hair. "I won't do that unless I'm one hundred percent sure I can be a family man beyond reproach. Just so you know before you decide."

"I'll stay," I whisper.

"What?"

"I'll stay," I say louder.

I'm neck-deep in shit, and yet I grin as a crazy lightness and joy fill every bone and muscle of my body.

CHAPTER 35

"I'll call you again tomorrow morning," Raphael says.

"Not before ten, please." I blow a kiss to my phone screen.

We hang up.

"Was that Raphael?" Pàpa asks, sitting down across the table from me.

I nod.

He shakes his head. "I still can't believe you hid your pregnancy from us and then hid Lily for six months. Six months, Mia!"

"Don't be too hard on her," Màma calls from the blanket on the floor where she's spent the past two hours fawning over Lily's every smile and sound.

What I still can't believe is their reaction.

Màma called me yesterday night, moments after Raphael had left my hotel room to fly to Paris and confront Gaspard. He'd offered to deliver my note while he was at it, but when I called Delphine, she refused to delegate her task. "He'll be all Raphael's after I'm done with him," she promised.

Lily and I were supposed to go back to Paris this morning, but that's not what happened.

On the phone, Màma told me Pàpa was on his way to bring the two of us home. They'd called all the hotels in and around Estheim—which hadn't taken long seeing as there are only three of them—and found out where I was staying. My parents wanted to finish the conversation. Besides, they couldn't bear the idea of me not staying at their house.

As we drove there, my hands shook and my chest felt as if I'd gotten trapped between two jostling elephants. I was on tenterhooks about our impending talk and Raphael's confrontation with Gaspard. Mine went a lot better than his, judging by the brief account he just gave me.

After Delphine handed the creep my letter, which made him green in the face, Raphael took over and tried to reason with him. When that didn't work, he threatened him and ended up hitting him right there in the diner. A fistfight ensued. The owner called the cops, and the two were taken to the police station.

That's what I managed to pull out of him over the phone, and I'm hoping to hear more tomorrow night when Lily and I get back to Paris.

As for my parents, we ended up talking all night, and both of them responded to my revelations with remarkable equanimity. That and an immediate grandparental devotion to Lily. It started with "she's so sweet" the moment we walked in the door, then quickly escalated to "little angel," and reached "the most adorable, smartest, and prettiest little girl in the world" three hours later.

Pàpa leans in. "Does Eva know about Lily?"

I nod. "She's helped me a lot."

"Does she know about the video?"

I nod again.

"Good," he says. "She's level-headed, our Evie. I'm glad you trusted at least one family member enough to share your secrets."

"Pàpa, please—" I begin.

"We may have been too strict and too uptight as parents, but I thought…" He shakes his head, his expression pained. "Don't you know how much we love you? How could you doubt we'd take your news with anything but forgiveness?"

I turn to Màma for support, hoping she'll ask him to drop the subject. Except she doesn't this time. She picks up Lily and joins Pàpa and me around the table.

"Your dad isn't blaming you, *herzele*," she says.

"Of course not," Pàpa says. "I'm blaming myself."

Màma touches my hand. "We just want to understand why you chose not to lean on us when you were in trouble. We need to know what we did wrong as parents." She pauses before adding. "And I need to know where I failed as a shepherd."

"You did nothing wrong," I say. "Nothing at all. It's just…"

Màma's eyes bore into mine. "What?"

"There was this woman, Suzelle… She came here asking for your help years ago."

"How do you know that?" Pàpa asks.

"I overheard your conversations." I stare at my hands. "You said you'd think about it, and when she returned, you refused to help her. You reported her to the police instead."

My parents say nothing.

"So I figured your kindness was reserved for those who deserved it, and your forgiveness didn't stretch to… impure women."

I look up.

Both of them are shaking their heads, looking at me with a mixture of regret and sympathy.

"We were going to help Suzelle in every way we could," Màma says. "We'd prepared money, made arrangements for her lodgings, and secured a small job until she'd found her bearings."

I knit my brows, perplexed.

"Just to be thorough, I asked an old buddy from the vice squad about her," Pàpa says.

Màma smiles. "Cop habits die hard."

Pàpa's mouth compresses into a hard line. "Some of her story checked out. Suzelle wanted to escape from her pimp's clutches, all right, and she did want to quit her profession. Only it wasn't to get a second chance."

"Then why?" I ask.

"She wanted to start her own procuress business." Pàpa smirks. "When my buddy did a bit of digging, we learned that Suzelle had already recruited two teenage girls from the housing project on the other side of the river."

I put my hand over my mouth, dazed.

Pàpa nods and taps his hand on the table as if to say, so that's that.

"I'm going to make your favorite truffle ravioli. Would you like me to cook something apart for Lily?"

"We're good," I say. "I brought everything she needs."

"Did I tell you she's the most wonderful thing in the world?" Màma asks as Lily digs her little fingers into her grandmother's cheek.

Thank God I cut her nails last night.

"At least a dozen times," I say.

Pàpa's gives me a conflicted look as if he's on the fence about something.

"What is it?" I ask.

"There's no pressure, and please don't take this the wrong way, but will you bring your Raphael here sometime?"

"Only if you'd like to," Màma adds quickly. "And if he's up for it."

"I'd love to," I say. "And so would he."

The expression of relief on their faces is priceless.

Pàpa goes to the kitchen, refusing my offer to help him with the cooking, as always.

"He thinks you and I jinx his dishes just by touching the ingredients," Màma says before taking Lily to the garden to show her Pàpa's beautiful apples.

I wrap one of Màma's shawls around my shoulders, sit on the porch, and watch them.

For the first time in years I can breathe even if my future is far from being unicorns and rainbows. Gaspard will likely post the video. Genevieve will continue badmouthing me to Raphael and to everyone in their circle. Raphael may discover he isn't made for long-term relationships, after all.

Which is why I still haven't told him he's Lily's dad. I hate the idea he might think Genevieve had a point and I'm using our baby to tie him to me.

There's also the little matter of my upcoming defense, which I might fail, seeing how little I worked lately.

I'm aware of all that, yet I'm not worried. And that's because whatever force hurtles me over the edge, and however high the cliff, I know I won't splinter and burst to pieces.

There's enough love around me—and in my heart—to cushion my fall.

EPILOGUE

It's three days before Christmas, and Lily has a cold.

She's all stuffed up, but the bright side of her congested nose—at least from my perspective—is that when she closes her eyes after my lullaby, I know for sure she's asleep.

Because she snores.

And that's my cue to tiptoe out of her room.

It's been three months since Raphael knocked on my door and everything accelerated.

In October, Gaspard posted the video on the Internet and emailed it to Màma's official address despite Raphael's vigorous warnings.

She deleted the mail without opening.

As for the World Wide Web, I can only hope my sex tape will drown in the noise until we've forced Gaspard to withdraw it. Raphael has sued him on my behalf. The case is still pending, but it's clear we'll win. First, because what Gaspard did was against the law. Second, because

Raphael hired two hotshot attorneys while Gaspard was unable to afford any.

For once, there's fairness in the unfairness of life.

In November, I defended my thesis and earned the right to be called "doctor of philosophy."

Hello, everyone, I'm Mia Stoll, PhD.

In the days that followed, I landed the *maître de conférences* job.

Two weeks ago, Lily and I moved in with Raphael. Before we did that, he'd had to make a few… er, a *gazillion* adjustments to his lifestyle, as well as to his open-concept loft.

He says it was no trouble at all.

I have my doubts, but I like to think he says that because having us here makes him forget the inconveniences.

He and Genevieve had a falling out shortly after the weekend on Ninossos. He won't give me the details, but I suspect she trashed me again and he decided he'd had enough. Three days after Lily and I moved to Raphael's place, Genevieve's daddy bought her an apartment in Hollywood, where she'll try her luck as a producer for one of the studios.

I would've given her a "free tip" to specialize in evil witch biopics if we were on speaking terms.

Quietly, I enter the living room and head to the couch where Raphael sits, reading.

I'm about to confess that he's Lily's dad.

Actually, "confirm" would be a better word because I'm sure he knows. We've never talked about it, but some time ago I stopped lying about her age, and he took to calling her "my little *flammkuche*."

He must *know*.

"Of course I do," he says after I fess up. "But I wanted to hear it from you, once you were ready."

"Thank you for your patience."

"You're welcome," he says. "Actually, I didn't mind your silence so much. It allowed me to get used to the idea and readjust my priorities."

I smile. "How long have you known?"

"From the moment I laid eyes on her."

I frown in disbelief.

"Let me show you something," he says, heading to his desk.

I follow him. Raphael pulls a photo out of the top drawer. It's Lily, smiling her adorable double-dimpled smile. Except something is off…

"Her dress," I say, pointing at the picture. "Lily doesn't have a dress like that."

He smiles. "This isn't Lily. This is my mom when she was about the same age."

A few moments later, I realize my mouth is gaping. I shut it.

Still smiling, he sets the picture on his desk and gathers me to him.

I wrap my arms around his waist and breathe him in.

He ruffles my hair. "You know, I've gotten so used to your pixie cut I actually prefer you with less hair on your head now."

"Good," I say.

His other hand cups me between my legs. "And with a full bush here."

I snort against his chest.

Less than a minute later, we're half-naked, my ass on the edge of his desk and him buried to the hilt inside me.

"Don't hold back," I say, meeting his measured thrusts. "I want it hard and fast tonight."

"Yes, doctor."

A few minutes later, we clutch each other, spent.

He kisses my forehead. "Marry me?"

I gasp.

Raphael's heartbeat quickens against my chest. That he's nervous like this about my answer is pure delight.

"Baby, if you need time to think, I totally—"

"No," I say.

He tenses, making me realize how my reply sounded.

"No," I say again, "I don't need time to think. And yes, I'll marry you. If you're certain it's what you want."

"I've never been more certain about anything in my whole life."

We both grin like idiots.

"Actually," he says as his hand trails down my back to palm my ass. "I wasn't planning on proposing tonight… like *this*. I was going to do it in a more classical way and with an appropriately sized rock tomorrow at Le Jules Verne."

"*This* was perfect," I say, planting a kiss on his mouth.

His grin widens.

"Except one major flaw," I add.

"Which is?"

"What will we tell Lily the day she asks how daddy proposed?"

He frowns. "Hmm."

"We'll be forced to lie to her."

He raises his index finger. "I have a solution!"

"Listening."

"We'll do another proposal tomorrow at the restaurant. I'll get her to give you the ring."

"She might decide to put it in her mouth instead," I say.

"We'll keep it inside the case, then. It won't fit in her mouth."

"OK."

His face crinkles up in a smile. "That way, she'll be part of the proposal, too. And the day she asks about it, we'll have a cool, *true* story for her."

I kiss his chin. "It's a really sweet plan."

"It's because I'm a really sweet man," he says smugly.

I begin to roll my eyes but stop halfway. "You know what, Raphael d'Arcy? You actually are."

THE PERFECT CATCH

THE DARCY BROTHERS BOOK 3

ONE

NOAH

I *miss Oscar.*

The realization occurs to me as I walk across the lobby to the exit of the indoor swimming pool where we train. This morning's practice was focused on sprints, weightlifting, and shooting—in my case, stopping penalty shots. Our coach, Lucas, believes that if I perfect that, it could give the club an edge this season.

I agree with him.

This is why I spent the last hour blocking with every part of my body that happened to be closest to the ball, including my head. A broken nose is a price I'm prepared to pay if it helps my team win.

I step out of the building into the sticky midsummer heat of Paris.

Ugh.

If only I could go back and spend the rest of the day in the pool! Or, better still, I wish the pool would turn into a river flowing from here to the 19th arrondissement.

Wouldn't it be great to just swim home?

Letting out a resigned sigh, I head to my old Yamaha parked on the corner. While I plod there, I picture Oscar bounding up to me and wagging his tail.

After a hard day that starts with practice, then four hours of deliveries, followed by another grueling workout, Oscar is my best sedative.

It'll be hard to unwind when I get home tonight.

And it won't be easier in the morning when I wake up to an eerily quiet apartment. On the other hand, no one will jump on my bed, trail a wet tongue all over my face, and bark until I take him for a walk.

The past two mornings have been the laziest I've had in a year, ever since Oscar turned my bachelor's life upside down. I might have even enjoyed them if it weren't for that stupid plumbing issue in the kitchen.

My sink drain is clogged beyond DIY fixing.

I halt in front of the cafe a few blocks down the street. Ten minutes in an air-conditioned room with a Perrier, an espresso, and a *jambon-beurre* sandwich are just the thing before I jump on my scooter and head to the pizzeria for my shift. That a pro water polo player needs a job on the side is something both the French Swimming Federation and the European Aquatics League must be ashamed of. It's also one of the reasons our national team hasn't won any Olympic medals since 1928.

1928!

Perhaps I should've gone to Italy or Montenegro when I returned to Europe. Or Hungary, for that matter, where water polo is *the* national sport.

The barista hands me my coffee, sparkling water and sandwich while I try to convince my body it doesn't need more to recover from being pushed to its limits at this morning's practice.

To say I'm zonked would be an understatement.

Chewing the last bite of the *jambon-beurre*, I pull out my phone and type a brief message to my new landlord. His family name, by the way, sounds hilarious in French. Luckily for him, he's American—probably of German descent with that name—so it doesn't matter.

Dear Mr. Bander,

Could you please send a plumber to fix the clogged drain, or confirm that it's OK if I call one myself? I informed the previous owners about the problem three weeks ago, just before they sold the apartment. Madame Florent didn't have time to take care of it, but she promised she'd let you know.

Many thanks,

Noah Masson

This is my second missive to him on the subject. If he doesn't reply by Friday, I'll go ahead and call a plumber. I know tenants aren't supposed to take initiative like that without the landlord's prior approval. But how can he give it if he doesn't read his emails?

Still, it would be unwise to antagonize the man. He just purchased the apartment with my lease and has the power to kick me out as soon as it expires.

But I do need my kitchen faucet, dammit.

The one in the bathroom is so short I can't fit the kettle under it. No faucet and no Oscar make me cranky, which might affect my performance. We can't have that. Especially not now, when the team is in its best shape ever and getting ready for the French National Championship and the LEN Cup.

To lift my spirits, I remind myself that Oscar is having a great time now, running free in the Derzians' garden. Lucky bastard. While other dogs—and humans—suffer the heat in Paris, Oscar can breathe. He's spending the whole month at my neighbors' summer house in Brittany with his lady friend, the Derzians' genteel poodle Cannelle.

Oscar isn't genteel, though.

It's anyone's guess what canine *mésalliance* produced the wild combination of traits that is my dog.

He doesn't know any tricks, either.

In short, Oscar is a perfectly untrained brown-spotted mongrel—or a love child, if you prefer—who obeys my orders only when they align with his own desires.

Boy, I miss him.

WHEN I ENTER MY APARTMENT, half-conscious with fatigue after the shift at the pizzeria and the second workout, my plan for the evening is simple. A cold beer, a bit of TV, and beddy-bye.

Only, there's someone in the kitchen.

Seeing as my landlord is currently stateside and no one else has a key to this place, it can only be a burglar. And with all the noise he's making, a crappy one, too.

I rush into the kitchen.

Oh.

My bad burglar is a woman.

She turns around to stare at me, her right arm still

reaching up to open the cabinet where I keep my extra cash.

I make a lunge at her, pull her away from her prize, spin her around, and press her face into the wall. She doesn't offer any resistance, clearly taken by surprise. I shackle her wrists above her head and lean into her to keep her in place.

She mutters something and begins to wriggle. "Let go of me!"

"Not a chance."

She squirms and kicks my shins.

"Stand still until I figure out what to do with you," I say.

She jerks her arms, trying to free her hands.

Good luck with that, chérie. You're up against a guy who spends several hours each day training to improve his grip on a wet ball. And whose single hand is as big as both of yours.

Her next move is to push back.

My response is to press her harder against the wall.

Her ass is out of this world… not that one would normally notice that when restraining an intruder.

It's high.

Round.

Firm.

Perched on top of endless slender legs that I'm sort of squeezing between mine.

As she writhes and pants and I hold her down, a few unusual things occur. My lids grow heavy and my head drops closer to her ash-brown hair that springs in fluffy coils all around her head like a full, soft, warm halo.

The delicious scent coming off it enthralls me. A perfume? Nah, perfumes smell different. Can it be her shampoo, or conditioner, or another beauty product women use to style their hair?

She steps on my foot, hard, breaking me from my trance.

"Ouch," I say, my voice perfectly flat to show her I'm not impressed.

"Let go of me, you stupid man!"

She has a slight accent. American maybe?

"Now, why would I do that?" I tighten my grip around her wrists. "So you can leg it with whatever you've already stuffed into your bag?"

She twists her head to look me in the eye. "I'm *not* a burglar. I'm your landlady."

"Of course." I study her lovely profile. "Pleased to meet you, *Madame*. I'm Snow White and the Seven Dwarfs."

Did I mention her eyelashes are to die for?

Or that she has the lushest, most kissable lips in the universe, topped off by the most beautiful skin I've ever seen. It's smooth, luminous, and the color of coffee with a generous dash of milk.

A light bulb goes off in my head.

This woman isn't real.

She's a fantasy come to life. And not just any fantasy. She's *the* fantasy I've had ever since I hit puberty, come to life.

My free hand twitches as I fight the urge to touch her face.

What the hell.

Feeling this way about this woman is wrong. Not just because I don't know her, or because my mind should be free of any desires unrelated to winning gold in the upcoming season, but because Uma will be arriving in France any day now.

I hope.

"Please, *Monsieur* Masson," she says. "I can explain everything if you'd just stop *hurting* me."

I flinch. Hurting her is the last thing I want to do regardless of who she is and what she was doing in my apartment.

Gingerly, I release her delicate wrists and draw back a notch, planting my hands on the wall on either side of her.

Incidentally, I have a hard-on.

But then again, who wouldn't after a solid minute against a booty like that?

She turns around, jostling within the small space between my arms and chest, and glares.

I narrow my eyes. "So. Let's hear it. Who are you and what are you doing in my kitchen?"

"My name is Sophie Bander," she says, her black eyes boring into mine. "As I said, I'm your new landlady."

Bander.

If she's a thief, how does she know my landlord's ridiculous name? Is it possible she's telling the truth?

"The new owner of this apartment is, indeed, named Bander," I say. "But it's a *Mister* Bander."

She nods. "Mr. Ludwig Bander. I'm his daughter, and *I* am the official owner of this apartment."

Riiiiight.

I swallow and take a step back.

She jerks her chin up triumphantly.

First my ears and then my whole face flame with embarrassment.

I just manhandled my new landlady.

"I'm very sorry about this misunderstanding," I say. "Can we start over?"

Her expression softens. "Go ahead."

I nod a thank-you. "Hello. My name is Noah Masson. I live here."

"Hi," she says. "I'm Sophie Bander. I own this apartment."

"Pleased to meet you, ma'am."

"The pleasure is mine."

We stare at each other.

I rack my brain for something to say and blurt, "My passion is water polo."

"You play professionally?" she asks with a polite smile.

"Yes," I say. "Except, pro water polo isn't like pro football or tennis. Most athletes need a second job."

"Why's that?"

"The level of pay is much lower."

"So what's your second job?" She twists her fingers in her hair. "I bet it's as cool as water polo."

"I deliver pizzas."

"Oh." Surprise flashes in her eyes. "Well, I hope to become a professional, too, one day—in real estate."

"I'm sure you will."

She studies her feet for a moment and then looks up. "*Monsieur* Masson, I think I owe you an apology, too."

"Please, call me Noah," I say.

She nods. "Letting myself in like I did wasn't very professional of me… I should've waited until you replied to Dad's email. Or called me."

I frown. "I don't have your number… And what email are you talking about?"

"My father wrote you that I'd stop by this afternoon to discuss the plumbing problem. Didn't you get his reply?"

I shake my head.

She lets out a sigh. "I bet it's in your spam. Could you do me a favor and check?"

I fetch my phone and open the spam folder.

Smack in the middle of the first page is an unread email from Mr. Bander. So, he did reply to my first email. Only, his letter was sorted with the request to send me a million dollars from Nigeria and an offer for a penis enlargement pill with free shipping.

The subject line of Mr. Bander's note is, unimaginatively, "From Mr. Bander."

I show her the email.

Sophie points an elegant finger at it and shakes her head. "No wonder it went to spam. I *have* warned Dad not to put his name in the subject line when he emails people in France. Guess he forgot."

"Did you tell him why?"

She gives me a hard stare. "No."

I nod in sympathy. In her place, I'd have a hard time breaking it to a parent that his name means "to have an erection" in colloquial French.

"How come your French is so good?" I ask.

"My mom is French."

"Ah, that explains it."

Given that Sophie is a mixed-race chick and her dad sounds Germanic, I assume her French mom is black, maybe of West African or Antilles ancestry.

"I've always lived in the States," she says.

And that explains the accent.

"New York?" I ask. For some reason, she strikes me as a New Yorker.

She smiles. "Key West, Florida. Have you been there?"

I shake my head. Maman and Papa often took me to the US when I was a kid. We visited New York and San

Francisco several times. But I have no recollection of traveling to Florida.

My gaze flicks to her lips and lingers there.

She clears her throat. "So, about your drain problem. I was looking for the shutoff valve, so I can give the plumber its location. Do you know where it is?"

"You were close," I say, opening the cabinet next to the one she was about to explore when I came in.

"Great, thank you. I talked to a plumber who can come by tomorrow morning at ten. Will that work for you?"

"That's perfect. I can stop in between my practice and work."

"Is the phone number in your lease contract still good?"

"Yep."

She gives me a business card. "Feel free to email or call if you need something else. I'm here to help."

"Thank you, Ms. Bander," I say. "It's just the faucet. Everything else is in perfect order."

She starts for the foyer then turns around. "Please, call me Sophie."

"OK, and sorry again for the mishap," I say, opening the door.

"It was nice meeting you, Noah." Her lips turn up in a yummy smile. "Despite the mishap."

"You, too."

As her heels clack against the stairs, I wonder how she'd have reacted if I'd answered her earlier question truthfully. I do need something else right now—something she can definitely help me with.

I need to kiss Sophie Bander.

TWO

SOPHIE

His hard ridge against my backside, imprinting my flesh with its shape…

The scent of his sandalwood aftershave enveloping me…

His face a few inches above mine, his heart racing and his breathing ragged…

The feel of his tall, strong body pressed into mine—broad chest, flat stomach, muscled thighs…

I shake my head to drive away those images. Thoughts of that nature aren't just unusual for me—they're unheard of. They're weirding me out.

Besides, they're totally inappropriate in the workplace.

Grabbing the documents Véronique asked me to photocopy, I scoot down the hallway toward the pair of ever-humming machines behind the cluster of artificial fig trees.

This part of my job sucks.

But hey, I'm an intern and that's what interns do, right?

Except, unlike other interns at Millennium III—the biggest real estate group in France—I have the privilege of owning an actual property in an up-and-coming arrondissement of Paris.

How I convinced Dad to buy me a one-bedroom apartment here is a tumultuous saga that deserves at least three volumes.

The first one would be called *The Impossible*. In this installment, Dad says things like "It's out of the question" and "You're a total rookie with no real knowledge of what this business involves."

The title of Volume Two would be, *Dogged Perseverance and Relentless Nagging* and would cover the period between December and February of last year. That's when Dad resorts to more technical arguments such as "French real estate prices have been stagnant since 2008" and "I'm not convinced about investing in Paris, given the risk of another terrorist attack and how it might affect the market."

I had to dig up data showing that select French cities —in particular, Paris—still delivered a good return on investment. As for my knowing next to nothing about the business, I invoked my GPA as proof of how good a learner I can be.

The third and final installment of the saga would be called *The Impossible Comes True*.

In this volume, Sophie Bander finds the apartment and Ludwig Bander begrudgingly purchases it. They agree that she'll personally manage it during the six months of her internship in Paris from July through December. Then she'll return to Key West, asking Millennium III to take over.

Sophie is ecstatic.

Ludwig is happy that she's happy.

End of Saga.

The photocopier begins to spit page after page into the tray.

As I watch it do its thing, I tell myself I'm lucky in more than one way. My boss here is a top-performing agent who believes interns should do more than make copies or serve coffee to clients. Véronique actually involves me in her real work. Last week, she took me along to show an apartment to a prospective buyer. On Monday, I attended a negotiation. Two days ago, she asked me to draft a lease agreement and compile an inventory.

I had applied for this internship during my final semester in Miami, and received the offer the day of graduation. When I told Dad I was going to spend six months in Paris working for a real estate firm, his eyebrows almost crept under his hairline.

"May I remind you, princess, that *I* own a real estate firm right here in your hometown?" he said, vexed.

"I know, Dad."

"Do you?" He arched an eyebrow. "Do you also remember that I'd be thrilled to offer you a junior position in it?"

I looked down at my feet. "Uh-huh."

"So why on earth do you need to spend six months slaving for someone else in Paris?"

As I searched for the right words, comprehension lit his eyes. "It's your mother, isn't it? You just want to spend more time with Catherine."

His expression softened as he said Mom's name so much so that you'd think he wouldn't mind spending more time with Catherine himself.

But I know better than to nurture false hopes.

It's been several years since I stopped fooling myself that my parents would ever reunite.

Anyway, Dad was right. Being closer to Mom was a big part of why I was going to Paris. I don't see nearly enough of her. Summer holidays and an occasional Christmas or Easter break just don't cut it.

When my parents divorced ten years ago, I chose to stay with Dad in Key West. My friends were there. I loved my school. I loved the weather, the town, and the island.

But that choice came at a price—going through my teenage years without my mom by my side. Oh, we did talk on the phone, daily. We texted, emailed, and Skyped. All of that taken together, I've communicated with Mom a lot more than with Dad over the past ten years.

But all those disembodied conversations couldn't replace the comfort of her physical presence.

I missed those magical evenings, when I'd sit on the front porch to read, and she'd come out with her own book and two frosty glasses of virgin cranberry cooler. I'd move over, and we'd just sit quietly next to each other, sipping our drinks, and reading.

Her Parisian apartment doesn't have a porch or even a balcony. But no matter. I wanted as many of those quiet evenings with her as I could get before returning to Key West and putting my life plan in motion.

Said plan is, by the way, the other reason I'm spending six months in Paris.

I want to learn the ropes of Dad's business. But I want to start by learning them as a regular intern in a big agency where no one knows me, and no one will *go easy* on me. Dad's is the biggest agency in the Florida Keys, but most of his staff have known me since I was a toddler, and all of them treat me like a princess. It's sweet but not very helpful.

The second biggest agency belongs to our main competitor and sworn enemy Doug Thompson. For some weird reason, Doug is extra nice to me. Every time we bump into each other on Duval Street or at Cuban Coffee Queen and he greets me with a warm smile and a "How are you today, Sophie?" I barely nod in response. How can I be friendly with a man who's at war with Dad? Not just a rivalry, but a real merciless, no prisoners, no cease-fires, no-holds-barred war for dominion over the Keys.

Needless to say, applying for an internship with Doug wasn't an option.

I stick the scanned contracts into a manila folder and remove the staple from the asbestos survey report for copying.

As I feed it into the machine, I recall my last words to Dad before boarding the plane to Paris. "Six months is nothing in the big scheme of things. I'll be back before you know it."

His eyes drilled into mine. "Will you?"

"You bet." I gave him a bear hug. "I'll become a real pro and I'll make you proud."

He ran his hand over his close-cropped salt-and-pepper hair and wished me a good trip.

My heart pinches.

I love that man more than the world. What a shame his marriage fell apart!

Since Mom left, I spent countless hours poring over her and Dad's Parisian Polaroids from before I was born. The pics show an ethereal northern blonde and a strapping black dandy posing on Champs-Elysées, in Tuileries, in front of the Louvre, and in other landmarks of the French capital. They hold hands. Sometimes his arm is wrapped around her shoulders and hers around his waist. In my favorite picture they gaze into each other's eyes with such passion you'd think nothing could kill it.

I've never felt as much as a spark of passion for anyone, no matter how hard I tried.

Just as well—no good comes of it anyway.

I wonder why thinking of those old photos has reminded me of yesterday's encounter with Noah Masson. The man is eye candy, no doubt. But beyond his height and athletic build, my blue-eyed tenant looks nothing like Dad.

Not to mention that no one in their right mind would call me a northern blonde.

And yet… what is it about Noah that made me spend an hour last night looking for a mistake in his rental agreement that would warrant a revision? I ended up finding it—*qui cherche trouve*, as Mom likes to say. The previous owner had leased the apartment as unfurnished, even though she'd equipped it with everything from a bed to a vacuum cleaner. Dad bought it together with all the movable property, and Noah's new contract is for a furnished lease. But we'd neglected to change the notice period from three months to one.

While the copier reproduces the termite survey, I pull out my phone and tap.

Hello,

Can I stop by around 8 p.m. next Monday to discuss a small change in the rental contract and sign a new copy?

Best,

Sophie

THREE

NOAH

Lucas waits until the last man is in the debrief circle before he tut-tuts. "Four exclusion fouls, people. That's four too many."

We fake remorse the best we can. But we know that, in truth, the coach is happy with the game and proud of us. No amount of tut-tutting can disguise the glee in his eyes.

"Jean-Michel, Denis, your sprints need work, but good effort there." He turns to Zach. "Very good effort."

Zach—our center forward responsible for two of the exclusion fouls—wipes the pretend guilt off his face and grins.

"If you guys can stay committed," Lucas says, "you'll peak right in time for the national championship."

"We're totally committed, Coach," Zach says.

"We'll do what it takes," Denis chimes in.

Valentin, Jean-Michel and the rest of the team shout things like "Hell, yeah!" and "You can count on us!"

"That's the spirit." Lucas turns to me. "Great job

with the saves, Noah. Perfect. Technically, tactically—you nailed it. Give me more of the same in the championship and LEN Cup games, and I'll be a happy camper."

Lucas no longer bothers to hide how happy he is. And so he should be. The squad is in great shape. For the first time since Lucas started the club, we're truly ready to fight for gold medals, both French and European. That we just won a scrimmage game against one of the country's best clubs, annihilating them like they were a college team, is no stroke of luck.

"OK, back into the water now!" Lucas blows his whistle. "Chop, chop! Thirty minutes of shooting, followed by thirty minutes of strokes and lunges."

Valentin shifts his weight from one foot to the other. "It's my mom's birthday today. I was hoping to leave in time for the family dinner."

"Do you want that gold medal—yes or no?" Lucas gives our defender a hard stare.

"Yes," he mutters.

Lucas jerks his chin at the pool.

Valentin nods resignedly and jumps in.

When the workout is over, the team—minus Valentin—head to the nearest bar for the customary drink. Zach comes along, too. He's never available in the evening, so I look forward to chatting with him.

Call me a fanboy, but the guy *is* one of a kind.

Just a few years my senior, he's so together it's unbelievable. In the field, he's efficient and generous. Even though he's our hole player, count on Zach to go for an assist over a direct shot, if he believes the team would have a better chance of scoring that way. In addition to being our top scorer and team captain, he also runs a successful e-commerce business and raises a special-needs kid.

Alone.

Maybe he's found the secret to bending space-time.

"How much do you sleep at night?" I ask Zach after everyone has settled around our usual table and Lucas has ordered a round of drinks.

"Six hours," Zach says. "Why?"

I shrug. "I just don't see how you can do all of the things you do and find time to sleep."

"I have help."

"Dobby?"

He chuckles. "Nanny. She's the one who looks after Sam from eight thirty to six. So I can play water polo and operate my business."

"I see."

A crease appears between his brows. "Thing is… I know it's selfish, but I do wish she didn't have kids of her own."

"Are you into her?"

"No!" He laughs. "She's married and she's in my employ. So no way. It's just… If Sam had a live-in nanny, my mornings would be a lot less stressful. And I could go out in the evenings, maybe even date someone."

"How long has it been since you—"

"Long," he cuts in before I can finish.

"You should contact an au pair agency," I say.

Zach shakes his head. "Mathilde has been with Sam for the past three years. She's doing a great job, and Sam is attached to her. The only way I'm hiring an au pair is if she quits, which I hope she won't."

Lucas raises his glass. "Here's to *Nageurs de Paris,* the

best water polo club in France! Let's prove it to the rest of the country this year!"

Everyone cheers and chugs their drinks.

Zach turns to me. "What's up with you? Last time we talked, you were mad at your oldest brother for bugging you, and hoped your childhood friend would get her French visa."

"I'm still mad and still hoping," I say with a sigh. "Just as it looked like Sebastian might have given up, his wife took over. She writes *letters* to me. What do you make of that?"

Zach grins. "Like, real letters? On paper?"

"Yep. And she encloses photos with them."

"Of what?"

"Family gatherings. Portraits of my brothers and their babies. That sort of stuff."

Zach gives me a funny look, like he wants to say something but doesn't dare. I told him about my fucked-up family months ago. He knows I was born a d'Arcy du Grand-Thouars de Saint-Maurice. He knows why I prefer to go by Maman's maiden name and why I won't talk to my brothers.

So why that look?

"Don't you think…" He hesitates. "Don't you think your family deserves a second chance? Don't you want to meet your nephew and niece?"

"They're cute in Diane's photos—but no, thanks. I want nothing to do with the d'Arcys."

"What about your friend's visa?" Zach asks, clearly sensing that a change of topic is in order.

I roll my eyes. "The French consulate in Nepal is taking its sweet time."

"I can't imagine she's a security threat."

"Just the usual red tape," I say with a dismissive wave. "But my mother is pushing for her protégée, and my mother doesn't give up until she gets what she wants."

"That explains your brothers' doggedness," Zach says. "It runs in the family."

As much as I hate to admit it, he does have a point.

"It's kind of your mom to take an unrelated young woman under her wing," Zach says. "She's covering all the expenses, right?"

I nod. "Strictly speaking, it's the Marguerite Masson Foundation, of which she's the founding CEO."

"Respect."

"She loves Uma," I say. "You see, Maman always wanted to have a girl, but she had three boys instead."

"I never wanted to have anything." Zach lifts his eyes to the ceiling. "But, thank you, Lord, for giving me a boy. Girls are the sweetest thing, except I wouldn't know what to do with one."

I smile. "Uma is certainly sweet, but she has a backbone and an independent streak. She plans to find a job as soon as she gets here so she can repay Maman."

"Good for her."

"She's willing to wash dishes in a restaurant, clean houses, anything. I'm keeping my eyes open for announcements."

"I'll do the same." Zach glances at his watch. "Got to go. Mathilde has granted me two extra hours, but my time's up."

He fist-bumps the players, shakes hands with Lucas, and heads out the door.

The rest of us stay for another hour, speculating about which club we'll be playing against in the first round of the national games. We also discuss the strengths and weaknesses of the top clubs and their players.

Barring Lucas, I'm the go-to guy on the attackers' preferred shooting techniques, since I spend several hours a week studying them on tape.

As a goalie, you have to.

But the moment I leave the bar, my neurons settle into a new formation, and all I can think of on the ride home is Sophie's text message. My new landlady has found an error in the lease agreement. She wants to discuss it and sign a new contract. Is this a pretext to raise the rent? Or to get rid of me so she can occupy the apartment herself?

My gut tells me there's more to her initiative than just correcting a spelling mistake in the agreement. And I'm going to find out tomorrow if I'm right.

The weird thing is that I look forward to her visit more than I'm apprehensive about it. Actually, "look forward" is an understatement. I'm thrilled. There's this wild idea that's formed in the most primitive part of my brain. I've been trying to dismiss it as wishful thinking—and failing miserably.

What if the sexiest woman to walk the earth has invented an error in the agreement so she can see me again?

What if I'm not the only one who nearly lost it from our brief physical contact the other day? What if Sophie felt the same way and has been lusting after me ever since?

That's preposterous. I know.

And yet I doubt I'll be able to sleep tonight.

FOUR

SOPHIE

I ring the doorbell.

My white blouse is all buttoned up and tucked into my gray pencil skirt, and my new hairstyle is a lot more sober than the afro I had before. This morning, I spent two hours at my local Salon de Coiffure to get my curls tamed into a classy braided bob.

Until a minute ago, I also wore thick frame fake glasses. According to Sue, my bestie, they transform me from a twenty-four-year-old intern into a twenty-five-year-old yuppie. But I just took them off and shoved them into my briefcase. *Yes, a briefcase!*

I don't really know why.

"Your hair is different," Noah says after I step in and we exchange polite greetings.

Oh, shoot. He doesn't like it. *Not that I care, of course.*

"It's beautiful," he adds, giving me an appreciative nod. "Is this your usual hairstyle?"

"A special effort for my mom," I say. "She's crazy for small box braids."

It's true—Mom loves the look of "easy chic" this style gives me.

What I failed to mention is the last time I had the patience to get Mom's favorite hairstyle was three years ago. And now, this morning.

"Is that how she wears it, too?" Noah asks.

"My mom?" I snort. "She'd love to, but Caucasian hair gets way too damaged from box braiding."

He gives me a confused look. "I'd assumed your mother was black."

I blink. "Why?"

"Because…" He screws up his face as if to say, *Help me out here.*

I frown and raise my brows. I have no clue what he's struggling with.

"Because…," he tries again.

I nod supportively. "Yeeess?"

He gives a shy little smile that could charm a corpse back to life. "Because your dad is named Ludwig Bander?"

I crack up. "You're not the only one to assume he's white."

"He's not?"

"Nope. But there's an explanation."

"I'm all ears."

"When Dad was born, Grandpa wanted him to have a king's name. So, he looked up all the kings who came into the world on the twenty-fifth of August."

"And he found a Ludwig?"

"Exactly. King Ludwig of Bavaria, born on the twenty-fifth of August eighteen something something."

He cocks his head. "Did your father name you Sophie after a queen born on the same day as you?"

"Very smart." I bow in mock admiration. "Princess Sophie. That's what he calls me, by the way."

"Was it the only royal name available for your birthday?" he asks. "Not that I have anything against Sophie. It's a lovely name."

"The other option was Marie Antoinette, but Mom said, 'Over my dead body'."

He gives me a wink. "She should've said, 'Over my *guillotined* body,' given our last queen's unfortunate ending."

I giggle but force myself to stop, remembering I'm here on business in my capacity as his landlady.

It's time I started acting like one.

"How's your sink?" I ask.

"As good as new. Thank you so much for your help!"

"It's my job."

For a brief moment, we stare into each other's eyes as the air grows thick with something unspoken and totally inappropriate.

"Can I offer you a cold drink?" Noah asks, shifting his gaze to his hands.

"A glass of water would be great."

He strides into the kitchen and fills two glasses with water. Then we sit down at the table and I explain the change in his contract.

Noah's gray-blue gaze is locked on my mouth the whole time.

"So, are you OK with the new terms?" I ask when I finish.

He gives me a funny look. "Are you planning to reclaim the apartment?"

"No."

"Because if you are," he adds, "just tell me so I can start looking for a new place."

"I don't have a hidden agenda, really."

I hope he can see I'm telling the truth.

Noah stares at me as if gauging my sincerity and then nods. "OK."

"OK?"

"Yeah, I believe you." He picks up the pen I'd set on the table. "Where do I sign?"

I point at the last page. "Here, please, on both copies."

Thirty seconds later, I rip up the old agreement and push one of the new copies toward Noah. "For your files."

"Thanks."

I stick my own copy in the briefcase.

We're done. My business here is finished, and I can go home.

I *should* go home.

"More water?" he asks, pointing at my empty glass.

"I'm good, thank you."

Both etiquette and common sense dictate that I leave now. Which is exactly what I'm going to do. Soon.

The moment he stops looking at me like that.

Any second now…

"Did Mr. Bander buy a second apartment for you in Paris or are you renting?" he asks without taking his eyes off me.

"I'm renting."

"In this arrondissement?"

"In the 18th."

"Do you like it?" he asks.

"The part where I live, yes. Very much. Do you know rue des Batignolles?"

"Uh-uh."

"It's lovely. I'm close to my mom's place, not far

from work, and within walking distance from Montmartre."

"Sounds like the perfect location," he says. "My first year in Paris, I lived in the 18th, too."

I release a frustrated damn. "So much for my good ear for French accents! I'd pegged you as a Parisian."

"Your ear *is* good," he says. "I spent the first eight years of my life between Paris and Burgundy. Then Maman and I moved to Nepal."

"Nepal as in the country in the Himalayas?"

"Yes," he grins. "That one."

"Wow," I draw out. "Was it hard living there so far from home?"

"I didn't mind once I stopped missing my b—" He stops himself and his expression hardens. "France."

"Were you in the capital city?"

His face relaxes into a smile again.

That smile will be the death of me.

"Nepal's capital is called Kathmandu," Noah says. "And yes, we stayed there most of the time. Maman and I enjoyed a lot more comfort than the vast majority of people she was helping."

"Did she volunteer for a nonprofit?"

"She still does."

"You must be very proud of her."

"I am."

There's another stretch of silence, during which we stare at each other without uttering a word. Forgetting about decorum, I let my gaze caress his strong neck, firm jawline, and chiseled mouth before it reaches his eyes the color of the ocean on a rainy day.

Our gazes meet.

My heart races—faster, louder—until it starts to feel like a countdown timer in my chest.

What's happening to me?

Come on, Sophie, you're smart enough and big enough to know.

It's called sexual attraction.

Something I've never experienced before. Something I thought was beyond my reach. Which was fine by me, because—let's face it—what good has lust ever done anyone?

Lechery has ruined brilliant careers. Randiness has pushed people to make irrational decisions. Passion has messed up so many perfectly happy, accomplished lives… and for what? A moment's gratification?

My inability to be sexually aroused isn't a flaw as I've come to realize.

It's a blessing.

"Got to go," I say, standing up. "I need to hit the shops before they close."

Noah stands up, too. "Looking for something specific?"

"Folding chairs. I'd like to buy two inexpensive folding chairs for my studio apartment and a bright-colored poster to give it some personality."

"Do you know where to look for that sort of stuff?"

I nod. "BHV."

"BHV is pricey."

"So is everything in Paris."

"But not outside of it." He gives me a mysterious smile. "Have you been to Les Puces of Saint Ouen?"

"What's that?"

"A huge flea market north of Paris, next to the Porte de Clignancourt. If you want items with personality, that's where you should look."

"I would need a car to go there and I can't drive in Paris. Neither can Mom."

"Two folding chairs and a poster, eh? Is that all you need?"

I nod.

"Does your poster have to be big?"

"No."

"Then I have a solution."

I raise my eyebrows.

"My scooter," he says.

"It's kind of you, but if I won't dare to drive in Paris, I'm definitely too chicken to ride a—"

"That's not what I meant. I'll take you to Les Puces."

My jaw slackens. "You can't be serious."

"Why not?"

"Aren't you busy enough with your own life and obligations?"

"It's no trouble at all." He smiles brightly. "I've been meaning to go there, anyway. A friend told me about this bistro, Chez Louisette, where you can eat overcooked lentils, drink cheap beer, and listen to terrible covers of Edith Piaf songs."

My lip curls. "You make it sound so *enticing*."

"Trust me, it's great fun. Besides, now is the perfect time for me to visit Les Puces of Saint Ouen."

"Why's that?"

"I'm grounded in Paris between two water polo seasons, and I can't think of a better plan for next Sunday."

I hesitate.

"Listen," he says. "Will it help if I tell you I have a vested interest in taking you to Saint Ouen?"

"Maybe… Go on."

"I see it as a unique opportunity to ingratiate myself

with my new landlady. Who knows, I may never get another chance."

I raise both my hands in defeat. "OK, you convinced me. What time?"

"Nine thirty in the morning. I'll pick you up if you text me your home address."

"Texting as we speak."

I fish my phone out of my briefcase and a few seconds later, Noah's phone beeps with my message.

This isn't wise, Sophie, the voice of reason whispers in my head.

Don't I know that? I whisper back.

A Sunday outing with my sexy new tenant is as ill-advised as it gets.

But, man, I'm excited about it.

FIVE

NOAH

Maman video calls me via Skype over breakfast.

I mute the radio, prop my tablet up, and answer the call.

"*Bonjour, mon chéri*," Maman says.

Her hair, clothes and makeup are as impeccable as ever.

"*Salut, Maman*."

"I've missed you."

"I miss you, too, Maman."

"My sweet little boy." She gives me a smile tinted with nostalgia. "All grown-up and handsome. Just look at you."

I clear my throat. "Shouldn't you be at the office, bossing people around right now?"

She sighs. "I should, but… I took a day off."

"Are you OK? Migraine?"

"Yes." She rubs her left temple. "Uma's latest news triggered it."

My heart skips a beat. "Did something happen to her? Is she all right?"

"She's OK." Maman gives me a funny little smile. "But she must get out of here real soon. Sooner than we thought."

I sit back, waiting for details.

"Mr. Darji told her over dinner last night he'd been approached about her and expects her to be married by October."

"What?"

She rubs her forehead. "I knew this would happen. Last time I paid them a visit, Mrs. Darji said something about Uma being ripe for marriage, but I hoped it was just a general observation."

Uma is twenty-three, so by Nepali standards, she's close to *overripe*.

"But what about her plans? I thought the Darjis were proud of her talent, and that she was going to Paris to learn haute couture embroidery."

"They were," Maman says. "And now, all of a sudden, they aren't anymore. I had the most unpleasant conversation with Mr. Darji after Uma called me earlier tonight. She was on the verge of a meltdown, the poor thing."

"What did Mr. Darji say?"

"That the man who approached him about Uma is a Brahmin."

"Shit."

Maman smirks. "Certainly not from Mr. Darji's perspective. To him, it's a chance of a lifetime and an honor. You should've heard him rave about the match. How do you reason with someone who's ecstatic?"

I can't say I'm surprised. Brahmins are the high

aristocracy in Hindu societies, and the Darjis are Dalits—one of the lowest and poorest castes. Mr. and Mrs. Darji love their children, but I've always suspected their letting Maman encourage Uma's dreams wasn't because they believed in the economic emancipation of women. They just thought that beautiful, educated Uma was too good for street peddlers and manual workers of their own caste.

And then a Brahmin comes along.

No wonder he's ecstatic.

I exhale a heavy breath. "Does Uma want to marry the man?"

"Absolutely not!" Maman bugs her eyes out for emphasis. "She dreams about Paris, the Ecole Lesage, and…" She gives me that funny look again.

"What?" I prompt.

"She's in love with you," Maman blurts out.

For months now, there have been hints and allusions, but it's the first time Maman has actually said it.

I tilt my head to the side. "Oh, come on. We've been friends for years. I'd know."

"No, you wouldn't. Men are terrible at *knowing* things like that."

"What are you saying, Maman?"

"Nothing. Just that I've suspected for a while now that my lovely protégée is enamored with my darling boy." She hesitates. "I'd be just as ecstatic as Mr. Darji, if it turned out the feeling was mutual."

At a loss for words, I blink and stare at her.

This conversation starts to feel like the dreaded game situation when I'm on the wrong side of the goal cage with the opponent's top scorer at the two-meter line, and not a single defense player around to give me a hand.

Fortunately, I'm not in the pool right now.

I can dodge the ball.

"Can you speed up her visa?" I ask. "Is Uma prepared to go against her father's wishes?"

"To answer your first question, yes, I can. Remember *Monsieur* Strausse from the consulate?"

"Not really."

"Anyway, I'm going to call in a favor." She clenches her jaw. "Uma will have her visa next week."

"What about Mr. Darji's consent?"

She studies her hands. "Uma hopes the two of us can persuade Mrs. Darji, and that the three of us can make Mr. Darji change his mind."

"But you don't believe that, do you?"

She gives me a pleading look. I know that look. It was what I'd get every time I asked for more details about my father and my brothers. Especially Sebastian.

Maman told me once, five or six years ago, that it hurt too much to talk about it. Didn't I have all the facts? Didn't I *know* what my father had done to her, and how my older brothers took his side so he wouldn't disinherit them? Wasn't that *enough?*

She was right, of course. It should be.

I mean, it *is*.

Just as I'm about to say bye, Maman purses her lips, and her gaze hardens. "No, I don't believe we can convince Mr. Darji. I don't even think we can sway his wife. They see this proposal as a gift from the gods."

"So what will Uma do?"

"Why don't you call and ask her?"

"I will."

She nods and a few minutes later we hang up.

I finish my breakfast with a lot less appetite than before Maman's call.

When I get to the pool, it turns out I may not be the

only one with bad news today. At least that's what the look on Zach's face suggests, as he jumps into the water fifteen minutes after the practice has started.

Zach's *never* late.

"You OK?" I ask him when Lucas lets us rest a few minutes between leg conditioning and shooting drills.

He nods. "I'm fine. It's… I'll explain later."

Lucas blows his whistle, and Zach mucks up his first try from a perfect position. He mutters a curse before picking up the ball again and slamming it with all he's got. I jump high out of the water and block it. His next shot is going to be a lob. That's bad news for me, because Zach is one of the rare players who is able to do it right.

He throws, netting the ball.

By the end of the practice, he's fully recovered his legendary control, and the coach's face relaxes visibly as a result. Small wonder. Our captain isn't just our club's best scorer. He's quite possibly the best shooter in France and one of the best in Europe. While my moniker is "The Rock" due to blocking talents, we call Zach "The Nuke" as in a weapon of mass destruction.

"Is it Sam?" I ask him in the locker room. "Has he come down with something?"

He shakes his head. "Sam's fine. It's his nanny."

I raise my eyebrows. "Mathilde the Perfect?"

"Mathilde the Perfect is cutting her hours in half starting Monday," Zach says with a sigh. "I'll have to miss the afternoon practice, and possibly sit out the season. I'm at my wit's end."

"Doesn't she owe you a longer notice?" I tie the laces of my sneakers. "Is something wrong with one of her own kids?"

He rakes his hands through his hair. "Her older son

has been hanging with the worst cads at school. Almost got expelled last week for something that upsets her so much she won't even talk about it. The kid's only thirteen."

"Shit."

"She's cutting her hours so she can spend more time with her children."

"Can she afford it?"

"Unfortunately for me," Zach says with a smirk, "she can. Her husband is a security guard at a shopping mall, and he's about to get a promotion, so they'll manage."

"Hey, you should see this as an opportunity to get that au pair you've been thinking about!"

"Your friend Uma," Zach says. "Did she get her visa?"

"Not yet, but she will in a few days."

"You said she'd be looking for a part-time job as soon as she gets here, right?"

"Oh, I see where you're going with this." I give him a happy grin. "She will, indeed."

"Mathilde will keep the mornings, so I'm looking for an au pair to babysit Sam in the afternoon."

"Uma will be attending embroidery classes at the Ecole Lesage in the morning, and she'll be free in the afternoon," I say. "It's perfect."

"Do you think she'll do an occasional evening, too, so I can go out and 'get a life,' as you put it?"

"I'm positive. Uma's your man… er… woman," I say. "She's great with kids."

"Does she speak French? I'm afraid Sam won't understand any Nepali and his English is very limited."

"She speaks perfect French, as it happens. She went

to the same Lycée Français as me, thanks to Maman's Foundation."

Zach expels a relieved breath. "So, you think she'd be interested."

"I'll ask her later today, but I'm sure she'll be thrilled."

"Tell her she'll have a big sunny bedroom, between Sam's room and the guest bathroom. We'll sign a standard contract, and I'll pay her cash for every extra hour."

I nod. "We'll tell her parents she'll be working for a family, OK? If any Nepalis call your house, you're *married*."

"No problem." Zach smiles. "I totally get how that would reassure her parents. If necessary, I'll ask Colette to play along and talk to them over Skype when she stops by to visit Sam."

"She won't mind?"

Zach has maintained a good relationship with his ex for Sam's sake, but I doubt she's a generous kind of person.

"She'll do it," Zach says.

"Cool."

He gives me a suspicious look. "Is there something going on between you and Uma that I should be aware of?"

The question is so unexpected I lose my tongue.

"I didn't mean to pry," Zach adds quickly. "And you're free to say it's none of my fucking business. It's just… as her future employer and your friend, I'd like to know if she's *more* than a friend to you or *used to be* more than a friend. To avoid gaffes or awkwardness."

"It's a fair question," I say. "We've never been

romantically involved. But we used to be close growing up. She's a fantastic human being."

Zach cocks his head. "Is that a roundabout way of saying you'd like to be romantically involved with her?"

I remember Maman's statement that Uma is in love with me. Could she be right? What about me? Do I love Uma more than just as a friend?

"Relax." Zach pats my shoulder. "I'm her future employer not her older brother."

I pick up my duffel bag and stand. "If I were looking for a relationship, I guess Uma would be perfect. My mother certainly thinks so."

"Well done, buddy!" Zach grins. "You haven't even started dating the woman, but you already have your mother's approval." He stands and slings his duffel over his shoulder. "For what it's worth, you have mine, too."

"That's great." I give a tight smile. "But I'm not looking for a relationship at the moment. I want to focus on the games."

Which is why the attraction I feel for Sophie is best ignored.

Offering to take her to the flea market on Sunday was a deplorable lapse of judgment. But it's too late to call it off now. I'll be fine. I'll do my duty as a good tenant, making sure to keep it friendly and professional the whole time. And after we say good-bye, chances are we'll never see each other again.

"Oh, yeah, absolutely," Zach says. "I want to focus on the games, too. But I do look forward to having an au pair in the house so I can date again."

I give him a sympathetic smile.

"That is," Zach adds, "if I can figure out the new dating rules and remember how to ask a woman out."

It's my turn to pat his shoulder. "Fret not, my friend.

I happen to know a hot single woman who might be exactly what you need."

The moment those words are out, I wish I could take them back. A jealousy I've never felt for anyone before stirs deep inside me. It makes me feel like a character in the *Alien* movies who discovers that a horrible creature has quietly hatched and grown inside his gut.

The beast thrashes in anger and pain, roaring, "Sophie's mine!"

What the fuck?

"That would be fantastic!" Zach turns to me, his eyes bright. "Do you think you could arrange a chance encounter?"

"Sure thing." I force a smile even as the alien bellows so hard I can barely hear myself speak.

SIX

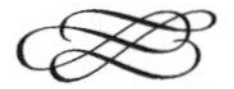

SOPHIE

"Hop on," Noah says, handing me a helmet and jutting his chin to the spot behind him.

The only thing his scooter has in common with the sleek two-wheelers Parisians favor is its general shape and presence of a motor.

"Did you find this… *thing* at Les Puces?" I ask, climbing on behind him.

"Don't worry," he says. "It's in a better shape than it looks."

Once I've adjusted the helmet, I put my arms around his waist, and off we ride into the hubbub and exhaust fumes.

By the time we're on the Périph'—the main ring road around Paris—I'm a wreck.

I knew the journey would be rough because of all the noise, traffic, and pollution along the way. Specifically, I'd anticipated muscle pain in my neck and shoulders because I'd spend the entire ride tense with fear that we would collide with a truck or fly off our iron horse on a sharp turn.

But an altogether different fear stiffens me.

As we slalom between cars, buses and bikes, I worry Noah could hear my heart pounding like crazy in my chest. What if he misinterprets it? What if he assumes I'm squeezing his hips between my thighs *not* because I'm hanging on for dear life, but because I enjoy the contact? The embarrassment of it! Just to think he might imagine that the constant friction between said hips and thighs excited me.

It does not.

And what if he assumed the reason I'm hugging him tight, my breasts flat against his back and my cheek pressed to the back of his neck, is not to increase my chances of survival, but because he aroused me?

He does not.

Nobody does.

What I'm feeling is adrenaline—not arousal. There's no way it's arousal. I don't *do* arousal. Never felt it before and not going to start now. Besides, the way I envision my future, I have no use for it.

Twenty or so minutes later, Noah turns off the Périph' and parks the scooter in front of a row of bric-a-brac stalls.

"*Et voilà*," he announces removing his helmet. "Welcome to Les Puces of Saint Ouen!"

I hand him my helmet and look around. "Where's the entrance?"

"Here," he says pointing to the cluster of scruffy peddlers selling knock off watches and handbags.

"Is this some kind of Platform Nine and Three-Quarters, and we're supposed to walk right through these people?"

He chuckles, shoving our helmets into the saddlebag.

"I suggest we go around them. There'll be two or three pretty gates inside the market."

"Promise?"

"Cross my heart."

"All right, then."

"Shall we?" He motions toward the stalls. "We have a lot of ground to cover."

I nod and follow.

For the next hour, we wander between booths displaying old stamps, kitchen gizmos, costume jewelry, vinyls, and all sorts of knickknacks. To some of these items, time has been as kind as to Jane Fonda. Others haven't aged quite so well.

I halt in front of a small boutique that sells vintage wedding dresses.

Ooh-la-la, they're pretty.

I'm not speaking about the 80s monstrosities with puffy sleeves and nylon skirts whose white has veered to gray. What I'm gawking at are the cream-colored ones cut in raw silk and lace.

The day I marry the man of Dad's dreams, I'll wear a dress like this.

When we pass a stand with dozens of severed doll heads organized by size and color, I wince and glance at Noah.

He shrugs. "To each his own bad taste."

"Let's move on," I say. "They creep me out."

"Did you know this is the largest flea market in the world, and one of the oldest?" Noah asks as we amble on.

"Really?"

"It was established back to the 1880s by ragmen called *biffins*."

I quirk my lips. "Someone's spent time reading up."

"Just doing my job as your guide for the day."

Another hour of exploring the main artery of *Les Puces* called rue des Rosiers, and the alleys that branch off it, and I find what I came here for. Actually, Noah was the one to spot the booth selling framed vintage posters. I picked an adorable, red and white *affiche* of a fifties movie *Mon Oncle*.

A dozen stalls further down rue des Rosiers, we stumble upon a furniture shop that carries folding chairs. They're in good condition—and cheap.

"Perfect," Noah says, tucking them under his arm. "Time for a well-deserved musical lunch at Chez Louisette."

"Aren't you buying anything?"

"I was hoping to find a toy for Oscar," he says. "But no luck."

"Who's Oscar?"

"My dog."

"You mean your *imaginary* dog?" I fold my arms over my chest. "I've been to your place twice and didn't notice any pets."

His lips curl up. "I'm flattered you think I'm a guy who'd have an imaginary dog. But Oscar is real."

I arch an eyebrow.

"He's vacationing in Brittany at the moment."

My second eyebrow goes up.

"With my neighbors," Noah adds.

"Of course." I school my features into a polite expression. "Has he sent you a postcard yet? Is he enjoying himself?"

"Last time I had him on the phone, he definitely was," Noah says, unfazed.

"Glad to hear it. What else did he say? Has he done any sightseeing?"

Noah grins. "I wasn't joking, you know. Oscar uses different sounds to express his emotions and needs, and I've learned to decode the most basic ones."

"So you speak Dog."

"I understand it."

"Give me an example."

"OK." He scratches the back of his head. "Let's see. He uses a unique frustrated growl to say, *My toy is stuck under the couch and my paws are too short to get it.*"

I smile. "One more."

"A high-pitched whining sound means *I need to pee.*"

"Another one?"

"When he purrs, it roughly translates as *I like what you're doing. Please continue.*"

I tilt my head to the side. "Oscar purrs."

"Oh yes."

"And you're *sure* he's real."

"You don't believe me?"

"Err… No."

"OK." He purses his lips. "Let's bet. If Oscar doesn't exist, you get a front-row seat for the first game of the season we'll be hosting."

"And if he does?"

"You'll join me and two of my friends for a dinner at the Moose."

"What kind of place is that?"

"A Canadian sports bar."

I agree to his terms before it hits me that no matter who wins this bet, Noah and I will have to see each other again.

For the next few minutes, we follow the GPS on his phone that leads us to Chez Louisette.

"In business since 1930," Noah says in a deep TV announcer's voice as he opens the door for me.

I step inside—and tumble into a time warp.

The place is rundown as if it hasn't been refurbished since 1930, but it glitters like a Christmas tree. Tacky garlands, pom-poms, and ribbons in red and gold hang from the ceiling. Mirrored balls and chandeliers dangle between the ribbons.

As if all of that wasn't enough, gaudy string lights add to the kitschy oomph of the room, drawing the eye to the performers' corner where a pudgy old lady belts out Piaf's "*La Vie en rose.*" A gentleman of matching build and age accompanies her on the accordion. Some of the diners sing along.

In the space between the tables and the bar, three or four couples dance a fast, bouncy waltz I recognize from old French movies that Mom and I watch sometimes.

I can't believe this place is real.

We sit down and order a beer for Noah, a sparkling water for me, and today's special for both, which is some kind of simmered dish.

The singer finishes "*La Vie en rose*" and moves on to the equally famous "*Non, je ne regrette rien.*"

"Do you have friends or family here in Paris?" Noah asks.

"My mom lives here."

"Are your parents separated?"

"Divorced."

"Mine, too," he says.

"Is your dad in France?"

Noah smirks. "His grave is."

"I'm sorry."

"I'm not."

My eyebrows shoot up.

"He was a nasty piece of work," Noah says.

"That's harsh."

"Why? My father was debauched, unreliable, tightfisted, and mean."

"Really? All of those things?"

"I'll give you an example. Several years after the divorce Maman needed money, so she swallowed her pride and asked him for help. He said no. So I swallowed my teenage pride and asked if he could please help her. The answer was still no."

"Was he broke?" I ask.

"Yes, but not in the usual sense of the word," he says cryptically, a grim look on his face.

My heart goes out to him. Despite my parents' divorce, I enjoyed a sheltered, happy childhood with both Mom and Dad doting on me and rich enough to get me almost anything I wanted. Noah, on the other hand, sounds like he grew up in poverty and rejected by his dad. It must've been hard for him.

"How was living on a shoestring?" I ask.

"We weren't poor," he mutters, turning away.

Great. Now I've hurt his pride.

Our food and drinks arrive, offering a much-needed distraction.

"How did you come to play water polo?" I ask, changing the topic. "Is it a popular sport in Nepal?"

His face crinkles up in a smile. "Nepalis prefer elephant polo."

"Have you played it?"

He shakes his head. "I guess I'm too French for that. Besides, I love water and swimming, and I love ball games like handball and basketball."

"You're sure tall enough for basketball."

"I did play it for a short while in middle school. But the day I tried water polo, I knew it was my sport."

The singer, who'd left the room momentarily, returns

to her spot. She nods to the man on the accordion and starts crooning, "*Padam… Padam….*"

"It's my favorite Piaf song," I say.

A middle-aged man and a woman two tables to our left stand up and launch into a bouncy waltz in front of the bar.

"Isn't this dance called *la java*?" I ask Noah.

"No clue," he says. "Want to give it a try?"

I blink at him. "Can you dance it?"

"Nope. But it doesn't look too complicated to me."

The temptation is too strong, so I set my glass on the table. "I might step on your toes."

"Step away."

He offers his hand, and we head to the improvised dance floor.

As we begin our clumsy stomp and whirl, all I can think of is Noah's hand holding mine, snug and tight. His other hand settles just above the low waistline of my jeans. His palm is huge. It wraps around my hip gently, but I can sense the strength in it, and I can certainly feel its warmth through the thin fabric of my tee. My skin prickles. What's weird about this is that I find his touch… pleasant.

"What's your function on the team?" I ask to take my mind off that troubling thought.

"Goalie."

"Was that your choice?"

"It was more by chance than by choice," he says. "When I joined the team in college, my coach needed someone to man the cage. I was the biggest guy on the team and, as it turned out after a few games, a natural at blocking."

"I envy you," I say. "I've been good at most things I've tried, but I've never been a *natural* at anything."

He gives me a wink. "Keep trying things."

When the song ends and we return to our table, Noah pulls out his smartphone. "So, let's get that bet settled."

"Now?"

He nods, tapping and scrolling on his phone until he finds what he's looking for. Holding up the phone, he shows me a dozen pictures of him and his furry companion. Then he shows me a short video of him scratching the dog's throat.

Oscar tips his head back and purrs. The sound he makes is low, soft and continuous, and it's definitely saying, *Oh yeah, right there, so good.*

"All right," I say, looking up at Noah. "You win."

He grins.

"So who are these friends of yours that I'll have the honor of meeting?"

"One is Uma," he says. "My best friend. She's arriving from Nepal this weekend."

"For a visit?"

"No, for longer." He gives me a weird look I can't read. "Forever, I hope."

His last words rattle me inexplicably.

"And the other one?" I ask.

"Zach, my team captain." Noah's gaze is trained on his beer as he adds, "He's a successful businessman and an all-around great guy. Zach is looking to meet a lovely young woman… like you."

Hey-ho.

I force a smile. "That would be great."

SEVEN

NOAH

I park my scooter a few blocks from Zach's house and head to his charming redbrick at the end of the street. Zach lives in Inry, a residential suburb of Paris that I'd never set foot in until Uma and I moved her things here.

She got her visa and arrived in France ten days ago.

The original plan had been that she'd stay in the Derzians' empty apartment until late August, when my kind neighbors return from Brittany. By then, she'd find a job and a room in a shared rental or in a student residence at Cité Universitaire. But Zach was eager for her to start as soon as possible. She did, and according to Zach, she hit it off with Sam immediately.

I'm happy about that, not in the least because I was the artisan of this arrangement. And it's fucking perfect any way you look at it. First of all, Uma will be able to return the grant money she believes others need more. Second, she'll be safe with Zach, whom I'd trust with my life, so Maman and I don't need to worry. Third, Zach got a huge weight off his shoulders. He can focus on the games again and start dating.

About that.

I called Sophie this morning to see if she was free on Saturday night for that dinner we'd discussed at the flea market. She said she was. I said "awesome" except awesome is the last thing I feel about it.

I keep thinking of our *la java* dance in that tacky bistro, two weeks back. We goofed around and I kept her at a safe distance from start to finish, but boy, was it hard. Just like the first time we met when I did a full salute within seconds of pinning her to the wall.

As we danced, the hand I'd placed on her hip as lightly as I could, itched to hold her harder. My fingers ached to caress her slim back. My palm burned to press into her hip so I could learn its exact curve and imprint its shape into my flesh before sliding lower to gloss her mind-blowing butt. As if that wasn't enough, the urge to crush her against my chest and claim her full mouth almost drove me to the brink of insanity.

Had the singer done one extra chorus of "*Padam… Padam…*," I might've lost control and done all of those things.

There's no denying that Sophie Bander is the worst distraction I've ever had to cope with. She draws me away from what's important. Worse, when I'm around her, my mind clouds over and I get this traitorous impression that nothing else matters. The season, Maman's work, Uma's future—all my goals and wishes pale next to my need to hold her.

What's even worse is that I doubt a night with her would quench my thirst.

Something tells me the opposite would happen. Having sex with her would make me want more sex with her, and the whole thing would spin out of control. Because that's who Sophie is. A dormant siren. A femme fatale pretending she's unexceptional. *Believing* she's unexceptional.

This… this *thing* has to be quashed before it's too late.

I ring Zach's doorbell.

Behind the door, someone stomps down the stairs.

"Let me get it! Let me get it!" Sam shouts excitedly.

A second person scurries to the door.

"OK, but you have to ask the *question* first," Uma says, laughing.

"OK! Who's there?" Sam hollers.

"It's me," I say, putting an eye to the peephole.

There's a silence. I picture Sam looking up at Uma for guidance. She says something I can't make out.

"State your first name and…" Sam commands before stalling. "…and…"

Uma says something again in a quiet voice.

"Last name," Sam shouts. "And step away from the peephole so we can see you."

"Let me help you, buddy," Uma says behind the door, lifting him so he can look through the peephole I guess.

I draw back, smile, and say loudly. "Noah. Masson."

"I remember you," Sam cries. "You're the goalie!"

The door opens, and I step in.

Ten minutes later, the three of us sit around the kitchen table. Uma hands Sam a mug filled with some unidentified beverage and makes a Nespresso shot for each of us.

"I'll be with you in a minute!" Zach calls from upstairs. "Just need to finish this conference call."

Uma prepares another Nespresso with more water—the way Zach likes it.

"So, how is everything?" I ask.

She grins and glances at Sam who's hiding his face behind his Winnie the Pooh mug. "Couldn't be better."

Sam sets his mug on the table. "Daddy's going to the lions tomorrow, and I'm staying with Uma for two days, and we'll watch *Lilo and Stitch* and *Leroy and Stitch.*"

I turn to Uma.

"Zach is going on a two-day business trip to Lyon," she explains, wiping Sam's mouth. "So, yeah, it's going to be a late night for us with Sam's favorite movies."

"Totally unfair," Zach says, walking in and sitting next to Sam. "I love that cartoon just as much as you do."

"You can join us next time," Sam says magnanimously.

Zach gives his shoulder a light squeeze. "Thanks, man."

When the boy runs away to play with his electric train, a deep crease appears between Zach's eyebrows. "I'm still nervous about going away for two days."

Uma hands him his cup. "You shouldn't be."

"You started only a week ago, and already I'm leaving you alone with him," Zach says, shaking his head.

"It's just one night." Uma sits down next to me. "Besides, you had no choice."

Zach turns to me. "I was hoping Colette would rise to the occasion for once… but that didn't happen."

I smirk as I picture Sam's mother serving Zach her standard response. Had Zach listened to her, Sam would be somebody else's responsibility now. But Zach *chose* to keep him, well aware of the boy's condition, so now Sam is Zach's problem. Not hers.

My teammate gives Uma an apologetic look. "Just say the word, and I'll cancel the trip."

"I know exactly what to do if Sam has a seizure. You should stop fretting." She stares into his eyes. "This trip is super important for your business, right?"

Zach nods. "It is. Otherwise, I wouldn't even consider going."

She shrugs.

"Uma's right," I say to Zach. "Stop fretting. You're leaving your boy in capable hands."

I mean it, too. Uma is the most dependable person in the world. She's kind, gentle, competent, and always in control. The kind of person I'd entrust with my life… and with my kid's life, if I have a kid one day.

Maman is right—she's perfect. It's humbling that a woman like that has feelings for me.

"Hey," Zach turns to me. "I never properly thanked you for arranging the outing next Saturday. Sophie sounds exactly like someone I'd want to date."

I shrug dismissively. "You'll thank me later if everything goes well. Did you find a solution for Sam?"

"I can babysit him," Uma offers.

"No way. You're coming with us." Zach gives her a wink. "Noah here would be *very* disappointed if you didn't."

"But what about Sam?" she asks.

Zach grins triumphantly. "Mathilde has agreed to come over for the evening."

"Cool." I stand up. "Thanks for the coffee, Uma."

She smiles. "Anytime."

"Will you be at the morning practice tomorrow?" I ask Zach.

He nods. "My train to *the lions* leaves at one fifteen."

~

WHEN I GET HOME, there's a letter in my mailbox. The handwriting on the envelope is Diane's.

Fantastic.

Yet another missive from my unwanted sister-in-law, who appears to be even more pigheaded than my brothers are in her refusal to let me be.

I plop onto the couch, tear the envelope open, and retrieve a sheet of paper. She's slipped in a few pictures, too, as per her habit. I set the photos aside and read the letter.

Dear Noah,

Sebastian, baby Tanguy, and I are spending another wonderful weekend at your estate. Take a look at the photos I enclosed. What do you think of the park? And isn't the castle absolutely gorgeous? The wild grapevine on the façade is so pretty against the old stones, you'd think I photoshopped it. (Just in case you do, please note I am not *that kind of girl).*

You should come and see it with your own eyes.

Oh, I will—sooner than you might expect.

Just so you know, I made several dozen large prints of that grapevine. They are framed and stacked in the storage room. They might come in handy should you choose to revamp the interior when you do the renovations, which are badly needed.

Pff. As if I cared.

Believe me, I'm not exaggerating. Chateau d'Arcy is falling apart. Given the thickness of its walls, the structure is in no danger, but the rest… If you set foot inside, I'm sure your heart will bleed. I tried to convince Seb to fix the worst of it, but he says it's not our place. He says he'll be happy to fund the works, so you won't have to deplete your trust fund for that, but you should take charge.

Do you think you could do that?

Hugs,

Diane

I lay the letter on the coffee table and lean back, clasping my hands behind my head. This note will go unanswered just like all of Diane's previous letters.

She seems to be a good girl. What a shame she had to ruin her life by marrying Seb, a.k.a. His Pompous Ass, Excellency Count Sebastian d'Arcy du Grand-Thouars de Saint-Maurice. My friendly sister-in-law is in for a lot of heartache the day she finally opens her eyes and faces the bitter truth.

Beneath the veneer of respectability, the country's oldest, richest, and most envied family has no honor. The way my late father and Seb treated Maman with Raphael's tacit consent is ugly. I'll never forgive them for that. My older brothers are unworthy of the riches they own.

If only my *Papa chéri* hadn't made a will!

Had he kicked the bucket without leaving one, his estate would've been divided equally between his three sons, according to French inheritance laws. Nothing for Maman, of course, whom he'd conveniently divorced.

But he did leave a will, and I can't legally dispose of my share until I'm twenty-seven.

Guess what? I'm turning twenty-seven in six weeks' time.

I feel a prick of conscience. It has nothing to do with my plans for the estate. But it has to do with how my cryptic answers might've led Sophie to believe I'd starved in Nepal.

When I told her Papa had refused to help Maman, I failed to mention that the money she was asking for wasn't for food or shelter. She needed a half million dollars for her foundation. The initial endowment having dried up and no new sponsors forthcoming, Maman's life's achievement was going down the drain.

But she and I were doing fine on alimony. More than fine. Compared to local standards, we were rich.

So why did I let Sophie think otherwise?

I guess it was the only way to stop her from asking more questions. She's my landlady, for Christ's sake—not my friend like Uma and Zach. She'll be gone by Christmas. There's no reason why I should share with her the fucked-up story of my life.

No reason at all.

EIGHT

SOPHIE

The first thing I see as we enter the Moose is a rustic stone wall behind the bar with a couple of flat screens tuned to hockey.

"How very North American," Uma says with a smile. "Not that I've been to North America, but that's exactly how I imagined a sports bar somewhere in Seattle."

"This one is more Montreal than Seattle," Zach says.

The place is lit by the dim glow of ceiling spots and at least a dozen wall-mounted flat-screen TVs. Polished wood and moose antlers dominate the decor.

The four of us had met by the statue of Danton at Odéon, which is spitting distance from here. I'd ridden the *métro* from work, Uma and Zach had arrived in his car, and Noah on his scooter.

Now that it stays warm after dusk, I revel in the pleasant coolness of this bar.

We make our way to the sitting area and pick one of the two vacant tables.

To our left, a large boisterous group is having a lively conversation in Quebecois French so thick you could slice it with a knife.

I jerk my chin in their direction. "Looks like we've found the place where Canadian tourists come to chill after a hard day's sightseeing."

"But that's a good sign, right?" Uma says. "Canadians wouldn't come here if this place wasn't authentic."

Noah smiles. "The main reason they come here is that there aren't a lot of sports bars in Paris."

Zach nods. "And even fewer where you can watch the Super Bowl, Stanley Cup and NBA playoffs in real time."

"And eat a decent poutine," Noah adds.

Zach raises his index finger. "*Pootseen*, please, if you want to sound Quebecois."

"What's a *Pootseen*?" I ask.

Noah and Zach exchange a meaningful glance.

"You'll discover soon enough," Noah says.

I think he was warning me, and I burst out laughing at his amusing air of mystery.

"Ladies." Zach looks from Uma to me and then to Noah. "Gentleman. Do I have everyone's permission to order your food and drinks?"

I narrow my eyes. "Depends on what you're ordering."

"You allergic to anything?" he asks.

I shake my head.

"Relax, Sophie," Noah touches my hand. "Nobody's treating you to fried crickets. We'll have Moosehead—a Canadian beer—and poutine."

I sigh. "Beer is fine. It's poutine that I'm worried about."

"Hang on." Uma rummages through her tote bag, muttering, "He used to do this all the time when we were kids—asking if I'd like a profiterole or a bit of *aligot* or a slice of *tatin*, and I had to say yes or no before he'd tell me what those things were."

"Did I ever trick you into eating something you hated?" Noah asks her.

"That's not the point." She pulls out a smartphone. "Ta-da! Don't you love modern technology? No more surprises. We're going to find out what poutine is in a moment."

Zach waves a server over, while Uma fumbles with her phone.

"Found it," she announces a few seconds later and begins to read out loud.

> Poutine was invented in Quebec under mysterious circumstances and in an undisclosed location sixty years ago. It has since become Canada's national dish. The classic poutine ("*la classique*") is made from hand-cut French fries topped with cheese curds (called *crottes de fromage* by locals, which means "cheese poop") and with hot brown gravy called *velouté*. Greasy and calorie rich, poutine is the ultimate comfort food.

Uma drops her phone back into her handbag and grins. "Sounds yummy."

Does she mean it?

I peer at her face and conclude to my horror that she does.

If I were a blunt kind of girl, I would've told these people what poutine sounded like from a health-conscious Floridian's perspective. It sounded like love handles, pimples, and a heart attack.

Zach turns to the waiter. "We'll have four Mooseheads and four classic poutines."

"Awesome." I bare my teeth. "Right up my alley. Can't wait."

I wonder if any of them can hear the sarcasm in my voice.

Noah hems before shifting his gaze from me to one of the TV screens. His lips are twitching.

Five minute later the server brings our frosty beers and steaming plates.

I stare at the huge serving of fries and rubbery cheese curds smothered in gravy. "This doesn't look very… appetizing."

"Don't be afraid to say it looks like shit," Noah says.

"The proof of the pudding isn't in looking pretty," Zach says. "It's in the eating."

With the fuck-it-all determination of a kamikaze pilot, I pick up my fork and knife. "All right, let's eat."

The cheese curds squeak in my mouth as I chew.

"I recommend you wash it down with beer," Noah says, his eyes riveted to my mouth. "It'll help your palate handle the shock."

Uma turns to me. "Isn't this the kind of food you're used to?"

I shake my head. "In Key West, we have lots of options to choose from. You can eat Cuban or vegetarian or French or… whatever. I usually go for French as I'm used to it."

"Sophie's mom is French," Noah says.

"That explains it." Zach gives me a bright smile. "I was wondering why your French was so good—barely a hint of an accent."

I acknowledge his compliment with a polite smile.

"What kind of place is Key West?" Noah asks.

"In one word?" I chew on my lower lip, thinking. "Relaxed. You'd like it."

"Tell me more." His eyes are on my mouth again.

Is that why I keep biting my lip?

I'm not in the habit of doing that—actually, I *never* do that. But there's something highly addictive in the way he stares at my mouth. The heat of his gaze makes me want to encourage him, makes me hungry for more.

Get a grip, Sophie.

I shrug. "In a nutshell—we have a tropical climate, the best beaches and sunsets, occasional hurricanes, and hordes of tourists on Duval Street." Winking, I add, "As well as lovely wood houses for sale via my dad's agency. Should anyone be interested."

An hour later, Zach settles the bill, and I use the occasion to study his face. The man is certainly good-looking. He's been the perfect gentleman throughout the dinner. So, why am I hoping Noah will offer me a ride home?

"Can I offer you a lift?" Zach asks me, standing up.

"I live in the 18th," I say. "You and Uma would have to make a huge detour and lose an hour, if not more."

This would be Noah's cue to jump in and offer that ride.

But he doesn't. He studies his shoes.

Uma turns to Zach. "Why don't I take the *métro* so that we don't delay Mathilde, and you take Sophie home?"

"I'll give you a lift," Noah says to Uma. "It'll be faster."

Shoot.

Inside Zach's Beamer, he makes small talk and I nod

as we drive north through the quiet city bathed in the soft light from windows and street lamps. The stereo streams jazzy French music. Add that to the air-conditioning and Zach's deep, masculine bass, and this *should* be a very pleasant ride. Romantic, even.

But it's confusion, not romance, that fills my mind right now.

My thoughts return to the Moose. The food sucked, but I truly enjoyed the company. Uma was totally sweet. Zach was gracious. Noah was… Noah. We ate, drank, joked, and pretended our "dinner among friends" wasn't really a double date, and we weren't really two couples in the making.

Couple Number 1—Uma and Noah, childhood besties teetering between friendship and something more.

Couple Number 2—Zach and I testing the waters to see if we click.

Do we click? I guess so.

In addition to being gorgeous, Zach is also a wealthy go-getter interested in a relationship. Unlike Noah.

Besides, he fits Dad's idea of a perfect catch to a T.

If I am to give the whole dating thing another shot and go out with someone while I'm in Paris, it should be him. In fact, I can't find a single reason why we shouldn't date.

My mind conjures up an image of Uma and Noah huddled together on his scooter.

It's decided.

If Zach asks me out, I'll say yes.

NINE

NOAH

I'm headed to the Parc des Buttes-Chaumont with a blanket, a pillow, an ultralight bivvy tent, and a cold beer stuffed into my duffel when my phone beeps.

It's a text from Sophie.

Are you asleep? I wanted to ask you a quick question, but it can certainly wait until tomorrow. Sophie

I tap a quick reply.

Awake. Shoot.

My curiosity piqued, I keep looking at the screen to read her reply as soon as it arrives. But, instead of beeping, my phone rings.

"Sorry for calling you this late," Sophie says. "I'd expected you'd be in bed already."

It hits me how much I like the sound of her voice. Feminine, velvety, sexy as hell. Even the most innocuous thing she says feels like a caress. I could listen to her say innocuous—and not so innocuous—things all day.

"Ten is a little early even for us larky athletes," I say. "Not to mention it's impossible to sleep in this heat."

"Tell me about it!" She lets out a sigh. "Why is it that no one has AC in Paris?"

"Because we don't believe global warming is real."

"Hmm." She doesn't sound convinced.

"Or maybe because we don't get heat waves every year, and they don't last long, so we hesitate to fork over several thousand euros on AC."

"That sounds more like the French," she says, a smile in her voice. "So what do you do to be able to sleep?"

"By 'you' are you referring to the French as a nation or me, Noah Masson, as a person?"

There's a brief pause before she replies. "You as a person."

"Tonight, I'm trying my luck outdoors. The town hall has opened several parks for overnight camping, so I'll be bivouacking in Buttes-Chaumont. I'm heading there as we speak."

"I'm not far from there myself," she says. "My boss and I were showing an apartment nearby, and then had a couple of drinks, so I'm still in the hood."

"Your boss takes you out for drinks," I say pointedly before I can stop myself. "How kind of him."

Shit.

That was totally uncalled for. The kind of relationship Sophie has with her boss is none of my business. She's my landlady, not my girlfriend.

"It *is* very kind of *her*," Sophie says. "I couldn't dream of a better boss for my first paid internship."

I wish I could bang my head against something right

now, hard. "Of course. That comment was way too macho, even for me. I'm really sorry."

"I forgive you," she says, her voice returning to velvety.

My shoulders sag with relief. "You said you had a question."

"I did."

"I'm listening."

"Err… Do you mind if I meet you in the park and I ask in person? I promise it won't take long."

Every nerve ending in my body perks up at "meet you" and dances a little jig at "in person." My pulse kicks into high gear and my cock stirs in my pants.

"It's about Zach," she says.

Oh.

Of course. Now that she's met him—and, no doubt, *liked* him—she wants to know more about him. What did I expect?

"Sure," I say, trying to sound pleased. "Can you be at the main entrance on the corner of Botzaris and Simon-Bolivar in ten minutes?"

"Fifteen."

"Great. See you there."

Thirty minutes later, we're sitting next to each other —me cross-legged and Sophie hugging her knees—on the blanket I've spread under a tree. She's wearing a flowy summer dress with a hem that bares her lithe calves and part of her thighs. My gaze travels down to her feet. They're clad in sandals with sexy straps that crisscross and snake around her slim ankles. Her toenails are painted dark red.

They are the most beautiful feet I've ever laid eyes on.

My chest clenches with longing.

Cut the crap, Noah.

That's way too much appreciation for a woman you're trying to set up with a friend.

Peeling my gaze off her, I look around. At least a hundred couples, groups, and individuals have set camp on the vast lawn, prepping for a night under the stars.

I pull the beer out of my bag and open it. "Want some? We better drink it while it's still cold."

"Thank you." She takes a swig and gives the can back. "That felt good."

Lifting the can to my mouth, I wonder if I'll taste Sophie. I wonder what her lush, delicious-looking lips taste like. What her perfect skin tastes like. What her little—

"How well do you know Zach?" she asks.

Talk about cold showers.

On the other hand, I needed this.

"Pretty well. We've been on the same team almost two years now."

"He seems like a nice guy."

"He is." I nod. "Better than nice. He's awesome."

"How come he's raising his kid alone?"

"Zach's ex-girlfriend didn't want the burden of a child with a chronic health condition."

"Oh."

"Sam's epilepsy is manageable," I add quickly. "He'll go to school next year like other kids his age. When he grows up, he can live a normal life, provided he takes his meds."

She nods.

"Look," I say. "I totally get it if you hesitate because of that, but you shouldn't."

"That's not why I—"

"Besides," I add before she can finish. "You can date

Zach without getting involved with his kid. Sam has two nannies and an adoring dad to take care of him."

She frowns. "That's not why I hesitate. It's just... I'm not sure I should start a relationship or even date, when I know I'm going back home in December."

"So what?" I shrug. "Why not have some fun while you're in Paris?"

"It's... complicated."

"Try me."

"You really want to hear it?"

I nod.

She snatches the beer from me, takes a good swig, and hands it back to me. "I'm frigid."

You? No way.

"Are you sure?" I ask.

She nods. "I've dated three different men, had sex with each of them, and never felt anything."

I study her face.

"Worse," she says. "I actually did feel something—pain and discomfort."

My hand touches her cheek before my brain can step in. "I'm sorry."

She doesn't jerk away.

"Now that I've adjusted my expectations," she says, running her hands down her shins, "I find lots of advantages to my condition."

My gaze follows her fingers that are wrapped around her ankles now. "Like what?"

"No distractions, no heartbreaks, no ill-matched boyfriends to be ashamed of later."

"I see."

The hell I do.

What I really see right now in the soft yellowish light of

the nearby streetlamp has nothing to do with ill-matched boyfriends. My world is focused on Sophie's slim ankles, the breathtaking arch of her soles and her long, callus-free toes.

Did I suddenly become a foot fetishist?

"Besides," she says. "I can be rational about picking my future life partner, and make Dad happy by choosing a man who meets his criteria."

"Which are?"

"Successful, ambitious, and gallant." She gives me a funny look. "Someone like Zach."

I glance up at her face. "Your dad has a lot of common sense."

"Gobs of it."

"He wants what's best for you."

"Absolutely."

"But... don't you ever wonder if there's a man out there who'd make you feel things that aren't pain or discomfort?"

"I do, but then I remind myself this is the way I'm wired." She sighs. "It would be foolish to wait for some fairy-tale prince whose kiss would wake me up from my sleep."

"You tried to have sex three times, right?" I cock my head.

She nods.

"That's not *a lot*."

She says nothing.

"Three disappointments aren't enough to conclude that's the way you're *wired*."

Sophie studies a tiny bug traveling down her hand.

"Tell me about each of those times," I say.

"I can't." She shifts her position. "Anyway, I should get going."

I glance at my watch. "It'll be midnight soon. I don't like the idea of you alone on the deserted streets."

"What's the alternative?"

I should offer to call her a cab. "Stay here."

"In the park?" She furrows her brow.

I point at my bivvy. "You'll be safer with me here than on the *métro*."

She peers at me.

I stare back, praying she'll say yes.

Because if she says no, I'm going to pack up and take the *métro* to the 18th with her, then try to catch the last train or hoof it back here. There's no way I'm saying good-bye now. I need a little more of Sophie tonight.

Please say yes.

She picks up the beer can and gulps down the rest of the liquid. "Are there any restrooms in this park?"

Fingers crossed this means yes.

"There's a toilet right there." I point toward a one-story building to our left.

She stands up. "I'll be back."

When she returns a few minutes later, I'm lying on my back with my knees bent and hands clasped under my head.

She lies down next to me, mirroring my position. "You'd expect to see more stars."

"This is plenty for Paris."

We stare at the night sky for a few minutes.

"My first time was with a classmate," she says. "We were sixteen. We were both of us so inept it's a small miracle we actually managed to get rid of our virginity."

I turn to look at her face. She's wincing.

"Not a happy memory, huh?"

She shakes her head. "I was *so* not ready."

"Did you let him near you again?"

"Nope. I broke up with him immediately. He cried."

"What about the second time?"

"The second boyfriend…" She's silent for a long moment. "Sophomore year. I didn't want to rush things, and he said he respected that. So we abstained for a while. And then…"

She expels her breath in a slow hiss.

"And then?"

"I agreed to have sex with him. I thought I liked him. He'd been perfectly likable before he stripped and started touching me." Her words come out fast and angry. "And suddenly, he was repulsive. His smell, his touch, his kisses…"

She releases another long breath.

I turn my head toward her. Sophie's jaw is set, her nostrils flaring, as she's reliving that situation.

"Did—" I begin to form my question.

"The third one," she says with an exaggerated nonchalance, "was the most pathetic experience of all. I was so not into it during foreplay that I went to the bathroom while he was looking for a condom, locked the door, and asked him to leave."

"Ouch." I say. "I wouldn't want to be in that guy's shoes."

She shrugs. "So I figured sex was overrated."

"Do you think you might be into women?"

"No. Definitely not."

"Good," I say.

"Why?"

"Because that gorgeous body of yours was made to be touched by a man."

She smirks. "Here comes the macho again!"

But she's wrong. My comment had nothing to do

with machismo. What I meant by "a man" wasn't abstract. The man I had in mind was specific and concrete with a birth name he'd chosen to discard years ago, and a straining cock he's choosing to ignore right now.

This man.

TEN

SOPHIE

For a moment Noah's eyes burn into mine, intense. He shifts closer to me, ever so slightly, and opens his mouth as if he's about to say something.

And then he blinks and looks away.

When he turns back to me a few seconds later, his expression is unreadable.

"I'm sorry," he says. "Feel free to gag me before I make another highly inappropriate comment."

I pull a face. "Gagging is so *Fifty Shades*. How about duct tape?"

"Really?" He frowns and shrugs. "If that's what floats your boat..."

"Did you pack any, by chance?"

He shakes his head.

I sigh. "In that case, there's only one thing left to do."

He gives me a quizzical look.

"Sleep."

"Good idea." He jumps up. "I'm going to open the bivvy and move the blanket inside, if you don't mind."

I stand up, too. "Won't we be too warm inside?"

"Don't worry." He unfolds the contraption which turns out to be a narrow one-person tent. "See the mesh on the sides? Keeps bugs out but lets air in."

I tip my head back and close my eyes hoping for a night breeze, but the air is as still and sultry as it was at midday.

"Not sure we want *this* air in," I say.

"The temperature will drop soon."

Opening my eyes, I glance at the bivvy. "It's going to be tight in there."

"Are you an aggressive sleeper?"

I smile. "I don't jump, kick, or snore in my sleep if that's what you mean."

"Me neither." Noah throws a small pillow into the bivvy. "We'll be fine."

He steps out of his flip-flops and climbs inside.

I remove my sandals. This is crazy. As in, *crazy exciting.*

When I crawl in, Noah has moved as far to the left as the tent allows, leaving me half of the available space and the whole pillow.

I turn to him, propping myself up. "Can you sleep without a pillow?"

He glances at it and then at me as if considering his options. "You're right. I'll need something."

Sitting up, he pulls off his T-shirt, folds it, and lies back down, tucking it under his head.

My lips part as I take in the glorious triangle of his torso.

Frigid or not, all that smooth, hard, chiseled *manliness*—this close—makes an impression.

Stop ogling his chest, Sophie!

I look at his hands instead. "They're big."

Shoot. Did I just say that out loud?

"You mean my hands?" he asks.

"Uh-huh."

He lifts his right hand and splays his fingers. "Having big hands is an asset for a water polo goalie. As is a large body size, arm span, speed of reaction, and a firm grip."

A firm grip. I swallow.

"Reaction speed is probably the most important feature," Noah says. "A shorter goalie who's explosive will get into the corners faster and block better than a big goalie who's slow."

"So, the ideal is a big explosive goalie, right?"

"Right."

I give him a wink. "Which is where you come in."

He smiles, blushing a little.

Aww. Could this man get any sweeter? I need a joke before my heart melts into a sticky mess. Any dumb crack will do.

"Don't take it the wrong way," I say, "but water polo players look a little funny."

"Funny how?"

"You know, with those bonnets tied neatly under your chins. And your chests are shaved…"

"It's to reduce drag and increase speed."

"Of course. But still…" I give him a sly smile. "It does reinforce the look."

"What look?"

My gaze flicking to his nipples, I mutter, "Baby look."

"Really?"

"Come on," I nudge him. "Can you deny that water

polo players look like babies? Huge, muscular, testosterone-fueled babies."

"Sophie." He arches an eyebrow in fake admonishment. "That was sexist and highly inappropriate."

I drop my head to my chest to show I regret my words. Which I don't. Not for a second.

"What's the word for a macho woman?" he asks.

"Hmm… Man-eater?"

He shakes his head.

"Femdom?" I try again.

"Warmer, but still off the mark."

"Butch?"

He sighs. "I'll have to write a letter to the Académie Française urging them to coin a word for women like you."

"Knock yourself out," I say.

"I'm going to propose *femcho*."

I snort. "That sounds perfectly ridiculous. Makes me think of that fluffy poncho I bought a few years back and never dared to wear."

"Hmm…" He rubs his chin, drawing my attention to the bulging muscles of his upper arm.

"Femcho accusations aside, how do you guys get so fit?" I ask.

He smiles. "We swim at least 2,000 meters during each workout, lift weights for body strength, and stretch for flexibility. Um… what else? We practice shooting and treading water until our arms and legs fall off. You know, the usual 'testosterone-fueled baby' stuff."

If I look at his mouth or his torso a second longer, I might squeal. Or make another inane comment. Or reach over and touch him.

Truth is, I have no idea what I might do because I've never felt this way before.

"Right." I turn away from Noah. "Do you think this light will go off at some point? I find it hard to fall asleep unless it's completely dark."

"Don't know," he says. "Never slept in a park before."

"I need to be at the office early. Do you mind if I set my phone alarm to seven thirty?"

"Mine is set to seven," he says. "I don't want to be late for the morning practice."

"Good night."

"Sweet dreams."

I breathe in the faint scent of Noah's aftershave and shut my eyes. The lawn where we're camping is a lot quieter now than it was half an hour ago, with almost everyone around us having crept into their tents and sleeping bags. I should be able to fall asleep easily.

Fifteen minutes later, I turn toward Noah again.

He's still flat on his back with his eyes wide open.

"The mesh on the other side lets too much light in," I say to justify my change of position.

He turns on his side to face me, folds his right arm under his head, and places his left hand between us, a bare inch from my breasts.

The heat coming off him and the scent of his skin—a touch of aftershave and a lot of Noah—messes with my brain. They take my thoughts and my senses to a place that's entirely new to me. I feel like I was beamed into a rain forest. It's hot, lush and full of surprises.

And scary.

"There's this theory in quantum physics," I say, scrambling to find my bearings.

He gives a crooked smile. "My fair landlady is a closet geek?"

"Not at all." I chuckle. "I just stumbled upon an article a few years back, and it stayed with me."

"What's it about?"

"The mechanics of touch," I say. "According to quantum physics, you can never really touch anything."

"What do you mean?"

"Everything is composed of tiny particles, right?"

He nods.

"Particles repel other particles of the same kind," I say. "For example, when you sit in a chair, you're actually hovering above it."

He furrows his brow. "Then why did my ass always feel sore after sitting in a chair through a double period at school?"

"If I remember correctly," I say with a smile, "it's because the waves you generate overlap with the chair's waves, and your brain misinterprets it as touching."

"So if I do *this*,"—he puts his hand on my hip —"I'm not actually touching you. Is that what you're saying?"

I swallow, trying to keep the smile on my face. "Yes."

He lets his fingers and the ball of his palm gently sink into my flesh without pressing or rubbing. With every second that passes, I feel my body respond to his hand hug. Through the thin silk of my dress, my skin tingles, and the flesh under his hand begins to burn.

Suddenly, the mischievous gleam in his eyes gives way to an entirely different expression.

My smile slips, too.

What's happening to me?

How did I go from pondering if I should date Zach

earlier this evening to wondering which direction Noah will move his hand—up to cup my breast or down to stroke my thigh. And how my body would react to it. And whether my need for him to do that is bigger than my fear.

What if this excitement I'm feeling isn't real and has nothing to do with a normal arousal a normal woman would feel? What if it's just wishful thinking? I may believe I'm aroused, but what will happen when he touches me more intimately? Will the illusion melt into thin air? Will my body stiffen with revulsion, just like it's done before?

The ironic truth is I'd be less anxious if I felt nothing —I'd know what to expect.

But with my body acting so out of character, setting my expectations high and giving me hope, it's just too scary.

"I don't think I'm ready for this," I say, butterflies in my stomach.

He doesn't respond for the longest moment with his hand on my waist and his eyes riveted to mine.

"That's OK," he finally says. "We should try to get some sleep."

Nodding with relief, I turn my back to Noah and push the pillow to the middle, offering him half of it. "I doubt it's comfortable sleeping on a folded tee."

He draws closer, laying his head on the pillow. I feel his warm breath on the back of my neck.

"Do you mind if I put my hand back where it was?" he asks.

"Suit yourself."

His hand returns to my waist and slides over to my belly. Should I tell him off for taking more than he was given? While I'm mulling over that question, he shifts, wrapping his entire arm around me and pulling me closer.

This is so much more than the authorized hand-on-waist that I lose my tongue momentarily.

Next thing I know he's pressing his chest against my back and snaking a leg over my thigh.

"Good night, Sophie," he says, his voice hoarse.

Recovering from my stupor, I finally move. But, instead of drawing away, I arch my body into him, looking for an additional point of contact.

There it is! The hard ridge I'd felt the day we first met when he'd tackled me in his kitchen. I love its length and thickness and the way it nestles against my derriere.

How shocking.

How totally inexplicable and sexy.

"Good night," I rasp, barely recognizing my voice.

What does the quantum theory have to say about this, I wonder? For years, it's been my handy justification for not reacting to a man's touch. Except I'm reacting all right to Noah's. Let's face it—I may not be as frigid as I thought.

How else can I explain that at the ripe age of twenty-four, and against all expectations, Princess Sophie was suddenly roused from her sexuality-free slumber?

I wish my savior were Zach the Successful Entrepreneur.

Or—even better—some hotshot business shark in Florida. But instead, it's Delivery Man Noah... *Damn!* Why did I have to be awakened by a guy who, on top of having neither money nor ambition, possibly nurtures a longtime crush on his childhood bestie?

How fucking ironic is that?

ELEVEN

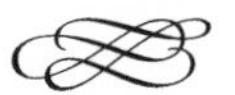

NOAH

Sophie and I head to my place, our feet sinking into the heat-softened asphalt with every step. If I focus on it, it looks as if it's steaming. Just like my brain.

The plan is to drop in, take a quick shower, swallow some coffee and toasts, and jump on my scooter. I'll give her a lift to her office and hightail it to the swimming pool.

We haven't uttered a word that wasn't *practical* since we woke up this morning.

Last night was… I don't even know what it was.

We drank a can of beer. Neglected to admire the stars. Chatted. Connected.

She flirted with me… I think.

I lusted after her, touched her, hugged her.

She let me.

But she wasn't ready for more. She suspects she's frigid.

As we lay down in the bivvy, I breathed in her head-turning scent and struggled to appease a raging hard-on.

Finally, in the wee hours of the morning, I fell asleep, still clutching Sophie to my chest.

I woke up to the alarm on my phone, a little dizzy—and very confused.

My mind is still muddled. The sticky heat that hasn't abated in weeks isn't helping. I can't wait to climb into the shower and let a cold jet lower my body temperature a notch. Perhaps it will cool my brain, too.

I glance at Sophie, but she won't look at me. She's eyeing an ice cream stand instead with an expression of desperate longing on her lovely face.

Halting in front of it, I touch her arm. "Ice cream break?"

She beams.

"What flavor for *Mademoiselle*?" the vendor asks.

"Strawberry cheesecake and chocolate chip cookie, please." Sophie opens her purse.

I beat her to it, placing a tenner onto the counter.

She scowls at me.

I scowl back.

She closes her purse and takes her cone from the vendor.

"Aren't you having one?" she asks me.

"I lost my sweet tooth with my milk teeth," I say, collecting the change.

"You should've let me pay," she says as we march away. "Five euros for two scoops is a ripoff."

"I delivered four pepperonis in the 6th yesterday, and the guy tipped me five euros." I shrug. "Easy come, easy go."

"Still…" She gives the frozen treat an enthusiastic lick. "So good. And exactly what I needed right now."

Watching her tongue flick in and out of her mouth, I struggle not to dwell on what *I* need right now.

"I hope the heat lets up by Saturday," I say to take my mind off those dangerous thoughts. "The Derzians are coming back with my dog, and I wouldn't want the poor thing to suffer the way he did before they left."

"Is he very furry?" she asks, turning to me.

"Not very, but enough to have a harder time than humans coping with the heat."

She gives me a sympathetic smile. "It's nice of your neighbors to take care of your dog like that."

I nod. "They're the best. Of course, it helps that Oscar and their own dog, Cannelle, get along like gangbusters, but still. The Derzians have been incredibly kind to Oscar and me ever since I moved into the apartment."

"Do they have children of their own?"

"A grown son and a daughter, both living abroad with their spouses and kids," I say. "The son is in China and the daughter in the US."

"You know where?"

"LA."

"Don't your neighbors want to move closer to at least one of their kids and grandchildren?" she asks. "Or are they such hardcore Parisians it would take a bubonic plague epidemic to get them to resettle?"

I chuckle. "As it happens, they *are* hardcore Parisians, even though they weren't born here. They're Armenians from Lebanon."

"Oh?"

I nod as we stop at the traffic light. "They visited Paris as tourists in the seventies and fell in love with the city. When war broke out in Lebanon and they fled, Paris was an obvious destination."

"They must've had a hard time rebuilding their lives from scratch in a foreign country."

"Apparently, it was easier than they'd expected," I say as we turn onto my street. "They made friends, found jobs, and felt at home within a month of their arrival. *Madame* Derzian is convinced the love they have for the city is mutual."

Sophie smiles. "So she believes Paris fell in love with them, eh? Just like that, at first sight?"

"Yep," I say. "Not immigration authorities, though."

She raises her eyebrows.

"When the Derzians applied for a residency permit, an immigration official said, 'You must understand—we can't allow everyone who loves Paris to stay here. If we did, we'd have to make room for at least a billion people. You should return to your home country.' "

"What did the Derzians do?" Sophie asks.

"They momentarily *forgot* they spoke fluent French like many Lebanese."

"And?"

"*Monsieur* Derzian spread his arms and said, 'Pardon. No speak French. Speak Armenian.' " I raise my hands, palms up, imitating *Monsieur* Derzian's gesture and accent. "The official didn't speak Armenian, which gave the Derzians an excuse to ignore his instruction and stay put."

She laughs. "How convenient! So your wonderful neighbors are illegal aliens?"

"Not anymore," I say. "They reapplied a few years later and were granted a residency permit."

We enter my building and rush up the stairs to my apartment. Which, technically, is Sophie's. Just another bit of weirdness she's brought into my life.

I hand her a clean towel and a new toothbrush. While she showers, I brew some coffee.

She comes out of the bathroom less than ten minutes later, smelling of my shower gel. "Your turn."

When I return to the kitchen, having washed and changed into clean clothes, Sophie has toasted two slices of bread.

I pour both of us some java.

She takes her cup from me and points to my toast. "Wasn't sure how you like it."

"With butter," I say, opening the fridge. "You?"

"Peanut butter and jelly."

I make a face. "Really?"

"I know," she says. "It's an affront to good—that is to say, French—taste. But it's stronger than me."

"I'm afraid I don't have either of those foods."

"No problem," she says. "I'll channel my French half and eat my toast with regular butter. We have to go in a few minutes, anyway."

I glance at my watch and nod.

"About last night," Sophie says, as I drink my coffee.

I set the cup on the table and stare at her.

"I feel guilty." She looks downward. "I sort of led you on and left you hanging."

"I don't—"

"I just want you to know I wasn't playing or anything." She glances at me and looks down again. "I did enjoy being touched by you. It's just… I don't know if I can handle another disappointment if it turns out that I am hopelessly frigid, after all."

"Sophie Bander," I say in a know-it-all teacher's voice. "You are *not* frigid."

"How can you be sure?"

"Because you want me."

She looks up at me again.

I hold her gaze.

She mustn't suspect how much I'm gambling here.

Both of my claims—that she isn't frigid and that she wants me—are based on a gut feeling, not certitude. Especially the latter one. For all I know, it's Zach she'd rather hook up with. He'll probably take her to dinner one of these days, charm her, date her, pamper her, and marry while the iron is hot.

"You know what?" she says at length, her gaze still locked with mine. "I think you're right. It does look like I want you."

I suck in a sharp breath.

She tilts her head to the side. "So what are you going to do about it, Noah Masson?"

TWELVE

SOPHIE

I get off the *métro* and march toward Parc de la Villette where I am to finally meet Noah's dog, Oscar.

We'll walk around the park—seeing as dogs aren't allowed inside—and head to Noah's for a bite and chilled *rosé*.

I didn't take my backpack as I have no intention of sleeping over even if it's Friday night. Véronique has tasked me with showing an apartment at ten tomorrow morning, all by myself. This fills me with a ridiculous amount of pride… and anxiety. I've spent the last two evenings revising my notes about the apartment and the neighborhood and rereading the survey reports. When I get home tonight, I'll go through everything once again, and one last time tomorrow morning before I meet with the clients.

There's a second reason I'm seeing Noah this evening, and it makes me even jitterier than tomorrow's baptism of fire.

Lovemaking.

It's always so smooth and easy in movies, but it's been the opposite in my personal experience. Just thinking about doing it again makes my hands clammy.

I'll think about Oscar instead.

Even though I'm a cat person and have no clue how to act around a dog, meeting Oscar doesn't stress me at all. Probably because Noah has told me his dog is part feline.

Yesterday afternoon right after I hung up with my soon-to-be lover, Zach texted me that he'd had fun at the Moose and we should get together again sometime.

I replied:

Definitely, as friends.

He texted:

Sure, no problem.

In the evening, I went to Mom's and told her about Zach and Noah, fully expecting a rant on my lack of common sense. Instead, she declared that Noah sounded like the kind of guy I needed.

Mom's eccentric like that.

She never sees the world the way Dad and I do.

To any rational observer, *Zach* is the kind of guy I need. The kind of guy who'd be *right* for me.

Such a bummer I don't want what's right! Not at this juncture, in any case.

I spot my *wrong* kind of guy and his wrong kind of pet from afar. They're engrossed in a game of catch. Noah hurls a stick. His four-legged friend races after it and brings it back. But instead of giving it to his master, he keeps it between his clenched jaws, bounces around Noah, and wags his tail.

Noah picks up another stick and throws it. Oscar drops the one in his mouth and zooms to snatch the second stick. When he returns with it, Noah pets him and hurls the first stick.

"Doing what you do would drive me mad," I say after Noah and I exchange greetings.

"It's not so bad," Noah says. "Oscar loves this game."

I point at the stick in Oscar's mouth. "Isn't he supposed to give that to you?"

"I'm sure he's considered it." Noah shrugs. "But he prefers to keep it for himself."

"How very… un-doglike."

"I told you he's part cat."

I smirk. "Yeah, you did."

"It's not just the failure to fetch, there are other symptoms." He crouches and begins to play tug-of-war with his dog. "Oscar takes five or six catnaps during the day, with the first one beginning a few minutes after he wakes up in the morning."

"Why does he even bother waking up?"

"So he can relocate to my bed."

"Right."

"But I can close the bedroom door for the night," he adds quickly. "Oscar will take his first morning nap in his own bed."

I finger my watch strap. "Can you make him purr?"

Noah nods. "Oscar, sit!"

Oscar looks at him, then at me and then at Noah again. After Noah repeats the command three more times, Oscar sighs and sits down. Noah squats next to him and rubs Oscar's throat. The dog makes a soft guttural sound you wouldn't expect from a canine. Noah scratches him behind his ears, and Oscar purrs louder.

"Satisfied?" Noah asks me.

"Awed," I say.

When we get to his apartment, Oscar rushes to his water bowl and drinks thirstily.

Noah kicks off his flip-flops. "You can keep yours on, if you want."

"No problem." I slip out of my clogs. "The floor looks clean enough."

"It *is* clean," he says, heading to the kitchen.

I follow him.

Noah opens the *rosé* and pours me a glass. "At what time do you usually eat dinner?"

"Nine-ish. Typically a salad or a bowl of soup."

"I made a Caesar salad with chicken breast and mixed greens," he declares not without pride and glances at the clock on the wall. "Will you be hungry enough in an hour?"

"Think so."

A loud snore comes from the TV room, and I give Noah a quizzical look.

"Oscar's last nap before bedtime," he explains.

"Is he… *snoring?*"

"Uh-huh."

"Cats don't snore." I quirk an eyebrow. "Neither do dogs, to my knowledge."

"He's also part human," Noah says, bounding around the table to plant himself next to me.

"Of course he is."

Noah's gaze settles on my lips and my heart begins to pound.

I point to the *rosé*. "I thought you were a beer buff."

"Nah. I'm a wine person. I only drink beer in July and August to prevent my body from overheating."

"A wine lover, huh?" I tilt my head to the side, eyeing him up and down.

He smirks. "I don't fit the image of a wine connoisseur, do I?"

I smile apologetically.

He shrugs. "Appearances can be deceptive."

"So can words." I jut out my chin in defiance. "What can you tell me about this wine, for instance, since you're a *connoisseur*?"

Picking up the bottle, he says, "Côtes de Provence Saint Victoire, 2015 vintage. A great Provence *rosé*. Dry with a hint of berries. It's excellent with chicken, so be sure to leave some for the meal."

I lift my glass to my nose and sniff. "Anything else?"

"This wine comes from the vineyards of the Négrel family in Provence," Noah says. "They've been making it for 200 years."

My eyebrows crawl up. Could he be bluffing, inventing all this stuff on the fly? Unlikely. But even if he is, he deserves kudos for creativity.

"Cheers," I say.

"Cheers." He touches his glass to mine.

We stare into each other's eyes as we drink.

Noah's blue gaze holds such unambiguous intent, I cannot but respond. His desire is contagious. This man has accomplished quite a feat, come to think of it. He turns me on. I know I'll enjoy his touch and I'm almost certain I'll like his kisses.

It's what he'll do afterward that has me on edge.

The doorbell rings.

Oscar runs to the foyer. When Noah and I get there, the dog is sitting in front of the door, wagging his tail.

He looks at Noah with an almost palpable joy in his black eyes, like he knows who's on the other side and is happy to see them.

Noah opens the door to a coquettish gray-haired woman.

Oscar begins to dance around her until she pets him and lets him give her a few generous licks. Then she straightens up and notices me.

"Oh my!" She turns to Noah. "I'm so sorry. I didn't know you had company tonight."

"That's all right, Juliet," Noah says. "Meet my friend Sophie."

Juliet grabs me by the shoulders and cheek kisses me. "So pleased to meet you, darling."

"The pleasure is mine," I say, unsure how to act around this exuberant woman or what to think of her.

"Hamlet and I just realized we've left our phone charger in the summer house," she says to Noah. "I was wondering if we could borrow yours until I go to Darty tomorrow and buy a new one."

"Sure thing," Noah says, heading down the hallway.

To the bedroom, I presume. Which I'll most likely discover later tonight. I exhale a shallow breath.

"Hamlet—that's my husband—is too dependent on his phone," Juliet explains to me. "Email, Facebook, Solitaire… Me? I only ever remember I have a phone when someone calls me. Are you a smartphone addict, too?"

"I'm somewhere between you and your husband," I say with a smile.

She smiles back. "You're even prettier than Noah said."

"He told you about me?"

"Just that he's been hanging out with a lovely American girl."

"I see."

Noah returns with a charger and hands it to Juliet.

"Guess what," she says to him. "I'm making your favorite *boreks*, tabbouleh, and dolma next Sunday."

Noah widens his eyes. "All three at once?"

She nods smugly. "Why don't the both of you come over for dinner?"

"You *must* taste Juliet's dolma," Noah says to me before I can invent a polite excuse. "It's out of this world. And her *boreks* are to die for."

"What's a borek?" I ask.

Juliet gives me a sympathetic look, sighs, and shakes her head as if to say she's really sorry about my sad *borek*-less life. But she doesn't offer a definition.

Neither does Noah.

"I have a prior—" I begin.

"That's settled, then." Juliet pats my cheek. "See you at dinnertime next Sunday, darling."

She waves good-bye to Noah and crosses the landing to her apartment.

I wait until Noah has shut the door behind her and cross my arms over my chest. "Did I just get signed up for a dinner with total strangers even though I was saying no thanks?"

He gives me a please-don't-shoot-me look. "You don't have to go if you really hate the sound of it, but trust me, you'll miss out on the best dolma this side of the Seine."

I sigh and unfold my arms. "Fine, fine."

"Cool," he says, grinning.

"I assume I just met *Madame* Derzian, right?"

"Correct."

"And her first name is Juliet."

He nods.

I narrow my eyes. "And her husband's name is Hamlet."

He nods again.

"They are *well matched*." I bite my bottom lip to stifle a smile.

"Don't laugh," Noah says.

"Sorry."

"I mean, don't laugh *yet*, not until you hear what they've named their children."

"Tell me."

"Their son's name is Romeo, and their daughter is called Ophelia."

This is too precious to be true. "You're messing with me."

"I swear I'm not," he says, drawing closer. "It's their Armenian sense of humor. Ever heard of Radio Yerevan?"

I shake my head.

"They're famous for their political jokes," he says. "My father was a big fan."

Is there a touch of nostalgia in Noah's voice at the mention of his "nasty piece of work" dad? Something doesn't compute…

"An example?" I ask.

He wrinkles his brow. "I can think of only one right now, and it isn't political."

"That's OK."

"Radio Yerevan was asked, *What's an exchange of opinions?*" Noah pauses for effect. "Radio Yerevan answered, *It's when you enter your boss's office with your opinion and walk out with his.*"

I giggle, following him back to the kitchen.

Noah sets his glass on the table. "Back to the Derzians. Obviously, Juliet and Hamlet didn't fall in love to form a Shakespearean couple. It was a coincidence."

"That's good to know," I say, wondering what his next move will be.

"Both names just happened to be popular among Lebanese Armenians at the time." He takes my glass from my hand and places it next to his. "But their children's names are quite intentional."

"Why?" I ask.

"It was Juliet's idea. Apparently, Hamlet wasn't too keen, but she couldn't resist the temptation."

I shake my head in fake reproof. "Women."

"Hear, hear!" He encases my face with his big hands and stares at my mouth as if he wants to devour it.

I suppose, that's exactly what he wants given the hunger in his darkened eyes.

"I sometimes wonder," he says, his gaze still on my lips, "if women enjoy watching a man almost lose it with want."

His voice is hoarse and incredibly sexy.

Those hands on my cheeks, that voice, that look…

"Wonder no more," I murmur. "They do."

Without any warning, his mouth is on mine. He presses a soft kiss to my lips and my eyelids drop. Stroking my face, he brushes his lips over my chin, jawline, and throat, before returning to my mouth.

I kiss him back. His lips are warm and a little wet from the wine.

While both of his hands still cup my face, Noah sweeps his tongue over my lower lip. He lingers in the right corner of my mouth, kisses it, and moves to the left corner.

I force my eyelids to open so I can watch his face

while he's kissing me like this. What I see is sexy as hell. His eyes are glazed over with desire, his ruggedly handsome face flushed with need.

I don't know about women in general, but admittedly frigid Sophie Bander enjoys watching a man almost lose it with want.

If that man is Noah Masson.

"Sophie," he rasps against my mouth.

A shiver runs down my spine.

He slides the tip of his tongue between my lips, coaxing me to open them.

I do, gladly.

Next thing I know, we're both lost in a hot, raw, openmouthed kiss. I feel lightheaded as his tongue thrusts against my palate and strokes the inside of my teeth. When he caresses my tongue, I stroke his, getting drunk on his delicious wine-infused taste. I hear myself moan softly.

I could cry with how sweet this moment is.

Why didn't anyone tell me kissing could feel like this?

Even with our mouths joined, there's still a good inch between our bodies. Noah slides one hand down the side of my neck. For a few moments, he rests it—hot and fingers splayed—at the back of my shoulders. Then, applying the tiniest amount of pressure, he nudges me closer until my nipples touch his chest.

Through two thin layers of fabric, the contact sets off a spark, electrifying me. My nipples are engorged and rock hard. I had no idea they could be like this.

Noah's kiss grows hungrier, rougher. Gripping the back of my head, he draws me as close as possible without crushing me against his chest.

I delve my hand into his soft wavy hair as I revel in

being held like this, kissed like this, desired like this by a man I haven't been able to stop thinking about since meeting him.

When he breaks away, I follow his lips, hungry for more.

"Sophie," he says, taking a step back. "Wait. There's something I need to ask first."

With an enormous effort, I steady myself and focus on his eyes.

He takes a deep breath. "Are you sure it's me you want?"

THIRTEEN

NOAH

She blinks. "What?"

"I wouldn't want to…"—I search for a good word—"derail you."

She stares at me, still confused.

Cut to the chase, Noah. Ask her the question you know you should've asked already, before you brought her here, before you pulled her into your arms in the bivvy.

Even if it means shooting yourself in the foot.

I tip my head back for a second and look straight into her beautiful eyes. "What about Zach?"

"Ah," she breathes out as comprehension hits her.

"Isn't it *him* you really want?"

"I do," she says. "I mean, not *your* Zach, but someone like him in a couple of years when I'm back in Key West and ready to settle down."

I exhale slowly.

She smiles. "But right now, here on my Parisian internship-slash-holiday, it's *you* that I want."

My shoulders sag with relief.

Keeping Sophie for me when I'm supposed to set

her up with Zach still doesn't feel kosher. But, at least, I know where I stand now. Sophie isn't kissing me because she can't decide between me and Zach or because Zach is taking too long to ask her out.

She's kissing me because she chose me.

Even if it's just for the duration of her Parisian holiday. Actually, that's fine by me. More than fine—it's perfect. Haven't I, too, been thinking of another woman for when I'm ready to settle down?

I peer at Sophie, taking in the bounty the universe deemed appropriate to drop onto my lap.

She chuckles softly. "You look like you just won Olympic gold."

"It feels that way," I admit.

Taking a step toward her, I back her against the wall, lean in, and place my hands on either side of her face.

Her smile slips, giving way to a wild mixture of emotions that flicker in her expressive eyes. There's desire and excitement, for sure, but there's also anxiety. Not surprising, given her history of ham-handed men.

I'll tread softly.

"Bébé," I say planting a gentle kiss to her forehead. "If I start doing something you don't like, or don't feel ready for, just say it. OK?"

She nods, her expression relaxing. "Go easy, please?"

"I promise."

She places her hands on my chest, stroking it. Her lovely fingers trail my collarbones, my throat, run down my shoulders, and then return to my chest.

"You're perfect," she says. "Better than my secret fantasy."

"What's your fantasy?"

She cocks her head. "Don't you know the meaning of the word *secret*?"

"Have mercy!" I plead. "Now that you disclosed you have a secret fantasy, you *must* tell me what it is, or I'll wither and die of frustration."

She hesitates for a brief moment and shrugs. "Oh well, here goes. My secret fantasy has always been a blue-eyed American football quarterback."

A happy grin spreads on my face, no matter how hard I try to suppress it.

Her gaze zeroes in on my pectorals. "But I'll take a French water polo goalie any day."

"Take him today," I say, catching her chin between my thumb and forefinger.

And then I kiss her hard, the way I've been dying to kiss her for several weeks now.

She lets me. Better than that, she responds, delving her hands into my hair. Her heavenly breath—chocolate, wine, and Sophie—makes me wild with lust. As I explore the tender interior of her mouth, a sense of urgency comes over me. I haven't forgotten my promise to go easy, and I'm fully prepared to freeze the moment she lets me know it's too much, or too soon. But until that moment, I'll push my sweet Sophie to see how far she'll let me go.

I break the kiss.

She sways, panting, her eyes glazed with desire.

"Bedroom." I say. "Unless you want me to take you right here up against this wall."

Say yes.

The image of Sophie impaled on my cock, back to the wall, makes my hands tremble. I picture her in that position—legs locked around my waist, breasts bared and bobbing as I pound into her with all I've got.

Jesus Christ.

What happened to not rushing it? So much for my

self-control... The need in my loins is killing all my good intentions. This woman has bewitched me.

The moment those words form in my mind, shame hits me in the solar plexus, making me choke.

What's wrong with you, man?

Blaming a woman's charms for your own failure to show restraint is... cheap, to put it mildly. It's what bad lovers do. It's what rapists do.

Say no, Sophie.

She blinks and swallows. "Bedroom."

Thank you!

I grab her hand and lead her through the TV room to the bedroom.

It's bathed in the golden light of the setting sun as we enter.

I turn to Sophie. "Too much light?"

She nods.

I go to the window and draw the curtains, leaving a narrow gap. When I return by her side, she's already taken her shorts off and is reaching for the hem of her tee. I watch, mesmerized. She pulls it up over her tummy, breasts, and over her head.

Spellbound, I follow her every move.

Sophie lowers her arms and drops her T-shirt to the floor.

I suck in a sharp breath, awed by what she's uncovered to my eyes.

Wrapped in a flimsy cotton bra with a floral pattern and a tiny pink bow tie in the middle, her pert, full breasts are the best gift I've ever received. They're perfection itself—the very essence of femininity. Her erect nipples pebble the fabric in the center of each breast.

I kind of knew already her breasts were out of this

world—summer materials don't leave much to the imagination—but seeing them like this robs my lungs of air.

I yank off my T and take a step toward her.

She reaches for my belt and tugs on it. My breaths come shallow and fast, as she undoes the buckle and draws the zipper of my jeans down. Slowly, she works my pants down my hips and thighs. When they fall to the floor, I step out of them.

She stares at my tented boxer briefs.

If only I could tell if it's anticipation or anxiety that heaves her chest!

She unclasps her bra, freeing her gorgeous boobs. I cup the left one, and nearly growl with the pleasure of it. Her breast is firm, soft and smooth, and it fits snugly in my palm as if it belongs there. Which it does.

I cover her right breast with my other hand, and just hold her like that for a moment.

She smiles. "Big hands and a good grip are definitely an asset, huh?"

"I'm glad you agree," I mutter as I begin to fondle the treasure in my hands and kiss every inch of her face.

A good ten minutes later, I slip my thumbs into the waistband of her panties and push them over her hips and down her thighs.

My hand slides between her legs before she's done shaking her panties off her ankle. I can't wait. Backing her to the bed, I yank off my briefs, crawl up, and loom over her.

Beneath me is a woman hotter and more beautiful than anything I've ever seen.

Regardless of what she believes, she was made for sex *with me.*

Pressing the ball of my palm against her mound, I

rub and slip a finger inside. She's wet. Not soaked, but definitely wet. I pull my finger out and position myself at her entrance.

"I don't have protection," she says.

"Not to worry, I got a whole pa—" I begin, my gaze trained on the thatch between her legs, before I realize she's hyperventilating.

I look up.

She swallows hard, clearly panicked, her eyes darting to the door.

Fuck.

"Bummer," I say. "I don't have any, either."

The relief in her eyes makes my chest clench.

I roll off her and lie on my side. "That second guy you told me about… Did he rape you?"

"No," she says. "Maybe. I don't know. I *did* agree to have sex with him. I told myself it was bound to be better than the first time. But once we were naked, and he started groping me and kissing me… suddenly, I didn't want it anymore."

She searches my face as if her default assumption is that I won't understand.

"Did you tell him you wanted to call it off?" I ask.

"Yes, but he wouldn't listen. He explained later that he'd been too far gone by then. I couldn't seriously expect him to be able to stop at that point."

"Did you believe him?"

"I guess." She furrows her brow. "I don't know how men function."

"Psychopaths aside, we function like humans," I say. "Not savage beasts. If we *want* to stop when a woman says no, we *can* stop."

I turn away and reach for my underwear on the floor.

She tugs at my arm. "Wait. I'm not saying no to… everything."

I tilt my head to the side. "You'll have to be more specific."

She looks away, blushing.

If I were a true gentleman, noble in my heart and not just on paper, I'd let her off the hook at this point. I'd make suggestions and ask her to respond with a yes or no. But I'm too keen on hearing her talk dirty.

"Come on, Sophie," I encourage her. "You can do it."

She grimaces. "Do I really have to spell it out?"

"I'm afraid you do."

"Oral sex," she mutters under her breath.

I cup my ear. "Beg your pardon? Did you say something?"

She chews on her lower lip, looking utterly miserable.

I can't believe how much fun it is to tease her.

"Oral sex," she repeats louder. "I'd like some oral sex, please. If that's OK with you."

I struggle to keep a straight face. "Would you like to give me a blowjob or do you prefer that I go down on you?"

"You," she whispers.

I push her legs apart and sit between them.

Suddenly, I don't feel like joking anymore.

I bend down and nuzzle the insides of her thighs. Then I kiss her folds openmouthed, spreading her with my fingers. I give her a hard, long lick and dip my tongue in. She tastes like sex in its purest form. Sweet, spicy, addictive.

I probe her, pushing a little deeper with each thrust of my tongue. She begins to whimper. That's all the encouragement I need to involve a finger, so I can lick her at the same time. Sophie's whimpers turn into moans, and soon she's writhing on the bed and gripping my hair.

My cock aches.

The temptation to shift so I can grind it against her, or—even better—so she could caress it is so strong I almost give in. But, in the end, I don't budge. Tonight isn't about me—it's about Sophie.

Only her.

When I glance up at her face, Sophie's eyes are closed, her mouth slightly open, and her cheeks flushed. So hot. Feeling her arousal bathe my finger in warm waves, I go harder, greedier, sucking and nipping at her flesh.

She tenses and spasms around me.

With a growl coming from a deep, previously unknown place in my chest, I lick her orgasm clean.

Then I stretch out by her side and gather her to me.

She gives me a heavy-lidded look, lifts her head, and takes my mouth in a smoldering kiss.

When she breaks it, I stare at her face. "Did you like your taste?"

"I did." She grins. "Is that weird?"

"Not in my view, *bébé*." I run my thumb over her lips. "Then again, my view is remote and unfocused right now."

She gives me a quizzical look.

I open my arms and spread them like a bird's wings. "Cause I'm flying."

FOURTEEN

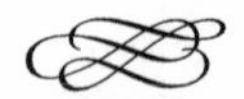

SOPHIE

I wake up to Oscar licking my face.

"Yikes, get off me, beast!" I shoo him away from my head, wiping my mouth, chin, and cheeks with the sheet.

Noah levers his body into a sitting position and nudges Oscar toward the edge of the bed. "Bad boy."

Honestly, he could've put a little more heart into his admonishment. At least for show.

When the dog jumps to the floor, Noah turns to me, smiling. "Congratulations."

"For what?"

"On Oscar's upgrading you from harmless to lick-worthy."

"Does he upgrade everyone so fast or should I feel proud and special?" I ask archly.

"Definitely proud and special." He gives me a wink. "And not because of Oscar."

"No?"

"He got nothing on *me*."

"How so?"

His smile broadens. "When I first saw you, it took me less than ten seconds to upgrade you from harmless to lick-worthy."

Memories of last night flood my brain, and I turn away, hoping he won't notice my flaming ears. "Can I go to the shower first?"

"Of course."

I roll out of the bed, kneel, and sift through the pile of clothes on the floor, looking for my underwear. I find my bra, but not my panties.

"Oops," Noah says, leaning over the other side of the bed and prying my lacy boy shorts from Oscar's mouth.

The garment is wet as he holds it up for me.

Seeing my hesitation, he balls it into his fist. "I'm—*we*—are very sorry about this. I'll wash it."

"I can't go home commando."

"May I offer you a pair of my briefs or Speedos?" he asks with a smile dancing in the corner of his mouth.

I jerk my chin up. "This is *not* funny."

"You're right," he says. "I'll have a word with Oscar."

He jumps out of the bed, hunkers next to his dog and schools his features into a stern expression. "That was badly done, Oscar. Very bad."

Oscar listens carefully, his big sad eyes locked on Noah.

"In this house, we don't munch on our guests' underwear without permission," Noah continues, his tone falsely stern. "You should be ashamed of—"

Oscar rears up and gives Noah's nose a happy lick.

Noah shuts up mid sentence, a grin breaking across his face.

I shake my head. "If that's how you discipline him, I see why he does as he pleases."

"Have you ever tried scolding someone while they're licking your nose?"

"No, I haven't."

He pets Oscar. "Thought so. F.Y.I, it's impossible."

"If you say so." I let out a resigned sigh. "Hey, I'll take you up on your offer of underwear."

He opens one of the drawers in the closet and rummages through its contents.

"This should do the trick," he says, handing me a pair of stretchy boxer briefs.

I grab them and head to the bathroom.

Twenty minutes later, I enter the kitchen. It smells of freshly brewed coffee and warm pastries.

I point at the croissants on the table. "Microwave?"

He screws his face up in exaggerated affront. "Please. I bought them in the *boulangerie* downstairs while you were in the shower."

"Now I know why my friend Sue suggested I spend a night with a Frenchman," I say before biting into a delicious roll.

"And why's that?"

"This *perfection*"—I hold the croissant up—"with fresh coffee early in the morning. So worth all the hassle."

His lips quirk as he points to the bottle of *rosé* from last night. "I'd say *this* was worth the hassle.

I cock my head. "You're well informed about wines for an athlete who grew up in Nepal."

"The French are born well informed about wines," he says. "Ask your mother, if you don't believe me."

"I may not know much about wines," I say, "But I do know a thing or two about vineyards."

"How come?"

"We had a two-day workshop at the agency last week on vineyard property sales. I learned an awful lot."

"Like what?"

"Like, whether the estate has a winery or only a vineyard, the type of grapes it grows, the age of the vines, their yield, if there's staff already on payroll, and lots of other things. All of them affect the price of the estate."

"I had no idea," he says, looking impressed. "Would love to hear more."

I smile, flattered. "Sure, but bear in mind I just had a crash course. There are specialized brokers out there who can immediately say if the estate is going to be profitable."

"I think your knowledge will suffice for my purposes," he says enigmatically.

Before I can ask him what he means, my phone wakes up in my purse, emitting Dad's ringtone.

I answer it.

"Hey, Princess, I have great news," Dad says. "Last night, Doug Thompson insisted we go out for a drink—"

"Our archenemy Doug Thompson?"

"Not anymore. He confessed he's in love with you, can you believe it?"

"No," I say.

"He's been in love with you for years now," Dad plows on, "and he'll do anything for a chance to win your heart."

I'm too flabbergasted to respond.

"If you and Doug hit it off, we could merge our two agencies and become an undisputed market leader. We'd have no rival in the Keys. We could develop the Parisian thing you started into a real agency, and—why not—open one in Miami."

He's so excited I can hardly believe my ears. "Dad, I—"

"You don't have to say or do anything about it right now," he cuts in. "I just wanted you to begin seeing Doug in a different light. If he's no longer our competitor, he's exactly what you want in a man."

This conversation is getting way too sensitive.

"Can I call you back in ten minutes?" I ask.

There's a brief pause before he says, "You're not alone."

"That's right."

"At eight in the morning," he adds pointedly.

His voice is icy now compared to the warmth it bubbled with seconds ago.

"I'll call you back," I say and hang up.

Noah hands me a fragrant cup of coffee. "Drink this before you run away."

I gulp down the contents and give him a smooch.

As soon I'm on the street, I dial Dad.

"You've met someone," he says.

"Maybe."

"Is he black?"

When did race become a factor?

"No," I say. "Neither is Doug Thompson, last time I checked."

"It's different."

"How?"

"Doug is a local, a native conch born and raised in Key West."

"Is that a virtue?" I ask with a touch of sarcasm.

"Yes, it is," Dad says. "It means he has roots here. It

means he can put up with our summers, and he won't run away after a few years to a cooler climate."

Sheesh.

This is about Mom as much as it's about Doug. I should've seen it coming.

"I take it he's French," Dad says.

"Yes."

"Catholic."

"He isn't religious."

"Even worse—an atheist."

"I don't think he's an atheist—he just doesn't give religion much thought. His passion is something else."

"What?"

"Water polo."

"Hmm. Is he a pro? Is he making good money?"

"Water polo isn't like baseball or soccer. It doesn't pay very well. That's why he has a part-time job."

"Doing what?"

I hesitate. Dad isn't going to like this. *Oh, well.* "He delivers pizzas."

Silence.

"Dad?"

"You're dating a pizza delivery man."

I don't comment.

He clears his throat. "Does your delivery man have a college degree?"

"Um… I don't know."

"So, basically, he's a loser," Dad says before adding, "Euro-trash."

"Oh, come on!"

"He'll pull you down, Sophie, can't you see that?"

"Dad, I don't plan on marrying him." I pout in frustration. "Shouldn't you be happy I'm finally dating someone?"

"You're dating someone who lives in Europe and delivers pizzas. No, I'm not happy."

"He's a wonderful person," I say, "and a gifted goalkeeper."

I wish I could mention Noah's additional gift that I discovered last night, but this is Dad, not Mom.

"A pizza guy." He laughs bitterly. "Ain't he a catch?"

I say nothing.

"What's his name?" Dad asks.

"Noah Masson."

"Just keep your head on your shoulders, Princess, will you?" Dad's tone is placating now. "You're young and inexperienced, and this Noah person… Can you promise me you won't do anything rash?"

"No problem," I say and we hang up.

Big problem, actually.

Despite Dad's outright disapproval and my own misgivings, I may have crossed the red line already.

I may be falling for Noah.

FIFTEEN

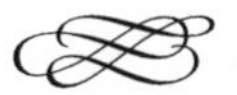

NOAH

I stare at Diane's latest missive while my mind processes what I've just read.

Dear Noah,

Jaqueline tells me you visited the chateau last week. That's such good news! I shared it with Sebastian who didn't comment, but his eyes lit up with renewed hope. Did the place bring back any childhood memories? Did it call to you? I want to believe it did.

Sidenote: I'm not usually this sentimental. It's the baby blues. It'll pass (fingers crossed).

Anyway, back to the reason I'm writing. Thinking about your visit to the estate made me realize something. Since you've been refusing to meet with Seb, or even Raphael, you may have never had a chance to hear Sebastian's side of the story.

I'm going to give it to you in this letter, and you can do what you want with it.

Marguerite ran out of money and asked Sebastian to donate half a million to her charity shortly after your father passed. I believe you know that much. What you may not know is that the company was on the brink of ruin at that point.

Sebastian said no to her because he was investing his personal inheritance—every last cent of it—into Parfums d'Arcy. If he'd sent her the amount she was asking for, there was no chance he could save the company. Almost a thousand workers in France and abroad would have lost their jobs. I'm not saying it was the only factor in Sebastian's decision, but it was a major one.

What would you *do in his place? Would you forego the last chance to save the family business so you could help people in a foreign country? Maybe you would. But Sebastian chose differently. And his choice doesn't make him a bad person.*

Seb asked Marguerite if she could put her foundation on hold and volunteer for other nonprofits while he's saving the business. She wouldn't hear of it.

Two years later, Parfums d'Arcy turned a modest profit. Your brother offered it to Marguerite, even though he was hoping to reinvest it into the company. She told him she'd found another solution, and no longer needed the d'Arcy money or his help.

So, there you have it—Sebastian's side of the story.

On another note, we are all hoping to see you at Raphael and Mia's wedding. Please come. It would be the best wedding present Raphael could dream of. Trust me.

Diane

I'm not going. When you cut someone off, there's no point in doing it *partially*.

Do I believe her version of Sebastian's side of the story? Could it be true? Is it possible that my brothers aren't moved by greed alone? Was Sebastian really concerned about the fate of his workers? Did he really offer his first profit to Maman?

Have I been judging him too harshly?

As for Raphael, Maman always says he was too young at the time and too easily influenced.

Speaking of Maman, something in Diane's letter bothers me more than the possibility I've been wrong to cut my brothers off. It's the response Maman gave Seb when he finally offered some money.

She told him she'd found another solution.

This "other solution" could only be Pierre Sorrel, the foreign ministry official who helped Maman get French government funding that year, and the years that followed. The ultimate jerk who made her pay for his help with her body.

That's what she told me the day I came home from school earlier than usual and saw him in our living room. He had his back to the door, ass naked, pants around his ankles. Maman was on her knees in front of him…

My hands ball into fists as I remember the scene.

What wouldn't I give to unsee it! I was fourteen and Maman was my hero, a warrior for social justice, a saint. When Sorrel ran out, and she confessed that what I'd seen was the price she was paying to continue her work, I resolved to kill him. I spent countless sleepless nights plotting his murder to save Maman from his clutches.

But the one time I actually had a chance at fifteen during a garden party at the French Embassy, I couldn't do it.

That's why I'm so mad at my brothers.

That is why I can't forgive them.

But… why didn't Maman take Sebastian's money when he offered it so she could be free of Sorrel? Was her pride stronger than her misery? Or was she less miserable than she led me to believe?

I shake my head.

This is all conjecture based on secondhand information from a woman who's far from impartial. Diane loves Seb, and she goes out of her way to justify his actions. Quite successfully, in fact. Every time she writes, I end up questioning things I've always known to be true.

I crumple her letter and toss it in the trash can. The next one she sends me will end up there unopened.

Anger pulsing in my veins, I grab my backpack and head out. Sophie and I have a train to catch.

We're traveling to Burgundy.

It's my second trip there in the space of a week. I went to the Chateau d'Arcy last Saturday to talk with the housekeeper, Jacqueline Bruel. Since my twenty-seventh birthday two weeks ago, I'm the legal owner of the estate, which means *Madame* Bruel is in my employ.

Not for long, though.

When Jacqueline and I chatted last week, I asked her to make sure the staff clear the premises from two to six this afternoon so I could spend a few hours there on my own and decide what I want to do with it.

I lied. My decision is made. It was made years ago. I'm taking Sophie to the estate today so she can give me an initial assessment and a ballpark price. Then I'll entrust it to one of those specialized brokers she mentioned.

And then I'll sell it.

When Sophie and I climb out of the cab and walk past the wrought iron gates, the air smells of roses and grass. Bumblebees and other summer bugs buzz over the neatly trimmed hedgerow.

A soft breeze makes thousands of oak leaves rustle along the gravel driveway. An English-style park of vast lawns sprinkled with sprawling trees and colorful flowerbeds begins to our left and stretches behind the castle. A vineyard spreads outward from it, covering the soft slopes of the hills to our right.

All of this is such a contrast to the smells, views, and sounds of Paris that it's hard to believe we left the city less than three hours ago.

Oscar would love it here.

He'd chase butterflies and roll on the grass to his heart's content, and there'd be no one to kick him out because it's a no-poop zone.

"Your friend Sebastian is smart to sell his chateau in the summer." Sophie fills her lungs with air and looks around. "I've been here less than a minute and already I'm in love."

I give her a stiff smile, wondering if I'd named my imaginary friend "Sebastian" by coincidence.

Hardly. I guess it was an unconscious attempt to give this charade a touch of truth.

Sebastian, Raphael and I, and generations of d'Arcy

boys and girls before us, spent many happy summers here. Raph and I always got in trouble, climbing trees we were too chicken to descend, chasing the housekeeper's pet goose around the park and playing hide-and-seek where we weren't allowed to.

What a shame my easygoing middle brother sided with Seb when Maman needed him!

Unlike his younger siblings, the always serious Sebastian spent most of his waking hours in the library, reading clever books. I'm sure it's in the library that he first hatched his plan for world domination.

"Again, why is your buddy selling this?" Sophie asks.

"He needs money."

"And he's stuck abroad, right?"

"Right." I turn away. "Where would you like to begin?"

"What are my options?"

"The park, the vineyard, or the house."

She points her chin to the stairs leading up to the ornate entrance. "Let's see the castle first."

"Sure," I nod before clapping my hand to my forehead. "Almost forgot. We won't have time to check it out, but you should know there's a grotto with rock art just a short hike up that hill."

I point in the direction of the d'Arcy Grotto.

"Is it part of the estate?" she asks.

I nod.

"Is the grotto any good?"

"It has the oldest prehistoric rock paintings in France," I say, a proud note creeping into my voice. "Ice Age about forty thousand years ago. I remember the magnificent mammoths and reindeer. Lions, too."

"Did you stay here as a kid?"

"Yeah."

"How sad," she says.

"That I visited the estate as a child?"

"No, silly. That your friend is selling his childhood home."

"It isn't sad," I say. "He doesn't care for this place."

Really, he doesn't.

SIXTEEN

SOPHIE

"How old is this chateau?" I ask when we've reached the top of the stairs.

Noah unlocks the beautifully carved entrance door. "More than four hundred years."

"Is it listed as a historical monument?"

He nods.

"It means the new owners won't be able to make any big changes without a special permit," I say.

Noah gives me a worried look. "Why would they want to make big changes?"

"Does the chateau have an indoor swimming pool and a spa?"

He shakes his head.

"Non-European buyers would likely want those things."

"Right."

I look around, taking in the vast foyer flooded with soft light, the marble flooring, the imposing chandeliers and fixtures, and the majestic staircase that leads to the second floor.

"This way." Noah motions to a drawing room on the other side of the foyer.

The chipped marble under our feet changes to an intricately set art parquet. The floor creaks with every step we take, but it's beautiful. Small honey-colored panels—probably oak—come together in large diagonal squares. I've seen this design before. I close my eyes, recalling what Véronique taught me about traditional French flooring styles.

"Parquet de Versailles," I announce with pride, pointing down. "That's what this pattern is called."

Noah smiles. "Good to know."

"Don't you go all smug on me, goalie." I jerk my chin up. "You brought me here so you could hear my opinions on this property, did you not?"

He drops his head to his chest. "*Désolé*. I did."

"I tried to look up this estate last night, but I couldn't find a chateau called Thouars-Maurice."

"No?" He stares out the window.

"Are you sure you got the name right?"

"I'll check with my buddy," he says. "Maybe the official name is slightly different."

"I bet it is."

Peeling my gaze off Noah, I look around. "This room is… unbelievable."

He grins. "It's called Salon Bleu."

I can see why. The walls are covered in faded blue murals depicting pretty shepherd girls frolicking with naughty shepherd boys in bucolic settings. I doubt Noah will be able to give me the age of these murals, but they must be at least a couple hundred years old.

The only mural-free wall has tall French doors that open to an English-style park, some of which we saw from the front of the building.

The view takes my breath away.

Surveying generous lawns that meld into meadows to meet woodlands in the distance, I declare that this is the most beautiful sight I've ever seen.

Even the ocean sunsets back home can't compare.

"This view is gold," I say to Noah. "Make sure nothing obstructs it when buyers come."

"Your word is my command."

"If I were you—or your friend—I'd put a big comfy armchair right here." I point to the space between the fireplace and the French doors. "And an open book on top."

"Wouldn't it look messy?"

"It will look lived-in and help the prospective buyers imagine themselves in this salon."

"Very clever."

"Just a little realtor trick."

"Got any others up your sleeve?"

I give him a cocky *what-do-you-think* look.

He grins and pulls me to him. "I love it when you act naughty."

"This is nothing, babes," I purr, emboldened by his compliment. "You haven't seen me naughty yet."

Nobody has seen me naughty yet, to be exact, but there's no need to mention that.

Noah's hand makes its way down my back and lingers on my backside. "Let me show you the great hall before we make it to the bedrooms."

I raise my eyebrows.

He couldn't possibly be suggesting what I think he's suggesting.

Or could he?

He takes my hand and leads me to another salon, bigger and grander than the one we just admired.

There's a small pedestal table planted in the middle of the ballroom. A bottle of red wine, a corkscrew and two stemmed glasses form an inviting group on top of it.

Noah picks up the bottle whose label reads, *Coteau de la lune*. While he's studying it, I spot a note, written in a neat schoolteacher's hand.

We hope you enjoy this twenty-year-old Pinot Noir—the chateau's last vintage.

Jacqueline, Greg, Deolinda, Fabrice

I show the note to Noah. "Who are these people?"

"The staff."

"Are they invisible?"

He smirks. "They've taken the afternoon off so we can snoop around undisturbed."

How unusual.

Noah opens the bottle and pours a little wine into one of the glasses. He sniffs it, takes a sip, and fills both glasses.

"*A la tienne,*" he says, touching his glass to mine.

I take a small sip. The wine is full-bodied and rich in subtle flavors I wish I could identify. One thing I'm sure of—the chateau had a damn good vintage twenty years back.

"Do you know why they stopped making wine?"

"Sebastian's father died," Noah says. "He'd been the *vigneron* of the family."

He sets his glass on the table. "Come on, let's go. We have a dozen bedrooms to check out, not to mention the park and the vineyard."

As I follow him up the gorgeous but rickety staircase and down a long hallway, I notice how dilapidated the castle is behind its regal grandeur and refinement. It's squeaky clean, but no amount of dusting and polishing can hide the mildew stains on crumbling walls or the huge cracks in the ceiling.

"When was this castle last refurbished?" I ask Noah.

"In the sixties."

He knows quite a bit about this place. Of course, his friend Sebastian probably gave him all the important details.

Noah opens one of the doors and motions me into a spacious room. "This is the lord and lady's chamber."

"The floors will need to be refinished here," I say. "And the walls treated and replastered."

After that we check out a magnificent wood-paneled library and five or six smaller bedrooms with en suite bathrooms. Some of them have paintwork or fabrics on the walls, others boast ceiling beams and antique bathtubs. All are as delightful as they are run-down.

In one of the rooms, he backs me to the wall and kisses me until I'm weak in the knees.

"Tomorrow?" he asks, staring into my eyes.

I know what he means without needing to ask. "Tomorrow."

He flashes me a big, sexy grin.

I grin back, excited and scared in equal measure.

"Want to look at the vines now?" he asks, drawing back. "Or continue exploring the remaining guest rooms, drawing rooms, wine cellars and the kitchens?"

I glance at my watch. "Our train leaves in less than two hours. So, yeah, let's see the vineyard."

We exit the castle and head toward the hillside, passing a small chapel, a fountain and an incredibly romantic *orangerie* on our way.

"Would you happen to know the estate's annual upkeep cost?" I ask.

He shakes his head.

"Can you ask your friend? I'll need that info to determine the price."

"I'll be sure to get you that info within a day or two," he says, before adding, "It must cost a small fortune to keep an estate like that."

I nod. "Whoever buys this, had better have deep pockets. Or tap into the huge revenue potential of the estate."

"Paying guests?"

"Yes, among other things," I say. "If I were the owner, I'd immediately apply for permits to restore the chateau and convert one of the wings into a hotel."

"You think the historic monuments committee would allow it?"

"If the request is vetted by a good architect and shows how the new income-generating activities will fund the preservation works and the return of the castle to its former grandeur, I'm sure they will."

He gives me a sidelong look. "Do you have other *income-generating* activities in mind?"

"You bet!" I begin to unfold fingers on my left hand as I tick off ideas. "I'd rent out the great hall for receptions, and that huge central lawn for music festivals and events. I'd restart the winery. I'd set up a gift shop and hire a guide to do daily tours of the chateau—"

"We—," he cuts in, "I mean, Sebastian already allows guided tours of the grotto."

"Good," I say. "But clearly not enough."

We walk in silence for a few more minutes. The colors and shapes of this amazing estate regale my eyes. This place deserves so much more love than it's currently getting. Delicate floral scents fill the hazy midafternoon air, which become more pungent when we reach the vines.

"How many hectares?" I ask.

"Err…"

"I'll need that info, too."

He smiles. "*Oui, M'dame.*"

We stare at the rows of trellised plants.

"Are the castle's cellars big?" I ask.

"Very."

"And the equipment, do you think it's still there?"

"I'm sure it is."

"That's an additional source of income!" I grin, bubbling with enthusiasm. "The new owner could start a sort of cooperative winery. Small growers with no facilities of their own could rent space and equipment in the chateau's cellars. Even amateurs could pay to get their bespoke wines. That's how it's done in the US, especially in California."

Noah says nothing.

He's crouching among the vines, stroking their trunks and running his fingers along the shoots. Reverently, he caresses the leaves and gently cups a bulging, vibrant bunch of ripe grapes, as if weighing it in his hand. When he snaps off a juicy red grape and tosses it into his mouth, his lids drop and an expression of rapture appears on his face as he savors it.

He opens his eyes and surveys the plot, mumbling, "I didn't realize someone still tended these vines…"

"When were they planted?"

"Decades ago, by Sebastian's grandfather."

"Well, maybe your buddy Sebastian feels it's his duty to keep these vines alive."

Noah turns to me. "Maybe."

"Do you know if this vineyard is rated grand cru?"

"It is."

"Wow. Good for Sebastian—it adds huge value." I blow out a sigh. "I think he's mad to sell this."

"He needs—" Noah begins.

"Money," I finish for him. "I know, I know… But if I owned this estate, there'd be only one way it would change hands." I pause for effect. "Over my dead body."

He gives me a funny look. "How far would you go to get your hands on a property like this?"

"Far."

"Would you marry its current or future owner, even if you'd never met him and didn't have any feelings for him?"

"Feelings shmeelings." I say what I always say when Mom or Sue become too sentimental. "All they do is cloud your judgment and lead to disappointments down the road."

"Does that mean you'd marry him?"

Does it?

Oh, who cares—I'm just making a point.

"Duh," I say, rolling my eyes. "In a wink."

SEVENTEEN

NOAH

"This is Hamlet and me age twenty-one." Juliet points at an old, photo in the big album on Sophie's lap. "This picture was taken in Beirut a few months after our wedding."

The women sit next to each other on the couch, looking at Juliet's family pictures. Hamlet and I lounge in roomy armchairs on either end of the coffee table.

Oscar and Cannelle have fallen asleep at our feet—Cannelle balled up on top of her favorite cushion and not making a sound like the gently bred lady she is. Oscar is lying on his back, hind legs wide open, and snoring happily. Being himself.

We're sipping post-dinner coffee from tiny cups. It was brewed Oriental-style which, according to Juliet, is "the only sensible way to drink coffee." While we're at it, we also wolf down a large number of small honey-soaked baklava.

The coffee was home-roasted, ground, and brewed by Hamlet. His lovely wife baked the baklavas. The Derzians know I'm not a big fan of desserts. *I* know that leaving their house without eating at least one baklava is simply not an option.

I crane my neck to look at the photo. Hamlet wears flared pants and a red shirt open down to his stomach to reveal a hairy chest. His hair is big and his mustache reminds me of Tom Selleck. Juliet is dressed in a ridiculously short skirt and platform shoes. Her long hair is parted in the middle. She wears a braided headband around her forehead.

Sophie gives our hostess a surprised look. "A miniskirt? In Lebanon?"

"Of course." Juliet shrugs. "Every self-respecting fashionista had one of those back in the day."

"You're the coolest hippie I've ever seen," Sophie says.

Juliet lets out a nostalgic sigh. "I used to have such pretty legs."

"Me, too," Hamlet echoes from his armchair, misty-eyed.

Sophie giggles.

Hamlet turns to his wife. "She thinks I'm kidding. Show her our Saint-Tropez pictures."

Juliet turns a few pages until she finds the Saint-Tropez pics. It's a series of four color photographs immortalizing the couple on the famed Riviera beach. Their bodies are fiercely tanned. Juliet is clad in a tiny, low-cut bikini. Hamlet stands next to his wife with an arm around her shoulders, proudly hairy everywhere with only a tiny scrap of bright blue fabric covering his boy parts.

My water polo Speedo would qualify as conservative next to Hamlet's Chippendales outfit.

I open my mouth to thank God that the Borat-style

mankini wasn't invented until this century, when he gives me a narrow-eyed *don't-you-dare* look.

"It's true," I say. "Both of you have pretty legs."

Hamlet turns to Sophie. "Told you."

"You're a beautiful couple," Sophie says.

Juliet smiles. "We were destined for each other, and not just because we both had Shakespearean names. We were born the same year and our mothers were best friends."

"That's a good start." I grab the chance to give an outlet to my censored sarcasm. "But from there to call it *destiny*..."

Hamlet leans in. "When I proposed to Juliet for the first time, I dropped to my knees and asked her to be my wife before God and man."

"I said 'no way,' " Juliet says.

Hamlet nods. "My heart sank. Had I been blind? Could it be that Juliet didn't love me the way I loved her? So I asked her, my voice trembling, 'Why not?' "

He marks a pause.

I glance at Juliet, expecting her to pick up the tale, but she gazes at her husband, clearly unwilling to interfere with his show.

"What did she say?" Sophie asks.

Hamlet waits a few more seconds before answering. "She said, 'Because proposing on both knees is lame.' "

Sophie gasps at such extreme shallowness and turns to Juliet. "Really?"

Juliet nods.

"What did you do?" I ask Hamlet.

"What else was I supposed to do?" He shrugs. "I rearranged myself in the proper kneeling position and asked her to marry me again."

Sophie smiles. "And she said yes, right?"

"She said no."

I wonder why this time. Was he too poor for her liking? A cabinetmaker with no connections and no family money, did she believe he wasn't good enough for her? Was she hoping to snag a sheik or, failing that, a wealthy *homme d'affaires*?

A smile turns up the corners of Hamlet's lips. "I asked her why not again. She rolled her eyes and said, 'Because we're twelve, silly.' "

Sophie bursts out laughing.

I chuckle, too, absurdly relieved.

"I proposed again when we were eighteen," Hamlet says, grinning.

Juliet smoothes her hair back. "I said yes, but I made him wait two more years until we turned twenty."

Hamlet reaches over and pats her hand. "You were totally worth the wait, sweetheart."

Sophie and I thank our hosts and stand up.

"She's a keeper," Juliet whispers in my ear while she cheek kisses me good-bye. "Don't mess it up, boy."

I think of all the omissions, half-truths, and outright lies I've fed Sophie about who I am and where I come from, and my stomach knots.

It's quite possible I've already messed it up.

EIGHTEEN

SOPHIE

Noah opens the door and glances at his watch. "We're back home and it's only nine. Three cheers for same-landing dinner parties."

"I like your neighbors," I say.

He smiles. "You might like them less next time when Juliet will keep you hostage until you've seen her children's albums. An album per child per year."

"Why didn't she do it this time?"

"She knows I have an important game tomorrow, so she took pity."

Tomorrow, Noah, Zach, and the rest of the team are playing the first national championship game of the season against *Olympique Toulon*. The game will be in Paris. And Noah gave me a premium ticket.

"See?" I say. "Your neighbors *are* lovely and they really like you."

"They really like Oscar."

"Him, too, but if I didn't know, I'd assume they were your family."

Noah's expression grows bleak, and he quickly

crouches to pet Oscar. Clearly, he doesn't like to talk or even be reminded about his family. Since we met, I've told him tons about my mom, my dad, my friends, and my childhood. He's told me almost nothing. I've pieced together that he grew up in Burgundy and later in Nepal where he hung out with Uma before returning to France. His mom stayed back in Nepal. He loves her. His father died years ago, I'm not sure from what. Noah hates him because he refused to help his ex-wife and his son when they were in a tight spot.

That's about it, really.

Could Noah be embarrassed by his modest origins? He doesn't strike me as a status seeker, and he talks about his pizza delivery job without a problem. Not that he talks about it much. The only things he's always happy to discuss are Oscar and water polo. And maybe the Derzians—at least, until my uncalled-for comment.

I chide myself for being so gauche, but when he nudges Oscar toward his crate and stands up, there's no unease or hesitation in his eyes.

Uh-oh. It looks like someone remembered the plans we made for tonight.

Noah runs the tips of his fingers over my cheeks, jawline and lips, featherlight. "Are we still on?"

I nod, taking deep breaths so I won't tremble.

He steps back and scoops me up into his arms and carries me to the bedroom.

I ask him to pause as soon as we're inside and pull the door shut behind us. When my feet touch the floor, I decide I'm going to be adventurous. I know I can trust Noah not to hurt me. He'll stop the moment I say stop. Granted, I haven't known him very long, but I know the important part. The part that matters, the part that defines him.

Noah wants me, but he won't let his desire control his actions. After all, I spent two nights in his arms without him trying to cajole me to have sex or—worse—force himself on me. And without me having to say no more than once.

You can do it, Sophie!

Tentatively, I cup his bulge through his jeans.

Surprise flashes in his eyes before his face relaxes into a satisfied grin. "Just so you know, I totally approve of the way you're going about this."

"Shut up and unbuckle that belt," I say, settling into my brand-new seductress persona.

He executes.

I undo his jeans and slowly push them, together with his underwear, down his narrow hips and muscled thighs. He loses his T while I'm at it. When he's stark naked, I zero in on his proud manhood and touch it. Reveling in the wonderful contrast between the warm, velvety skin and the hardness it encases, I run my fingers up and down before wrapping them around him.

His flesh throbs against my palm.

My core grows heavy in response, pulling, aching for him.

Suddenly, his hands are everywhere. Noah unbuttons, unclasps and pulls my clothes off, stroking every part he uncovers. All the while I keep pressing my palm against his length, letting go of it only for two brief moments so he can strip my bra and shirt away.

He rakes my bared body with a scorching gaze. Then he bends down, his mouth closing over my right nipple and his big hand cupping my breast. His other hand rubs my belly and slides between my legs.

Ooh, it's welcome there. So very welcome.

Noah's gaze is scalding when he lifts his head and stares into my eyes. "You're dripping wet for me."

"So are you," I say, running the pad of my thumb over his tip.

He grins.

I give him a satisfied smirk. Who knew Frigid Sophie had a sex kitten in her?

Suddenly, Noah lets go of me and jumps onto the bed. The next moment he's flat on his back, a condom in his hand. "Come here."

I climb on the bed and sit on my heels next to him.

He rolls the condom on and lays a hand on my hip. "Ride me?"

That's not quite how I expected him to initiate our first full-blown lovemaking, but I'm game. I straddle his hips and begin to lower myself on him, very slowly, listening to my body's reactions. There's no trace of pain, no discomfort—just pleasure. Noah's hands are on my hips, hot and strong, but he isn't trying to accelerate my descent by pushing me down. Nor does he lift his hips.

When I'm fully impaled, I wiggle a little, loving the feel of him inside me. He thrusts tentatively. I push down to meet him.

Soon, we establish a rhythm, moving in perfect synch.

"*Bébé*," he rasps after a while. "I can't hold out much longer."

I bend over him and kiss his lips. "That's OK. I don't know if I can come like this, anyway."

His expression is still hesitant, so I add, "But I've *really* enjoyed this ride."

He nods, and tightens his grip on my hips. I let him lift me up a little and hold me steady where he wants me. His thrusts come faster, harder, the cadence accelerating to frantic. A minute later, his face contorts and he groans his pleasure.

I climb off him.

He turns on his side and puts his hand on my mound. There's a question in his eyes.

"Yes, please," I say.

He begins to caress, varying the amount of pressure and the pace, asking me if he should move left or right, go faster or slow down. Inhibited as I am about dirty talk, his simple questions make it incredibly easy to guide him, coaxing more and more joy from his hand.

Something begins to build inside me, and then I come, gasping at the sweetness of the release.

When the last wave of pleasure subsides, I turn to Noah. "Good job."

"Sorry you didn't get a vaginal orgasm." He strokes my upper arm, before resting his hand on my shoulder. "I was hoping we'd come together."

I blink. "Are you kidding me? I've just had *penetration*, and I enjoyed it. I *loved* it. You have no idea what that means to me."

He smiles. "Tell me."

"It means I can stop lying to myself that being frigid is great, that frigidity rocks, because it gives you protection against dumb choices."

"It doesn't?" he asks with fake innocence.

I roll my eyes. "Only death gives you protection against dumb choices. All frigidity has *really* given me so far is a feeling I was missing out on a lot of fun and on an important part of human experience. A feeling that I was… defective."

"You're perfect, *bébé*," he says.

I give him a mischievous smile. "Maybe I am now that you've untwisted my vagina."

His grin becomes so big I fear the corners of his mouth might crack.

Pressing a hot kiss to its left side and then the right, I add, "This *bébé* will always be grateful for that, Noah Masson, no matter how things end between us."

When I find my seat on the deck level, Uma and Sam are already there. Uma is armed with blue pom-poms and Sam, a blue foam hand. Sam is wearing a jersey with a big three on the front. I imagine it's Zach's number.

"Hey!" Uma greets me with a bear hug. "I'm glad you made it. This is going to be fun."

Her warmth and genuine friendliness make it hard to resent her, and yet I do. For what she means to Noah. For the possibility of their future together and even for their shared memories.

Why couldn't this Himalayan rose be less sweet? Or less pretty?

Thirty minutes later, the game is in full swing, and the three of us are cheering our heads off. Noah's team is winning. All the white caps seem to be in top form, but Noah's and Zach's play is wicked. By the second quarter, Zach has scored four goals and Noah has saved as many. He's on fire. I can see now what he meant when he told me about the importance of a big arm span, strong hands, and "explosiveness" in the goal cage.

And he's cunning.

Time after time, I watch the goalie of *Nageurs de Paris* lure Toulon's attackers into aiming at the side of the goal cage he's left unprotected. Only he hasn't. The moment they take the bait and shoot, he leaps out of the water and blocks the shot with an incredible precision.

It's also fun watching him get all bossy and bark at the defense players to move left or right, keep their eyes on the ball, or slow down a specific attacker.

The commentator raves about Noah.

"Tremendous save by the goalkeeper!"

"Strong hands!"

"Noah Masson continues his amazing set of saves!"

"Goalkeeper did well—what a fabulous stop!"

The man is in love.

Unfortunately, Toulon's players are just as inspired as the Parisians, if not more. They dominate the field, shooting so often and in such a perfectly coordinated and well-practiced way that they net the ball as often as the Parisians, even with Noah guarding the goal.

At the very end of the final quarter, one of the Parisian players commits a major foul, and Toulon sets up for a penalty. Everyone in the audience holds their breath. Noah explained to me that a water polo penalty shot is so hard to stop, it's almost always a sure goal. And to make matters worse, the score is tied. If Toulon scores, they win the match.

The attacker takes his time preparing, and then fakes a shot. Noah hardly budges, his eyes glued to the ball. After two more fakes, the real shot comes, powerful and precise. I brace for the worst.

Noah blocks with his head, rushes to the ball, catches it, swims forward, and passes it to a teammate. The player passes it on to Zach, who slams it into Toulon's cage.

Everyone freezes, watching the trajectory of the yellow ball as if in slow motion. The second it flies above the goalie's hand and hits the net, the arena roars with excitement.

"What a save!" the commentator shrieks. "What a shot! Unbelievable!" He chokes on his delight and begins to cough.

The white caps cheer and throw up their arms, fists clenched. It's over. Time to pop the bubbly.

Nageurs de Paris won.

NINETEEN

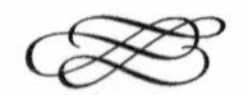

NOAH

N*ageurs de Paris* opened the season with a win against *Olympique Toulon* and went on to defeat three more clubs—on their home turf, as it were.

Today we played in Paris again, trouncing Aix-en-Provence, 14–6. Lucas is very happy. As per our recently established tradition, he's treating all his men, together with their partners and children, to celebratory drinks. We've already finished the requisite bottle of champagne and switched to beer, wine, and sodas for the kids.

All four of them are having a blast at the moment with a silly game organized by Denis.

He's placed four small paper bags on the floor—one for each kid—and has them take turns at picking theirs up with their mouths. They aren't allowed to touch the bag, or the floor, with their hands. When they fail, Denis asks them to jump on one leg while singing. When one of them succeeds, Denis picks up his scissors and cuts a centimeter or two from the top of that kid's bag.

"What's the point of this game?" Uma asks him.

"The one with the shortest bag when I say stop, wins." Denis smiles. "Want to play?"

Turns out she does, and so do Sophie, Zach, and all the other adults in our group.

When the children are done, we line up by the wall and look at Denis.

"What's the prize?" Julien asks.

Denis pulls a small bag of gummy bears from his backpack.

Jean-Michel stares. "Seriously?"

"I'd planned this for the kids, remember?" Denis shrugs before scratching his head. "Hmm… I got only one more paper bag."

We wait for him to find a miracle solution.

"OK," he says. "Different rules for grown-ups. This will be an elimination contest. If you pick up the bag when your turn comes, you stay and I crop it. If you fail, you're out."

Over the next forty-five minutes the café's patrons witness a competition almost as fierce as the one we just had in the pool. Only this time it's every man for himself.

Lucas is the first to be eliminated, followed by Jean-Michel and his girlfriend, Valentin, Julien, Denis's wife, Uma, Zach and the others. Sophie and I are the last *men* standing.

The bag barely rises above the floorboards now.

Valentin moves from one eliminated contender to the next, taking bets. Sophie gives me a mischievous look and begins to circle around the bag, swinging her arms to encourage cheers.

"Go Sophie!" Zach shouts.

"Traitor," I mouth to him.

Only I'm the traitor, seeing as I've stolen his would-be girlfriend. And he's being remarkably gracious about it.

Sophie rolls up her sleeves and does a few ear-to-shoulder stretches. "Fifteen years of beach yoga, people!"

The masses cheer.

She waits for them to go quiet before adding, "Four years of cheerleading!"

The audience chants her name.

"Heading to the top, U-S-A!" she chants, launching her fists in the air.

Watching her enjoy herself like this, completely uninhibited and infectiously exuberant, is a pure joy. If I wasn't her opponent, I'd be cheering her at the top of my voice.

But as it is, I have to defend the Tricolor.

I strike a bodybuilder pose exhibiting my biceps. "*Vive la* France!"

"Go Noah!" Uma hollers.

I put my hand over my heart and drop my head in recognition of her support.

"*Mesdames, Messieurs,*" Denis says, taking on a commentator's voice. "We are about to witness the final round of this tournament. A battle of the titans. A battle of civilizations! Eagle versus rooster. Doughnut versus croissant. Marilyn Monroe versus Brigitte Bardot. Elvis—"

"Get on with it," someone cuts in.

"All right, all right!" Denis turns to Sophie. "Your turn."

She plants her feet wide, entwines her fingers behind her back and starts lowering her torso with almost no visible effort. God, she's bendy! She sure wasn't lying about yoga and cheerleading.

Hmm, I wonder why she never mentioned either of those to me.

We may still be in a gray zone between dating and a relationship, but what we have is definitely more than casual sex. Or am I getting ahead of myself? After all, Sophie still has her life plan, and I'm probably just a fun distraction on her "Parisian holiday." The man who "untwisted" her vagina.

Maybe that's why she hasn't told me about her yoga and cheerleading passions.

Unless it's because I haven't been forthcoming about my own life, either.

Thing is, I'm not ready to tell her the truth yet. But I certainly want to know more about her. I'd like to hear what it was like growing up in Key West, I want to know what books and movies she likes, where she stands politically.

And I wouldn't mind a private demo of her yoga skills.

In fact, I'll ask for one tonight.

In bed.

My cock twitches when I picture Sophie arranging her gorgeous body in one particular posture.

"Dude, it's your turn now," Denis's voice snaps my attention back to the present moment.

Squatting in front of the bag, I try to grab it with my mouth—and fail.

Denis strides toward Sophie, takes her hand, and yanks it high. "Elastic Girl is the winner!"

Sophie jumps up and down, shouting, "Woohoo! Take that, frog-eaters!"

My phone rings in my pocket with Maman's ringtone. She must calling to ask about the result of the game.

I excuse myself and step out of the bar.

"Did you win?" Maman asks.

"Yes, we did."

"Congratulations!"

"Thanks, Maman." I hesitate. "Can I call you back tomorrow? I'm out celebrating with the team."

"Is Uma there, too?" she asks.

"Yes."

"What about that American woman you've been enthusing over lately? Is she there, too?"

"Yes. Why?"

"Are you dating her?"

"Yes."

Keeping this from Maman is pointless. Just as is keeping pretty much anything from her. Sooner or later, she'll find out, and she'll be upset. We don't want that.

When Maman is upset, she becomes emotionally unstable and gets horrible migraines. A couple of times she's even had suicidal thoughts. The one time I upset her *seriously*, she filled the bathtub with hot water, wrote a farewell note to me, and was about to set her plan in motion, when I came home from school.

At the regular time.

Is it unkind of me to think she hadn't actually meant to kill herself? Anyway, I've learned over the years to avoid doing things that would upset her.

Maman is silent for a long moment. I don't need to see her face to know she's rattled. Uma is the girl she's always wanted me to be with.

That was my intention, too.

But not anymore.

"I'll be in France next week," she finally says.

"Cool."

"I've decided to attend Raphael and Mia's wedding."

"Really?"

"Yes. Did you get their invite?"

"I tossed it in the trash, same as their engagement party invite, Lily's christening party invite, and all other RSVPs I've been receiving from the d'Arcys."

She doesn't comment.

"I'm surprised you're going," I say.

"So am I, but… Since Raphael visited me last year, I've done a lot of thinking."

"And?"

She sighs audibly. "He was too young at the time. We cannot hold him responsible for sticking with his older brother who'd been a father figure to him ever since his Papa engaged on the path of debauchery."

"That may very well be, but—"

"You should go, too. For my sake. I'd like you and Raphael to make up."

What?

"You don't have to decide right now," she says quickly. "Go back to your friends, and we'll discuss this in person in three days."

When I return to the bar, Sophie is sipping her wine at the long table. I sit down next to her.

She offers me a gummy bear. "No hard feelings?"

"None." I turn to her. "You won fair and square."

She beams.

I take the candy from her hand. "Thank you for sharing the bounty."

"How's your mom?"

"Fine," I say. "She's coming to Paris next week."

I almost add "for my middle brother's wedding"

before remembering I've never mentioned a middle brother to Sophie. Or any brother, for that matter.

My lovely girlfriend shifts in her chair to face me. "Tell me something. Why did you leave Nepal two years ago?"

"So I could join a good water polo club and play professionally."

It's what I always say when asked that question.

"Oh yeah, I remember!" She smiles. "Nepalis are more into elephant polo than water polo, right?"

"Yep."

But not quite.

On those rare occasions when I look into my soul, I see a more complex answer. There's the water polo, of course, but there's also… Maman. The truth is, regardless of all my love for her and my admiration for what she does, I needed a break. I needed to put some distance—more precisely, a dozen countries and a couple of seas—between us.

Sophie offers me another gummy bear.

I open my mouth and she feeds it to me. Unable to resist the temptation, I kiss the tips of her fingers. She stares into my eyes, biting her lower lip.

Suddenly, nothing else matters. All I want is to be alone with her in my bedroom. Or in her bedroom. Or anywhere we won't be disturbed. With no match to play tomorrow, not even a practice session in the morning—Lucas has given us two days off—I'm planning to pleasure her until she begs me to stop. Judging by the way she's looking at me right now, she won't object to my plan.

Sophie's purse rings.

She pulls out her phone and gives me an apologetic smile. "It's Dad. I better answer it."

While she's outside, I go over to Uma and Sam. The boy declares that I played well, but I'm not as good as his dad who's the best player in the world. Uma grins and ruffles his hair. Nodding in agreement, I look around for Zach. He's sitting at the other end of the table, half listening to Julien talk about something animatedly.

His eyes are trained on Uma.

If I didn't know Zach better, I'd say he's leering.

But I must be wrong.

Zach is the ultimate gentleman, and Uma is an ingénue from a very conservative background with no family in France. She's his employee. And his teammate's best friend. Those are lines he won't cross, if I know him at all.

Zach blinks as if waking up from a trance and says something to Julien.

I turn back to Sam and Uma, shamefaced. My sick mind must've misread Zach's expression. He's overprotective of his son. No doubt it's Sam he was staring at—not Uma.

When Sophie returns, her smile is strained.

"Something wrong?" I ask.

"No." She gives me a funny look. "Dad's here in Paris. I'm sorry, but I have to go home."

TWENTY

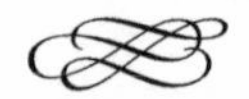

SOPHIE

Dad lets go of me after the longest hug in Bander family history. No wonder, considering this has been our longest time apart.

"I hope you haven't had dinner yet," he says petting my braids. "I booked a table downstairs."

Downstairs must be the hotel's restaurant.

What with all the drinks and gummy bears I've consumed this afternoon, I'm not hungry, but I won't ruin Dad's evening by saying no to his invitation.

"At what time?"

"About now."

"Great," I say. "Let's go."

"So, how do you like living and working in Paris?" Dad asks once we're seated.

I smile. "A lot."

He doesn't look pleased to hear that.

"Sophie," he says in a tone that bodes nothing good for me. "I won't beat about the bush. I'm concerned."

"Is that why you flew in?"

He nods.

I poke and push my food around the plate, waiting for Dad to continue.

"How's Catherine?" he asks instead.

Stalling, eh? "Mom's doing great. She got the post she's been vying for, so she's happy."

"Good," he says. "Is she seeing someone?"

I lift my eyes from my plate. Dad wears his poker face, but I detect emotion in his eyes and a bit of anxiety in his voice.

Interesting. "No," I say. "She isn't. Why are you asking?"

"Just curious."

Don't read too much into this, Sophie.

They've been divorced almost a decade, and I've lost count of false alarms and broken dreams of their reunification. It just isn't happening.

Mom loves her movie critic's job, especially now that she got hired by the biggest daily in the country. When she lived with us in Key West and Dad called her Cat, she submitted movie reviews to dozens, maybe hundreds of periodicals, but her English wasn't good enough to allow her to express herself with the same witty elegance she does in French. She landed other jobs—and hated them. She tried to be a stay-at-home mom and hated that, too. She missed her parents and friends. And she loathed the Keys weather ten months out of twelve.

While Dad's business expanded and took more and more of his time with every passing year, Mom became increasingly withdrawn and sad. Her doctor gave her antidepressants, but they didn't seem to help much. With hindsight, I don't think Mom was depressed. She just never managed to make Key West her home.

When I turned fourteen, she announced she had to

go back to France or she'd go crazy. She begged Dad to follow her. He refused.

The rows they had that year! He'd tell her she was capricious and irresponsible to ask him to abandon a flourishing business and uproot me just because she didn't like the fucking weather. She'd call him self-centered and unfeeling, since he couldn't see it was a matter of survival for her.

After months and months of arguments, they finally agreed to disagree. Mom was returning to France, Dad was staying put, and I was asked to choose.

Talk about impossible choices.

In the end, I stayed with Dad. It wasn't just about picking him over Mom. It was choosing what I knew and cherished over the unknown. I loved my school and my friends, our big house on Elizabeth Street, the shows on TV, the cheerleading, the beach…

"Your daughter?" someone at the table on our left asks Dad, breaking me from my reminiscences.

A stylish woman in her mid-forties is looking from me to Dad.

He nods.

The woman gives Dad a coquettish smile. "Stunning, just like her dad."

I take a closer look at her. Blonde, fit and well groomed, she's clearly flirting with Dad. Her friend, a plump brunette of about the same age is scrutinizing Dad's hands for a wedding band.

I smile politely, struggling not to roll my eyes.

This happens all the time. Dad gets hit on by women of all ages, colors, and sizes. He's held up well—in fact, *very* well—but it's not just that. He has that Denzel Washington air about him—poised and strong with the tiniest hint of intensity and an even tinier smile hiding in the corner of his mouth.

It wreaks havoc with women's brains.

The funny thing is he doesn't seem to care. Since the divorce, he's had a dozen dates and a couple of short-lived relationships, but nothing serious. When I ask him, he says he has no time and he's already married—to his job.

"Thank you," he says to the blonde and turns away without a second glance.

I search his face. "Spit it out, Dad. What are you so concerned about that you flew all the way here, abandoning ship at a busy time?"

He studies his food for a moment before he looks me in the eye. "I worry that you'll decide to stay here at the end of your internship."

"What makes you think that?"

"The way you speak about that *boy*, Noah Masson."

"The *boy* is twenty-seven," I say. "And you're totally overreacting. It's just a summer fling… er, summer and fall fling. I haven't changed my plans."

"Yet," he says. "You haven't changed them *yet*. But I can see it coming a mile away. You've never sounded so… into someone before. In fact, you've never *been* into someone before."

I wave my hand dismissively. "Let's not jump to conclusions."

He sighs. "Anyhow. The other reason I'm in France is that I'm invited to a high-society wedding next weekend. Will you accompany me?"

I arch an eyebrow. "I didn't know you had high-society connections here."

"I have many connections in many places that you

aren't aware of," he says. "So will you come? I wouldn't want to go alone."

"Sure. I'll keep you company, Dad. It'll be my chance to wear that big-ticket gown I brought with me and never had an opportunity to show off."

"The one you wore to your graduation? I love that gown," Dad says.

"Me, too."

When we're done, he walks me to Mom's where I'll be sleeping over tonight. My place is farther away, and Noah's is across the city. Besides, it would be too awkward asking Dad to put me in a cab so I can spend the night with a man. A man he clearly disapproves of.

Luckily for me, Mom doesn't.

"I've never seen you so into someone before," she says at some point in our now-traditional kitchen table confab.

Funny how she gives a positive spin to the words Dad had uttered with horror earlier tonight.

"It may turn out to be nothing," I say.

"Sure. But it may also turn out to be something beautiful and lasting. You have to let it blossom."

"Dad worries I'll give up on my future to be with Noah."

Mom says nothing.

"Isn't that what *you* did?" I ask, before adding, "And regretted it?"

She takes a heavy breath. "I never regretted marrying your dad, or having you. It's just… I know how much you and Ludwig love Key West, but that place was slowly killing me."

I take her hand over the table and give it a squeeze. "I'm sorry, Mom. I didn't mean to—"

"I saw Ludwig earlier today," she says, interrupting me.

"You did?"

They haven't met in ages.

"The years have been kind to him," she says, smiling.

"So have they been to you."

"That's what Ludwig seems to think, too." She pushes a strand behind her ear. "He said I looked just as smashing as when he first laid eyes on me."

I can't believe my ears—or my eyes. "Mom, you're blushing."

"No I'm not. Anyway, it doesn't mean anything."

I cock my head. "What's the deal? Did he just show up on your doorstep?"

She laughs. "Nothing so dramatic. He called and said he was in Paris in a hotel not far from me and asked if I wanted to have a coffee for old times' sake."

I wait for her to tell me more about their *coffee*, but she changes the topic.

As I listen to her talk about the latest movie she saw and the review she was writing for it, I can't help wondering if my parents still have feelings for each other.

The other thing I wonder about is whose hunch about Noah will carry the day. Will our fling turn into something more? Will I change my plans and stay in France so I can be with him? Or will he be willing to move to Key West to be with me?

Sheesh.

I should learn to live in the present moment, and stop building castles in the sky.

They're known to crumble at the slightest puff of wind.

TWENTY-ONE

NOAH

"When will you come over again?" Sam asks me.

"In a couple of weeks." I scoop him up and sit him on my lap at the garden table.

Uma comes out of the house carrying a tray loaded with three glasses of iced water and three bowls of ice cream—regular for her and me, and a special homemade concoction for Sam. After an hour of playing tag, this is just what we need.

"Is it normal for late October to be so warm in Paris?" she asks.

"No, this is much warmer than the norm." I ruffle Sam's soft curls. "Your dad and I are playing two major tournaments this season, so we'll be away quite a bit."

He nods, a solemn look on his face. "I know."

Uma sits down across from us and gives Sam a wink. "I'll arrange a bunch of playdates with your chums Evan and Mo while your dad and Noah are traveling."

Sam's eyes light up.

"Besides," Uma says. "I have some outings planned for us."

The boy's eyes are sparkling now. "To the movies?"

"Yes, but not only." Uma leans in. "We're also going to the zoo and to the circus."

Sam jumps off my lap, bounds around the table, and wraps his arms around Uma.

She kisses the top of his head. "Listen, why don't you watch a couple of *Diego* episodes, while Noah and I discuss some boring grown-up stuff?"

He grabs his bowl and scoots into the house.

Uma points at the untouched water he left behind and sighs. "He's got his priorities straight… Hang on."

She picks up the glass and carries it into the house. Through the open window, I hear her negotiate with Sam around ice cream, water, and Diego.

When she returns, I ask her about her embroidery school. She says she's learning a lot and loving every moment of it.

"Good." I smile and point my chin to the house. "It looks like you're not too unhappy about your part-time job, either."

She beams. "Sam is the sweetest kid I've ever met."

"How is it going with Zach?"

"Fine." She looks down at her ice cream bowl.

"Uma?" I narrow my eyes. "Is there something you want to tell me?"

She shakes her head before lifting her eyes to me. "But I have a question for you."

I lean in. "Shoot."

"Is Sophie still in the dark about who you are?"

Not quite the question I expected. I nod.

"Why?" she asks.

"It's complicated."

She scowls.

I duck my head in mock panic.

She lays her hands on the table. "I get it that you don't want to be associated with the d'Arcys, and you don't want strangers to know your real name. I respect that. But you did tell Zach. Why not confide in Sophie, too? I'm sure your secret will be safe with her."

This is awkward.

Uma may be an innocent, but she's far from stupid. I'm sure she's figured out by now that Sophie and I have become more than friends. Does it bother her? If she's still in love with me, I don't see how it wouldn't. Yet, she seems to genuinely like Sophie and believes she deserves my honesty, which my girlfriend totally does.

"You're right," I say. "As a matter of fact, I've decided to come clean with her next time I see her."

Hopefully next week, what with her father having monopolized her free time.

Uma lets out a relieved sigh. "Good decision."

We sit in silence for a moment.

"Did you go to Raphael's rehearsal dinner?" I ask. "Maman told me she was taking you along."

Uma slaps her forehead. "I was going to tell you about it! Can't believe it's been a week already…" She shakes her head. "Time clearly moves faster here than in Nepal."

"Definitely," I say.

She tilts her head to the side. "Are you coming to the wedding tomorrow?"

"No."

"You should."

"Did Maman put you up to this?" I lean my elbows on the table and rub my face. "She keeps saying Raphael can't be blamed for Sebastian's choices."

"Marguerite is right." Uma takes a breath. "Anyway, I really enjoyed myself except for a bit of weirdness at one point."

I raise my eyebrows.

"I overheard a conversation." She shifts uncomfortably. "Someone called Marguerite when we were hanging out on the patio. After she asked who was calling, she just listened for a long time, and then…"

Uma falls silent, hesitating.

"What did she say?" I prompt.

"She said she was thrilled to hear their interests were aligned. She asked whoever was calling to let her think about it and she'd call him back."

"Probably a potential donor."

"That's what I thought, too." Uma gives me a funny look. "But when she phoned that person back a few minutes later, she said, 'I'll call you tonight to explain the details, but if my plan works, you'll return to Florida with your daughter'."

I gasp.

Was her caller Sophie's dad? Have they joined forces in plotting to separate us? That would explain his sudden visit and keeping Sophie busy every evenings with various activities.

I glance at Uma. She looks like she's about to burst into tears.

"What's wrong?" I ask.

"I shouldn't've told you." She wrings her wrists. "Marguerite has always been so kind to me, and I feel like I'm betraying her… It's just that what she's doing is wrong… and unfair to you and Sophie."

I give her a long stare. "Uma, I must be blunt here. Aren't your interests aligned with Maman's and Sophie's father's? Don't you want Sophie to go away?"

She blinks. "Why would I? She makes you happy—it's obvious. And I'm your friend."

A light bulb goes off in my head.

Uma isn't in love with me. It's been Maman's wishful thinking the whole time. She saw something that wasn't there, and she made me see it, too, through her sheer will and power of persuasion. Because she wanted her favorite son to marry her chosen protégée.

That's just so Marguerite.

She is all about benevolence, only her benevolence comes at a price—control over the lives of those she cares for.

"Oh, my God!" Uma claps a hand to her mouth. "You think I'm in love with you."

"I—"

She shakes her head. "Of course you would. I'm sure that's what Marguerite has told you."

I close my eyes for a moment, thinking. "Has Maman told *you* that you're in love with me?"

"Yes, a million times. And that you're the reason I came to France."

"And I'm not."

She shakes her head. "It was for the embroidery school. And to escape an arranged marriage without my parents' losing face."

I run my hand through my hair. "Did Maman tell you *I* was in love with you?"

She nods.

My jaw clenches.

"Don't worry." Uma smiles. "I never bought it. You do love me, I'm sure, but only as a friend. I've never caught you looking at me the way you look at Sophie, or the way… other men look at me."

"For the record," I say, "I've never caught *you* looking at me that way, either."

She smiles.

We sit in silence for a long moment and then I stand up. "I better tell Sophie the truth before her dad does it."

Uma nods. "And, please, come to Raphael's wedding."

"I will."

If not to make up with my brothers, then to confront Maman.

TWENTY-TWO

SOPHIE

As I admire the wedding venue, which is a sumptuous *hôtel particulier* in the heart of Paris, I wish I had my phone to take a selfie. I would send it to Noah, just to show off. Only, my phone has gone missing since yesterday lunchtime. I've turned the office and my apartment upside down, and called myself from Dad's phone multiple times, but nada.

It was probably stolen from my purse during lunch.

I'm not too upset, though. All my data is backed up on the cloud, and the phone was an old model with a cracked screen. Dad announced he was buying me the newest and coolest model tomorrow. Because he feels guilty. Beats me how choosing the restaurant where my phone got stolen makes it his fault, but hey, if Mr. Bander needs a pretext to pamper his *princess*, I won't stand in his way.

The *maître d'hotel* directs us to the patio where pre-dinner drinks and sophisticated-looking snacks are being served. I understand the church wedding was held yesterday, in Alsace, where the bride's mother is a pastor.

It was only family and closest friends. This morning, a bigger ceremony was held at the town hall of their arrondissement, and now it's the dinner party for a much larger circle.

Which—lo and behold—includes Dad and me.

A good-looking French woman in her fifties approaches us with an adorable little girl in her arms.

"Ludwig! I'm so glad you could make it." She tilts her head toward the baby. "This is Lily, my granddaughter, courtesy of the newlyweds."

Dad points to me. "This is my daughter, Sophie."

"Pleased to meet you, Sophie," the woman says. "I'm Marguerite."

Noah's mom is called Marguerite, too. Must have been a fashionable name for that generation.

I smile. "*Enchantée*. And congratulations on your son's wedding!"

"Thank you, darling." She looks at Dad. "I'm happy to be here, but I'm also anxious to get back to work."

"I know what you mean," he says.

She turns to me. "I run a charitable foundation. The manager and staff are perfectly competent, and yet… You see, I'm a very hands-on philanthropist."

She smiles and eyes me up and down.

"*Magnifique*," she says to Dad, giving him a meaningful look.

His nod is cursory but just as meaningful. "Yes, she is."

Why do I get a feeling they've included me in some game they're playing without explaining the rules?

"Have you met Raphael and Mia yet?" Marguerite asks.

I follow her gaze to the stunning couple surrounded by a group of guests across the room.

"Not yet," I say. "But I'm looking forward to it."

A boyishly pretty young woman with a professional camera around her neck, is walking toward us. A step behind her is a handsome albeit aloof man holding a baby boy in his arms.

"Will you excuse me for a moment?" Marguerite gives us a perfunctory smile and scoots off.

The woman with the camera halts next to us. "Hi, I'm Diane, the unofficial photographer of this wedding."

She holds out her hand.

I shake it.

"*Chéri*," she says to the man holding the baby. "Will you and Tanguy stand over there for a quick pic?"

The man goes to the designated spot and poses.

When she's done, Diane turns to me again. "I hope we can chat later, when I'm done with my official and unofficial duties."

The stiff man passes the baby to a middle-aged woman—a nanny, I guess—who takes him out to the garden.

He extends his hand. "Sebastian d'Arcy."

I shake it, after which he shakes hands with Dad.

Dad turns to me. "This young man is Count Sebastian d'Arcy du Grand-Thouars de Saint-Maurice, owner of one of the most successful businesses in Europe."

I've never seen a count—or any aristocrat—before.

Am I supposed to *curtsy?*

Nah. He isn't the Queen of England, after all.

Weird how Dad stressed the man's title and fancy name. Is he so impressed he forgot he's American, and a *conch* to top it off? In Key West, we aren't given to formalities. Dad usually calls everyone by their nickname, regardless of status or position.

Something else bugs me.

It's the last part of count d'Arcy's long name. For some reason, those words sounded familiar… Wait a minute! The chateau Noah took me to in September was called Thouars-Maurice. And its owner was called Sebastian. This cannot be a coincidence. No effing way. Count d'Arcy du Grand-Thouars de Saint-Maurice is Noah's buddy Sebastian.

Fancy that!

"I visited your amazing estate last month," I say to him with a smile.

His eyebrows rise from which I deduce Noah hasn't told him he'd asked me to give him a hand selling the property.

Then again, why would he? It's not like either of us is getting a commission.

Count d'Arcy opens his mouth as if to say something, shuts it, and gives me a polite smile. "I'm glad you liked it. The estate is my brother's, actually."

"Raphael's?"

"No, my *other* brother's."

Curiouser and curiouser.

I'm sure Noah said the owner of the estate was his friend Sebastian, not his friend Sebastian's brother. But why on earth would he lie about it? Why would anyone bother lying about such an unimportant, minor detail?

I must've misunderstood.

But why didn't he mention his friend was a count? Probably because Sebastian's title doesn't mean anything to Noah. It doesn't define Sebastian in Noah's eyes.

Fair enough.

What I really can't explain is why Noah told me his friend was in need of cash, when Sebastian d'Arcy clearly isn't.

Maybe Sebastian's *other* brother is. I'll have to ask Noah—

Who's right here, barely a dozen feet from me, chatting with the bride. And with Uma.

What is he doing here? What is Uma doing here?

D'oh! This is his friend's brother's wedding. Noah was *invited*.

And he chose to come here with Uma.

"Excuse me," I say to Dad and Sebastian, and begin making my way toward Noah.

"So, should I call you Dr. Mia Stoll, PhD?" I hear him ask the bride.

"That would be overkill," she says.

"Dr. Mia Stoll then," Uma suggests.

The bride shakes her head. "Too pompous."

Noah cocks his head. "How about just doctor, like in *Doctor Who*?"

The bride grins. "How about just Mia?"

Noah and Uma exchange a comically dubious look and nod in unison. "Yes, doctor."

I join the trio amid peals of laughter.

Noah's smile slips and blood drains from his face the moment he sees me.

"Sophie!" Uma gives me a hug. "So nice to see you here!"

I mumble something. Mia says something and I respond to her. Hopefully, my autopilot is using context-appropriate expressions.

Uma hooks her arm through Mia's and walks away with her.

Noah and I stare at each other.

"Sophie," he says. "I feared this would happen… I tried to call you all day yesterday—"

"I lost my phone."

He swallows. "I went to your place, and I waited, but you didn't come home…"

"Dad took me out, and then I slept over at Mom's."

"That's what I thought." He draws a breath. "Has he… Has he told you about me?"

A sense of foreboding seizes my chest. "What do you mean?"

"I guess he hasn't, then." Noah's lips compress into a hard line. "He just brought you here instead."

My chin begins to tremble.

"I haven't been completely honest with you," Noah says.

I stare at him and, suddenly, I *know*.

All the jagged pieces of the puzzle fall into place, forming a picture that explains everything.

"You're Count d'Arcy's *other* brother," I say.

He nods.

"You're the owner of the estate you took me to last month."

He nods again.

"Why?"

Before he can respond, I lower the pitch of my voice and say mockingly, "I'm Noah Masson, a goalie and a pizza delivery man."

The muscles on his face are so taut they look like they might snap at any moment.

"Why the charade?" I ask.

He grabs my hand. "It wasn't a charade, Sophie. I *am* Noah Masson, goalie and pizza delivery man. That's who I've chosen to be."

"And yet," I smirk. "Your brother is a filthy-rich

count and you yourself are worth at least fifteen million."

He says nothing.

"You never even mentioned you had a brother," I say. "Two of them!"

"I didn't mean to—" he begins.

I fake a male voice again. "I'm renting a tiny apartment from you and helping my friend sell his estate. Oh wait, it's *my* estate! My mom volunteers for a charitable foundation. Oh, wait it's *her* foundation. Uma is just a friend. Oh wait, she's actually my *fiancée* with whom I came to my *brother's* wedding."

"She isn't!" Noah almost shouts. "It's not what it looks like."

A few heads turn toward us.

"With you, nothing is what it looks like," I say.

"Sophie, please, can we go somewhere private, so I can explain my reasons… and apologize properly?"

"Don't bother." I yank my hand from his and look around.

Dad is leaning on the wall near an elaborate flower arrangement, watching me anxiously.

I run to him. "Will you take me home?"

He nods, and five minutes later we're in a cab, zooming away to my apartment.

When the mansion vanishes from sight, I wipe my eyes with the back of my hand and turn to Dad. "Will you take me home to Key West?"

TWENTY-THREE

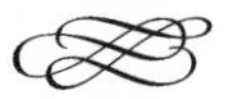

NOAH

Oscar gives me a wounded look, followed by a frustrated growl and a long vibrato whimper. That particular sequence means, "Why aren't you sharing that sandwich? I thought we were friends."

"You've put on weight, buddy." I pet him. "The vet says we have to watch your diet."

Oscar whines some more and scampers to the gap between the cupboard and the wall where he stays for a long moment. Coming out, he heads straight to the TV room and climbs on the couch for his midafternoon nap.

I've always wondered what he does in that corner. Maybe it's his meditation room where he performs a breathing routine, reminds himself life isn't so bad, and recovers his mojo. Another possibility is that he keeps a stash of naked lady dog postcards in there to be perused in times of emotional crisis. Whatever happens in that nook clearly works, because he always emerges from it cheered up.

I wish I had a place like that.

Because if this isn't a time of emotional crisis for me, then I don't know what is.

Sophie didn't answer my calls for the next two days following the wedding. When I called from the intercom of her building, she wouldn't buzz me in. Then I left for Athens for a LEN Cup game. The team stayed on for a couple more days to visit the Acropolis and explore the local night life.

Zach and I flew back. I went to Sophie's office straight from the airport. Her colleagues told me my landlady had to cut her internship short and return to the States for personal reasons. A friendly young woman told me *Mademoiselle* Bander had hired the agency to take care of my lease.

"I'm here to help if there's anything you need," she said, giving me her card.

"Thank you, everything's fine."

Heading out the door, I wondered how she'd have reacted if I'd told her the truth, which hasn't changed since July.

I need to kiss Sophie Bander.

So badly that I'm seriously considering going to Key West to try to smooth things over with her. I screwed up, there's no doubt about that. But I did have mitigating circumstances.

Sophie always told me she was going to marry the man of her father's dreams. She had a life plan for her future as a Floridian real estate mogul. She was going back to Key West at Christmastime to start it off. What we had wasn't serious.

Cut the crap, Noah.

These are not "mitigating circumstances." They are cheap, pathetic excuses. The bottom line is, Sophie had been honest and frank with me from start to finish.

And I lied to her.

No wonder she's mad at me.

The problem is I can't go to Key West right now. My team needs me. For the first time since Lucas established the club, we have a serious shot at becoming national champions. We're in the middle of a crazy season, competing in two overlapping championships, *Championnat de France* and the LEN Cup. We train several hours a day, and we travel all the time.

I had to quit my pizza delivery job.

Lucas tells us that now that *Nageurs de Paris* has won enough games to be taken seriously, he has big plans for the club. His first step will be to hire a publicist who will raise sponsor money and get advertising contracts for players.

Let's hope that happens, and soon.

Because I'm running out of funds. The estate hasn't been sold yet. Heck, I haven't even had time to hire an agent. And even when I do, it's not like I intend to keep the proceeds. Assuming Sophie's ballpark is correct, most of the fifteen million will go to Maman's foundation as planned. There will also be a huge tax to pay, and maybe even lawyer fees if Sebastian contests the sale.

Which he might, seeing how much he's attached to preserving the d'Arcy patrimony.

Is that such a bad thing?

I startle at the thought that came out of nowhere. Well, not quite. Ever since Sophie and I went to Burgundy, my mind keeps conjuring up images of the trained vines, of the view on the park from the Salon Bleu, and of Sophie gawking at the down-at-the-heels grandeur of the castle.

"This place is magnificent, for sure, but not just on

the outside," she said as we were leaving. "It has a beautiful soul. I hope the new owner can see it and love it the way it deserves to be loved."

My doorbell rings as I swallow the last bite of my sandwich. Oscar wakes up for a split second, then shuts his eyes again, in what I choose to interpret as complete trust in my capacity to handle the intruder.

It must be Maman.

She's taking me to a "lovely" new restaurant she's discovered in my neighborhood, and that's why I just ate a sandwich. Maman's "lovely" restaurants tend to be of the kind that serve beautifully presented itty-bitty portions that never leave me sated.

I let Maman in, glancing at my watch. The reservation is for seven, so I have a full hour to ask her the questions I've been burning to ask since Raphael's wedding.

She heads to the TV room and sits as far from Oscar as she can. She says he's too scruffy. She isn't entirely wrong.

"You invited Mr. Bander to Raphael's wedding just so he'd bring Sophie along and she'd find out the truth about me," I say without a preamble.

She gives me a long stare. "You shouldn't have lied to her."

"You're right, I shouldn't have. And you should've stayed out of it—or advised me to come clean. But, instead, you used my mistake to advance your agenda."

"I had your best interest at heart," she says. "And the same goes for Ludwig who was very concerned that his only daughter would ruin her future."

"By being with me?"

"By abandoning her dreams for an infatuation."

It was more than an infatuation, I burn to say.

Why else would it grow with every passing day and week, instead of fading away? Why else would it feel so right, like I found the woman who was made for me?

But I keep silent, afraid that saying those things out loud will make Sophie's departure even harder to bear.

"By the way," Maman says. "I'm glad your peccadillo led Ludwig to me. What a wonderful, upright man! He believes in charity as much as I do. I'm sure it won't be long before he donates a sizable amount to my foundation."

"No doubt." I squint at her. "So the pair of you came up with a genius fix to the problem Sophie and I created."

"Don't be so cynical," Maman says before simpering. "I must admit, our fix *was* brilliant in its simplicity and effectiveness."

"Just listen to yourself!"

She shrugs. "I did nothing wrong. Sophie is a nice girl, but she's wrong for you."

"Because *you* know who's right for me."

"As it happens, I do." She arches an eyebrow. "Uma."

Of course.

Maman's gaze softens. "She loves you."

"Yes, she does," I say. "As a friend."

"Don't be silly."

"She told me that herself."

Maman blinks, visibly confused. "She couldn't have."

"And yet she did. Maman… I can see how she and I may look like a great match. Only, we aren't drawn to each other."

"You're just saying it to spite me." She rearranges her legs and smoothes her skirt. "You're upset."

Sarcasm contorts my mouth. "No kidding."

"All I wanted was your happiness."

"Did it occur to you to ask if I'd already found my happiness before you walked all over it?"

She blinks again.

Bile rises in my throat. "Tell you what, Maman, you should order some puppets for the foundation and start staging shows."

She shifts uncomfortably. "I'm not sure that's a priority for the children we're helping."

"It won't be just for them—it'll be mostly for you. Your puppets will do *exactly* what you want them to do. And your shows—every single one of them—will end exactly the way you want them to end."

She lifts a trembling hand to her face and rubs her left temple, an expression of suffering on her face.

Migraine.

A.k.a., my cue to apologize and take back everything I've just said, because I've suddenly realized she's right. Because that's how we roll.

But not anymore.

Neither of us speaks for a while.

Then Maman stops rubbing her temple and gazes into my eyes. "I love you, Noah. Please believe me when I say that everything I've done was dictated by that love."

"Oh, I do believe you." I nod for emphasis. "But here's the thing. Your love has soured me. It's poisoned my relationships with Seb and Raph, and now also with Sophie. I'd say something's wrong with your love."

She sniffles and dabs her eyes, which would normally shut me up.

But not this time.

"Your love is broken, Maman," I say. "It needs some serious fixing."

She stands up and storms out the door.

I don't try to stop her.

Instead, my thoughts return to the estate. The more I think of it the less I see how Sophie's enthusiasm about it reflected badly on her. She was just being herself. Candid and genuine. Refreshingly honest. Awestruck by something exceptional—and vocal about it.

Isn't that a thousand times better than hypocrisy?

TWENTY-FOUR

SOPHIE

Watching the sun dip into the Gulf of Mexico, coloring the sky all shades of purple, reminds me of the view on the park from Noah's castle. I'd announced it was the most beautiful vista in the world, even better than Key West sunsets. I had raved about the chateau and its grounds, and even declared I would do anything to lay my hands on it. Including marrying someone I didn't have deep feelings for.

The shame.

That conversation is, without a doubt, the single most mortifying episode of my life. Just remembering it sets my face on fire. Why, oh why, did I say those things?

I was *making a point.*

And Noah took it.

With a sigh, I scoot from the middle of the bench to the side of the boat, hoping that Doug's friends Tim and Rosalind won't notice my flaming cheeks.

"What do you think, babe?" Doug calls out from behind the helm. "Gorgeous, huh?"

I've lost count of the times I almost asked Doug to call me *bébé*. He probably would as a tribute to my French side. Only there's a risk that hearing him say *bébé* would make things even worse for me. Getting over Noah has been hard enough—I don't need a daily reminder of what he murmured when he made love to me.

It's been only two months, but it seems like my Parisian holiday ended an eternity ago. And yet, it seems like yesterday.

"The sunset or your boat?" I ask Doug, turning my head to give him a bright smile.

Rosalind and Tim chuckle.

"The boat." Doug grins back, proud beyond measure of his shiny new yacht.

"The best view ever!" I say.

Just to think I was a girl who couldn't get the hang of lying no matter how hard she tried.

That girl is gone.

The new me has grown up and figured it out.

Watch me. "Hey, I'm getting a little queasy," I say to Doug, pulling a sad face. "Could you drop me off at the pier?"

He gives me an aww-you-poor-darling look. "Sure thing. Do you mind if we continue without you?"

"Not at all!"

This one isn't a lie. Doug's friends are OK, but we have zero shared interests and nothing to say to each other.

With Doug, at least, I can talk shop.

When I'm finally alone in the house—I've moved back in with Dad until I find a new apartment—I fix myself a cranberry cooler and sit on the porch.

Halfway through my drink, my phone rings in my

pocket. It's Noah. I never pick up when he calls me, expecting each call to be the last. But he's been at for eight weeks now, sometimes daily, and there's no sign of him relenting.

Dad says I should just block his number. He's right —that's the best thing to do.

I answer the call.

"Sophie?" he sounds incredulous.

"Yes. I picked up just to ask you to stop calling."

See? I'm so good at lying now it's scary.

What I really picked up for is to hear his voice. And also because it's been so damn hard to stop thinking about him, to forget his eyes, his smile, his lovemaking…

"I'll stop calling if that's what you want," he says. "But will you please hear me out first?"

I huff out a sigh. "It's OK, Noah. I'm not mad anymore. You hid things from me because you had no reason to reveal them. We weren't in a serious relationship."

"Is that what you think?"

"Yes, and I think my dramatic departure from your brother's wedding was utterly ridiculous. I hope you didn't have much explaining to do."

"You've changed," he says.

"Amen to that. What about you? Did you sell the estate?"

"I donated my trust fund to Maman's foundation and kept the estate."

"What will you do with it?"

"Seb and Raph are chipping in with enough to cover the renovations and initial upkeep."

"Seb and Raph, huh? The brothers you hated so much you wouldn't even mention their existence."

There's a brief silence before he says, "I'm done with hate."

Good for you.

"How's the championship looking?" I ask.

"We trounced Bordeaux and Nancy and defeated Marseille, which nobody expected, seeing as they practically own the national championship. Next week, we're headed to Strasbourg for the finals."

"Good luck."

"Thank you, I'll need it." He hesitates. "Not just for the match, but for… everything. The delivery man is now saddled with a huge estate, a crumbling chateau, and a once-profitable winery. I don't even know where to start."

"Hire a manager or bring in an associate."

"I've been thinking about that, too," he says.

"Stop thinking—act."

He chuckles.

"It was nice talking—" I begin.

"Would *you* like to be my associate and spearhead all of the cool projects you came up with in Burgundy?"

Whoa.

"Thank you for offering," I say, "But I'm going to say no."

"Sophie, I—"

This time it's my turn to cut in. "I'm about to get a marriage proposal."

"From whom?"

"A lovely local man—our biggest competitor, as it happens. Well, ex-competitor now."

"Has your ex-competitor penciled a date onto your calendar?" he asks with sarcasm.

"In fact, he has. Next Saturday at Louie's Backyard."

Why I'm giving him the time and place, I do not know. It's not like he's going to fly in from France and *save* me.

Anyway, I don't *need* saving.

There's a pause before Noah speaks. "I take it you intend to say yes."

"You bet."

I do intend to say yes, despite my panic attacks in the middle of the night, doubts, and the knowledge I'll never feel about Doug the way I feel… *felt* about Noah.

"Isn't it too soon for a proposal?" he asks. "You couldn't have dated him more than two months."

"Why wait? Doug and I are a great match, personally and professionally."

Except, my body still refuses to allow him more than a no-tongues smooch every now and then.

It's back to frigid for me.

Doug says he doesn't mind. He claims that my *decorum* is one of the things he likes about me. I never gave him the reason why I left Paris earlier than planned, but he's come up with an explanation of his own. That city was too decadent for Sophie Bander. Doug is extremely proud to be dating the most uptight woman in Key West.

The image of Noah's blond head between my widespread thighs with my fingers delving into his soft hair as I guide him flashes before my eyes.

It's hard to believe that woman was me.

But what happens in Paris, stays in Paris.

"You told me once," Noah says, "that you avoided emotions because they cloud your judgment."

"So?"

"Can't you see that's what's happening to you now?

You're letting an emotion cloud your judgment. And it isn't even a good emotion."

"What are you talking about?"

"Anger."

I say nothing.

"You are still mad at me," he says. "And you want to hurt me as much as I hurt you."

"It's not about you! I'm over you. I'll marry Doug because he's the kind of man I've always wanted to end up with."

"Listen to me, *bébé*. Don't repeat my mistakes. I let anger guide me for years, but things weren't as black and white as I thought. The villains had redeeming qualities, and the saint… wasn't so saintly."

"So you turned your back on Marguerite?"

"Of course not. I still love her, and I admire her commitment to philanthropy. But I'm no longer the tool of her revenge."

"I'm glad to hear it," I say.

"*Bébé*—"

"Take good care, Noah."

And with that, I hang up.

TWENTY-FIVE

NOAH

The first thing I see as I get off the plane is a big sign on the passenger terminal: WELCOME TO THE CONCH REPUBLIC.

I smile.

Sophie told me how Key West jokingly "seceded" from the United States in protest for something back in the eighties. I knew the locals enjoyed their fake independence, but I didn't quite expect a sign at the airport.

Another surprise is that it isn't as hot as I was bracing myself for. But it *is* mid-December.

It's almost *winter*.

After I pass through customs, I head to the taxi line. The hotel I'm booked at is out of town and pricey, but that's what you get when you reserve last minute. And let's not even talk about my business-class airfare; it's the most I've ever paid for a ticket. Actually, for anything. I emptied my savings account and I'm overdrawn, but I didn't touch the estate renovation account that Seb and Raph set up.

It had felt wrong.

Climbing into the cab, I give the driver the address. Amusement flickers in his eyes, but he just drops my duffle into the trunk and drives off.

Exactly one minute later, the cabbie pulls into the front yard of a large wooden mansion with a sign that says, "Marnie's Bed and Breakfast."

It would've taken me five minutes to walk here.

"Twenty dollars," the driver says, pointing to the price list taped to the outside of the car.

I pay, grab my duffel, and head for the entrance of the bed-and-breakfast. In my peripheral vision, I spot something unusual a couple of meters to my left. It's a toy iguana that someone has placed under the palm tree.

Must be the local version of the garden gnome.

The iguana tilts its little head and scurries up the trunk of the tree.

Noah, you're not in Paris anymore.

By the time I've checked in, showered, changed into a fresh set of clothes and returned to the lobby, it's already dark.

"How far are we from Louie's Backyard?" I ask the guy at the front desk.

"A twenty-minute drive. Twenty-five, tops."

"Can you call me a cab?"

"I just tried for another customer," he says, "but the wait is about thirty minutes right now. There's the Poultry Farmers' Convention—"

"Never mind. I'll walk there."

"It's too far for a walk," the concierge says. "You could rent one of our bikes."

I could—and I do.

Any chunk of time gained at this point, even if it's just a five-minute nugget, may change my life.

The concierge gives me directions, hands me a helmet and a lock, and sends me on my way.

It's not until I'm riding in the dark along a narrow strip between the ocean and the highway, my eyes veiled by wind and rain, that I admit I should've walked.

The bike isn't the problem—it's me.

I'm the weak link, wasted from two consecutive flights and too little food. The receptionist said it was easy-peasy. "Just ride along the water past the AIDS Memorial, Higgs Beach, and Casa Marina until you see Louie's Backyard."

Maybe, instead of trusting him, I should've asked for a map or, at least, for a description of the AIDS Memorial. As it is, I'm riding blind, separated from the ocean on my left by a low guardrail and from the highway on my right by nothing. I have no clue where I am.

Suddenly, my front wheel meets an obstacle, and I fly off the bike and over the guardrail.

Fuck!

At least, I won't drown, I tell myself as I fall.

Thump! Splash!

I don't, but it isn't thanks to my swimming skills.

It's because my bum hits the sandy bottom of the ocean, and I topple over on my side.

The water is so shallow it barely covers me, even lying down.

I lever myself up to a sitting position and laugh, feeling both relieved and ridiculous for expecting a serious plunge.

When I push open the door of Louie's Backyard, I'm soaked to my bones and sore in several places. Did I mention it's nine?

I spot Sophie at a table by the window, with a well-groomed man in his early thirties. There are two empty dessert plates on the table, a check folder, and some change.

Fuck.

He must've proposed by now.

"Hi," I say to both before training my gaze on Sophie. "Can we talk?"

"Noah!" She moves to stand up but then sinks back into her chair.

The man surveys me.

I stare at Sophie. Water drips from my hair and clothes, forming a puddle on the floor. All I can think of is whether I am too late or if there's still time to talk Sophie out of marrying this guy.

He turns to her. "Who is this?"

"Someone I met in Paris," she says, looking shaken.

He searches her face. "Should I *ask* him to leave?"

There's a clear implication of potential violence in his tone, should I unwisely decline his request.

Dude, I may be drenched, but I'm still bigger than you.

My gaze is locked on Sophie's mouth. Boy, how I've missed it!

I hope she says "don't" to her beau. I pray she doesn't say "get out!" to me.

Sophie gives him a weak smile. "I'm sorry, Doug. There's some unfinished business Noah and I need to discuss."

She stands up.

Doug stands too. "Are you sure?"

She nods.

"Call me if he tries anything funny," he says.

"I will." She marches toward the exit.

I follow her. Once outside, she continues to walk

briskly. I settle into a stride next to her. Ten minutes later, we're on an empty beach.

Sitting down, she hugs her knees and looks up at me.

I slump to the sand by her side.

"Talk," she says with her gaze on the water.

"Did you say yes to Doug?"

She keeps looking straight ahead. "What if I did?"

Fuck.

I drop my head into my hands.

"I said no," she breathes out.

I turn to her.

She's looking at me now, and even in the dark, I can see the turmoil she's going through in her eyes.

"I'm stupid," she says. "Doug is really a perfect catch."

"Then why did you say no?"

"I can't imagine… making love to him."

On impulse, I grab her hand. "I love you, Sophie."

She blinks. "What about your amazing Uma?"

"She's still amazing and will always be." I lift her hand to my lips. "But she has no effect on the pace of my heart or on the stiffness of my cock."

I press my lips to the back of her hand, remembering her skin. *Ooh, the bliss.* Flipping her hand over, I kiss the inside of her palm, her wrist, her fingers.

"Shouldn't you be in Strasbourg now?" she asks.

"I should—and yet I'm here."

She frowns. "But it's the finals, the chance to win that gold you've been dreaming about—"

"We have a substitute for each player, including me. No big deal."

The crease between her eyebrows deepens.

I exhale a long breath. "OK, here's the truth. They might lose. If they do, they'll hate me. Actually, they hate me already. I hate myself for walking out on them like this."

"You shouldn't have!"

I stare into her expressive eyes. "I have no regrets, Sophie. If you're willing to give me another chance, I'll quit everything and move here."

Her eyes widen. "You would?"

"In a heartbeat."

She tilts her head to the side, her expression still concerned.

"Maybe I can find a water polo club to join here," I say, winking. "Or a pizza joint in need of delivery men."

She draws closer and peers into my eyes. "You'd really do that for a second chance with me?"

I nod.

Her lips part slightly.

I lean in and claim them. Soft, full, warm. Holding her face, I sweep my tongue over her lips. She parts them, letting me in. *Sweet Jesus, that taste!* I drink it in, pushing my tongue deeper. Can't get enough of her. Fifty-seven days of craving this, of starving for her, of waking up with a hard-on, furious for being torn out of the dream where I could hold her.

I'm never going without Sophie that long again.

Ever.

When we break the kiss to catch our breaths, she leans her forehead against mine and murmurs, "I'll go to France with you."

I draw back and study her face, incredulous.

She smiles.

"Are you sure?" I ask.

She nods. "I love you."

I gather her to me and kiss her again, hungrily, thoroughly.

A few moments later, she draws back. There's a mixture of surprise and elation in her beautiful eyes as she guides my hand under the hem of her dress.

I gloss my fingertips up her inner thigh until they meet the material of her panties. It's moist. I apply more pressure, sliding my fingers a little farther.

The fabric isn't just moist—it's sopping wet.

If we weren't on a public beach, I'd unzip my jeans, sit her astride my lap, and drive into her like a madman.

"*Bébé*," I murmur, slipping a finger under the panties and into her hot slickness.

Her eyes roll in her head.

When she focuses on my face again, her expression is unexpectedly determined. "We need a room."

"Will my hotel do?" I withdraw my finger.

"Yeah." She reaches for her purse and stands. "Let's go."

I remain seated, waiting for my arousal to die down.

It takes time, what with Sophie's eagerness messing with my willpower.

But that's OK, because the urgency in her voice is a gratification in its own right. As for the hunger in her eyes, it's worth the championship gold I forfeited by coming here.

It's worth all the gold in the world.

TWENTY-SIX

SOPHIE

When we enter Noah's room after a half-hour power hike, both of us need a shower.

So we take it together with a condom for company.

As soon as we've washed the sweat and sand off each other, Noah puts the condom on and backs me against the tiled wall. I moan from the joy of having his body pressed to mine. He kisses me gently, then harder, and then applies himself to getting me to the point of arousal I was at on the beach.

It doesn't take long.

Truth is, I think I could get there just by looking at his wet muscled chest or peering into his blue eyes I could drown in—have drowned in.

I'm beyond salvation.

He murmurs my name as he fondles my breasts and sucks my stiff nipples. His hands roam my body, rubbing, gripping, squeezing.

When he bends his knees to hoist me high against him, I throw my arms around his neck and bracket his waist with my legs. My body tenses with need as he devours my mouth. All I can think of is the thickness at my opening and how much I want it. My core is heavy, aching, pulling, begging for the feel of it.

I'm ready.

So ready I'm on the verge of exploding.

And that's exactly what I do, seconds after he buries himself in me hilt-deep.

The orgasm is shockingly, achingly sweet. It pushes everything else outside of the confines of my world. It connects my core with my mind in a profound, almost supernatural way, stealing my breath.

When it ebbs, leaving me both sated and hungry for more, I realize I've just experienced pleasure like nothing I've ever known before.

I want this again—I *need* this again—as many times and as often as Noah can handle.

"Did you just…?" he asks, not daring to utter the word.

I nod.

"Good girl." His face expands into a smug grin.

I grin back. "Wouldn't mind another one."

He stops smiling and slams into me. This thrust is sharp and rough, unlike the long stroke he used to enter me, but it's so exquisitely erotic I gasp.

He begins to hammer, and all I can do is grip his neck and cling to him, letting the pleasure build inside me. My fingers dig into his flesh as he pounds, fierce, abandoning himself to his own need. Our bodies strain together, muscles taut, blood rushing, hearts throbbing.

With every withdrawal, I feel emptier than before. With every push, I'm propelled closer to another climax.

When it ripples through me, making me cry out,

Noah growls and lets himself come, too. Our voices mingle as our bodies quake with pleasure.

Afterward, we towel each other off and climb into the bed.

"Another one?" he asks, looking keen and awfully pleased with himself.

"Enough for tonight, I'm wasted."

He cups my cheek. "Tomorrow morning, then."

"First thing," I promise.

He strokes my face, when I notice a small crease between his eyebrows. "Something wrong?"

"Your life plan." He frowns. "What about your dream of becoming your dad's associate and the biggest realtor in Florida?"

I touch the hollow above his collarbone and rest my hand on his strong neck. "Every good plan allows for adjustments. I'll launch my conquest of the world from Paris."

He stares into my eyes for a long moment. "How about launching it from Burgundy?"

"Are you asking me to run the estate so you can keep playing pro water polo?"

"Yes."

"I'd love to," I say, "but that would make you my boss, which would be—"

He presses a finger against my lips, shushing me. "I'm not asking you to run *my* estate as a manager. I'm asking if you'd do me the honor of running *our* estate, as my wife."

EPILOGUE

SOPHIE

I look around the great hall of the Chateau d'Arcy, filled with music, light and people—just the way it was built to be—and grin, satisfied.

It's been an eventful couple of months for Noah and me.

Zach had surpassed himself in Strasbourg, scoring like a madman. Not just Zach—every single player did his darnedest to help the club snag the gold medal. Problem was, they couldn't be as focused on offense as in the previous games because the substitute goalie needed more help than Noah to block the opponent's incessant attacks.

Strasbourg had won gold for three years straight for a reason.

At the end of the last quarter the score was tied, and the referee announced a penalty shootout.

Under normal circumstances, that would've been a perfect opportunity for Noah's perfect saves. But he happened to be across the ocean at that moment, trying to make an entirely different kind of catch.

His club lost.

Back in Paris, *Nageurs* was still celebrated for the silver—a first for the city—but all the players could think of was how close they'd been to the gold.

Strasbourg's coach retired in late January, just as he'd been planning to, and Lucas succeeded him as head coach for the national team.

The day after we landed at Charles de Gaulle, Noah showed up for the workout at the pool. He was fully prepared to be roasted by Lucas and his teammates and kicked out of the club.

He did get roasted, but in the end, Lucas chose to give him a second chance.

"If you pull another stunt like that on me," Coach said, "you're dead."

Noah swore he wouldn't.

Seeing as he had absolutely no intention of proposing again.

Seeing as his first proposal got accepted.

And that brings me to the reason why the great hall is bustling with smartly dressed people on this frosty late-February evening.

Noah and I are celebrating our engagement.

Everyone's here.

My mom, looking young and flirty in her shimmery red dress.

My dad, tall and fit and all Denzel-y.

Marguerite, making eyes at him.

A bunch of philanthropists and high-level officials Marguerite has invited so she can tell them about the foundation.

Noah's brothers Raphael and Sebastian, their wives Mia and Diane, babies Lily and Tanguy, and some of their in-laws.

Sue and two other friends of mine from back home.

Uma, dazzling in a gold and silver embroidered sari.

Jacqueline and the rest of the estate staff.

Noah's entire team with their plus-ones.

The Derzians.

Oscar.

Jazzy music is playing in the background, and several couples are dancing.

Noah is talking with his brothers whom he's been spending a lot of time with lately. Raphael says something funny or—judging by the mischievous expression on his face—naughty, and both Noah and Sebastian burst out laughing. It's incredible how thick the three of them have grown over just a few months. Of course, the two older brothers had been close from the start, but Noah had barely spoken to either of them since Marguerite whisked him off to Nepal when he was eight.

I guess blood *is* thicker than water.

Their blossoming bromance aside, the trio is easy on the eyes, with Noah being the tallest, brawniest, and blondest of the lot.

I really should stop ogling my fiancé like that—there'll be plenty of time for it when the guests are gone.

With an effort, I peel my eyes away from him and look for Diane's sister, Chloe, who's an architect and property flipper. I want to consult with her about the renovations we're planning in the spring.

As I scan the crowd for a petite woman who meets her description, I catch sight of Marguerite sashaying toward Dad.

"Ludwig!" She touches his arm. "Finally, we can catch up."

"How have you been?" he asks politely.

When I'd learned about Dad's involvement in what Noah and I now refer to as the "Parents to the Rescue Conspiracy," I cold-shouldered him for a week.

Then I forgave him.

He's my dad.

I know he sent a fat check to Nepal last month, and Marguerite wrote back that she'd like to show him how grateful she was, when they met in person.

Ugh.

"I've been busy," she says, "but also thrilled to launch all those new health, housing, and literacy programs with the money that came in over the last few months."

"I'm happy to hear that."

"Now, Ludwig," she says in a husky voice. "About that promise I made in my letter—"

"Ah, there she is," Dad interrupts her, waving to Mom. "Cat, over here!"

When she's close enough, he grabs her hand and pulls her to him.

"*Comment ça va,* Marguerite?" Mom asks with a tight smile.

The other French woman's smile is just as cursory. "*Très bien,* Catherine."

"Cat is my girlfriend," Dad says to Marguerite.

Oh. My. God.

I knew he'd taken Mom to dinner a few times, but him calling her his *girlfriend* means that the rekindled relationship has progressed to a whole new level.

A mischievous smile dances in Dad's eyes.

Oh, how I love that smile.

Marguerite turns to Mom. "I thought you were divorced."

"We are," Mom says.

Dad lifts her hand to his lips. "I hope we'll put an end to that unfortunate situation soon."

What?

I freeze.

Mom gasps.

"Am I a fool to hope for that?" Dad asks her.

She narrows her eyes at him. "Are you asking what I think you're asking?"

He nods.

She screws up her face. "What if we botch it again?"

"We won't," he says. "I promise. And just so you believe me, I'm no longer the manager of my agency. My new associate Doug Thompson will take care of the day-to-day business so I can spend at least half the year in France with my two beauties."

This is too good to be true.

Mom's face expands into a beaming grin. "Then it's an *oui*."

"Congratulations," Marguerite mutters and retreats hurriedly.

"Whee!" someone squeaks in delight, clapping her hands.

It may or may not be me.

I dart to them and pull both into a big hug.

"Guys," I say. "You just made my most cherished dream come true."

Mom and Dad gaze at each other, eyes glistening.

I smooch each of them on the cheek. "Will you lovebirds excuse me for a moment? I need to share this scoop with my *fiancé*."

As I make my way to Noah, who's now discussing something with Zach, he turns to me and looks into my eyes.

A little miracle happens.

Despite all the laws of physics—quantum or otherwise—despite the distance between us, I feel him touch me in the deepest, most intimate way.

Soul to naked soul.

AUTHOR'S NOTE

One of the earliest Olympic sports, water polo is a national pastime in Hungary, Serbia and Montenegro, and is very popular in most of Europe. But it's incomprehensibly underfunded in other parts of the world, including France and the United States. Things are changing in the US, though, where water polo is the fastest growing sport. No wonder, considering the achievements of the national men's team (Olympic silver at Beijing) and, especially, women's team (Olympic gold at both London and Rio).

For the purposes of this story, I invented several water polo clubs, tweaked the schedules of various competitions, and threw in a fake fact or two, such as Paris winning a silver medal in the national championship.

But I've tried to stick as close to reality as possible.

COMPANION NOVELLA

CLARISSA & THE COWBOY

What happens when a hunky farmer and an uppity bluestocking get stranded in a cave with a 40,000-year-old phallus on the wall?

A sizzling-hot and hilarious romance, that's what!

CHAPTER 1

NATHAN

Anne-Chantal gives me a knowing smile and pushes my ticket across the counter. "Here you are."

"Thank you."

My tone is polite and hopefully formal enough to discourage any comments she might be tempted to make.

"The tour starts in five minutes," she says.

I nod and, exhaling a sigh of relief, move to turn away.

"You're *really* into prehistoric cave art these days, aren't you?" she says, tilting her head to the side.

"What's wrong with enjoying—"

"Nathan," she butts in, arching an eyebrow. "This is your fifth tour of the Darcy Grotto since January."

Not that you've been counting or anything, I itch to say, but decide against it.

Anne-Chantal is one of Ma's bosom friends and a frequent guest at the farm. Even though she sometimes boxed my ears when I was a kid, I owe her respect.

Anyway, busybodies are inevitable when you live in a village where everyone knows everyone.

"Fifth, you say?" I feign surprise. "I guess I *am* really into cave art."

With that, I shove the ticket into the pocket of my jeans and march to the area where two dozen visitors are waiting for our guide, Dr. Penelope Muller, to show up and start the tour.

Her scrawny assistant Nina arrives first and delivers her introductory spiel. "It's going to be chilly inside the Grotto. So, if you left your coat or jacket in the car, you might want to go get it now."

Several people dash out.

As before every tour, I can't help wondering if Nina ever eats anything beyond the occasional lettuce leaf. If I wasn't wary of giving her false hope, I'd take her to the farm and make her sample our dairy products.

If Girault cheese and butter don't transform her into a foodie, then nothing will.

"Nathan, hi! You're back." Nina smiles and tucks a strand of hair behind her ear.

We cheek kiss.

Like her boss, Nina isn't a local. But she claims she loves Burgundy with its lush vegetation, gentle rivers, and hills. She also loves country life. And, above all, she loves farm animals. Especially, cows. Nina's most cherished dream? To settle down in the region and become the wife of a dairy farmer.

At least that's what she told me when we bumped into each other about a month ago, in early February, at the opening of the cattle fair in Auxerre.

I asked her if her boss shared her aspirations.

"Clarissa?"

"Um… I thought her first name was Penelope?"

"It is." Nina played with a lock of her hair. "Clarissa is her middle name. She doesn't care for her first name and only uses it professionally."

Clarissa.

I took a moment to adjust my go-to fantasy in which I whisper "Penelope" while pushing hilt deep into her welcoming heat. As sexual fantasies go, this one is as much vanilla as it is a pipe dream. Thing is, I've never been with a woman—let alone someone as refined and far removed from my world as Dr. Muller—who could fully accommodate my length.

I wouldn't call myself a freak of nature, but there's no denying I'm larger than average. A lot larger. My neighbor and friend Celine once suggested I should book an appointment with a specialized surgeon to see if they can "trim" my "thingy" a bit.

"I know a woman who had her breasts reduced from an F cup to B cup, and it changed her life," Celine said.

No way in hell was my answer.

Then she came up with another idea. Why not try full penetration with a professional first? To be honest, I'd toyed with the idea a few years back, but I couldn't bring myself to pay for sex.

"That's because you aren't desperate enough," Celine offered when I rejected her second scheme. "Unlike the average farmer, you never had any trouble getting laid."

My guess is that by "average farmer" she meant herself.

Anyway, when I asked Nina what Clarissa thought of Burgundy, she rolled her eyes. According to her, Dr. Muller will get out of here as fast as lightning the day her research at the Grotto is done.

Of course, she would.

I don't know where Nina gets her romantic notions about country life from, but running a big farm is one of the hardest jobs I can think of.

A cheerful "hello" uttered in the world's most pleasing voice brings me back to the present moment.

Clarissa has arrived, sharp on time.

Dressed in a silky white blouse, black pants, a tailored black jacket and a pretty scarf around her neck, she's as classy as ever. Another friend of mine, Danny, who came along on my third tour, claimed she wasn't beautiful. Then again, Danny's standard for female beauty is Pamela Anderson from *Baywatch*.

Clarissa's breasts are pert little handfuls, nowhere near Pamela's cup range. The tip of her thin high-bridged nose looks down. She wears glasses, very little makeup, and has naturally brown hair.

And yet… to me, she's the sexiest thing alive.

Maybe I have a hand fetish.

Clarissa's delicate, long-fingered hands are out of this world. But they aren't the only thing she has going for her. On my first and fourth visits, she wore a skirt, giving me a chance to see her shapely long legs. Not just see them—study them, caress them with my gaze, and commit their lines to memory.

Then, there's her voice. Its clear, velvety sound makes my heart beat faster. Her intelligent gaze turns my brain to pulp. So much so that I still haven't plucked up the courage to ask her my prepared questions during the tour and ask her out after the tour.

Clarissa's competence and subtle humor leave me in awe.

As for the grace with which she carries herself, it has my cock on speed dial.

"Stop staring. You'll burn a hole through her,"

Anne-Chantal whispers with an amused smile on her face as she sails past me.

Great.

I can see her calling my mother the moment I'm out of earshot to tell her what she thinks about my *fifth* visit. Blanket denial combined with insinuations that the woman is so bored with her job she sees things that don't exist will be my best line of defense.

Anne-Chantal unlocks the heavy door and ushers everyone in before closing it behind us. I guess the animals painted on these walls are too precious to risk some moron creeping in at night and spraying his own version of a wild beast over them.

"Bone fragments and tools made by the Neanderthal man who lived here some 60,000 years ago were found in the Bison Cave and Hyena Cave," Clarissa explains as we begin the tour.

Having taken it four times already, I know what comes next, even though she does improvise a lot. The group hangs on her every word, staring at the masterfully painted reindeer, mammoths, rhinos, and horses.

"The beautiful Paleolithic art you're looking at," Clarissa says, "is the work of the Cro-Magnon—the modern humans—who moved in here some 40,000 years ago."

As she takes us to the Mammoth Hall, the largest of the interconnected caves, she explains that until two decades ago, no one knew about the existence of the paintings. Tourists came to the Grotto to admire its stalactites, stalagmites, and underground lakes. They were given a piece of stalactite as a souvenir at the end of the visit, and they left unaware that these caves held an extraordinary human-made treasure hidden under a layer of calcite.

As we progress from cave to cave, I keep staring at Clarissa. She doesn't look at me, not once.

All too soon, the tour is over.

Several visitors surround Clarissa to ask their questions.

I hover by the entrance for a few minutes, and then stride out and get into my car. As I drive off, I decide that I should forget about her. It's foolish to expect Dr. Muller, a lady and a scholar, the young and ambitious curator of the Darcy Grotto Museum, to care for a local farmer.

She could also be frigid.

Alternatively, she could be only interested in older men.

Or women.

Or group sex.

And even if I did manage to get under her skirt, what would be the point? I'll give her my heart—she practically has it already—but the moment there's an opening in some fancy museum in Paris or another big city, she'll zoom out of here like a meteor.

Ah, the voice of reason!

Thank you.

I'm giving up.

CHAPTER 2

CLARISSA

After dessert, everyone moves to the drawing room, splitting into small groups. The butler serves a selection of sweet wines for ladies, whiskey and eau-de-vie for gentlemen, coffee for me, and a spiced chai tea for the mayor's wife.

Genevieve sits down by my side on the sofa and spends a few moments watching me watch Sebastian and Diane.

"I'm sure he's brought her here with the sole purpose of making you jealous," she says, pointing her chin toward the couple.

Oh, I doubt it.

For the first time in months—make it a year—young Count Sebastian d'Arcy du Grand-Thouars de Saint-Maurice has come to a house party at his family estate in Burgundy with a woman on his arm. And, to make sure there was no doubt in anyone's mind as to her status, he introduced her as "Diane, my girlfriend."

A tomboyish checkout clerk, Diane is nothing like

the regal heiress he dated last year. Nor does she have much in common with the overachieving me, or any other woman I've ever seen within flirting distance of Sebastian.

Perhaps that's why he's into her.

Because, he *is* into her.

There's no way the desire in his eyes when he looks at Diane is fake. Besides, why would he bother scheming when he knows he can have me anytime? Nothing has been said between us, but I've dropped enough hints and given him more than enough seductive smiles and glances over the last year.

He *knows*.

And I know that he knows, even if my self-proclaimed friend Genevieve seems to believe I'm a nerd with zero emotional intelligence.

Last time Genevieve and I crossed paths was at Raphael's birthday party here at Chateau d'Arcy. I had too much to drink, which had the unfortunate effect of blunting my instincts and loosening my tongue. Genevieve confessed to me she was in love with the middle d'Arcy brother and her childhood friend, Raphael. I admitted I had the hots for the oldest brother, Sebastian.

"Here's to snagging the two most eligible bachelors in France!" Genevieve raised her glass. "Sebastian is worth a billion, and Raphael isn't far behind."

"It'sh not about his money," I slurred.

"Naturally." She gave me a wink. "I would never imply something so vulgar."

My ears still burn with shame every time I remember that exchange.

Truth is, it *is* a little bit about his money.

Not in the sense that I'm eager to lay my hands on

one of the country's oldest and biggest fortunes. Even though I like nice clothes as much as the next woman, I'd rather make enough to buy them myself than latch onto a man with deep pockets.

No, the way money affects my feelings for Sebastian is subtler than that.

Never mind that he owns a huge fragrance company, multiple houses in France and abroad, a Greek island, a private jet, and one of the largest estates in Burgundy. What matters is that said estate includes the Darcy Grotto and the adjacent museum that I curate. And that makes Sebastian the lucky owner of one of the most ancient and remarkable Paleolithic rock-art caves in Europe.

It's as if owning those cave paintings were his personal achievement, as if he'd *created* them or, at least, discovered them himself.

Sebastian is handsome and cultured, albeit aloof. I decided he was very attractive the day I first met him. But I can't help wondering if I'd be just as impressed if he were a local librarian or a mail carrier.

Or a dairy farmer.

I tune back in and realize Genevieve has been talking to Diane. She must have said something mean, because Diane purses her lips and there's a hard look in her eyes as she glances at me.

Wait a second! Why is she looking at me*? What did Genevieve say?*

Panic seizes me as I consider the possibilities.

Apart from inviting me to dinners and house parties at the castle—along with the mayor, his wife, and a bunch of other people—Sebastian has never said or done anything to suggest he was interested in me. What if Genevieve told Diane otherwise? What if she told Diane he and I were seeing each other?

As I sit there, petrified, embarrassment warming my ears and dampening my palms, Sebastian takes Genevieve's place on Diane's right. The next moment, he's kissing her in a way that's too intimate to watch.

That's it, I'm out of here.

Easier said than done.

Sebastian intercepts me before I have a chance to sneak out of the room. He says I should stay, for my safety. He hates the idea of me driving home alone on poorly lit countryside roads.

"You'll sleep at the castle," he announces in a tone which makes it clear the matter is closed.

Next, he calls the housekeeper and asks her to get one of the guest rooms ready.

I mumble thank you and sit down again, not daring to look at anyone—especially, Diane—and bracing myself for more mortification.

Mercifully, Yves Fournier, the mayor of Verlezy, remembers he wanted to discuss something with me. He sits down on my left, his wife Josephine takes the spot on my right, and the three of us spend the rest of the evening plotting how to dovetail the Grotto's outreach with Verlezy Primary's extracurricular activities.

When I finally go to bed, it's one o'clock in the morning.

The emotional shock inflicted by Sebastian and the never-ending discussion with Yves and Josephine have left me drained, which explains why I drop off the moment I shut my eyes. But it doesn't explain the dreams. *One* of the dreams, to be more exact—the one I've been having nearly every night for a couple of months now.

In it, I'm alone in the smallest cave of the Grotto and feeling uncommonly and inexplicably aroused. The warm flickering glow of several candles lights the room, and there's a musky smell in the air. I lean against the wall and touch myself as I picture *him*. Right on cue, *he* materializes by my side, leans into me, and covers my busy fingers with his large hand. His mouth descends onto mine as he rubs my bud, and I feel a long finger slip inside me.

Oh, oui! Right there. More, please!

He adds another finger and pumps deeper, faster—

I can never remember if he makes me come, but I always—always—wake up wet.

Shocking, I know.

What's even more scandalous is that the man in those dreams is not Count Sebastian d'Arcy. Nor is he one of my five ex-boyfriends. He isn't a faceless stranger conjured up by my imagination, either.

He's *Cowboy*.

Aka the dairy farmer who's taken the tour of the Grotto half a dozen times since January, and whom I often spot at various local events.

I don't know his name.

Since I'd never date him, I'm not even interested in learning it. If ever he tried to hit on me or if a common acquaintance formally introduced us, I'm sure we'd have nothing to say to each other.

For one, he has no interest in archeology. Whenever I sneak a peek at him during the tour, he's staring at me, not at the paintings on the walls.

And, I don't care for farming.

So, when I find myself in the same room as him, I pretend I don't know who he is. To make my point even clearer, I avoid acknowledging him with a hello or a nod.

He's never on my mind in daytime.

I don't look forward to his next visit or to a chance encounter in the village.

So why those dreams?

CHAPTER 3

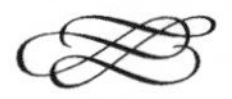

NATHAN

My new Workaway volunteer, Lorenzo, points to the trimmed part of the hedge. "How am I doing?"

"Not bad at all!" I nod in appreciation. "You're a natural."

"It's because I've done this before."

I try not to smile as he intones his remark with a singsong Italian accent, adding an "eh" at the end of each word.

"May I?" I take the shears from his hands and clip the little branches that stick out.

Two years ago, Ma planted this hedge around the nicest cottage on the farm after we decided to turn it into a guesthouse for tourists. In spring and summer, they come for fishing and hiking in the area, or just to get away from the city and enjoy some peace and quiet.

I hand the shears back to Lorenzo. "All yours."

The young software engineer from Florence and his girlfriend arrived two days ago, and will stay through

May, working four hours a day in exchange for accommodation and food.

When they're gone, I'll take in two new people. The farm has three single-story cottages on its grounds, built by my grandfather and updated with modern amenities by Pop.

I occupy one of them so that Ma and I don't crowd each other's space. The second cottage is for paying guests. The third one—only big enough to serve as temporary lodgings for a single person or a couple—stood empty for years because Ma preferred to put up visiting family and friends in the main house.

So, it made an awful lot of sense to host Workaway helpers in addition to the farmhands we hire when there's too much work.

I should've thought of it myself, but I didn't.

It was Celine's idea. She learned about the program three years ago from a friend, and posted an ad for her organic produce farm the same day. Her first helper was a giggly middle-aged school teacher from Germany. The woman went above and beyond with every task she was given.

Since then, Celine has been hosting a nonstop influx of *Frauen*, with an occasional Dutch or Austrian woman thrown in. All of the ladies fall in love with Burgundy and with Celine's farm. They delight in the food and wine she serves them. Most come back the following year. And some of them fall in love with Celine.

Anyhow, Ma and I decided to give the Workaway thingy a shot, despite our initial skepticism. When milk prices are low and labor costs high, you need to get creative to keep a big dairy farm profitable. Besides, only an idiot would pass up on a highly motivated workforce that's happy with payment in kind and with beautiful landscapes for a bonus.

We welcomed our first volunteers two years ago, and never looked back.

Celine was right to insist.

"Hey, neighbor!" a familiar voice calls.

Speak of the devil.

Celine waves hello as she walks through the gate and gives Lorenzo a bright smile. "Hey, new guy!"

"I'm Lorenzo," he says.

She fist-bumps me and cheek kisses Lorenzo. "My name is Celine. You alone here or with a partner?"

"My girlfriend Paola is inside." He points to the cottage.

Celine turns to me. "Did you talk to her?"

"Paola?"

"No, silly! The *cave woman.*"

"Can we discuss that later?" I give Celine a pointed look.

She glances at Lorenzo. "Oh. Sure."

Since we were teenagers, Celine and I have always kept each other updated on our progress—or lack thereof—with the objects of our fixations.

Celine's is rarely a specific person. It's a type. She digs men that are nerdy, skinny, sensitive and preferably bespectacled.

I blame it on Harry Potter and that actor, Romain Duris, both of whom she was hung up on as a teenager. Her more recent crushes—Tim from *The Office* UK, Jim from *The Office* US and Chandler from *Friends*—haven't exactly helped either. I've tried to get her to appreciate guys like Terminator and Rambo by making her watch my favorite 90s action movies, but that was a total waste of time and effort.

Celine may be one tough cookie, but she's hopelessly attracted to men who have less muscle than she does.

I'm not saying there's something wrong with guys like that. Problem is they don't go into farming. While there's no shortage of musclemen among my brothers in plows, you'd be hard pressed to find a skinny nerd.

Come to think of it, you'd be just as hard-pressed to find stylish, eloquent and graceful female archeologists around here. I'm pretty sure there's just one, and she's afflicted with a strange condition that makes me invisible to her.

It would've been so much easier if Celine and I were attracted to each other!

We'd become lovers and I'd marry my spunky, dependable neighbor who hides a nice body under her checkered shirts and baggy jeans, and comes from a long line of farmers. To top it off, Ma loves Celine with all her heart. We could be very happy together...

But no, the naked guy Eros, God of Horniness, has a sick sense of humor.

My phone lights up with an alert sent to it by the calving sensor in the barn.

"Got to go," I say, standing up. "Gabrielle is in labor."

Celine draws her eyebrows. "You have an alert for that?"

"It's a pretty nifty app," I say with pride, heading to the barn. "Had it installed two weeks ago."

Celine marches next to me. "Could be a false alarm."

"I guess I'll find out."

I pick up the sanitizer, gloves, and wipes from the tool shed and race to the barn.

Celine follows, hot on my heels.

Turns out it isn't a false alarm—Gabrielle is in labor. And, by the looks of her, it won't be an easy one.

I had a feeling this "petite" heifer would have a tough time calving, and unfortunately, I was right. She's fully dilated, her water sac has broken, and the calf has presented as it should—front feet first. But it's too big. And that must be the reason it's stuck in the birth canal.

Looks like a C-section situation to me.

"Time to call the vet," I say to Celine.

"You're sure we can't handle it?" She crouches down and stares, trying to assess the odds. "You and Brigitte managed just fine last time."

Yeah, I wish Ma was here now, but she's on a long-overdue vacation in Provence.

Celine pulls out her phone. "I can snap a pic and send it to her—to get her opinion."

My gaze shifts from Celine to the heifer.

I really don't want to mess this up. Gabrielle and the calf are too valuable to take unnecessary risks.

"We don't need my mother's opinion," I say, all doubt gone from my voice. "We need a vet."

An hour later, it's over.

I have to go fill out a dozen or so forms required by the EU red tape every time a calf is born, but the important thing here is that he *was* born. And he's healthy as is his mother.

"So, how did the Grotto tour go?" Celine asks me when the vet is gone and we've tucked in Gabrielle and the calf.

"Same as last time. Clarissa ignored me so profoundly I lost my nerve."

"You didn't go up to her after the tour?"

I shake my head.

"Did you at least ask your question during the tour?"

"Nope. Didn't have the guts. I'm giving up."

"You're pathetic, Nathan Girault."

I arch an eyebrow. "Says the grown woman with *Harry Potter* posters everywhere in her house."

"Yeah, well, at least I take action. On those rare occasions when I meet a man who fits the bill, I make sure to talk to him, to give him a chance to size me up, and to…" She lets out a heavy sigh.

"What?"

"Let me know he isn't interested."

"So, what's the point?"

"The point is in not giving up. Because you never know."

I shake my head.

"Promise me you'll go back there next week and initiate a verbal exchange," Celine says.

"What for? It's hopeless. I bet that even if I do, she'll just wave me off. I'm too *rustic* for her."

"Then you'll get closure."

Good point. Besides, what do I have to lose?

"One last time, next week," I say. "I promise."

"That's my boy!" Celine gives me a pat on the shoulder and goes home to cook dinner for her *Frau*.

CHAPTER 4

CLARISSA

Jean-Philippe has been the curator of the Museum of Archeology in Paris for at least a decade.

He's been a good friend of my parents for at least twice as long, which is one of the reasons I'd refused his offer to take over as the Paleolithic art curator when the current one retires in a few weeks. All the scandalmongers whispering about nepotism behind my back, staffers citing my family name in hallways, unlucky contenders rolling their eyes as if to say, the old boys are looking after their own… *Grrr!*

If only I could impress upon every single museum curator and archeologist in France that my parents never intervene on my behalf!

But I can't, nor do I believe it would help. Even if I wore a sign across my chest that said exactly that, chances are nobody would believe me.

Except, it's the truth.

Mother and Father hate owing favors to other

people—even to good friends. And they love knowing that my achievements are my own.

As it happens, I love knowing that, too.

Then why am I dialing Jean-Philippe's number at this juncture?

Sebastian d'Arcy, that's why.

True, the count had never overtly flirted with me, but I'd convinced myself flirting just wasn't in his character. I had deluded myself that his interest in the Grotto and his frequent invitations to gatherings at the chateau had meant more than neighborly solicitude and a genuine interest in the rock paintings discovered on his estate.

I was such a fool!

"My dear Penelope, it's so good to hear your voice!" Jean-Philippe says on the other end of the line. "To what do I owe the pleasure?"

I hesitate for a moment and confront the issue head on. "That job you mentioned two weeks ago—is it still up for grabs?"

"I've done a bunch of interviews, but I'm not entirely happy with any of the candidates." There's a brief silence. "Why? Have you had enough of sweet Burgundy and want to move back to Paris?"

"I've changed my mind about the job. It's too good to pass up."

"When I made the offer, you told me you preferred to be a big fish in a small pond rather than a small fish in a big one. I'm just curious—what gives?"

"It's like you said," I lie. "My small pond is beginning to feel like a tiny fish bowl."

"I knew it!" He chuckles, pleased with his perspicacity.

If only he knew how far he is from the truth!

"You were born for the ocean, *mon enfant,*" Jean-Philippe says when he's done chuckling. "Your parents have no doubt about it."

My stomach clenches at the brutal accuracy of the latter observation. Jean-Philippe is right. What with being dyed-in-the-wool atheists and certified pessimists, Mother and Father believe in me more than they have ever believed in anything.

And *that* is the root of the problem.

"With the TGV train, Auxerre is less than two hours away from Paris, right?" Jean-Philippe asks.

"That's right."

"So, you can easily zoom to the Grotto, if you need to check something for your research, and be back within the day. Isn't that convenient?"

"It is, indeed."

"Send in your application straightaway," he says. "And expect to be called for an interview very soon."

"Thank you."

"The job is as good as yours, but we'll need to do it by the book."

"You'll be accused of favoritism no matter how we do it," I say.

He chuckles again, unfazed. "Let me worry about that, *mon enfant.*"

After I hang up, I email him the application form I'd already filled out, my CV, and a letter of motivation.

That was easy.

If everything goes to plan, I'll hand in my notice in April and move back to Paris. Another archeologist will take over as the curator of the Grotto. As for *this* archeologist, she'll have no reason to cross paths with Sebastian d'Arcy ever again.

My phone beeps, reminding me it's time.

I shut down my computer, grab my jacket, and head over to the cave for the daily tour.

The first thing I notice in the crowd waiting in front of the entrance is the strapping, sun-kissed man who towers above everyone.

Cowboy.

Immediately, I avert my gaze, refusing to acknowledge him and denying him the chance to acknowledge me. It's rude, and God knows I feel guilty doing it, but so far, my selective blindness has worked at keeping him from approaching me.

He hasn't even dared to ask a question!

And that is great on more than just the obvious level of sparing both of us some awkwardness. The second, less obvious and more twisted, level is that I expect him to say something dumb if he opens his mouth. Call me a prejudiced snob, but I just can't picture this country hick asking an intelligent question about the paintings. Or even about stalactites.

Beats me why, but I don't want to hear him say something embarrassingly inane. It would pain me to watch the others in the group—most of them tourists from big cities—choke down giggles while stealing glances at the thickheaded hayseed.

After all, I've had sex with that hayseed repeatedly in my dreams!

Nina hands me my flashlight and we start the one-hour tour, which continues without any incidents. Cowboy keeps silent. Others ask lots of good questions about the techniques our ancestors used to paint the animals on the walls. In the Mammoth Hall, everybody gapes in awe at the beauty of the creatures on the ceiling.

I realize just how much I love this place, and that I'll miss serving as a tour guide. It won't be part of my new job in the Paris museum, which has dedicated personnel for that.

When we're done, Nina accompanies the group to the exit. I stay behind for a moment, intrigued by a detail on one of the horses in the Dance Hall that I hadn't noticed before. Or, to be more exact, I had noticed it, but hadn't realized its significance.

I pull my phone out and begin to dictate my observations.

When the Grotto grows quiet, Nina returns by my side. "Ready to leave?"

"Not yet," I say. "You go ahead—I'll lock up."

She nods. "See you at the office later this afternoon?"

I glance at my watch, at the painting, and at the five other horses in the cave that I'd like to study more. "This might take a while, so I can't promise I'll be there before closing time."

"OK." She waves goodbye.

I wave back.

Half an hour later, I'm done. It's only five, so I will catch Nina at the office. She'll be the first to hear my new theory. I smile, brimming with enthusiasm and pride as I stride to the gate. Once I've aired it with Nina, I'll have her transcribe my dictated notes while I call Father.

And after that, I'll go home and begin researching and building arguments to support my hypothesis.

Grinning like an idiot, I pull the door toward me. It resists. I push the handle down and pull harder. The door still resists. I stick the key into the keyhole and try to turn it at the same time as I push the handle down. No luck. I jerk it up. No effect whatsoever.

Oh great.

I whip out my phone but, just as I feared, there's no service. Why, why didn't I listen to Nina and switch to her cell phone carrier? She can usually use her phone close to the gate, while I must leave the Grotto and get away from the limestone to get one or two bars.

OK, let's take stock of the situation.

Everyone is gone. The door has malfunctioned. I'll keep trying, but if I don't manage to open it, I'm stuck here until eight-thirty in the morning.

The light coming in through the upper part of the door made of thick, burglarproof glass is growing dimmer by the minute. In an hour or so it will be dark. I can work through the evening, using my flashlight and my phone. But what about the night? There's nothing to lie on or to cover myself with. And even if the temperature in the Grotto is constant, it'll be too cold for my silk shirt and cotton jacket.

I'm so screwed.

"Dr. Muller," someone calls from the recess to my left.

My eyes widen as I spin around.

Cowboy takes a step forward. "Apologies if I spooked you."

I'm still too startled to produce a verbal response.

He gives me a sheepish smile. "I stayed behind, hoping to ask you about that painting over there."

I look in the direction he's pointing.

"Is that a child's hand?" he asks. "Looks like that to me, but since you never commented on it, I wasn't sure."

Oh, so he did look at the art and not just at me!

He even listened to my commentary.

Finally, my tongue recovers its mobility.

"It is a child's hand," I say. "But, much more importantly, do you have a phone?"

CHAPTER 5

NATHAN

"Yes," I say. "I do."

"Can I use it?"

I fish my phone out of the pocket of my jeans and hand it to her.

"*Merde!*" She points at the screen.

I raise my eyebrows, surprised to hear her curse.

"*Merde, merde, merde!*" She squeezes her eyes shut, takes a deep breath, and opens them, looking calmer. "No signal."

"Try another spot?"

She shakes her head. "If it doesn't work here, it won't work anywhere else in the cave."

"Would you like me to have a go at the lock?"

Her eyes light up. "Will you? You might be better at this sort of thing than I am."

She hands me the keys.

I begin to tinker with the lock, which shows no intention of giving in. But I've never been a quitter, so I persist.

Clarissa folds her arms over her chest and watches me.

This sort of thing, huh?

She must be referring to all the nonintellectual, *physical* stuff that I do with my hands day in and day out. Does she know what my occupation is? Then again, do I look like the eggheads Celine raves about? Nope. I look like someone who could easily gobble one of them for dinner.

"Damn lock!" I puff, frustrated with my lack of success at the "sort of thing" I'm supposed to be good at.

When I hand the keys back to Clarissa, she narrows her eyes. "Did you have something to do with this?"

I frown. *Whatever does she mean?*

She stares at me and then at the lock.

My frown deepens.

She curls her lip as if to say, *Should I draw you a picture?*

Comprehension hits me. Exasperation and anger come next. "Really? Is that what you think?"

"We never had the slightest problem with this lock," she says through her clenched jaw. "It's been tampered with. And, yes, I think it was you."

"Hell, no!"

She blinks, taken aback at the vehemence of my reaction.

OK, calm down, Nathan, and put your cards on the table. Given the circumstances, it's the best thing to do.

"The first time I took your tour," I say, "it was to learn about the paintings."

I pause, searching for words.

"And the second?" she prompts.

"The second time was to get a better look at you." I

cock my head. "And so were the third, fourth, and fifth times."

She juts her chin up. "So, you admit to interfering with the lock?"

"I admit no such thing. Today's tour was my last attempt to establish eye contact and get a sense of how you'd react to me. When that failed, I lingered so I could walk out at the same time as you and strike up a conversation. That's all, Clarissa. No foul play."

I fold my arms across my chest, mirroring her posture, and wait for her to decide if she believes me. For a long moment, neither of us moves. Clarissa glares at me, and with every passing second, I lose hope.

Now that my righteous anger has dried up, there's no denying that the situation does look fishy from her vantage point. In her place, I'd probably suspect me of trapping her here, too.

Do I come across as a stalker?

Is she *scared* of me?

Jeez, and then I up and call her Clarissa, when I'm not even supposed to know her middle name!

Just as I begin to panic, she sighs and gives me a feeble smile. "Nina told me you've been asking her lots of questions about me."

I nod, still too tense to smile back.

"Nathaniel Girault, right?" She holds her hand out.

"Nathan, please." I shake it, relief washing over me. "Sounds like you've asked her a question or two of your own."

Clarissa's smile widens. "Nina likes you. She was disappointed when she realized what you were after when you chatted with her."

"I didn't mean to—" I begin.

She waves her hand dismissively. "That's OK. Nina's over it. I believe she's been dating someone lately."

"Good for her." I hesitate, before asking, "Am I off the hook, premeditation-wise?"

"Hmm… Considering all the good things Nina and Anne-Chantal have said about you… I guess you are."

"Anne-Chantal?" *Meddling old—Urgh!* "What did she have to say?"

"Not much."

Clarissa's smile grows playful—the most kittenish I've ever seen on her.

God, I love that smile! I want to drink it in.

"She said she's friends with your mom," Clarissa says, "and that you've been her favorite since your most tender age."

I roll my eyes skyward.

She tucks her bottom lip in with her teeth. "Your champion also reported how she changed your diapers when you were a baby, and that you were the cutest and sweetest baby boy she'd ever laid eyes on."

Shoot me now.

"She also said"—Clarissa pauses to gaze at me with an innocence that's so blatantly fake it isn't even trying to pass for authentic—"that you've grown up to be the handsomest young man in the area, and quite possibly in the whole world, that you're single at the moment, that you work really hard running your operation, which is *big* and *profitable*, that—"

"Enough. Please." My face is on fire.

"I'm sorry." She surveys me. "It was unkind of me to tease you like that… even though I wasn't exaggerating. She really did say all of those things."

"I'm sure she did."

"Please don't be angry with her. She meant well."

"Uh-huh."

I'm not angry, but I'm having words with Anne-Chantal next time she shows up at the farm.

Clarissa picks up her flashlight. "Since we're stuck here, anyway, I'm going to head back into the Dance Hall to work for a bit."

"Mind if I tag along?" I point my chin at the flashlight. "I can hold it so your hands are free."

She hesitates a split second and hands me the flashlight. "Sure. Thanks."

We backtrack to one of the inner caves, where she halts in front of a horse painted in black charcoal and ochre, and points to its hooves. "See how the feet are twisted in an unnatural way?"

I bring the flashlight closer to the hooves and study them. "You're right."

"I believe this painting had an educational value. The artist was trying to show, perhaps to children, what tracks this animal would leave."

I tilt my head to the side and inspect the horse's feet again, this time considering Clarissa's hunch.

"It might seem like small fry to you," she says. "But to a young archeologist, that kind of finding could potentially be huge. Career-making huge."

I turn to her. "I don't think it's small fry. As someone who spends most of his days around animals, I think it's an amazing insight. You should be very proud of yourself."

She beams happily.

One more Clarissa smile I'd never seen before!

As I peer at her lovely face made even lovelier by her toothy grin, time seems to stop. She stares back as her smile fades slowly, and her cheeks begin to redden. I lean forward ever so slightly, my eyes still locked with hers. Clarissa's hand shoots to the side of her neck and strokes it. When my gaze shifts to her mouth, her blush deepens.

Could that mean…?

Does Ice Ice Baby, as Celine sometimes calls her, want me?

Emboldened I take a step forward.

As if waking up from a trance, Clarissa jerks her hand from her neck and balls it into a fist.

I freeze.

She pulls the zipper of her thin jacket all the way up and turns toward the wall. "Do you mind pointing the flashlight at the horse's feet again?"

"Of course."

She turns her phone recorder on and describes every part of the horse and every tiny detail of its twisted feet. When she's done describing, Clarissa begins to develop her theory on the "educational" function of the painting. From there, she talks about the purpose of cave art in general.

When she pauses to collect her thoughts, I toggle the flashlight off. "Saving your batteries."

She says nothing, but it's obvious she's uncomfortable in the dark. So, I pull an app on my phone that lights up my screen instead. The light is dim but it will do.

"Not worried *your* batteries will die?" she asks.

I shake my head. "They'll die on the altar of science."

"Father could've said that." She chuckles. "*Without* the tongue-in-cheek."

"Really?"

"He'd say, 'Penelope, the advancement of science should always be uppermost in your mind.' "

I lower my brows. "You're messing with me. Nobody speaks like that."

"He does."

"What would your mom say?"

"Hmm." She rubs her chin, thinking. "She'd say, 'Penelope, there's no progress without sacrifice.' "

"OK, you *are* messing with me. There's no way both call you Penelope when you prefer Clarissa."

"But *they* prefer Penelope, and that's what they call me."

"They must have a nickname for Penelope." I wrinkle my brow. "Ellie?"

"No."

"Nellie?"

"Uh-uh."

"Pen?"

"They don't use diminutives."

"OK." I hesitate before asking the next question. "Why do you prefer Clarissa to Penelope?"

She sighs. "You mean, it's just as long, right?"

"No—"

"It isn't entirely wrong," she says. "But my closest friends call me Clarissa. They've done so since we were in Cambridge together—"

"You went to Cambridge?"

Of course, she did.

Clarissa nods.

I lean against a stalagmite column and cross my ankles, trying to play it cool. "I went there, too."

Her brows fly up.

"For a visit," I add. "The summer I backpacked around Europe with my buds."

She smiles.

"So, you like the name Clarissa?" I ask.

"I don't like the name as such, but I like being called it."

"What do you mean?"

"When someone calls me Clarissa, it momentarily erases from my mind the litany I grew up with."

"Which is?"

"That I'm a fourth-generation archeologist on both sides, and that I'm destined for 'great things.' "

"Ouch," I say. "Heavy stuff."

"Very heavy. But as Clarissa, I can be a regular girl who sometimes goes to the movies to watch a dumb comedy and who enjoys shopping for clothes."

"In short, who has fun."

She nods.

"Are you an only child?" I ask.

"Yes. I wish I had a sibling, so he or she could carry half of my burden."

"Amen," I say. "I could sign under that."

"Only child, too?"

"Yeah…"

"The future of the farm? The savior? Last hope of the rural world?" She gives me a wink. "Daddy's hero?"

"Yes, to the first three, but not to the last one. It's Pop who was my hero."

"Not anymore?"

I run my hand through my hair. "He passed ten years ago."

"I'm sorry." She hugs herself and rubs her arms.

"You're cold."

"A little."

"Here, put this on." I take off my padded leather jacket and hand it to her.

She shakes her head. "Are you crazy? You'll freeze."

"It would take more than this for me to freeze," I

say, laughing. "Besides, my sweater is a lot warmer than what you have under your flimsy jacket."

"How about we swap?"

I tilt my head to one side and just stare at her, letting her realize the ridiculousness of her proposition.

"Right." Her gaze shifts from my face to my chest. "You could throw my jacket over your right shoulder."

I snort.

"Or the left one," she adds, a smile crinkling her eyes, "if it's more sensitive to the cold."

"How about a compromise?"

"Listening."

"You put my jacket over your jacket, and we transfer to the nook where I was waiting for you," I say. "It has a bench to sit on and it's closer to the door, in case someone notices one of us is missing and comes looking."

"Deal! My mind is too foggy now to continue working, anyway."

Murmuring a thank-you, Clarissa turns toward the wall. I help her into my jacket, which hangs down to her mid thigh, and with sleeves so long her hands get lost.

She turns back toward me, smiling, closes her eyes and takes a deep breath, flaring her nostrils.

Uh-oh.

Seized by panic, I scrutinize her for signs of disgust. What if my jacket reeks of manure or—worse—sweat, both of which I've grown desensitized to over the years? I make a point of keeping my body and clothes clean, but people have different thresholds for smells.

"Holy cow!" She opens her eyes.

My panic level is about to go through the rock above our heads.

Clarissa grins. "Feels like I've been dropped into a sea of testosterone."

Is that a bad thing? Or good?

"It's surprisingly homey," she says, answering my unspoken question.

Homey.

I let out the breath I was holding. Even if "homey" is a Parisian euphemism for "smelly," in situations like this, the best thing to do is stick to the facts.

Fact number one: She didn't return my jacket.

Fact number two: Right now, she's pulling its collar up as if to take in more "homeyness."

All is not lost.

I point my phone's light at the ground so we can see where we step and offer her my hand.

After a brief hesitation, she pushes the sleeve of the jacket up to free her beautiful hand and places it into my open palm. Her touch is soft—and electrifying. I close my fingers over her hand, and start walking slowly. We reach the nook much too soon.

With difficulty, I let go of her hand.

Clarissa scoots to the right side of the bench and pats the space next to her. "Plenty of room for both."

Nodding, I sit down and place the phone between us.

An awkward silence follows, during which I try hard not to think about the sleeping arrangements we'll need to discuss soon.

Except, that's all I can think about.

Even the smartphone next to me—the ultimate twenty-first-century gadget—makes me think of a medieval "sword of honor" trick I'd read about somewhere. A knight would place it between himself and a lady who wasn't his wife if circumstances forced them to sleep next to each other.

Thing is, Clarissa may well be a lady who isn't my wife, but I'm no knight in shining armor.

I fully intend to use our circumstances to my advantage.

CHAPTER 6

NATHAN

"It's eight," Clarissa says, looking at her wristwatch. "The best thing to do now would be to sleep, but it's too early, and… um… I don't think I can sleep sitting, or lying on the cold floor, for that matter."

Aha! I wasn't the only one thinking about our sleeping arrangements.

It's very tempting to suggest that my body would make for an excellent mattress, but I hold my tongue. While she obviously has a sense of humor, she's still a refined city girl, unaccustomed to the plainspoken ways of the country.

Tread carefully, Nathan.

"You can try to sleep on the bench," I say.

"What about you?" She clears her throat. "That's the only bench inside the Grotto."

"I'll be fine on the floor."

A deep crease forms between her brows.

Not good. She's fretting.

Time to change the topic. "Just before you stopped recording, you said something about how that horse's twisted feet could change our idea of cave art."

"Yes, well, I was getting ahead of myself." She tucks her hair behind her ears. "I'll need a lot more evidence and research before I can make that claim in public."

"Humor me—I'm not here to judge you."

She gives me a sidelong look. "This stays between us, OK? I may be completely off the mark here."

"Mum's the word." I draw an invisible zipper over my mouth. "If I *really* need to talk about it, I'll unburden myself to my herd's head cow. She's second to none at keeping secrets."

Clarissa gives me a nod. "OK. So, you see, archeologists are still not sure why cave dwellers made art. One big theory is that they would get bored, sitting around after a meal, not doing anything special. So some of them made up tales. Others made graffiti."

"It figures. I sing when I'm bored."

"Will you sing for me?"

"Maybe later." I flash her a smile. "But, please, go on. Is there another theory?"

"The other big theory is that making those paintings was part of some ritual."

"What kind of ritual?"

"Nobody knows."

"Hmm…" I scratch the back of my head. "I don't like that theory."

She raises her eyebrows. "Why not?"

"It's too easy." I shrug before saying, in what I hope is a professorial voice, "When clueless about why folks did what they did, call it a ritual."

She turns toward me—not just her head, but her

entire body—and leans forward. "That's exactly how I feel about it."

"So what's *your* theory?"

She stares into my eyes for a moment, before speaking. "The horse in the Dance Room would suggest that at least some of the paintings were made with the purpose of recording and transmitting practical knowledge. They had an educational function."

"Makes sense to me."

She beams. "Really?"

"I'd wager that paint was a lot harder to produce in those days than now, so if I were a caveman, I'd make sure my art did double duty."

She blinks and stares at me like I've just given her a map to the Holy Grail. "That's an excellent point, Nathan!"

"Happy to help, ma'am."

"Naturally, I'll need to find many other examples in other caves before I can postulate a theory," she says.

I give her a solemn nod. "Naturally."

"I wouldn't want to make a fool of myself." There's that crease again.

"Mum's the word, trust me."

She nods. "I trust you."

We stare into each other's eyes for a long moment. Clarissa's gaze is filled with excitement, and something else, something a pessimist would describe as warmth, and an optimist, as longing.

I'm an optimist.

My body tenses, aching for her touch. My hand on the bench burns to inch closer to hers and brush it. But my instincts tell me it's too soon. Clarissa is just beginning to see a man with a functioning brain behind the jacked hick.

She isn't flirting with me yet.

Hold your horses, Nathan.

"Speaking of horses," I say before correcting myself, "I mean, education, do you think that was also the purpose of *that* shape?"

I stride to the opposite wall and point the beam of the flashlight up at what looks like an erect penis.

She comes near me and says without batting an eye, "The phallus?"

What a handy word! "Yes, the phallus. Do you believe it was a teaching aid for a lesson in human anatomy?"

She smiles. "That's a bit far-fetched but can't be excluded."

"Do you think it's life-size?"

"I don't think so." She tilts her head to the side and squints. "It's much too large."

Er… not really.

"There are men," I say, "Living men, who would compare favorably."

My traitorous eyes dart to my fly before I look up at the wall again.

Clarissa is silent.

No giggling, no comment, not a sound.

Shit. I went too far.

Discussing cave-art phalluses is one thing, but drawing her attention to my real cock is quite another.

She's going to bristle. She won't want to speak to me anymore.

"Those men, they sound… *intimidating*," Clarissa finally says, laughter in her voice.

My whole body slackens in relief. "They aren't! Their… phalluses aren't *freakishly* big."

"Then, how would you describe them?"

An adjective, quick! One that would both reassure and entice her, one that won't be too vulgar or too—

Her lips twitch. "Would you call them *fulfilling*?"

Yes! "That's exactly what I would call them."

My eyes drill into hers.

She holds my gaze and begins to stroke the back of her neck as she did earlier in front of the horse with twisted hooves.

Dude—she's flirting.

In fact, she's beyond flirting.

Consciously or not, Clarissa is *seducing* me.

My eyes wander over her face and body. Suddenly, brushing her hand is not enough. It won't even scratch the surface of my wanting.

Need to hold her, all of her, need to press her to me.

My control snapping, I place the flashlight on the ground, lunge forward, and grip her shoulders. The next second, my lips descend on hers, kissing and coaxing her to open up. I pull her closer to my chest, almost crushing her soft breasts. My hands roam freely, exploring the shape of her.

So fucking good.

Clarissa doesn't resist me, doesn't push me away. Better still, her eyes become hooded as she melts into me. She wants me, there's no doubt about it, but… she's too passive. Her arms hang at her sides. She's turned her face up toward me, but she hasn't parted her lips.

Is this her way?

Nah. It doesn't track.

Driven, independent women like her don't make inert lovers. Something's holding her back.

"Rissa," I whisper against her mouth. "It's OK. Let go—I have you."

I have no idea why I called her Rissa. Nor do I fully

understand what I've asked her to let go of. But, somehow, it feels right. Both felt right.

On a gasp, she parts her lips.

I push my tongue between them and devour her sweet mouth. Can't get enough of her taste. Standing on tiptoe, she kisses me with passion. As our tongues dance together, she lifts her arms and grips my neck.

I back her against the closest stalagmite column, and allow my erection to prod her tummy through her layers of clothing.

Will she shrink from it?

Rissa moans softly and pushes into me. Sweet Jesus, she's pressing her taut stomach against my cock. I begin to grind, all while kissing her and fondling her breasts.

And then her right hand lets go of my neck and settles, fingers splayed, on my bulge.

Inert, you say?

Bending my knees, I reach for the hem of her narrow skirt and push it up her smooth thighs. Up, up, up, until the skirt is bunched around her waist. Then I make quick work of unzipping both jackets.

Need to see her.

Tearing my mouth from hers, I draw back a notch and look at her. "Oh my God, Rissa…"

The sight before me is sexier than anything I've seen.

My cock twitches beneath her palm. She smiles.

She's killing me.

Her legs, clad in tight little boots and stay-up stockings, are long and shapely. Made to be stroked and kissed. She's wearing black panties with a bit of lace. I picture them dangling from one of her ankles, her legs wrapped around my waist, ankles crossed, squeezing me as I fill her.

Whoa, going too fast, Nathan!

I shoo that image away… only to make room for another one in which her legs are on my shoulders.

That's it, I must touch her. I simply can't go on living if I don't.

I cup her between her legs and find she's already wet.

"Yes, please," she whispers, nuzzling the side of my face.

I must have died and gone to heaven.

She throbs under my fingers, pressing into them. When I push the crotch of her panties aside and slip in a finger, she lets out a ragged moan and clenches her muscles around it. I'm loving how wet and eager Rissa is. What I'm loving a lot less is that she's tight.

Much too tight.

Truth is, calling my cock "fulfilling" rather than "freakish" doesn't shrink it to… manageable proportions. I'm not complaining. Better too large than too small, right? But experience tells me she might recoil when she sees it.

With her hand still on my cock, she gives it a gentle upward stroke. "You weren't lying about your size."

My lids grow heavy. "Why would I?"

"Men often do."

She trails her hand down, then up again. Her fingers reach the buckle of my belt and stop there.

Will she undo it? Will she free my cock and stroke it, skin to skin? What will her expression be when she looks at it?

My hand is still between her legs, but I've stopped thrusting.

She takes my wrist and pulls my hand away from her. "We'll continue this later."

"Promise?"

"Oh, yes."

I wait for her next move.

Slowly, she unbuckles my belt and opens the fly of my jeans. Her gaze locks with mine as she fumbles with my underwear, freeing my raging erection.

Her fingers begin to explore me, but she won't look down.

Is she panicked by what she'll see? I try to read her expression, but I'm too crazed with lust to play shrink.

"Look at it, Rissa," I say softly.

She gives me a tight little smile and lowers her eyes. "Oh my."

Hooking my index finger under her chin, I tip her head up to see her face. Rissa's eyes are wide, but there's no distress or, worse, dread in them.

That's a start.

"You were telling the truth," she says. "The one on the wall can't hold a candle to it."

I arch an eyebrow in mock affront. "I'd never lie about something so sacred."

She giggles.

So far so good.

"It's too big for me," she says just as I begin to relax.

"You don't know that."

She looks down and studies me. "It's absolutely gorgeous, Nathan, but if you… it'll hurt me if you—"

"Shush." I press a finger against her lips. "Hurting you is the last thing I want."

"I know."

I brush a gentle kiss on her mouth. "You don't have to decide anything now. We can just fool around and see where it leads us."

"OK." She gives me a relieved smile and tightens

her grip on my cock. "I've never seen anything like this. It's a privilege."

"Is it?"

She nods. "May I?"

Before I realize what she's asking, she squats and gives the tip of my cock a tentative lick. I shudder, my hips twitching involuntarily. She licks again and again, stroking the base with her hands, squeezing gently and kissing it.

When she looks up at me, her gaze is dark and intense.

"I'll come if you don't stop now," I rasp.

"That's OK."

"No." I grab her shoulders and pull her up. "Ladies first."

"You fiend," she protests. "I was enjoying myself!"

"I have principles."

"They are too old-fashioned."

I shrug.

"So what do you suggest?"

"For starters,"—I hook my thumbs into her lacy panties at the sides and pull them down—"we get rid of these."

She helps me remove her panties. I leave the rest of her clothing on, so she won't be too cold. Her pubes are dark and only lightly trimmed, which is a godsend for a man who's never liked bald pussy. Reaching down, I play with her moist curls and spread her folds, exposing her hooded little bud. My breath hitches and my cock pulses like crazy as I stare at her.

She lets out an amused snort. "You look like you could eat me."

"That's the plan."

She chuckles.

"Lean back on the column," I say, my voice coarse.

She does immediately.

I kneel before her and settle her right thigh on my shoulder.

And then I carry out my plan.

CHAPTER 7

CLARISSA

Nathan tongues me like I'm the world's most delicious ice cream.

His fingers stretch and probe.

I tangle my fingers in his hair as I moan.

He abrades my sensitive skin with his evening stubble, and I love it.

When my legs begin to tremble, he wraps his big hands around my bottom and squeezes, his mouth still doing its magic between my legs.

In a rush of heat and exquisite pleasure, I shudder. Then another wave, and one more. Barely conscious of my surroundings, I hear myself making strange noises, mumbling between groans and whimpers. "Oh God... Nathan... I can't... Oh God." It's too much. I want him to stop.

I don't want him to stop.

As I ride the last aftershock, he strokes my hips and trails his tongue up to my stomach. He rises and leans his forehead against mine.

I encase his face between my hands and kiss him deeply.

A long moment later, we break the kiss. Nathan stares at my face and then at my bared sex, his gaze scalding me.

"Still hungry?" I tease.

He doesn't respond, doesn't even smile back.

Heat creeps up my neck and cheeks.

Who knew being selectively undressed like this would make me feel more bared—and more turned on—than full nudity?

My heart quickening, I lower my gaze to his enormous shaft. I want it as much as I'm apprehensive about it. What will I do when he presses its tip against my entrance? How will my body react? Can I stretch enough to receive it without pain?

But he said I didn't have to decide yet.

He said we could just fool around.

Gingerly, I palm him and begin to stroke up and down his hot length. He groans, one hand on the column next to my head, the other on the side of my neck. I rub a little harder, curling my fingers around him. He throbs against my palm.

I look up into his heavy-lidded eyes. "May I?"

A nod.

Finally.

I've been burning to press my lips around it since I first saw it. As I explore its hard shape, its cordlike veins and the softness of its skin against my lips and tongue, I feel like an ancient priestess performing an act of worship.

If that phallus on the wall is life-size, then the man it was attached to must have had quite a following. I envy his groupies who were no doubt sturdier than I am and more apt to accommodate him.

Were all the women Nathan slept with able to take him in? Would he tell me the truth if I ask him? It's damn tempting to ask.

Except, I won't.

Asking him about his exes might give him the wrong idea. Regardless of how he makes me feel or what happens here tonight, I'm not going to date a farmer from Verlezy. We belong in different worlds, and the only bridge between those worlds is our lust.

Lust fades away. Complications remain.

OK, if tonight is all we have, I'd better shut that chatterbox in my head and let my hair down.

I increase my pace and the amount of pressure, feeling him grow even harder, thicker and bigger than he already is. Wetness pools again between my legs. My core is heavy, empty, wanting to be filled.

"Rissa," he murmurs. "Careful, or I'll come."

I lift my eyes to him.

He smooths his hand on my cheek, his eyes drilling into mine, searching.

With my hands tight on his shaft, I pull back a little and bite my lower lip. "That's the plan."

"Really?" He searches my face. "You don't mind the mess?"

"I have tissues in my purse."

"You sure?"

"Oh yes, I always carry a pocket pack—"

"I mean, are you sure you want me to come on your face?"

It takes me a moment to adjust to the rawness of his words. I'm not used to that. The men I've dated before I got too busy—and too picky—would never talk to me like that. They'd use euphemisms and avoid crude words at any cost. But they never went down on me with so much passion… if they did go down at all.

Slowly, I nod.

He trails the pad of his thumb over my mouth. "You know, you've let me do that already in my fantasies. Many times. But I had no idea you'd be up for it in real life. I thought you'd be squeamish."

"Appearances can be deceiving," I say, omitting to mention I've never actually tried a facial before.

The mere thought of such an act had appeared distasteful. Degrading, even.

Except, with Nathan, it doesn't.

He grips the nape of my head and guides me gently back to his groin. A few enthusiastic minutes later, his face contorts in pleasure and pain. I find that both beautiful and empowering.

"Shut your eyes," he prompts, visibly struggling to hold his peak off a little longer.

I do just before his warm seed hits my face.

He growls, pumping.

When he's done, I lick my lips to taste him and laugh nervously, feeling a little awkward.

"Don't move," he says. "And don't open your eyes."

Noises, steps, then his voice again. "I have your purse here."

He opens it so I can dip my hand inside and find the tissues. Taking the pack from me, he wipes my eyes, my forehead, and my cheeks.

"Do you mind if I use some of the water from the bottle in your purse?" he asks.

"Please."

He wipes my face again with a wet tissue. "All clean."

Smiling, I open my eyes.

He collects the tissues and tosses them in the trash can next to the bench. "You must be thinking this was crazy."

"It was fun," I say, standing up.

I pull the hem of my skirt down, ignoring the aching and clenching in my center.

One can't have everything. He's too big for me.

But even without penetration, I just had the sexiest time in my life, and that will have to do.

Nathan picks up the now-flickering flashlight and offers me his hand. Back at the bench, we sit down next to each other, our knees touching.

He turns to me. "Will you come sit on my lap?"

"I thought you'd never ask!"

The frankness of my reply startles me.

Nathan looks a little surprised, too.

And happy.

The moment my butt touches his thighs, he puts his arms around me and pulls me closer. "Rissa."

That moniker, said in a deep, gravelly voice feels like a caress. Loving. Tender. Doing unwanted things to my heart.

Watch out, Clarissa.

I trace his firm jawline. "I have a nickname for you, too, you know."

"Tell me."

"Cowboy."

He laughs. "Did you just come up with it?"

"No, that's what I've been calling you since your fourth visit when Nina told me what you did for a living."

"I'm afraid what I do is a lot less romantic than what

you see in movies," he says, before cocking his head. "So, you spotted me a while ago."

I nod, caught red-handed.

He gives me a long look, and I know what he's thinking even if the question never comes.

I give him an apologetic smile. "I didn't want to give you a chance to ask me out."

Wow. That came out a lot more brutal than I intended.

"I figured that much," he says.

"Why didn't you ever ask me a question during the tour?" I smooth the back of my hand against his cheek, enjoying the prickliness of his stubble. "Everyone else did, but you never said a word. You just stared."

He shrugs. "I had lots of questions, but I thought they were dumb. I didn't want to ruin my already slim chances with you."

"The questions you asked tonight, and the observations you made were anything but dumb," I say. "Even my parents would concede that much."

"I take it they have lofty standards?"

I roll my eyes. "You have no idea. I'm a fourth-generation archeologist on both sides, so they expect me to be the next Champollion."

"The name sounds familiar... Who's that?"

"The guy who cracked Egyptian hieroglyphs in the nineteenth century."

He nods. "That's a tall order."

I skew a smile. "Not for Penelope Clarissa Muller. They seriously expect the Nobel Committee will one day have to add a new prize category in archeology just to celebrate my achievements."

"You're lucky," he says.

I draw my eyebrows together. "Is that a joke?"

"Nope." He kisses my hand as I trail it across his mouth. "You have parents who believe you're super smart and can do anything."

"Do you realize the pressure that puts on me? I feel that no matter how hard I work, I'm bound to disappoint them."

"Right," he says. "I hadn't considered that part."

I peer at him. "What about your parents? I bet your mom thinks you're a national treasure, and your dad must have been very proud of you."

"It's hard to know what Ma thinks of me," he says with a smirk. "Except that it's my sacred duty to make sure it's handed down to the next generation."

I frown.

"Don't get me wrong," he adds quickly. "Ma has a great personality and she loves me. It's just… well, let's just say she may not be convinced I'm the brightest pea in the pod."

My jaw falls. "Why would you say that?"

"Maybe because she and Pop took me out of regular school at sixteen and sent me to an agricultural *lycée*."

"It wasn't what you wanted?"

"I didn't really have time to stop and consider what I wanted. Dad had been so sick, and then I had to deal with the funeral and all the paperwork because Ma was too devastated. She could barely make herself get up in the morning… And then we were hit by the milk crisis."

"I remember seeing angry farmers on TV," I say. "They blocked roads and dumped manure in front of administrative buildings."

"Yeah, well, you'd be angry, too, if you had to pay 45 percent in taxes when the milk price was pushed down to two hundred euros per ton."

"I believe I would." I kiss his nose. "Do you think

you would've gone to college, if circumstances had been different?"

He slips a hand under the double layer of our jackets and cups one of my breasts over the blouse. My lids drop with the joy of his warm, big hand on my petite breast.

"Honestly," he says. "I'm not sure I would've gone to college. I did OK at school, but I was never an A student."

I caress his strong neck. "Few boys are at that age. They just take longer to grow up than girls."

"Anyway," he says. "It wasn't in the cards. The year Pop died, his friend and our neighbor—my bestie Celine's dad—took his life. Several farms went belly up… But for Ma, selling our farm was out of the question. It was Pop's legacy. He'd sacrificed himself for it."

"What do you mean?"

"He died of cancer caused by pesticide exposure. You see, he'd been in charge of spraying since he was ten, and he'd never used a mask or gloves."

"How awful!"

He nods.

"You loved him very much, didn't you?" I ask.

"I worshiped him."

We stroke each other in silence for a while.

I wonder if Nathan will ask me if he can see me again. For his sake, I hope he doesn't. He won't like my reply.

"Do you have a boyfriend in Paris?" he asks.

I shake my head, dreading the next question.

But when it comes, it isn't what I expected. "How long has it been since you had sex?"

"A long time." I hesitate. "Eighteen months."

He sucks in a breath, but says nothing.

The flashlight battery dies a few minutes later.

When Nathan moves to turn his phone on, I grab his hand to stop him. “We should try to get some sleep.”

“Yes, we should.” He picks me up and lowers me onto the bench. “Put your head on my lap, and lie down.”

“What about you?”

“I can sleep sitting,” he says. “I’ve done it before.”

I stretch out on the bench and fall asleep within minutes with my face to his groin and his hand in my hair.

Anne-Chantal’s laughing voice wakes us up in the morning. “What a picture!”

I sit up and look at my watch. It’s seven in the morning.

Thank God, she showed up to work an hour early!

When I glance at Nathan before I return his jacket, he’s peering at her, eyes narrowed and eyebrows lowered. That prompts me to pay closer attention.

The cashier doesn’t look shocked to discover us here.

She doesn’t even look surprised.

In fact, she looks mighty pleased with herself.

CHAPTER 8

NATHAN

Ma is back from her vacation, cooking a homecoming dinner.

Celine, Frau Lotte, and Lorenzo are also in the kitchen, supposedly giving Ma a hand, but are really just sipping wine and talking about organic fertilizers. That is, Celine is doing most of the talking and the others are doing most of the sipping.

I can hear everyone's voices very distinctly from the computer room where I'm toiling with an endless EU questionnaire. Ma never touches them, but one day she's going to have to sit down and learn. I hate paperwork as much as she does, so it's only fair that we take turns.

After Anne-Chantal freed us yesterday morning, Rissa said she needed to go home for a few hours. She had her own car and didn't need me to give her a lift. Once she left, I tried to pressure Ma's chum to confess to jamming the lock.

She folded her arms across her generous bosom. "Someone had to do something. It was becoming unbearable to watch you waste away like that."

"So, you confess—"

"I confess to nothing at all." She lifted her chin to the locksmith working on the door. "He'll confirm it was a malfunction."

I rolled my eyes, not bothering to ask Marcel, our village locksmith and Anne-Chantal's dear husband, for confirmation.

Before I left the Grotto, I discreetly placed my phone under the bench, next to an eyeglasses case that must have fallen out of Rissa's handbag. With a bit of luck, she'd be the one to find it when she came looking for her glasses. That would give her a pretext to get in touch.

Still under the spell of our intimacy in the cave, I was hopeful, almost certain she'd show up last night. Or at least reach out via Anne-Chantal, inviting me to come by and collect my phone.

But she didn't.

Not last night, nor this morning before work. And now, with a rainstorm howling outside, bending trees and threatening to blow roofs away, there's no way she'll turn up.

The doorbell rings.

I open the door, expecting Lorenzo's girlfriend Paola, who always arrives at least twenty minutes late.

Except it isn't Paola—it's Rissa.

"Your phone," she says, handing me the device.

"Thank you."

We stare at each other.

"I better go," she begins.

"Stay." I clear my throat. "Ma is cooking boeuf bourguignon tonight, her specialty. We have a few people over for dinner."

She hesitates. "I don't want to intrude."

"Don't be daft." I point to the uproar outside. "It'll

be safer to drive back in a couple of hours when the storm quiets down."

She glances at the sky, at her car, and then back at me. "OK. Thank you."

When we enter the kitchen, four pairs of eyes zero in on her and shift to me.

"Hi everyone," she says, giving them a timid little smile.

Well done, Rissa!

If I were in her place now, with Celine, Lorenzo and —especially—Ma eyeballing me like that, I think I'd just go into a stupor.

They all greet her.

"This is Clarissa," I say. "I invited her to join us for dinner."

Celine jumps up and puts an extra plate, glass and silverware on the table.

Respect, she mouths to me when Rissa isn't looking.

Lorenzo fills her glass. Ma stirs the brew on the stove with her back to us. I wonder what she's thinking.

The doorbell rings again, and this time it's Paola.

Ma announces that the food is ready and can everyone please sit down.

I serve.

"If I knew we had a special guest tonight, I would've laid the table in the dining room," Ma says, taking her serving of fragrant bourguignon from me.

Celine pats her hand. "Your kitchen is just as presentable, Brigitte."

"I know," Ma says. "But still."

Paola turns to Rissa. "Are you a local farmer, too?"

Celine snorts.

"I'm an archeologist," Rissa says with a smile. "I curate the museum at the Darcy Grotto near Auxerre."

Lorenzo perks up. "We were planning to go there next weekend!"

The conversation flows smoothly, mostly between the volunteers, Celine, and Rissa. I keep silent, listening and staring at Rissa.

So does Ma.

When Lorenzo, Frau Lotte and I finish our second servings, Ma ushers everyone to the TV room for tea and cookies.

Rissa giggles over something Celine whispers in her ear. I swallow my cookie and scoot closer on the couch to where Rissa is sitting.

"What about the public library in Auxerre?" she asks Celine.

My friend sighs. "All female stuff."

"Have you tried your luck in Dijon?" Rissa asks. "It has several libraries."

Oh, I see. Celine has told her about her hot nerd fetish.

"I have," she says. "And I even spotted there two adorkable guys who were totally my type and weren't wearing wedding rings."

"And?" Rissa leans forward, bright-eyed.

Celine shrugs. "And, crickets. Both made it clear they weren't interested."

"Um... Have you considered tweaking your look a little bit?" Rissa asks her.

"Why would I do that?"

"It's the combination of cropped hair, lumberjack shirt, roomy jeans, Doc Martens, and posture." Rissa smiles softly. "It might be giving the men who don't know you the wrong idea."

"Which is?"

"That you're into women."

Frau Lotte, who seems to have overheard Rissa's last remark, turns to Celine, disappointment and shock in her eyes. "You're not?"

Celine blinks, flabbergasted.

Frau Lotte mutters something that sounds like a curse under her breath.

"Jeez, I had no idea." Celine looks at Rissa and at Frau Lotte. "Really?"

Both women nod.

"But I love my lumberjack shirts!" Celine says. "They're part of who I am. And you can't expect me to wear heels on a farm!"

"Of course not," Rissa says.

Celine puffs, stands, and carries her plate to the kitchen. When she reappears in the TV room, her expression is determined.

"Thank you, Brigitte, for the delicious dinner," she says to Ma. "So happy we met, Clarissa! Night, everyone. I'm turning in early so I can process this… revelation."

"I'll be happy to paint your nails and teach you how to use makeup," Paola offers.

Celine nods a thank-you and marches out the door.

One after another, the volunteers retreat to their sleeping quarters. Ma yawns, declares she's too knackered to stay up and heads to her bedroom upstairs.

Rissa and I are the last ones left in the room.

My heart pounds in my chest.

If she didn't mean to spend the night with me, she would've left by now. *Right?*

I stare at her lips.

She stares at mine.

Suddenly, she stands. "Thank you, Nathan. I had a wonderful evening."

"Want to have a look at my cottage before you drive off?" I blurt.

"You don't live in the farmhouse?"

I shake my head and stand. "Follow me."

The moment we enter the cottage and I pull the door closed, I'm kissing her. She kisses me back, opening her mouth to let me in. I thrust in my tongue deep and hard, while my hands tug at her coat.

She lets me remove it.

I'm so impatient my hands are shaking as I throw it over a chair. Her hands are just as unsteady when she pulls on the sides of my jacket.

I shrug it off.

We kiss and kiss, starved for each other, drinking each other in. My mouth latches to her soft lips with an almost bruising ferocity I've never known before and a need I'm unable to control. This woman was made for me. I know it in my bones.

Just like I know she'll let me take her tonight.

That's why she's here.

She's going to give it her best shot despite her misgivings and fears that she's too small for me.

I let go of her mouth.

She gasps, eyes glazed with lust.

"I'll be gentle," I whisper near her ear. "I won't give you more than you can take."

She nods once, her nod a profession of trust.

As my hand grips her waist and pulls her to me, my other hand unzips her silky black pants. They fall to the floor and she steps out of them. Slipping a hand inside her panties, I press two fingers to her cleft and rub. She moans. When I plunge them inside her, her moans turn into whimpers.

I kiss her again, pushing my tongue deep, fucking

her mouth with it. She grows unsteady on her feet, leaning against me for support. A few more thrusts of my tongue and fingers and she collapses against me.

"Aah," she groans raggedly into my mouth.

My cock is so hard it threatens to make a hole through my jeans or burst them at the seams.

That's it, I'm taking her within the next five minutes or I'll explode.

I pick her up and carry her to the bedroom. We yank on each other's clothes and underwear until we're naked. I open a condom. She helps me roll it on.

I nudge her to lie on her back and rake my gaze over her. "So beautiful. I'm going to kiss you absolutely everywhere, but right now I need to be inside you."

"I need you inside me."

Her face is flushed with an almost desperate longing, and she's dripping wet from my earlier caresses.

It's now or never, Nathan.

Positioning my tip at her entrance, I rub it against her wet curls and push in just a notch. Slowly, her opening begins to stretch, adjusting to me.

She lifts her head, propping herself on her elbows. "I want to watch you enter me."

Another small thrust, then another. More stretching. My gaze travels between her pussy and her face looking out for signs of discomfort. But there are none. Encouraged by that, I thrust again, this time harder.

A throaty gasp escapes Rissa's lips and she arches her back.

Still no sign of pain.

With another push, I'm sheathed deep inside her.

I withdraw slowly and thrust again, careful not to hit her womb. "How's this?"

"It's wonderful," she says. "Absolutely fucking wonderful."

Dropping her head back to the pillow, she grips my neck and wraps her legs around my waist.

As I pump in and out, pleasure builds, held back only by my promise not to give her more than she can take.

"Faster," she commands.

I increase the cadence, and soon we're moving against each other fast and hard like a well-oiled machine. Given how happy she looks and sounds, I'm tempted to push harder still, but I rein in that urge.

As things stand, I don't know if I'll see her again. But if I hurt her, even inadvertently, I can be sure as hell that I won't.

Closing my eyes, I thrust, faster and faster. She writhes beneath me, completely open, throbbing around me, trusting me to give her what she craves.

A few more thrusts, and her pussy begins to spasm. I burn again to push a little deeper while she's riding her orgasm, but I deny myself. This will have to do. This is already so much more than I could hope for.

Crying out my name, Rissa shudders. A tremor shakes her legs and her body, while her mouth opens, forming a beautiful *o*.

The sight of her abandon sends me over the edge.

With each spurt of my seed, the pressure subsides, making room for joy, and a flying sensation that lifts my hard body as if it were a feather.

Afterward, we cuddle in the soft glow of the night-light.

"Turns out I'm roomier than I thought," she says with that deliciously sly smile of hers.

"Told ya."

"Was it good for you? If it was at least half as good as it was for me, I can die happy, and be really, really proud of myself."

I frown in mock concern. "Please don't die just yet. Now that I got a taste, I need more."

She smiles, but gives no promises. Then she looks away.

Not good.

"Did you ever envision selling the farm and the land?" she asks, turning back to me.

"It isn't mine to sell—well, half of it at least. It's Ma's."

"Of course," she says. "And, from what you told me, she'll hold on to it until her last breath."

I nod.

Something infinitely sad flashes in her eyes before she turns away again.

I bring her hand to my mouth and kiss the inside of her wrist. "Farming may not be the most profitable occupation these days, but the land here in Burgundy—and we own a good chunk of it—increases in value every year. That said, Ma's attachment to this land and to this farm is purely sentimental. It was Pop's whole life."

"Is it your whole life, too?"

"Good question." I scratch my head. "I don't know any other life to compare it to."

"So, you have no idea if you'd enjoy doing something else more than operating a dairy farm?"

"I don't think I would."

We lie in silence for a long moment. This conversation isn't about farming, of course. It's about us. It's about the possibility of us being together.

"Do you think you could enjoy living on a farm?" I ask.

She laughs. "I'd be the most ridiculous farmer in the world!"

"I said *live* on a farm, not operate one."

She shakes her head. "In fact, I'm going back to Paris in two weeks, to be part of an extensive research team in one of the capital's best museums."

"What?" I turn on my side and peer at her. "Why? You've only been here a few months!"

"Almost two years, actually," she says. "You only *discovered* me a few months ago."

What do I say to that? That I'd do anything to turn back the time and *discover* her earlier, much earlier? That I'd give a hand to have Anne-Chantal stop by and give me a ticket to a guided tour of the Grotto on Rissa's very first day as its curator? It would be the truth. But there's no point saying it now.

We hug each other.

As I drift away, my body light from the lovemaking and my heart filled to the brim, a heavy, dreamless slumber swallows me up.

RISSA WAKES up at dawn and sneaks out while I pretend to be asleep.

The moment she's out the door, I begin to ache for her.

I tell myself it's just my body. My cock, my hands, every limb, and muscle on me.

But not my heart.

It can't be my heart.

Because it takes more than two nights to fall in love.

I must've read that in one of Ma's psychology magazines when I was bored and out of other reading material.

The irony of the situation is that I know Rissa wants me as much as I want her.

But Dr. Penelope Muller wants something else.

And, unfortunately for me, she wins.

CHAPTER 9

NATHAN

The traditional Farewell to Winter Ball is in full swing.

OK, the ball isn't a *real* tradition because it hadn't existed until twenty years ago. Then one year, Josephine, the wife of our eternally reelected mayor, introduced the extravaganza and got the d'Arcy family to sponsor it.

I guess that's the reason Count Sebastian d'Arcy is always in attendance.

And the reason the good citizens of Verlezy and the neighboring villages gather in the town hall, suffer through a speech or two, and then eat, drink, and dance into the wee hours of the morning.

Celine and Ma always drag me to the ball.

They don't do it for my sake, mind you. I'm just the inextricable owner of the two male arms they like to lean on when entering the town hall.

This year is no different.

No, it *is* different. While I'd normally look forward to chugging down some beers with my buds and maybe sneaking off with a local woman, tonight I'm not in the right mood for either.

I haven't been in the right mood for twelve days now, ever since Rissa spent a night at my cottage and announced she was going back to Paris.

"Oh, come on!" Celine nudges me with her elbow. "Stop sulking."

I force a smile.

"Do you notice something different about me?" she asks.

I study her face. "You're wearing lipstick."

"What else?"

"Um… mascara?"

"Yes!" She beams. "Anything else?"

"If this is a quiz, do I get a beer for three correct answers?"

She rolls her eyes and huffs.

"She's wearing a skirt," Ma says. "A skirt!"

I look down to verify that improbable claim. It's safe to say I've seen Celine almost every single day of her life—she's two years my junior—and never, not once, has she worn a skirt.

But today she is.

"It's not too awful," she says. "As long as I remember to keep my knees together when I sit. But the heels, they're killing me."

As if to confirm her statement, she trips and spills some of her beer on the floor.

Ma pats her cheek before pulling a small pack of tissues from her handbag, reminding me of Rissa.

I sigh. Everything reminds me of Rissa these days.

My friends Danny and Mo wave from the middle of the room and saunter over. As Celine and I chat with them, I can't help wondering if Rissa will make an appearance alone or in the company of her colleagues.

"Hey, Nathan!" someone calls from the entrance.

A moment later, Thomas, my second cousin on Pop's side, joins our group. "Good evening, Brigitte."

"Haven't seen you in… forever." Ma gives him a hug. "What are you doing here?"

"Just passing," he says noncommittally.

Thomas studied advanced mathematics but instead of applying for academic jobs when he graduated, he chose to use his math skills in banking. Turned out to be a great move. For the last six or seven years, he's been working for an investment bank in Dijon, developing financial models, and amassing millions.

"So, what do you do for a living?" Danny asks Thomas.

He pushes his eyeglasses up the bridge of his nose. "I'm a mathematician."

"Hot nerd alert," Celine whispers to me.

I take another look at Thomas, and it hits me how much he fits her type.

She should totally go for it.

But the poor thing is too awestruck to utter a word. She downs her second glass and mumbles, "Need another one."

Poor Celine.

Ma and I exchange a look as Celine scurries away.

When Danny and Mo move on, Ma arches an eyebrow at Thomas. "So, what did you say you were doing here?"

"I'm looking for a house to buy."

"Moving to the country?" Ma asks.

He smiles. "No, just as a getaway. And a quiet retreat for when I want to do some hardcore math."

Celine slips and falls in the center of the room, causing a commotion. She's prone on the floor, her face next to her spilled champagne.

Thomas and I rush to her and help her to her feet.

Her cheeks are crimson. "This is the first and last time I wear heels!"

She takes a step and halts, cringing.

Thomas squats next to her. "Which foot?"

She points at her left leg.

He removes her shoe, takes her foot in his hands and begins to press various parts of it. "Does it hurt here? And here? What about here?"

She shakes her head to each of his questions, gazing at him as if he was an apparition. Next, he palms her ankle and asks her to take another step.

"Sprained but not broken," he declares, standing up.

While he helps her limp toward the nearest chair, I go to the drink table to get her a new glass. When I return with it, Celine and Thomas are sitting next to each other, chatting. Her foot is on his lap.

"It's best to keep it elevated until she gets home and applies ice," he explains.

Celine's expression is dreamy, like she can't believe this is happening to her.

"Do you go to the library often?" she asks him.

He shakes his head.

I bug my eyes at him from behind Celine's back.

"But I love reading," Thomas adds quickly. "I have a big library at home."

I was over at his place in Dijon a few weeks ago. There was no library there, big or small.

You're digging your own grave, man.

"In my Paris apartment," Thomas says.

Oh, I see what he's doing. He's hoping to seduce

Celine locally and confine their fling to Burgundy. That way, she'll never see his Paris apartment and have a chance to call him out.

"Would you like to see it?" he asks her.

Celine tilts her head. "Your library?"

"Yes." He stares into her eyes. "I'll be working from Paris next month, and if you can take a weekend off and visit me, you can borrow as many books as you want."

"Thank you," she says. "I will."

I leave them to their own devices, hoping that Thomas won't wait too long before telling Celine he doesn't read outside of math and finance, and that he's a banker. Scanning the room, I spot Ma who's found Anne-Chantal and a few other cronies. *Good.* Anne-Chantal will give her a lift, which means I can go home.

The door opens, and before I've even turned to see who it is, I know it's Rissa.

As soon as she spots me, she makes a beeline in my direction. "I was hoping to find you here."

"Aren't you supposed to be packing?" I say. "That is, if you're still leaving the day after tomorrow."

She smiles. "Most of my stuff is already in Paris, and I'll come and get the rest next weekend."

I say nothing. There's nothing to say.

She moves closer. "I've been… thinking about you."

"Of course," I say, expelling a bitter snort. "That's why you called and texted *all the time.*"

"Neither did you."

"You're the one who sneaked out in the morning." I give her a hard stare, even as my hands burn to touch her, to press her to my chest. "You're the one who's leaving."

She nods and looks down at her feet. "I wanted to ask a favor."

"Ask."

She probably wants me to keep her boxes until next weekend, seeing as there's plenty of room on the farm.

Her eyes are still downcast as she says, "Will you make love to me tonight, one last time?"

CHAPTER 10

CLARISSA

He takes a few endless moments to consider my unorthodox request, and eventually he says yes.

We drive to my spartan apartment in silence.

I hope he'd back me to the wall and kiss me as soon as we get in like when we went to his cottage. Except he doesn't. We stand in my entryway, avoiding each other's eyes.

Nathan presses his mouth into a hard line.

My heart clenches in my chest.

I've grown familiar with this feeling ever since Nathan and I spent that night in the Grotto two weeks ago. Still, it leaves me perplexed. How can a man I barely know suddenly matter so much? Why do I feel so sad leaving him behind? Why do I hunger for him as if he were the only one for me? As if I were in love.

It's perfectly absurd!

Worse, it's ridiculous, shallow, and downright moronic.

Oh, I have tried telling myself it's not him, it's his size.

More exactly, the incredible sensation of being stretched and filled so completely. I've never experienced it before, and I'm unlikely to experience it again.

Perhaps not even tonight, if the way things are going is any indication.

But, deep in my soul, I know it's not just his cock or his lovemaking. It's also the way we connect, the way he makes it easy for me to be candid, to be myself, the way he moves, the way he looks at me. The way everything about him feels right.

Suddenly, a truth I've been choking for days breaks its invisible chains and barrels out. "You're by far the best thing that happened to me since I came to Burgundy."

He says nothing.

"Come away with me," I beg.

"There's nothing for me in Paris."

"Not true! I know a lot of people there, I'll help you find a job, and then—"

He shakes his head.

Oh, Nathan.

I take a step toward him. "Then tonight is all we have."

His gaze sears me.

"Here I am," he says. "Mad at you for leaving, and at the same time, craving you, dying to bury myself in you."

God help me, I'm dying to let you.

"I ache, Nathan. I feel empty inside." My voice is hoarse with lust. "Please."

His chest rises and falls and his eyes grow darker.

I take another step and slip a hand under the hem of his sweater, flattening it against his hard stomach.

Suddenly, his hands are everywhere on my body, my face, in my hair. Sweaters are pulled over heads, shirts unbuttoned, and belts hit the carpet with a thump.

I lead him to the bedroom where I remove his underwear. He bares my breasts, sweeping his tongue over my stiff nipples. As he alternates between them, his hand slips inside my panties and I moan at his touch.

Reaching down, I touch him, too.

Ooh, that sweet thickness! It belongs inside me.

"Tell me what you crave," he murmurs. "I want to hear it."

"Your hot skin against mine. You on top of me, around me, in me."

He groans. "Rissa."

I gaze at his massive shaft. Then I kneel and lick the underside, every vein on it, the tapered head and the small slit.

My center throbs, heavy, needy.

Nathan pulls me up. "I want to come when I'm inside you."

"Here, I bought the biggest condoms I could find." I hand him the pack.

He glances at it. "They'll do."

Climbing on the bed, he stretches himself on his back. "Will you try to take me in as deep as you can?"

I nod, removing my panties.

He places his hands on my hips as I settle on his broad tip and begin to lower myself slowly, his expanse stretching me, filling me. With every breath, I impale myself a little more, take a little more of him, almost weeping with the joy of it.

When he's as deep as last time, I pause.

"It's OK, baby, no need to push more." He frowns in concern. "I wouldn't want to hurt you."

"You're not hurting me."

The crease between his brows remains.

"I stopped to feel your shape inside me," I say, rocking my hips, my voice coarse with lust and emotion. "I can take more."

"Rissa—"

"I want to take more."

As I push myself a little more down his throbbing shaft, he cups my mound and begins to stroke. His gaze is a silent plea. Wetness gushes in me, and I open a little wider still, slide down more, caressing him with my inner muscles, until his tip hits my womb. I draw in a breath and bear down a little more, making that contact tighter. There's no more room inside me for him to invade.

"Oh, Rissa," he rasps. "Sweetheart, I'm in to the hilt. So deep."

Lifting his head, Nathan stares at where we're joined. I stare, too, lightheaded, sweat running down my forehead. I wipe it from my left temple.

He reaches up and wipes my forehead and right temple with his big hand. "I've never been so deep in a woman, didn't think it was possible."

His shaft twitches inside me, making my eyes roll in my head.

Through the haze, I hear him say, "Thank you for this gift."

And I fall apart, my legs shaking uncontrollably.

He waits until I've ridden my first orgasm, then lifts me up and lays me on my back. "Want more?"

"Yes."

"Hard?"

"Yes."

Nathan slams into me, making me yelp and cling to him, digging my fingers into his back. He pumps deep and fast, no longer anxious he might hurt me, no longer trying to control himself. I should be wary, but instead I spur him with my heels, urging him to penetrate me deeper, take everything, breach my womb if he must.

My second orgasm is the most powerful I've ever had. He thrusts relentlessly, and I come and come, crying out his name. His face contorts as he comes, too, his pleasure consuming him.

When he collapses on top of me, I breathe him in, kissing his face and squeezing his tight butt.

"If I didn't know better, I'd say you really liked me," he mutters, pushing my damp hair from my forehead.

"I do."

He pulls back a little and stares into my eyes. "Stay in Burgundy, with me."

"I can't." I hold his gaze. "Come with me to Paris."

He shakes his head.

I almost beg him to at least come visit me occasionally, before I stop myself.

There's too much intensity, too much passion between us. I don't want compromises. If we aren't going to be together fully—body, heart, and soul—then it's best we make a clean cut now and never see each other again.

CHAPTER 11

CLARISSA

Yes, I know I said a clean cut.

But that was before I spent a month in Paris—in my favorite season of the year, among new colleagues who turned out to be much kinder than I'd feared—feeling so lonely I cried myself to sleep every night.

It had been a mistake to stay the night at Nathan's cottage. It had been an even bigger mistake to take him to my place in Auxerre. If I count the night in the Grotto, that's three nights we've spent together.

Only three nights, for heaven's sake.

So why do I miss him so much—in my flesh, in my bones, in my soul? Why can't I move on?

"It was nice seeing you again," Nina says, breaking me out of my bleak thoughts. "And thank you for those exquisite chocolates!"

"Oh, it was nothing."

"You kidding? They were delish! Did you see how fast they disappeared? I've noted the name of the shop to be sure I buy some next time I'm in Paris."

"Glad you liked them."

"Will you come down to the Grotto again, or do you have everything you need for your research?" Nina asks.

"I think I'm good, at least for a while."

She nods, her eyes on the road.

"Thanks again for driving me to the train station," I say. "You really didn't have to—I could've called a cab."

She waves dismissively.

"How do you like your new boss?" I ask.

"He's OK… bit boring though. We had more fun when you were around."

I smile. "What about the guy you were dating?"

"Still dating." Her lips twitch at some private thought—no doubt a good one, judging by her smug expression. "It's getting serious."

"Hey, I'm so happy for you!" I pat her shoulder before blurting, "Have you seen Nathan Girault since I left? The farmer I got trapped in the Grotto with…"

Please, keep your eyes on the road, Nina!

I'm blushing so furiously that if she looks at me now, she'll imagine all kinds of crazy things he and I might have done while we were trapped.

And she'd be right.

"I haven't seen him," Nina says. "But Anne-Chantal talks about him sometimes."

Do I have the guts to ask her what exactly Anne-Chantal has said?

Nina glances at me, sympathy in her eyes. "He's been working really hard. And *not* dating anyone."

I turn away and stare out the window.

Three minutes later, she pulls up at the Gare d'Auxerre-Saint-Gervais and I get out. We hug. Nina drives off. I enter the station and find my platform on the flap display. The clock on the wall tells me it's time to go. With a determined nod to no one in particular, I rush to my platform.

"The TGV to Paris leaves in three minutes," a woman announces over the loudspeaker.

I adjust the straps of my backpack, drop my head to my chest in defeat, and march back into the lobby.

This train will leave without me—I'll take the next one in two hours.

My hands are shaking when I pull out my phone and call Nathan, telling myself he might be somewhere with no reception. Or he might not pick up, too busy harvesting or taking care of his cows.

Even if he does answer the phone, there's no reason to expect him to drop everything and drive thirty minutes here and thirty minutes back to his farm just so he can say hi to me. No reason whatsoever. What's going to happen is that I'll eat a solo dinner at the station bistro, check my emails, and take the next train to Paris at eight o'clock.

Forty minutes later, Nathan sits down next to me at a small table on the bistro's terrace.

Clad in worn jeans and a white tee, he looks even brawnier than I remembered. My gaze caresses his body and lingers on his suntanned face.

God, how I've missed him!

We don't say much for the first five minutes.

To calm down, I try to focus on the sounds and smells of the bustling station.

Freshly brewed coffee. Gas. Waiters zooming back and forth, balancing trays.

One of them brings us coffee and iced Perrier.

A chime sounds, followed by the woman on the loudspeaker who delivers the usual security announcement. Travelers rush into the building, gazing up at the displays. Others drag their luggage out and wave to the nearest cabbie.

I have a hard time breathing.

Nathan's left arm and leg are almost touching mine, and his masculine scent makes my head spin, reminding me of our first night in the Grotto. My heartbeat is so wild, I'm not even sure I'm capable of speech right now.

"How's the new job?" Nathan asks.

Inhale. "Fine." *Exhale.* "You?"

"Busy, as usual."

I nod.

We sip our drinks without looking at each other.

Is he over me?

Was he ever into me, to start with?

I sneak a peek at his broad chest. It's heaving. *He's nervous!* Unless, of course, it's normal for a big guy with so much muscle and a strong heart to breathe like that.

My train leaves in less than an hour.

Speak now, Clarissa, or forever hold your peace.

Except, what I intend to say will make me look pathetic—more pathetic than I've ever felt in my life.

I can't say it.

I *won't* say it.

I *am* saying it, because it's my voice that murmurs, "Will you come visit me one of these days?"

He turns toward me and stares.

I hold his gaze.

"Rissa..." He sighs before shaking his head.

I don't like his sighing or his frowning or his shaking his head. I don't like it at all.

"It's been hard forgetting you," he says. "Really, really hard. But I'm working on it."

"I've given up."

He takes my hand and presses it to his lips.

"Please, Nathan, can we give the long-distance thing a shot?"

"The long-distance thing is for college kids." He smirks. "Not that I would know."

"It isn't just for kids!"

"Anyway, I can't. Not with you."

I search his face. "Why not?"

He lets go of my hand and turns away.

"Why not?" I ask again.

"Because…" He turns back to me—his eyes filled with anger and desire and regret. "Because of who I am. Because I'm tied… I'm *married* to the family farm. I'm bound to my land and to the herd."

I chew on my lips as desperation sets in.

"If I start a long-distance relationship with you…" His frown deepens. "Fuck that, if I as much as spend one more night with you, I'll ditch everything and move to Paris."

I swallow. *Yes, please!*

"Do you know how many times I've envisioned that since you left?" His expression is unbearably hard. "And here's what I think would happen. I'd move in with you and become a kept man. I would idle my days away in a city where I don't belong and where my skills are useless. You'd begin to resent me."

"Sounds very… apocalyptic."

He doesn't respond.

I squeeze my eyes shut before opening them. "Fine. Stay here. I'll do the moving."

"What?"

"I'll quit my job and move in with you. I'll do my best to adjust, to help you with the farm, learn your way of life—"

"That's nuts. You can't just—"

"I'm in love with you."

He shuts his mouth.

"I'm in love with you," I say again, my voice cracking.

"You *want* me." He furrows his brow. "It's called lust."

"Oh, I want you all right, but what I feel is so much more!"

"I don't get it." His gaze bores into mine. "I mean, I totally get why you'd *want* me, but not— You called me Cowboy, remember? What would a smart, cultured woman like you find in an uneducated hillbilly?"

I cup his face, shocked by how little he thinks of himself, by how blind he is to his own wondrousness. Should I mention his loyalty first? Or his drive? What about his decency, his kindness, his humor—

Nathan puts his hand over mine and squeezes gently. His eyes are so sad it breaks my heart.

"I'll… draw up… a list," I say through tears.

Pulling me to his chest, he wipes away my tears with the pad of his thumb. "I love you, babe."

I eye his mouth, my heart swelling with hope.

Kiss me.

He kisses my forehead. "You're the most amazing woman I ever met, Rissa, and I sure as hell won't let that woman ruin her life."

CHAPTER 12

NATHAN

Summer is here, and our cows now spend their days outside, roaming freely and grazing to their hearts' content.

Earlier this week we moved the last calves born in April out of their hutches. In a couple of months, the males will be sold to feedlots, and the females will be raised to become milking cows like their mothers.

Life goes on.

"You're unhappy," Ma says as we clean the barn.

"I'm perfectly satisfied with my existence."

"Oh really?" She tilts her head to the side. "Is that why you never smile anymore?"

I frown. "Yes, I do."

"Nope. You haven't smiled once since your Clarissa left for Paris."

"She was never mine," I say. "And she has nothing to do with this."

We finish in silence and head for the house to have lunch with our volunteers. But before we go in, she stops in her tracks and turns to me.

"What is it, Ma?"

"I want to tell you a story."

"Now? Here?"

She nods. "I've never told you this and it's been gnawing at me."

"OK."

"In your last months of middle school when you told your teachers you were going to continue at an agricultural *lycée*, your father and I received a visit."

"Who?"

"Your principal. She said it would be a waste of talent to send you to a vocational school, that you should be encouraged to go to college and study economics, law, medicine, engineering—anything you wanted—because you had the capacity for it."

"What?"

"She said you had a good head for math. She showed us your grades."

"They were nothing special."

Ma lets out a sigh. "That's what you think because that's what your dad put in your head."

"What are you saying, Ma?" I narrow my eyes. "I know what my grades were. I saw them, remember?"

"Yeah, but you misinterpreted them. Your dad managed to convince you that only straight-A students should go to college. But your grades were solid."

I fold my arms over my chest and stare at her.

"Your principal said, 'Consider this—Nathan gets those grades without even trying. I know he helps you with the farm when he should be doing homework.' "

"What did you say?"

"I wanted to ask her more questions, but your father exploded. He started yelling at the woman."

Ma tries to imitate his voice. "What's wrong that?

What's wrong with agriculture and running a dairy farm? How do you think your favorite milk, yogurt, and cheese land on your table? Why the hell is it a waste of talent if Nathan chooses the life of a farmer?"

I find it hard to picture Pop yelling at my school principal like that, and yet I don't doubt for a second that Ma is telling the truth.

She shifts uncomfortably. "Your principal asked if the life of a farmer was what *you* wanted, what *you'd* chosen. Your dad said yes."

"We'd discussed it at some point," I say, jumping to his defense.

"I was there when you did," Ma says. "It wasn't a discussion. It was a monologue—his."

"Why are you telling me this now?"

"To come clean." She gives me a weak smile. "I'm just as much to blame as your dad for robbing you of choices."

I smirk. "So, I should hate both of you now."

"I hope not," she says. "I adore you. So did your dad. He was a good man."

"I know that."

She nods. "I loved him deeply, and he was sick, and I… I refused to see what he was doing to you, how he was undermining your self-confidence."

"Ma—"

"At that age," she interrupts me, "kids aren't supposed to think they have no choice but to honor the decisions that were made for them. They're supposed to think the sky is the limit."

"How do you know I wouldn't have chosen this life anyway even if I was encouraged to look elsewhere?"

"I don't know that," she says. "But what I do know is that keeping the farm in the family was more important to your dad than anything. It was the destiny he'd chosen for himself and for you, and I was too weak to argue."

"Is this about…?" I pause, looking for the right words. "Ma, are you trying to set me free to be with Ri — Clarissa?"

"It's more about... making amends to you, my boy. And, yes, I'm also trying to set you free to live the life you choose."

I clasp my hands over my head and stare at her for a long moment. "Whatever choice I make, we're not selling the farm."

She raises her eyebrows.

"Because if we do," I say, "Pop's sacrifice would've been for nothing."

EPILOGUE

CLARISSA

I'm in London for the decade's biggest conference on cave art, organized by the Royal Archaeological Society.

If I don't get up, I'll risk being late for my own presentation. Yep, Dr. Penelope Muller Girault is slated to open the conference with a talk on the educational function of upper Paleolithic cave paintings.

Luckily, I don't need to take the Tube to get to the conference held at the British Museum. All I need to do is cross Russell Square.

Problem is, it feels too good to be in bed—and in Nathan's arms.

Around this time three years ago, we walked out of the Darcy Grotto into the sunlight and said goodbye to each other.

I thought that was it.

Boy, was I off the mark.

A lot happened in the months that followed the "cave incident." I moved to Paris and started a new job at the Museum of Archeology. Celine, who's my BFF now, fell madly in love with Nathan's cousin Thomas. I knew he'd felt the same way about her when a week before her first visit, he bought hundreds of books and ditched the home cinema in his Paris apartment to install a wall-to-wall library.

They married five months later.

In July that year, after a cathartic conversation with his mom, Nathan had an epiphany. He realized life didn't have to be black or white. And, as far as his farm was concerned, it didn't have to be all or nothing.

He and Brigitte sold half of their land, which fetched them a small fortune. To increase their profit margin from what was left, they converted his cottage into a second guesthouse and transitioned to organic farming. It was a relatively easy switch, what with the herd being a grazing one to start with.

Nathan hired a manager to help Brigitte operate the farm. He partnered with Thomas, and together they opened a fancy store in Auxerre. The store sells mouthwatering yogurts, cheese, ice cream, and other premium dairy products in funky packaging.

When he called me in September to ask if I was still interested in him, my "Yes, I am!" tumbled out in a rush of mad joy before he'd finished his question. The truth was, I'd been borderline suicidal all summer, and I was seriously considering an unsolicited relocation to the village of Verlezy. And, possibly, a hunger strike.

Good thing he'd announced he was moving to Paris before I had a chance to say that.

Nathan and Thomas are now proud owners of three Girault's Finest stores in Paris and five in Burgundy. The plan is to expand into Belgium next.

With an effort, I roll off my husband's chest and head to the bathroom. "Call Brigitte!"

"Why, do you doubt my mother's capacity to look after a garden gnome?"

"May I remind you the garden gnome in question is now superfast and primed for mischief?"

"I'll call her," he says.

In fact, I don't doubt Brigitte's skills as a grandmother for a second, but I know how much she enjoys early morning briefings with her son. He enjoys them, too, but he gets sloppy when traveling abroad.

I can't believe it's been three years!

Three years, one kid, seven articles, one monograph, two hundred new cows, eight Girault's Finest stores. And counting.

"What about the Tokyo job offer?" Nathan asks when I come out of the shower.

I glance at my watch, which says I need to be out the door within the next five minutes. "I wrote them yesterday with a 'very honored but can't.' "

"Rissa, you said it was a fantastic opportunity when they'd reached out to you. I don't want you to sacrifice your career—"

"Nobody's sacrificing anything," I declare. "I have an excellent job in Paris. Tokyo will wait."

He draws his eyebrows together in confusion. "Until when?"

"Until you're ready to open stores in Asia."

"You think Thomas and I can pull that off—stores in Asia?" he asks, grinning.

I bend down and kiss the top of his head. "I think the sky is your limit, Cowboy."

EXCERPT

Dear Reader,

I hope you enjoyed the **Darcy Brothers box set**!

Would you like to follow Uma and Zach as their red-hot chemistry boils over?

Their story, **PLAYING WITH FIRE,** is the most emotionally intense romance I have written yet.

It's also Book 1 in the **PLAYING TO WIN series**.

If you liked the DARCY BROTHERS books, you'll adore the **PLAYING TO WIN** romances.

Guess what? The **complete series** is now available on Amazon, in one convenient box set.

3 hunky French athletes.
3 passionate women.

3 hot and tender love stories.

Sound like something up your alley?

Here's a sneak peek!

Uma snatches the chocolate from the box and darts out the door into the garden. I drop the box and run after her.

She shoves the chocolate in her mouth.

"Cheater!" I narrow my eyes in what I hope is an intimidating glare. "You're going to pay for this."

She bolts, trying to get back into the house.

I block her way, towering over her. Uma retreats, turns around, and runs to the other end of the garden. I follow, hot on her heels. She doesn't shriek, no doubt, so she won't wake up Sam, whose window is open above us.

For two or three minutes, I chase Uma around the garden in silence. I'm faster, but she's nimbler. Besides,

I've no clue how I'm going to make her "pay" for her theft, so I'm not really putting my heart and soul into the pursuit. On our third round, Uma ducks under my arm and hightails it into the house, across the kitchen, and toward the stairs.

She's hoping to make it to her bedroom and lock herself in.

Not happening.

Accelerating, I close the distance between us. She scrambles up the steps. I grab her shoulders from behind, putting an end to her delusion that she can outrun me. Giggling, she tries to break free. I wrap my arms around her to hold her. She stops thrashing. I pull her into me, tightening my hold. She stops laughing.

For a few moments, neither of us moves or makes a sound, pressed against each other, panting.

Her chest heaves underneath my forearms.

I press them lightly against her little breasts, her nipples…

My heart throbs in my ears.

A caveman's impulse to sling her over my shoulder and carry her somewhere private where I can have my way with her surges up somewhere in my gut, both shocking and tantalizing me. To resist it, I plant my feet firmly into the step and refuse to move a single muscle in my body.

With Uma one step higher on the staircase, her nape is perniciously close to my face, making my struggle harder than it already is. Her silky black hair is gathered into her usual bun that's gotten messy from all the running.

I stare at her delicate neck.

Want to kiss it.

Dying to kiss it.

Can't.

Because… reasons… good reasons… if I could just recall them.

There!

She's Sam's nanny.

That's good, but not good enough…

She's my friend's almost fiancée.

Sort of.

Anyway, she's inexperienced and clearly not thinking straight right now.

Very good.

I relax my embrace enough for her to duck and slip away.

Only she doesn't do it.

Instead, she leans back into me.

~

ABOUT THE AUTHOR

Alix Nichols is an unapologetic caffeine addict and a longtime fan of Mr. Darcy, especially in his Colin Firth incarnation.

She is a USA Today bestselling author of sexy, funny, riveting books which will "keep you hanging off the edge of your seat" (RT Book Reviews) and "deliver pure pleasure" (Kirkus Reviews).

At the age of six, she released her first romance. It featured highly creative spelling on a dozen pages stitched together and bound in velvet paper.

Decades later, she still writes. Her spelling has improved (somewhat), and her books have topped the Amazon charts around the world. She lives in France with her family and their almost-human dog.

Connect with her online:
Website: alixnichols.com
Facebook: facebook.com/AuthorAlixNichols
Pinterest: pinterest.com/AuthorANichols
Goodreads: goodreads.com/alixnichols
Twitter: twitter.com/aalix_nichols

Made in the USA
Middletown, DE
09 August 2018